CHOICES LIKE RIVERS

NANCY JACKSON

Copyright © 2020 by Nancy Jackson

All rights reserved. No Part of this book may be reproduced in any form or by any electronic or mechanical means, including information storage and retrieval systems, without permission in writing form the publisher, except by a reviewer who may quote brief passages in a review.

Hardback - 978-1-7348946-1-5
Paperback - 978-1-7348946-0-8
eBook - 978-1-7348946-2-2

Published in the United States by Wild Ideas Press
Edmond, Oklahoma

This work is a work of fiction. Names, characters, businesses, organizations, places, events, and incidents either are the product of the author's imagination or are used fictitiously. Any resemblance to actual persons, living or dead, events, or locales is entirely coincidental.

Book Cover Design by
Angela Westerman of
AK Organic Abstracts
AKOrganicAbstracts.com

It is common to thank God for guiding our hand at our craft. But, for me this process has been much more than just Him guiding my hand.

It is difficult to explain, but it has been as though He was literally pouring the stories, the books, through me as I wrote. I felt each word as though I were hearing it, reading it for the very first time. I never knew what the story was truly about or what would happen until He poured it through me.

So when I dedicate this book to my Father God, it is much more than what these simple words can convey. I am truly honored that He chose me as the vessel who was privileged enough to put this book, and all the others, onto paper.

I only hope that this book touches your heart as much as it did mine!

CONTENTS

Chapter 1	1
Chapter 2	5
Chapter 3	24
Chapter 4	43
Chapter 5	63
Chapter 6	82
Chapter 7	100
Chapter 8	120
Chapter 9	139
Chapter 10	156
Chapter 11	175
Chapter 12	194
Chapter 13	211
Chapter 14	230
Chapter 15	249
Chapter 16	269
Chapter 17	292
Chapter 18	311
Chapter 19	330
Chapter 20	349
Chapter 21	367
Epilog	382
Author's Note	389
About the Author	391

CHAPTER 1

Sharon - June 1978

On the morning of June 15th, 1978, she walked into the front door of the police station. She was five years old and dressed in a pillowcase for a dress and a thin piece of rope tied around her waist for a belt. Her makeshift shoes were strips of old cloths wrapped tightly around her feet.

She stood just inside the door unsure of what to do. Her blonde hair was disheveled, with bits of bark strewn throughout. But what everyone noticed the most were her big blue eyes.

The activity in the room slowed, then stopped completely as she stood there chewing on her finger, frowning in indecision.

Sharon Paulson walked over to the little girl and knelt down. "Sweetie, can we help you?"

The little girl looked at Sharon for a brief moment before responding. She removed her finger from her mouth as she searched Sharon's face. It was as if she was looking for something, a sign maybe of what she should do or say next.

"My mommy told me to come here."

"Your mommy? Where is your mommy?" Sharon asked, glancing behind the little girl.

"I don't know." Then, almost as an afterthought, she partially turned and pointed back out through the glass door. "Out there."

The other officers in the room rushed out to see if they could find her mommy. But, they found no one in the parking area. They continued to spread out, looking up and down the street, but found no one that could be this girl's mother.

"What's your name?" Sharon asked. Waves of compassion tinged with panic, surged through her.

"Molly Sue."

"Molly what is your last name?" Sharon asked.

Molly just looked at Sharon. It was clear that she didn't know her last name, or maybe didn't understand what Sharon was asking her. Molly's big blue eyes only continued to search Sharon's face.

Sharon took Molly Sue by the hand and led her into the back room where they made coffee. It was an old file room they had made into a makeshift break room. She picked Molly Sue up and sat her in a chair at the table, realizing that the pillowcase was the only thing she was wearing.

"Are you hungry?" Sharon asked.

"Me ate this morning when I woke up."

Sharon took an apple that she had brought with her lunch and poured a small glass of orange juice from a canister she kept on hand. She then set them on the table in front of Molly Sue.

"Here you go, just in case." Sharon was nervous. Her mind was racing, and she was trying to determine why this sweet little girl was alone. Her mind could only conjure up the worst scenarios.

Molly Sue just sat quietly and looked at the apple and juice while she continued to chew on her finger.

"You don't have to eat them if you don't want to, but if you do, it's okay," said Sharon, nervous energy causing her to ramble.

When Molly Sue continued to sit there, Sharon picked up the apple, took it to the sink and began to slice and peel it. Unsure of what to do, she felt compelled to help this little angel. Once peeled and sectioned, she then sat the apple back down on the napkin in front of Molly Sue.

The apple and juice continued to sit there untouched. "Molly, do you know why your mommy said for you to come here?" Her question was met with only a slight shake of Molly's head, her blonde curls bouncing.

"Where's your daddy?"

"Daddy?" Molly Sue asked, dipping her eyebrows in thought.

"Yes, do you have a daddy?" Sharon was trying to push down the panic that wanted to rise and overtake her. Again her question was met with only those big blue eyes gazing back at her. *There must not be a daddy*, thought Sharon.

Just then, Officer Anthony Sproul peeked around the doorframe and motioned for Sharon to step out. As soon as Sharon stepped into the hallway, He said, "We can't find any sign of her momma. The town is quiet, and we have been up and down the street. The other officers are continuing to canvas the adjacent stores now. There is no sign of her."

CHAPTER 2

Sharon - April 1970

Sharon Paulson sat with her face to the sun. The day was beautiful, and it was nice to have a good day after the cold and windy spring. She wanted her mood to be light and airy just like the beautiful day that whirled around her in the budding trees, and singing birds, but she just couldn't force herself to comply.

Sadness crept over her like a suffocating blanket and she looked down at her hands. The nail polish she had applied only two days before was now chipped and peeling away. She picked at the chips and pulled away what she could.

Graduation was only a month away. This wasn't exactly how she had pictured her *launch into life after high school* beginning. A tear slipped out, and she reached up to brush it away. She knew she should go back to class, but didn't think she could look everyone in the face right now.

The warmth of the large boulder felt comforting and so she remained. She wrapped her arms around her legs and rested her head on her knees. *What am I going to do?*

Her stomach knotted, and she began to cry in earnest. *My father will kill me*. A vision of her father's face sat firmly before her. Then a vision of her mother's disappointed face surfaced there beside his.

By her best guess, she was now just over three months pregnant. The party last January had swept away her inhibitions and when Rory touched her, she had melted into his arms. It was true that it had been her first time, and Rory was not her boyfriend. But even if he were ready to drop everything and marry her, it would not ease the situation.

Should I even tell him, Sharon wondered? They hadn't gone out again since that night. In fact Rory didn't even act interested in her anymore. He was now dating another girl and to Sharon, it seemed as though they were serious.

Well, there was no use crying over spilled milk. She had to do what she had to do. She just didn't know if she should wait until after graduation to tell her parents, or tell them now. By then, she would be well over three months along and her tight bellbottom jeans were already cutting into her.

Standing up, she knew for her parents' sake, she should wait and let them enjoy the pleasure of their first child graduating. The news could wait, and then they would decide together what she would do.

She reached down to pick up her books and purse and the button popped off her pants. It pinged against the rock and rolled down the hill. Sharon felt her hopes roll away with the button. Could there possibly be a good outcome to her situation? If so, she couldn't imagine it.

She tried to picture herself raising a baby. She knew nothing about babies. It would saddle her mom with the burden of caring for it.

Sharon envisioned her mom juggling her job as it was. She always rose early to prepare breakfast for their family and then rush off to her job as a legal secretary. It was Sharon's chore to clean the breakfast away and stack the dishes for washing later.

Her younger brother had trash and yard duties, so Sharon helped her mom with cleaning the house, doing laundry, and cooking. Her mom was very efficient and could juggle a lot in her life. But Sharon knew she could only do so much. Because her mom loved her job, she dealt with the other responsibilities so that Sharon's father would continue to allow her to work.

If a baby came along, what would happen then? Would her mother have to leave the job she loved? Sharon thought she would throw up, and she did.

As she bent over, losing the breakfast her mother had prepared just an hour earlier, she noticed the small green sprouts of spring reaching up from the nearly warm earth towards the warmth of the sun. Spring is their new beginning. Each fall they die, and each spring they have a new start, a new life.

Sharon wasn't sure why, but those tiny green sprouts gave her just a small bit of hope. If they could have a new start, maybe she could too.

She stood, took a deep breath and resolved herself to do the hard things she needed to do. She would raise this baby and she would do whatever she needed to do in order to do that. The books on her hip were heavy, and she was glad that soon she wouldn't have to be challenged with school on top of everything else.

She shifted the books and walked along the edge of the school property, making her way to her old '65 Ford Fairlane. The door creaked as she opened it and the vinyl seats were already hot from the morning sun.

Where could she go? If she went back home, she risked accidentally running into one of her parents who might happen home for some unforeseen reason. Her younger brother Calvin would be at school. With nowhere to go, she just sat in her car.

So, I earn $1.60 per hour at the drugstore. If I can go to work there full time, I'll have around $64 a week. That seemed like a lot to Sharon since working only part-time while going to school, the most she had ever earned in a week was around $24.

But who will take care of the baby while I work? If Mom is at work all day and so is Dad, how can I go to work too?

She felt depression threaten to overtake her again. It was all so overwhelming. How could she ever do this? She must be stupid to think she could take care of a baby. Once again, the tears started to fall. Her arms felt too heavy to lift to the steering wheel, so she just sat looking out at the high school.

Shame had kept her from talking to anyone about her situation. She didn't know anyone who had gotten pregnant before they were married. At least she didn't think she did. The age of Aquarius and free love was just a tiny glimmer on the East and West coasts. Its light hadn't yet shone to her small town in the South.

None of that felt right to Sharon, anyway. She wanted a home and a family. This jump start was not the way she had seen her having that dream though. She thought she would go to college, get a career and meet a handsome man. He would court her and they would fall madly in love. Then they would have her dream wedding and then a baby.

Sharon placed her hands over her abdomen and looked down where the tiny life's little story was beginning. *I will try little baby, I will try to be a good mommy.*

The bell for class change began to ring, signaling that first hour was over. Sharon reached up and turned the key in the ignition and backed out of her spot. Anxiety rippled up her spine as she drove home. She had nowhere else to go, so she would go where she knew. As she drove, she kept telling herself, it would be okay. *Somehow, it will be okay.*

Sharon - June 1978

Sharon pulled a chair up to the table where she had sat Molly Sue. The little girl had grabbed hold of Sharon's heart the instant she had walked through the door. As her eyes traced the outline of the bright blue eyes framed with thick lashes, Sharon kept telling herself that this little doll was not hers.

Even though she kept reaffirming that fact over and over in her mind, her heart was not listening. Her heart had already fallen in love with the tiny little cherub.

Molly Sue sat quietly as if she knew how to be a good girl. She didn't seem to be afraid of Sharon or of being in the police station. *Where has she come from and what has happened to her mother,* Sharon wondered?

"Molly, is your mommy hurt? Why did she tell you to come here?" Sharon asked.

Molly's eyes searched Sharon's face as if the answer to the question lay there.

"Is your mommy sick or hurt?" Sharon rephrased and repeated the question.

"Mommy not feel good," Molly Sue's tiny voice finally answered.

"If you can help us find her, then we can help her feel better," said Sharon. "Can you help us find her?"

Sharon stood up and reached her hand out. Molly Sue only hesitated for a moment before taking Sharon's hand and sliding off of the chair. The feel of the tiny hand in Sharon's palm felt familiar, yet it shouldn't be. It felt like it belonged.

As they walked back into the front room of the police station, the hustle that Molly Sue's arrival had caused was gone. They could not find her mother and so life went back to its normal routine and flow.

"Anthony, any luck?" Sharon asked.

Anthony shook his head as he glanced down at Molly Sue. "Jim and David are still out looking."

Sharon nodded and walked toward the front door. The double glass doors were shielded from the sun by the deep overhang on the front of the building. The parking lot was two rows deep and across the street was the elementary school and playground.

Molly stood quietly by without comment. She once again had the end of her forefinger in her mouth. Sharon realized that at Molly's level, all she could see were the cars parked up to the curb. She reached down and lifted Molly Sue up to hold her. Once again she was reminded that the pillowcase was all the clothing she had on. *I have to fix that and soon*, thought Sharon.

Sharon pushed one glass door open and stepped out onto the front sidewalk. It was a beautiful morning and the small town was quiet and lazy. School was out for summer break and most people were at work on that Thursday morning.

Two boys on bicycles raced down the sidewalk and nearly ran Sharon over. Stepping to the side, Sharon instinctively wrapped her arms further around Molly Sue to protect her. In return, Molly buried her small blonde head in the crook of Sharon's neck.

Before Sharon could call out to the boys, they realized their error and simultaneously called back to her, "Sorry Miss Sharon!"

"That's much better! I would hate to have to call your mommas," Sharon called after them.

"It's okay sweet girl. Those boys are gone," Sharon spoke softly to Molly Sue.

The only sign that she had heard Sharon's words was a slight tilt of her head and a bright blue eye that peeked out through blonde curls. This was the first sign of fear that Sharon had witnessed. Molly Sue continued to cling to Sharon.

When Sharon grinned at Molly Sue, she finally raised her head and looked around. "The boys are gone. It's okay now. We need to go get you some new clothes."

She turned with Molly Sue and went back inside the station. "Anthony, I'm going to take Molly Sue and help her get cleaned up and get her some proper clothes. Tell Bill where I've gone. He can call me at home if he needs me, or if I'm not there, I'll be back soon."

Sharon sat Molly Sue back on the floor. "Let's go get my purse and we'll go." Molly Sue looked at Sharon and for the first time, she smiled.

Their medium sized town was small compared to a city, but it had a few different stores to shop at. Sharon knew exactly where to take Molly Sue. The Dryden Dry goods Store had tons of cute little girl clothes, shoes, and accessories. Often Sharon had longingly looked at the little dresses and hair bows before sadness took over and she walked away.

The bell jingled above the door as they stepped in. Gladys turned from behind the counter and nodded a greeting to Sharon. Then her eyes grew round and questioning.

"Gladys, meet Mollie Sue. She came to visit us at the station this morning." Molly Sue looked up at Gladys and shuffled behind Sharon to hide.

Understanding the subtle cues from Sharon's face, Gladys commented, "What a pretty little girl! And so well behaved too."

Soon a little blonde head slowly emerged behind Sharon's leg. Big eyes blinked as she looked at the lady behind the counter.

Gladys picked up a sucker and came from around the counter. She knelt down low to Molly Sue's height and held it out to her. "Would you like a sucker?"

Sharon knelt down, taking the sucker from Gladys. "It's okay. It tastes great." Sharon pulled off the paper wrapping and licked one side of the sucker, then handed it to Molly Sue.

Molly Sue took the sucker and timidly touched the end of her tongue to it. As soon as the grape flavor resonated on her tongue, her eyes sparkled and she put the entire sucker into her mouth.

Sharon and Gladys stood up. "Thank you Gladys. She just walked in our door this morning and so far we can't find any sign of her mother. The guys are out looking now.

I'm here to get her some clothes and then take her home with me and bathe and dress her."

Gladys looked down at Molly Sue as grape colored drool dripped out of one side of her mouth. "She sure is beautiful, isn't she?" Gladys asked. "I don't know when I've seen a little one this captivating."

"I know. My heart went out to her the moment I saw her. Of course any child walking in alone like that would tug at my heart, but she just grabbed something deep inside of me," said Sharon.

"Don't get too attached. Her mother will turn up and then you'll have to let her go. This little one will break your heart if you're not careful."

As Sharon looked down at Molly Sue, she knew Gladys was right. She didn't want to get too attached, but this little angel walking into her life felt like a long-lost piece of herself had suddenly reappeared. She kept telling herself that Molly Sue was not hers, but somehow that didn't help.

"I got some new little dresses in just yesterday. Let's go back and look," said Gladys.

It was hard for Sharon to hold back. She wanted to buy every single dress. She had managed to put back quite a bit out of each paycheck into her savings through the years, but she still had to watch every penny and not be frivolous.

When it was all said and done, she had bought three dresses, two pair of pants, three tops, a nightgown, two pairs of shoes, socks, panties, and hair bows. When Gladys was through ringing it all up, it came to a whopping $66.39.

The air rushed out of Sharon. Her salary of $9,500 a year was slim, making this a big extravagance. But, she was happy to do this. She reached in her purse and pulled out her checkbook, checking her register to make sure she did indeed have enough in her account to cover the purchase. She realized she would have to transfer some money over from savings for the check to clear.

"Gladys, I'm going to give you this check and go straight to the bank to transfer some money from my savings to my checking account. I don't think I expected my purchase to tally up so high."

"If it would be better for you, I can just put this on your account and you can come in and pay me later." Sharon thought about that. It would save her having to take Molly Sue to the bank where they would face having to answer more questions.

"You know it would save me a trip to the bank right now. That would be great. I'll be back in by tomorrow at the latest to pay you."

"No problem! I can't wait to see her in her new clothes."

Molly Sue stood by holding tightly to the empty sucker stick. A line of purple syrup ran from the corner of her mouth to her chin. *I wonder if she has any idea what is going on*, Sharon wondered.

It was a quick walk back to Sharon's car which she had parked in the station parking lot. She went in briefly to check on the status of the search. "Have you guys found Molly Sue's mother yet?" Her brow was pinched in concern as was Anthony's.

"No, nothing at all. And everyone that we have questioned knows nothing about her either."

"I bought her some clothes and I'm going home to bathe and dress her. I'll probably feed her some lunch and then be back."

Anthony nodded as they were leaving the station.

Sharon opened the passenger door to her 1976 Mustang II. It was white with a dark royal blue racing stripe and had a Cobra II engine. It was one of the few luxuries that Sharon afforded herself. She got teased that she had only bought the car because it was just like the original car on the TV show, Charlies' Angels, but she didn't care. Who knows, maybe she had.

She sat Molly Sue on the black vinyl passenger seat and told her to sit still. By the time Sharon had deposited the shopping bags in the car's trunk and slid in under the steering wheel, Molly Sue hadn't moved an inch. *My goodness she is well behaved.*

Even though she hadn't moved, Sharon could see some anxiety on her little face. "What kind of car does your mommy have?" Sharon asked.

Molly Sue just looked at Sharon. Her face showed worry, and it looked like she might be about to cry. "Does your mommy have a car?"

When she didn't answer, Sharon started the car and the powerful engine roared to life. Molly Sue began to shake and cried out. Her hands flew to her face and covered her eyes.

Sharon immediately turned off the engine and pulled

Molly Sue over into her lap. "It's okay. It's okay." She crooned as she rocked Molly Sue in her lap.

She got the distinct feeling that Molly Sue had never been in a car before. The thought was ludicrous in this day and age, but she felt certain that was the case. "Molly, this is a car," Sharon said as she rubbed her hand over the steering wheel.

Molly's hands came away from her face and she watched as Sharon turned the wheel back and forth. Molly sat forward and touched the wheel. "You can turn it if you want to."

Placing both of Molly's hands on the wheel, she showed her how the wheel turned. Soon, Molly had forgotten her fear and was happily playing, turning the wheel back and forth.

"I'm going to start the car again, okay?"

Molly Sue looked at Sharon and she nodded. Sharon pulled the seat lever and slid the car seat back enough to accommodate both she and Molly Sue. "You want to help me drive?" When Molly Sue nodded, Sharon once again turned the ignition.

Sharon placed her left hand on the wheel and shifted into reverse. Molly's hand followed the turn of the wheel, no longer afraid. The little girl on her lap felt just right to Sharon, as if she had sat there many times before. Molly Sue seemed full of joy, the fear long gone by the time they pulled into the driveway of Sharon's small bungalow.

"Now it's time to play dress-up," said Sharon. She opened the car door and sat Molly out on the driveway where she waited quietly for Sharon to retrieve the bags from the trunk.

As they walked toward the house, Sharon once again pondered just how right Molly Sue's hand felt in her own. It was as if that was where it had always belonged.

SHARON - JUNE 1970

Sharon lay on her bed, curled up on her side. She could not escape the horrific depression that engulfed her every day. The bright sunshine beckoned her as it filtered through the lace curtains, but wanting no part of it, she shut her eyes.

Graduation had happened three weeks earlier and she would have loved to have enjoyed life's milestone and all the parties that had gone with it. But, the heavy weight she carried had overshadowed it all.

She had waited until a week afterwards to tell her family about the pregnancy. Until then, she had dug in her closet and found flowy tops that covered the top of her jeans which she had tied shut with a string, looping around the button, through the hole, and then back.

With all the excitement of the end of the school year, no one had ever noticed. Her mother had even thrown her a graduation party. Her mother's happiness had only grieved Sharon even more, knowing how the news would affect her.

Exactly one week after graduation at the Monday night

dinner table, Sharon told her parents. Calvin was also at the table, but Sharon hoped that his presence would help to temper their response.

It was somewhere between the last bites of dinner and before dessert, that she blurted out the words, "I'm pregnant."

It was such a sudden and out-of-place comment that her parents weren't even sure they had heard her correctly. Surely she hadn't just said that she was pregnant.

In the wake of their stunned silence, she confirmed her comment. Finally, after the once calm night had exploded into tears and shouts of anger, all were finally spent and quiet in the living room.

They had sent Calvin to his room, but Sharon was sure he was listening at the top of the stairs. Her father's rage terrified her. She had never seen him this violently angry before.

Her mother couldn't stop bawling and dabbing her eyes with her violet embroidered hankie. All Sharon could do was count the number of scalloped edges on each side as it bobbed up and down from eye to eye.

That evening had played on a loop over and over in Sharon's mind every day since. She wondered what she could have done differently to have made for a better outcome, but still nothing came to mind.

The deadly silence in their home lasted for five solid days. Then one day without warning, her father took her by the arm and marched her to their new Pontiac. She didn't dare ask where they were going.

Anger radiated off of him like heat from a furnace. She had never been afraid of her father, that is until she had boldly declared her new physical status.

They didn't talk as they drove. A few times she nearly got up the courage to ask where they were going, but timidity would soon take over and silence her.

After about an hour, they arrived at the nearest large city. He pulled the car into the parking lot of a small stand-alone brick building. It was clear that it was some kind of business, but what it was, was not readily clear to Sharon.

Her father reached for his car door, then paused and looked over at Sharon. There was pain in his eyes. The anger had diminished somewhat and now his face was contorted by extreme emotional pain.

His eyes were rimmed red, but he didn't cry. Then with a nod, he said, "Get out of the car."

Sharon opened the door and went to stand next to her father. They walked side by side to the door of the building and he opened the door for her.

Inside the clinical smell of antiseptic assaulted her nose. The room contained about a dozen or so metal chairs with orange vinyl padding on the seats and backs.

A counter stood directly ahead of them and suddenly Sharon realized her father was standing there talking to a lady on the other side who was handing him a clipboard.

When the realization finally hit her that they were at an abortion clinic, she panicked. She wanted to run, but where? She didn't even have her purse. She placed her hand on the door handle from an urge to flee, but just as she did, she caught her father's eye. The unspoken warning on his face was clear.

Obediently, without a word, she walked over and sat beside her father on one of the orange chairs. There were no others in the small room and the lady who had been behind the counter had disappeared.

She wanted to have the baby. She didn't know how, but with every fiber in her being she already loved the tiny little life that was growing inside of her.

Not daring to make a fuss, she sat quietly as tears dripped with a loud plop… plop… plop… on her bare legs.

She had no choice. She had almost no income, no husband, and no one to help her through this. All she needed was just someone to help her just a little, and she knew she could do it.

Once she had told her family, she had told her best friend. It was then that the first thought of an abortion had surfaced.

"Hey, just go have an abortion and get your life back," Lisa had said.

Lisa's words had hit Sharon hard. She wasn't sure what life Lisa had been referring to. Sharon lived a quiet and shy life. She didn't party, and neither did she have big career aspirations.

The thought of having an abortion had sickened Sharon, and she told Lisa so.

"Well, I think you're silly. You're young and there is so much left to do and fun to have. Having a baby will stop all of that. You don't want to have an abortion, just give it away."

Sharon had thought about that, but then she knew she couldn't just give a child of her own away. She had dreamed of being a mom since she was a small child playing with dolls. Neither an abortion nor adoption was the answer for Sharon.

Yet, here she was in an abortion clinic. Her father had intentionally not told her where they were going.

"I don't want to do this," Sharon said.

Her father deliberately laid the pen on the clipboard. "You will have an abortion. You are not yet eighteen and you will do as I say. You are too young to understand what having a bastard child will do to your life."

A bastard child. The phrase rolled in Sharon's mind. A bastard child. No, not my child. I would love my child and it would never be a bastard to me.

Soon the lady was back at the counter and her father rose to hand the clipboard back to her.

Sharon's blood pressure rose until it was rushing and pounding in her ears. She couldn't breathe and began rocking back and forth in her chair.

Suddenly her father turned towards her. The wailing she was making had startled him and he rushed over to her.

Torn between fatherly love and a sense of duty, he tried to stop her wailing and rocking.

"Sharon, listen to me. Stop this. You will see one day

that it is the right thing. Someday you will understand. Someday you will be grateful."

He grabbed her forearm and pulled her up. At the door to the back hallway a nurse met them with a hypodermic needle. Sharon couldn't hold them off. Between her father, the nurse, and the receptionist, they were able to sedate her into compliance.

She barely remembered the procedure. The doctor and nurse were like vague shadows moving about the room. Couldn't she just die along with her baby? Couldn't she just die?

Her father had been wrong. Two weeks later she still just wanted to die. She still didn't see that it had been the best thing.

CHAPTER 3

Sharon - June 1978

The sound of the large black phone sitting next to the sofa in Sharon's living room penetrated loudly into the bedroom where she and Molly Sue had been trying on all the new clothes she had purchased. She had made it a game and both she and Molly Sue were soon laughing.

"Hello," answered Sharon.

"Sharon, it's Bill." The chief of police, Bill Jacobs was her direct supervisor. "Anthony said you had taken the girl to your home."

"Yes, I did. She didn't have any clothes and so I bought some and brought her here to bathe. I hope that was okay with you." Sharon fiddled nervously with the black coil that connected the receiver to the phone base.

"Yes, of course. Jim and David have looked everywhere

they can think of to look. They have questioned everyone within a two-block radius of the station. No one knows anything about her or her mother. Once you get her all cleaned up, get on back here and we can take her picture and make flyers to post around town."

"Will do."

"Has she said anything about her mother at all?" Bill asked.

"Earlier I asked if her mother was sick and she said Mommy doesn't feel good. But that was it. I think as soon as we get the flyers made I will see if she can trace her steps back to where she came from. But she didn't even have any shoes, or underwear so I thought that would be a priority. She didn't act like her mother was in urgent danger, just not feeling well."

"Very good. I'll see you both when you get here."

Molly Sue stood in Sharon's bedroom door looking out into the living room where Sharon had been talking on the phone. Her eyes told Sharon she was curious about her phone conversation. Whether it was about the phone or the actual conversation, Sharon couldn't decide.

Sharon stopped in front of Molly and got down on her knees. "Molly, you said earlier that your mommy wasn't feeling well. Can you tell me about your mommy?"

Molly's eyes darted back and forth looking from Sharon to the room beyond and then back to Sharon. Big tears welled up in her eyes and she began to cry. "Mommy." She sniffed and cried.

Sharon thought her heart would break as she enveloped

Molly Sue in her arms. "Molly if your mommy isn't feeling well, can you help me find her so we can help her?"

She could tell Molly was trying to stop crying. She stood for a while and Sharon could tell she was thinking. Then suddenly, Molly Sue burst out into tears again. "I want my mommy. I want my mommy."

"Okay, okay sweet girl. Let's see what we can do about finding your mommy."

With her face all cleaned up and in one of her new pants outfits and brown leather shoes, they loaded back up into the car. Molly Sue crawled onto Sharon's lap expecting to sit and help her drive again, and Sharon let her.

The station was still as calm as when they had left it. Not wanting to use the mug shot wall to take her picture, they went outside and sat Molly Sue on a bench. "Smile for the camera," said Sharon. Molly Sue just sat quietly. *I wonder sometimes if she understands what I am saying*, she thought.

After taking a few shots to ensure that they might have a good one, Anthony rushed it to the darkroom to expedite development.

"Okay Molly, can you point to me which way you walked here from?" Sharon was attempting to talk in simple terms so that Molly Sue would understand.

The little girl turned and looked around. They were standing on the sidewalk in front of the station. "Here, let's go out a ways," said Sharon as she took Molly by the hand and led her across the street to stand by the schoolyard.

"Now that we are out of all those cars, can you look and see which way we should go to find your mommy?"

Again, Molly Sue looked. She turned around again and again, slowly at first and then almost frantically. When she began to realize she did not know which way to go, she began to cry again. "I want my mommy."

"Okay, Okay," said Sharon picking her up. An idea occurred to Sharon, and she walked back across the street to the station.

"Anthony, don't we have some paper and crayons somewhere?" Sharon asked.

"Yes, I think so." A few minutes of digging in cabinets produced a Big Chief tablet and a box of sixteen Crayola Crayons. "I think that maybe I can get Molly to draw me some pictures of her mommy and maybe she will remember something important."

Anthony nodded as Sharon walked back to the break room. "Molly, can you draw for me?" Molly's eyes lit up, and she nodded vigorously.

She eagerly took the tablet and crayons from Sharon. "Molly can you draw me a picture of your mommy?"

Molly Sue was already hard at work holding a crayon in her chubby little hand and drawing. Sharon wasn't sure if she had heard her or not. When she looked on the paper, there were two stick figures already begun. It looked to Sharon as though it were maybe her mommy and Molly Sue.

Then next to the figure of her mommy, Molly Sue began to draw a very large stick figure. It was considerably out of proportion to the size of her mother. But then that could just be a lack of perception or control on Molly Sue's part.

Once done with the large figure, she drew an arm with the hand firmly on the mommy. All three figures had smiling faces, but there was something about how Molly Sue had drawn the large figure with the hand on the mommy that seemed unsettling to Sharon.

"Molly that is a very good job. Can you tell me who these people are in your picture?"

Molly nodded and pointed, "Molly Sue, Mommy, Buddy."

"Is Buddy your daddy?"

Once again Molly Sue's eyes searched Sharon's as if she hoped to find the answer to the question there. "Molly, do you know what a daddy is?"

Molly shook her head. "So who is Buddy?"

Again, she could tell that Molly Sue didn't know how to answer the question. "Okay, can you draw a picture of where you live?"

Soon, a small box shape filled a clean sheet of paper. She drew a lot of trees and two windows, one on each side of the door.

Then Molly pushed that sheet aside and began another picture. *I think she is drawing her mommy again*, thought Sharon as she watched.

She used the yellow crayon to draw curly ringlets on top of the stick figure. Then there was a bed drawn as if the figure was sitting on the bed. Molly Sue drew a simple triangle dress in gray and then something very curious. She drew a bracelet around her mommy's ankle with the dark brown crayon.

Sharon picked up the pictures that Molly Sue had drawn and stood. "Molly keep drawing as much as you can remember about your mommy, Buddy, and where you live. I'll be right back."

As she walked down the hall to Chief Jacob's office, she thumbed through Molly's drawings. Bill saw Sharon as she came down the hall and stood to greet her. "What have you got, Sharon?" Bill asked.

"I had Molly draw pictures. I tried to have her show me, point to me, where she had come from, but she couldn't. It really upset her when she was looking and couldn't remember. So I thought I would have her draw pictures and maybe we could see something that might look familiar."

She handed the three pictures to Bill. "So this is her mommy, daddy, and her?" Bill asked looking up at Sharon.

"No, not according to Molly. I asked, and she doesn't seem to understand the word daddy, or father. She said that was Buddy, when I asked her."

"Does it mean anything that she drew him so much bigger than the other figures?"

"I have no idea," said Sharon. "Bill it may be a long time before we can find her mother and I don't want to call a social worker. If you are agreeable to it, I want to take her home with me. She's so well behaved, I think I can bring her here during the day or maybe find someone to help watch her during the day." There was a knot in Sharon's stomach as she asked. She didn't want Bill to say no.

Thumbing back through the pictures for the third time, not responding to Sharon's request, Bill finally looked up at Sharon. "Do you think that's wise?"

"What do you mean?" Sharon shifted from foot to foot.

"Will you get too attached to the girl? When we find her mother, she will have to go back to her, unless of course there was abuse."

"I don't see any signs of abuse. I bathed her and she looked healthy," said Sharon. She heaved a sigh and continued. "I understand. She isn't mine and as soon as we find her mother and get them situated, I will be fine with seeing them reunited." She could taste the lie like bitter gall as it left her mouth. She knew she would not be okay, even now, losing Molly Sue. But, she would do what she had to do.

"I think she sent Molly Sue here to get help, and now Molly Sue doesn't know how to take us back to her. She said that her mommy wasn't feeling well. I think we need to do whatever we can as fast as we can to find her mom." Sharon wondered if Bill was buying what she was saying. She knew the words were the words she was supposed to say, but the truth was, she wanted to run as far away from there as possible with Molly Sue and never come back.

Bill knew Sharon well. She had been his secretary as Chief for six years. He also knew that she had never married or had children, and not because she didn't love them. Every time he had seen a child come in the station, Sharon was the first to talk to them and make them feel welcomed. He knew she was getting in too deep with this little girl, maybe already had. But, it seemed best for Molly Sue.

"Okay. I know you'll take good care of her. I don't mind her being here when you're working, but I can't imagine that she would want to stay here all day long with nothing to do and nowhere to play."

A rush of relief flooded through Sharon. "I'll make it work. I promise. My friend Leslie keeps two kids for her neighbors while they work. I know she'll help."

Bill handed the pictures back to Sharon, but when she reached up to take them, he held them firm looking her pointedly in the eye. "Don't get your heart broke, Sharon. I mean it."

She nodded, and the papers slid from Bill's fingers. "I know Bill. I know." As she turned to leave his office, Sharon wiped a tear from her eye. Her heart was already breaking.

SHARON - SEPTEMBER 1970

The room was filled with the clickety-clack of a room full of typewriters. Sharon sat focused on the typing lesson she was to finish by the end of the hour. She enjoyed typing, and for the most part, she was pretty good at it.

"Grrr," she mumbled as she hit an 'r' instead of the 't'. She rolled up the paper and gently rubbed the typing eraser across the mistake. She knew if she was very careful, she could rub out only the space of the letter and it would keep the appearance of the assignment looking clean.

Satisfied that she had done a good clean-up, she rolled the platen back down and carefully lined up the row again. She singularly hit the 't' making sure it was exactly where it needed to be. Relieved, she scolded herself. *It takes way too much time to correct an error. I have to do better.*

She finished the assignment with only the one mistake. Once done, she pulled out the paper with pride. Proofreading her work to confirm what she already knew, she smiled. Only the one mistake.

The bell rang, and she hustled to gather her things and take the assignment to the instructor's desk. The wooden tray on the corner of the desk was surrounded by other young women attempting to get their assignments in so that they too could hurry off to the next class.

Sharon was one of the last to drop her paper onto the stack. Her next class was just across the hall so she knew she had plenty of time to get there and be seated.

She was enjoying business school. It was a good alternative to college and her parents had readily agreed. The drive from home each day was short, only about thirty minutes, but it gave her time to transition from the still awkwardness at home and the busyness of school.

This was week two, and she was settling in and gradually opening up to the other students. The unseen wall of separation she felt that divided her from the others never went away. It hovered in her mind like a dark grey cloud.

She was different than they were and had no desire to get too chummy with anyone.

Shame had devoured her summer. Her mother attempting to flutter around with heightened happiness only made it worse. She knew her mother was only trying to cheer her up by presenting a super happy environment. But that was not what she needed.

She needed honesty and vulnerability from them. Did they not hurt or have remorse for the decision they had made for her? She would never know because they refused to talk about it.

Lisa had been cavalier about it when she had tried to cry on her best friend's shoulder. She spewed platitudes that reaffirmed her previous opinions. "You'll be better off. You'll see."

Sharon soon stopped taking Lisa's calls. She just couldn't be around her anymore. With the severing of that friendship, she was completely alone. There was no one else that she could tell, so she carried her greatest burden, her greatest shame, her greatest regret deep inside where no one would know.

Moving forward was merely a decision. There was no other choice. Getting an education and then a job was a necessity. She had lost the desire to date so she would have to take care of herself.

Business school was something that interested Sharon, and it was a short two-year program rather than the four years that college would require. Honestly, it was probably the shorter path that attracted Sharon more than the occupation. Her desire to be out from her parents home drove her daily.

As Sharon slid into her seat, she smiled at the lady who sat to her right. They had developed a superficial friendship for the sake of school. A quick comment, a smile and a nod before the bell rang each day.

But this morning was different. Just as the bell rang, Sharon looked up to see the teacher standing next to a new student. "Class, we have a new student. She is starting a little late, so we will all need to help her get caught up. Please welcome Patty."

The class erupted into applause, all but Sharon. She couldn't. All she could see was the round mound protruding from underneath the maternity top that Patty wore. It had unexpectedly punched Sharon in the gut.

Numbness overtook her. She looked down at her accounting book and worked to open it to the correct page. But, she couldn't remember what page it was supposed to be. She flipped back and forth and then realized that she was assaulting her book in an almost frenzied fashion.

The classroom had grown quiet around her and all eyes were on her. She looked up and met their gazes with wet red-rimmed eyes. She gritted her jaw down tight, sat up straighter, and looked ahead to the teacher with steely eyes. She could do this, she had to do this.

The period seemed to drag on forever. It was normally a fifty-minute class, but Sharon's anxiety turned the teacher's words into white noise in her head. She looked ahead and nodded when appropriate. She had finally found the correct page, but when she looked at her book, the letters danced and taunted her.

As soon as the bell rang, Sharon lunged from her chair and was the first out the door. Around the corner, she leaned up against the wall and closed her eyes. She wanted to scream, throw a fit, anything that would release the agony she couldn't seem to escape.

"Are you okay," a gentle voice broke through her raging mental fog.

Sharon opened her eyes to see none other than Patty standing there before her with a look of genuine compassion on her face. *Why her*, Sharon thought?

Sharon nodded then burst out crying. Patty reached up and patted her arm, looking around. "Here, let's go where we can talk," said Patty as she guided Sharon down the hall and outside to a bench.

Robotically, Sharon let Patty guide her. There was something about Patty that resonated with Sharon. Maybe it was because she too, had felt a life growing deep inside of her. They had something in common, but then different.

Patty let Sharon cry silently once they were on the bench. It was as if she knew Sharon needed her tears to cleanse her from a deeply ingrained pain.

Then, when the tears had stopped falling, and they had begun to dry on Sharon's cheeks, Patty said, "I'm a good listener."

Could she dare tell her? What would she think of her? She shook her head and looked down at the stack of books on her lap.

"You don't have to. I'll just sit here with you and keep you company."

A glimmer of warmth began to rise inside Sharon. Acceptance. Someone accepted her. *But she wouldn't if she knew.*

"This is lunch period. Will you go with me to eat lunch?"

Sharon looked up at Patty. She wanted to go with her, but shame kept her back. "No, I'm okay. You can go on."

Patty smiled. "I really do want you to go with me. I don't want to go alone and I don't feel like I fit in with the other girls. For some reason I feel a connection with you. Please come with me."

Sharon looked at the sympathetic face and nodded yes. She needed a friend, but she would have to be careful to keep her secret safe. The irony of the friendship didn't escape Sharon and a short laugh burst forth.

"What?" Patty asked.

Sharon smiled and said, "Nothing. Nothing at all. Thank you."

Patty smiled too.

Sharon - June 1978

The night had been long and Sharon rose with fatigue as great as that when she had laid down.

Molly Sue had grown fearful as darkness had blanketed

the sky. She was growing tired, there had been no nap, and she wanted her mommy.

The day had been like a fairytale. They had shopped, colored, read books, and laughed. But at the end of the day, Molly Sue had grown sleepy on the short drive home. When the car stopped, it jarred her awake, and the result was a disgruntled child.

Sharon had picked her up and carried her inside amidst moans and vocal outbursts begging for her mommy. She had done her best to soothe Molly Sue, but little had changed her disposition.

With Molly Sue on her hip, she had made a simple dinner of soup and sandwiches. Molly Sue just sat looking at it after one solitary bite. Then, she slowly slumped forward and fell asleep with her head on the table.

Knowing she couldn't let her sleep there, Sharon was challenged with moving her to the bed without waking her. She was tempted to just let her sleep there for fear of waking her to more fits. She looked so angelic there asleep, and Sharon knew her fits had only been birthed from fear of losing her mommy.

She carefully scooped her up and walked to the spare room. It seemed so lonely in there and it was hard to envision leaving Molly Sue alone in there all night long. *What if she woke in the middle of the night alone and afraid?* Upon deciding that she would let her sleep with her, she turned around and headed to her own room.

Once successful at laying her on her bed without waking her, she gently removed her shoes and socks. Brilliant red patches covered her heals and other pressure points on her feet. *She hasn't worn shoes and they are rubbing blisters.* Sharon had been in such a hurry to dress her, that she had never thought about the consequences.

She retrieved the new pink pajamas and started to change her for the night, but stopped. She was sleeping and what would it hurt for her to sleep in her clothes for one night; she thought.

The light flicked off and left the room in darkness. Sharon left the door cracked so that a swath of light sliced across the bed.

Exhausted, she grabbed a bottle of cabernet and a glass. After scraping and stacking the dishes in the sink, she found her favorite chair and poured herself a glass. The television remained quiet. She had enough running through her mind to keep her engaged for the evening.

Soon, that familiar comfort she craved washed over her. She finished the bottle as sleep greeted her. But, it was short lived.

Suddenly, through a thick and overwhelming fog, Sharon struggled to come to terms with a noise in the background. Crying. It was crying.

Confusion clouded her foggy mind. *Why would there be crying?* Then she remembered Molly Sue. She sat forward and shook her head to clear her thoughts. Against the medicated call of her body, she pushed herself up and toward the room where she had laid Molly Sue.

There she sat up on the bed crying. As Sharon flipped on the light a terrified little girl with a red blotchy face sat entrenched in wracking sobs. Compassion pushed aside the remaining fog and Sharon scooped the tiny angel in her arms and rocked and crooned.

They spent the rest of the night in the overstuffed rocker, in the living room. Sharon had covered them both in a large afghan and had rocked and sang. When she would drift off, Molly Sue would pat her cheek to wake her to begin singing again.

By Sharon's best guess it had been around three in the morning when they had both given in to exhaustion.

The harried night had been enough to bring Molly Sue back to a bright eyed, and sweet young girl. Sharon on the other hand felt like throwing a tantrum herself. But she smiled anyway and popped a kiss on the top of Molly Sue's head.

Bathed and dressed, minus the stiff leather shoes, Sharon and Molly Sue left for the station. She had put the pair of tennis shoes she had purchased in her purse intending to purchase a pair of those little rubber thongs Gladys had shown her yesterday.

She had to be at work by eight and the store didn't open until nine, so she would carry Molly Sue around and let her walk in stocking feet inside the station.

"Good morning ladies," greeted Anthony as they walked in.

"Good morning," greeted Sharon in response.

Anthony looked at Sharon. Deep dark circles ringed the sockets of her eyes, and her hair was not the tidy 'do that it normally was. It was obvious she hadn't slept.

"Everything go okay last night?" Anthony asked.

Sharon nodded rather uncertainly, but Anthony figured it out. He had three young children of his own and he knew that new surroundings could cause a lot of chaos.

"Any sign of that person we were looking for?" Sharon asked rather cryptically. She didn't want to say the word mommy.

Anthony shook his head and Sharon headed on down the hallway to her office. A pile of pink message slips waited for her and a large stack of case folders as well. The day of playing with Molly Sue yesterday was coming back to bite her.

"Molly Sue, I have to get some work done. I'll get you the paper and crayons and you can sit and color for a while. Then we will take a break and go get you some shoes that won't hurt your feet, okay?"

Molly Sue nodded. She had woke quiet and compliant again, causing Sharon to almost completely forget the previous evening. She quickly prepared a play area in the corner of her office and as soon as Molly Sue was situated, she got to work.

An hour later, movement at her door caused her to look up. Bill stood there looking at Molly Sue, then over to Sharon. He nodded towards his office and Sharon knew he wanted to speak to her in private.

"Molly Sue, I'll be right in here if you need me. Please stay here and play. Okay?" Molly Sue nodded and watched Sharon walk away.

"We still have no word on the mother. We have put

flyers up around town, but I want to reach out to the local television stations and have them run something on the news. Someone somewhere is missing this child. If we can broadcast it wide enough, then we have better hope of finding them."

Sharon nodded and listened.

"Rough night?" Bill asked.

Sharon closed her eyes for a moment before opening them and answering. "Yes, it was. She cried for her mommy. We rocked in the rocker and I sang to her for most of the night."

"She seems fine now."

Sharon nodded. "Yes, she does. She was tired, and it was dark out. This morning she woke fine."

Then Sharon thought of something that had occurred to her in the night. "Bill, what if we look at missing person files county wide?"

"We've done that. I had Anthony call all the other county precincts and ask them to look through their missing person files. It took the entire day, but they finally all got back to me. No missing females that would be near this age."

"What about the hospitals? If her mother was sick, she may have been able to finally make her way to care."

"We did that too. Nothing."

Sharon was at a loss. She had thought hard to try to figure out a way to find Molly Sue's mother. The only two ideas she had had, Bill had just addressed.

"She hasn't worn shoes. She showed up here with rags

on her feet yesterday so I bought her some little leather shoes. Last night when I took them off, they had nearly blistered her feet. I will go get her some thongs as soon as the store opens. I guess I'll get her a few more things. It looks like she may be here awhile."

Bill glanced at the door between his office and Sharon's. Molly Sue stood silently looking at them. "Do whatever you need to do, Sharon."

CHAPTER 4

Sharon - December 1970

The loud shrill of the pink princess phone on Sharon's wall startled her as she laid down for a Saturday afternoon nap. She continued to lay there for a moment or two debating on whether she was curious enough to see who it was, to make her get up. The comfort of her bed had latched around her body providing the nest of refuge she so desperately needed.

Curiosity got the best of her, and she hurried to the kitchen to answer the phone. "Hello."

"Sharon, it's Lenny. I'm taking Patty to the hospital. She's in labor." Lenny's voice was loud and shrill. He was terrified and Sharon could hear it in his voice. Adrenaline shot through her own body and her mind raced through to determine what she should do right then at that moment.

"I'll meet you there," she said breathlessly.

The last three months had proven that Patty was indeed a good fit for a friend. Sharon hadn't been able to bare her soul yet regarding her pregnancy and then abortion, but her situation had matured Sharon beyond where the other classmates were. Sharon was drawn to Patty and truthfully, she was living somewhat vicariously through Patty's pregnancy.

Her heart was beating in her ears as she hurriedly rushed to the hospital. She had no idea what to expect or if she could even see Patty before they ushered her to the back.

"They took her on back," said Lenny as he met her at the glass entrance doors. The canned air rushed out and the doors whooshed to a close behind her.

"Okay, well, calm down. Let's sit over here." Sharon took Lenny by the arm and urged him to sit in the waiting room chairs. She sat on the edge of the seat in a chair that sat perpendicular to Lenny.

"How far along were her contractions?"

"Huh?" Lenny looked at Sharon with wide eyes.

"The pains. How far apart were the pains?"

Lenny's eyes shot back and forth as he mentally searched for the right answer. "I don't know." He looked panicked at Sharon.

She patted his arm. "It's okay. Let me go see what I can find out."

Sharon approached the nurse at the desk and asked if she could go back and see Patty. The nurse looked at her sternly, then finally nodded.

She could hear Patty huffing and puffing and screeching as she drew closer to the room. "Oh Sharon, come here quick," said Patty as Sharon appeared through her door.

Patty's hand was reaching out and anxiously waving for Sharon to take it. Her eyes were wide with panic.

Sharon took her hand and drew it close to her chest. "It will be okay," she said beaming.

Patty felt immediate comfort with Sharon being near. "Where's Lenny?"

"He's a mess, but he's here, or rather out in the waiting room. Will they let him in here?"

"Yes, but he wasn't sure if he could bear it. It isn't really common for men to be in the room during delivery. Will you stay with me?"

Dread filled Sharon with nausea and yet she felt compelled to be right there by her friend's side. "Yes, of course."

Finally, they reached the stage where Patty would receive an epidural and her pain became somewhat bearable. The nurses showed her how to breathe to ride through the pain of the contractions and Sharon helped.

She had little time to realize the bittersweet feelings that kept washing over her until Patty was holding her new baby son in her arms. At that moment, a wall of emotional separation sequestered her away. This was not her baby.

She was genuinely happy for Patty, but fresh pain from the trauma she had faced only months ago gripped her. Her baby would be two months old by now. A flurry of activity in the room went about her and then Lenny rushed into the room and was by Patty's side. That emotional wall proved to further push her away to the outskirts of the room.

"I think you should probably wait in the waiting room now. You did great helping her, but she needs time with her family now," said a well meaning nurse.

Sharon nodded numbly and walked woodenly to the waiting room. She dropped into one of the hard waiting room chairs. Her knuckles were white where she clutched her cloth purse in her lap with both hands as if it were a lifeline to sanity. She sat for at least an hour just staring ahead.

"Miss. Miss?"

Sharon finally realized that someone was trying to get her attention. "Yes?"

"Patty and Lenny would like you to come back to the room."

Sharon nodded and stood, but her feet wouldn't move. "Are you coming?"

Again, she nodded standing still. "Well, come along then."

She shook herself internally and forced her body to move forward. The closer to the room she drew, the louder her heart pounded.

The vision as she entered the room was one of a beautiful new family. Patty was holding the precious bundle and Lenny was standing beside her leaning in with his hand on the baby. This was her friend, her dear friend.

Suddenly the past seemed to fade and her love for Patty and Lenny broke through the crust of her woes.

Sharon smiled at Patty, then looked at the tiny baby. Tears broke free, not for her misfortune, but from joy at seeing this new life.

"Do you want to hold him?"

"Will they let me?"

"They aren't in here." Patty giggled.

Sharon sat her bag down and reached for the gently squirming life. "He's beautiful!"

"Hey now," said Lenny. "That's my boy! He ain't beautiful. He's handsome." They all laughed. But he was truly beautiful to Sharon.

Holding the baby, she knew she was meant to be a mother, and she knew that someday she would, that is if she could ever open her heart to trust again.

"Hey there little guy. I'm your auntie Sharon. Well, I'm not a real aunt, but sort of. I hope we will spend a lot of time together." Sharon held the baby naturally, and he soon closed his eyes and drifted off to sleep.

"Give that baby back to his mother." In rushed the nurse displeased with Sharon holding the baby. Reluctantly she handed baby Evan over to Patty.

"He's marvelous! You have free babysitting anytime you want it." Sharon was truly happy for her friend. Remorse and remembrance barely clouded her heart.

The five days that they insisted Patty be in the hospital seemed like forever to Sharon. She visited twice a day and was there when Lenny rolled them both out the front door on that last day. The nurse guided a cart holding bouquets of flowers and little gifts of baby-boy blue.

Back at Patty and Lenny's house, Sharon had arranged for a small welcome home party. Ten of their closest friends and family waited.

It was a great time, and Sharon loved planning and hosting the surprise for her, but if she were honest with herself, it could have been more fun. *Will this heaviness ever leave me? Will I ever feel normal again?*

Later that evening when Sharon stepped out into the cold December wind to go home, the depths of her loneliness and sorrow took hold. The busyness of the past week had suppressed it, but now the little family was home, there were no more parties to plan. Now Sharon was alone, really alone.

Once back at her parents' home, she dumped her coat and bag and walked to the kitchen. She knew they kept a bottle of red wine for a special occasions should they arise. She shuffled through items in the cabinet until she found it, pulled it out, and poured herself a glass. She was glad they were gone for the weekend.

The first sip left her sputtering and nearly choking on the strong flavor. But by the end of the bottle, she hardly even noticed how it tasted.

Sharon - July 1978

It had been two weeks and there had been no sign of

Molly Sue's mother. They had continued to post flyers and hand them out. The news stations ran stories at least twice with no response. The local newspapers also wrote articles and posted notices. Nothing.

There were the occasional crackpots who had wild stories and claims. But with one glance from Molly Sue, it was clear she knew none of them.

Sharon had gotten into a routine. Molly Sue was sleeping better at night and therefore, so was Sharon. She had purchased a few toys for Molly Sue, a doll and a stuffed bear. She played with the doll, but she rarely stepped a foot away from her bear whom she named Fuzzy.

Sharon had swapped out shoes routinely on Molly Sue's feet. She only allowed her to wear one pair for one to two hours until she would rotate them out for another pair. She hoped this would help toughen up her little feet so she could tolerate wearing shoes without discomfort. *I wonder what she wore in the winter? More rags?*

It was during those thoughts that anger would surge up in her that someone had forced this sweet baby girl to live in rags. There had been no physical signs of abuse, and honestly Molly Sue's behavior didn't show any signs of emotional trauma either. The mother she yearned for, had loved her. It was clear to Sharon that the lack of shoes and fancy clothes had not been from a lack of love.

Sharon's friend Leslie had agreed to keep Mollie several hours through the week. Both she and Sharon felt that just thrusting her into Leslie's home would not be good for

Molly, so Sharon and Molly Sue visited during the day while Leslie had the other children she watched.

At first, Molly Sue sat properly on the sofa next to Sharon, quiet but watchful. They never pushed her to go play. Then on the third visit Leslie's daughter Sherry came and just stood in front of where Molly sat. For what seemed like an eternity, she just stood while they both looked at each other.

"You want to come play?" Sherry finally said.

Molly Sue looked at Sharon for approval and when she nodded, Molly Sue jumped down and went with the other little girl. They had two more visits before Sharon felt comfortable leaving her. The station was only three blocks away. If Leslie needed her, she could be there quickly, but Sharon hated leaving her for even one moment.

When it was time for Molly Sue to go solo at Leslie's, Sharon discussed it at length with her. When they pulled into Leslie's driveway her new little friend was waiting for her on the porch. Molly flung the door open as soon as the car stopped and ran to the porch with Fuzzy in tow. Sharon didn't even bother to get out, just simply waived to Leslie and drove off.

Molly Sue hadn't even looked back and said good-bye. *If I am suffering separation anxiety now, what will happen when her mother is found?*

Each day, Sharon would take Molly Sue to work with her for a couple of hours, then take a break and take her to Leslie's. She would have lunch at Leslie's with Molly Sue, then pick her up after work.

Sharon wasn't much of a cook, and really wasn't sure what Molly Sue was used to eating, but she did her best. When they went to the grocery store, Molly Sue once again looked around in awe as if she had never seen a place like that before. The lights were bright, and the people walked randomly with carts half full. When a loud voice came over the loudspeaker, Molly Sue slapped her hands over her ears.

Sharon walked up and down the aisles showing her food items, boxes with pictures, and such, in an effort to try to discern what to buy, but Molly had little input. Macaroni and cheese proved to be a big hit, as did hot dogs.

They would eat a bite of dinner each night then watch a sitcom or two before shutting off the television. Then Sharon would dress Molly Sue in pajama's and pull her up into the rocker with Fuzzy and they would read and sing, giggle and tickle.

Sharon still couldn't bear to put Molly alone in the spare room, so once she fell asleep in her arms, she would put her to bed in her room.

Then, Sharon would relax with her customary bottle of cabernet. Usually she would fall asleep in the recliner, then wake an hour later and go to bed.

She liked the new routine, but had a dread in the pit of her stomach regarding the day when they would find her mommy. Still from time to time, Molly Sue would ask for her mommy with woeful big blue eyes peering at Sharon, but it was happening less and less.

A knock on Sharon's office door declared Bill standing there. She got the distinct impression that he had been standing there for a while watching her.

"What?" Sharon asked.

"You were lost in thought. What were you thinking about?"

Sharon looked around the room and back to Bill. She was uneasy, not wanting to confess she was thinking once again about Molly Sue. "Nothing in particular."

Bill sauntered into the room, shut the door, and took a seat in the chair in front of Sharon's desk. He sat for a few moments just watching Sharon. "We have to think ahead about what we will do with Molly Sue."

"What do you mean?" Sharon squirmed in her seat. Her skin prickled with anxiety.

"It doesn't look like we will find her mommy anytime soon. We need to find her a foster home."

A sharp intake of breath sucked into Sharon's lungs. "No!"

Bill sat patiently allowing his words to sink in. "We have to do what is necessary for her. We need to get her settled in case we don't find her mom."

"I want her!" Sharon frantically spoke. "I can be her foster mom. I can be Bill. I can. What do I need to do?"

"I know you do, but aren't you already in too deep?"

"I want to adopt her."

"You can't adopt her. She has a mother out there somewhere."

"I... I... I will be her foster mom." Sharon thought she

would collapse from panic. "It would be what is best for her. She is settled at my home and we have a routine. Please Bill don't take her from me."

Bill was calculating in his mind what was really best for Molly Sue. If Sharon got in any deeper and Mollie's mother resurfaced, it would kill Sharon. He really didn't think she would recover. Although, she was right. She had been good for Molly Sue and the little girl seemed to be flourishing.

"Let me make some calls," said Bill as he rose to leave. "One way or another, we need to establish a legal guardian until we find her mother should she need medical care or something similar."

"Bill, I'll do whatever I need to do." Sharon's eyes pleaded with Bill, her breath still.

"I'll try, but you know that the system will not want to place her in a single parent home."

"If we can go straight to a judge and keep her out of the system, they might. You know Judge Abernathy. Talk to him. Please. You can make him understand."

He nodded and walked away. "I'll do what I can."

Sharon felt the room swimming, as if the air had been removed out of the room. She suddenly stood, knocking over a stack of files. Stepping over them, she reached for her purse and hurried out of the building and straight to Leslie's. She needed to see Molly Sue.

SHARON - DECEMBER 1971

The new little Christmas stocking that Sharon had done in needlepoint hung beside her own simple stocking. She had done one for little Evan. He had added such joy to her life. He was walking now and when Sharon would babysit him; she was busy anticipating his every step.

Sharon had been tempted to venture out on a few dates through the past year, but all she could ever think of was the fear of talking about her past. She knew if she were to get close to a real relationship she would have to tell them and she couldn't bear it. For now, she was living vicariously through Patty, but that was okay until things in her life changed.

A sharp knock on the door sounded before it flew open ushering in a cold snow studded gust of wind with her friends Patty, Lenny, and baby Evan. They were having a little family Christmas party with just them.

Sharon reached for Evan as Patty and Lenny sat down a box of goodies, and then they shrugged out of their coats. Sharon pulled off Evan's coat and stocking cap and hugged him tight. He twisted around in her arms to look at the Christmas tree, bright with lights.

She walked over to the tree to show him up close and he drooled on a little fist as he looked up with bright eyes. Then suddenly without warning a tiny fist shot out and slapped at the tree. A glass ornament went crashing to the floor, shattering on impact.

"Oh, no!" Patty's voice came sharply from the kitchen.

Lenny presented himself quickly with a broom and a scolding for Evan.

"It's okay guys. I shouldn't have held him so close. He didn't know." Sharon didn't care about the ornament. The joy that the lit up tree brought Evan was what brought her joy, not the individual ornaments.

The friendship between the three of them had grown comfortable. It really felt more like they were indeed a family. Sharon had never known a friend as close as Patty. Once seated for dinner, Sharon looked around the table and her heart was genuinely full.

The warmth from the oven that now ticked quietly as it cooled, the warm glow of the light above, the interlacing of aromas from the various dishes and their seasonings, all immersed the room in a soft bed of comfort.

"So, you two ladies will graduate business school in a few months. What are your big plans?" said Lenny.

"Well, I have to get a full-time job," said Sharon. "I probably jumped the gun moving out of my parents' house so soon, but I couldn't take it anymore. This little garage apartment seemed affordable at the time, but I naively didn't figure in all the other stuff I would need to live on. I'm strapped!"

Both Patty and Lenny looked at Sharon. "We would up our babysitting pay if we could. Is there some other way we can help?" Patty asked.

"No. I didn't say that to alarm you or think I was asking for help. I just mean, the minute I can get a full-time job, I have to!"

"Where do you think you'll look?" Lenny asked.

Sharon laughed, "Everywhere. I've actually put in

several applications for part-time work hoping that I can get hired on somewhere that will transition me to full-time once school is over. So far no luck."

"I'll admit, I haven't thought about it too much. Going to school full time while being a mother is overwhelming. I've daydreamed about taking a few months off to stay home with Evan, but I know we don't have that luxury," said Patty.

Lenny sat looking towards his plate. Vacancy on his face was evidence of a faraway thought. "I wish I made more money so you could stay home full-time Patty." He looked over at her. Waves of love poured forth from his eyes. For a moment it was as if they were the only two in the room.

Sharon ate in silence studying her plate to give the illusion of privacy. Soon, she heard Patty clear her throat, and it broke the mood. Sharon felt eyes suddenly on her.

Looking up, Sharon realized Patty had a cocky grin on her face, then glanced sideways at Lenny. "By the way... There is something I wanted to tell you." Sharon looked from Patty to Lenny as they exchanged conspiratorial glances with each other.

"What? Are you pregnant again?" Sharon asked almost hoping she would say yes.

"What? Oh, no! Goodness no!" Patty's face wrinkled in distaste. "I don't think I could handle that on top of Evan and school right now."

Patty punched Lenny in the ribs. "You tell her."

Lenny rolled his eyes and wiped his mouth with his napkin. "There is this guy I work with…"

Sharon moaned out loud. "No! I don't want to hear it."

"Wait, Sharon. Listen." Patty attempted to quiet Sharon so she would listen. "He's a really nice guy. I wouldn't have encouraged this if he wasn't." Patty's eyes were pleading with Sharon to listen, so she shut her eyes and sighed.

Sharon gave in. "Okay. Go ahead and tell me,"

"Well, he has worked with me for six months. He is smart and funny, isn't that what girls like?" Lenny grinned. "No seriously. He really seems to be a nice guy. He saw you and Patty together the other day and was asking about you. I said I would talk to you."

Sharon's stomach had knotted up from the beginning of hearing of a guy being interested in her. Patty had questioned her several times about her dating, or rather not dating. As close as they had gotten though, she had never had the courage to tell her about the abortion or the effect it had had on Sharon.

Honestly, being with a man again terrified her. Yes, she wanted a home and a family, but seeing how quickly she could get pregnant caused her anxiety about it happening again before she was ready. She didn't want to have to date someone and then hold them at arm's length.

There was also the concern that she might not be able to get pregnant again after the abortion. She had heard rumors that was a huge possibility after having had an abortion. Not knowing for sure kept the hope alive for someday. But what if she really couldn't? Then she would have to tell her boyfriend or husband why. How could she share her deepest shame to anyone?

Lenny and Patty were talking about the guy at work. Sharon had missed most of their dialog while caught up in her internal dialog of anxiety. Coming back into focus, she smiled and nodded. "Well, maybe." She stood and began stacking empty plates to take to the sink.

The room grew quiet and neither Lenny or Patty said a word. The feeling that they had touched a nerve was profound, but neither knew why.

Sharon stood at the sink staring out at the blackness of the night. Her reflection faintly peering back at her, shrouded in the night's darkness. The tears that rolled down her cheeks were hot and she could no longer hold them back. The sudden feel of Patty's hand across her shoulders startled her.

"What is it? You can tell me." Patty's words were soft and gentle and convincing. A fleeting thought rushed by that maybe she could tell her friend the truth. But, could she really?

"I'll take Evan to the store. We'll leave you ladies to talk for a bit." Lenny already had Evan bundled and was heading for the door. As soon as it closed behind him, Patty was leading Sharon to the sofa.

The lights of the little Christmas tree bathed the room in shades of red, blue, green, and yellow. In the otherwise dim room, Sharon felt a sense of comfort. Her friend sat quietly beside her on the sofa just waiting, giving her time. Her friend's breathing penetrated the roar in Sharon's mind. The turmoil, the anxiety that she spent so much time trying to relegate to an unused portion of her memory.

She rested her forehead on her knees and wrapped her arms around her shins. Several minutes passed before she looked up and spoke. "My father forced me to have an abortion."

A sharp intake of breath penetrated the silence. Sharon braced herself. This was one of those moments where time would fracture or move forward. Was their friendship forged so deeply that it could overcome this deep, dark part of her past? Would her friend understand? Could she understand?

Sharon couldn't bear to look at Patty. After the initial reaction of shock, nothing was said, and neither moved. Was Patty waiting for more explanation or was she so shocked that she was at a loss for words?

Time ticked by as if caught in a surreal warp where seconds drew out as if they were hours. Neither knew what to say. Sharon wondered if she should continue, but what more was there to say? Patty didn't know how to recover from the shock, much less comfort her friend.

The single light hanging from the center of the kitchen ceiling flickered. It startled and caught their attention breaking the trance that only words can produce.

"I'm afraid," Sharon finally said. The words were dull and lifeless. Months of pushing them down flat inside herself had reduced them to mere words devoid of feeling.

Patty fidgeted in her seat. She focused her gaze on her friend's profile. The pain of her eyes and the dampness of her cheeks touched something in Patty and washed away all the shock. She reached out and pulled her friend close to her. "I'm so sorry."

The two sat for a few moments longer. The embrace created comfort that flowed from Patty to Sharon and it worked to push aside the resurfaced grief. Finally, when Sharon felt she could breathe again, she pulled away and sat upright. For the first time since her confession to her friend, she turned to face her. What would she find there? The eyes would tell her the truth.

But when Sharon looked at Patty, her eyes were full of tears yet to fall. The pain for her friend that rested there was sincere. And at that realization, out burst sobs of pent up grief and a flood of relief at the same time. She knew it would be okay.

"Tell me," Patty urged. "Tell me everything and anything that you want to tell me."

Sharon gave the short version of her pregnancy, the dilemma, and her father's solution to the problem. Patty sat by quietly listening.

"But Patty here is the thing. I'm afraid. I'm afraid if I get close to someone, I'll have to tell them. I don't even know if the abortion will prevent me from having kids. What if I can't and I haven't told and then I am found out?"

"Sharon, the man who is worthy of your love will understand."

"I just can't seem to get over it. The pain is horrific. When I lay down at night, I can't avoid it. It doesn't matter that it wasn't my decision. That almost makes it worse. I hate my father. I try not to. I know I should forgive him. I know he thought he was doing what was right for me, but I'm so angry at him. And my mother. She just stood by weakly leaving me to his brutality."

Sharon realized she was grinding her teeth. The unforgiveness in her gut was wrenched into a knot. She closed her eyes and breathed deep forcing her entire body to relax, acutely aware of each muscle and the tension it had absorbed. One by one, she worked to release them.

"I think that is one reason that I'm so attached to sweet Evan. I can love him and jump past all the unknowns and fears in my life. I can just love and enjoy him."

"I can't imagine how hard all this has been for you. And being there for me during the pregnancy and birth. How you must have been hurting inside. I never knew." Patty longed to express her deep heartfelt sympathy and consolation, but words didn't seem to express what she was trying to say.

"It was horrible at first. That day you walked into the classroom felt like someone hit me in the gut. Then you insisted on being my friend." Sharon snorted a tiny laugh and looked over at her friend. She was relieved that the worst was over and she had been accepted in spite of it all.

"And now, I insist that you go out on a date. I promise I would not even suggest it if I didn't think he was a wonderful man. You need to do this." When Sharon looked away, Patty repositioned herself to make eye contact. "Listen to me. This is a good thing. It will help you move forward and heal."

Sharon studied her friend's face. The abortion alone was her deepest pain, but its tentacles reached far and wide into other areas of her life. The unforgiveness, the fear, the lifeless despair. Maybe this one action would help to ease just a little of that.

"Okay. I'll go."

CHAPTER 5

Sharon - August 1978

Sharon and Molly Sue were in the front yard with flats of annuals surrounding them. They were digging in the dirt and planting flowers long past the time they should have been. But Molly Sue hadn't been there in May, so August would have to do.

Being so late in the summer, they had sold them to her at a significant reduction. It was already so hot that Sharon thought she would melt and it was only ten in the morning.

She sat back on her haunches and looked around at what they had left to do. Molly Sue was diligently pushing dirt in on the plant she had just put in the hole. She worked carefully to not break the stem as she pushed the dirt firmly down.

Once her task was complete, she looked up at Sharon and smiled. "Are we done?"

Sharon knew her face was beat red and drenched in sweat. Then an idea occurred to her, and she responded. "Not yet, wait here."

She walked across the yard and turned on the water hose. Acting as though she were going to water the flowers they had just planted, she walked over to where Molly Sue sat watching her. Then suddenly, she put her finger in front of the end of the hose creating a spray of water and showered Molly Sue.

The little girl squealed with delight. For the next thirty minutes the two of them played in the water as if they were both five years old.

Finally, they tumbled onto the lush grass and laid looking up at the blue sky. Molly Sue pointed at one of the white fluffy clouds. "That one looks like a pillow."

Sharon searched for a cloud she could point out. "Look. That one looks like a heart."

Then as the clouds thinned and the shade of the tree crept over them. They found peace just resting side by side.

As it neared lunchtime, Sharon rose and collected the remaining flats of flowers and placed them in a shady portion of the porch.

"Let's go get cleaned up and get some lunch."

With the flowerbed residue absent from their hands, They stood up to the kitchen counter and worked on sandwiches. Molly Sue pulled out four slices of bread from the bag with bright polka dots all over it.

Sharon layered homemade tuna salad on two of the

slices and Molly Sue covered them with the remaining slice.

"Let's get some chips," Sharon said and reached for a bag of potato chips.

They sat at the kitchen table where both could look out at the backyard. Molly Sue ate quietly and Sharon gazed off into the backyard, but saw none of it. A slight tug of her shirttail, brought her back.

Molly Sue smiled big. "Thank you, Miss Sharon."

"For what, Molly Sue?"

"For the food." Sharon thought how odd that a child so young, well any child for that matter would think to be thankful for food.

"That is very nice Molly Sue. Did your mommy teach you to be that way? To be thankful?"

"Yes. Sometimes we didn't have a lot to eat."

Sharon frowned. "I see."

"Mommy taught me how to make a garden and grow vegie-tables."

Sharon laughed. "You mean vegetables?"

Molly's head bobbed up and down. "But mommy and me called them vegie-tables. We would laugh at that."

"What kind of vegie-tables did you grow?"

Mollie Sue thought for a moment before answering. "We had tomatoes. We had onions." With serious eyes looking up at Sharon. "I didn't like onions very much."

Sharon tried not to smile.

"We had carrots and green beans. But when summer went away the vegie-tables went away too."

"Did your mommy not know how to can or freeze them?"

Molly Sue looked at Sharon with a blank look like she did so often when she did not know what Sharon was asking her.

Then, changing gears, Sharon said, "You know, there are onions in the tuna salad." She raised her eyebrows for emphasis.

Molly Sue looked down at the half of a sandwich that remained on her plate. "That's okay. If they are in the middle of something, they are okay." She then picked up the sandwich and took a bite.

Sharon watched as Molly Sue chewed the large bite. Everything that little girl did was endearing, or was it just that Sharon was so desperate to love her?

They continued to eat and chat, munching on the chips when they had finished the sandwiches. The shrill tone of the phone interrupted their conversation.

"Hey, it's Leslie. Do you two want to go to the pool with us?"

Sharon looked at Molly Sue. "You want to go to the pool?" Molly Sue just looked back at Sharon. "You know, to go swimming?" She knew what swimming was and smiled as her girls bounced in a profound yes.

"Does Sherry have an extra swimsuit that Molly Sue could borrow?"

"I think so. I'll check."

Less than an hour later Leslie, Sherry, Sharon, and

Molly Sue were standing, waiting to pay for entrance into the pool.

"Where are Mike and Brandon today?"

"They went to Mike's dad's farm. I'm not really sure what they will do out there. Help his dad do something."

"Two please. One adult and one child." Was repeated by both Leslie and Sharon as the girls peered out where the loud laughter and splashes of water were coming from.

Once inside, they found a place with two lounge chairs and got settled in. Molly Sue watched carefully to see what Sherry did and followed suite. "Molly Sue, do you know how to swim?" Sharon asked.

She nodded slightly. Her eyes were round and scanned the crowd of kids walking fast to keep from running, jumping in. Others were throwing big inflated balls at each other in the water. Still others were jumping from a platform. Molly Sue was chewing on her finger the way she had done right after walking into the police station that first day.

Sharon scooted over to the edge of the seat and pulled her close. "I know there are a lot of other kids out here, but see how much fun they are having? You'll have fun too." Sharon stood and took Molly Sue's hand. "Let me go with you. We'll get in together."

Molly Sue walked close beside Sharon as she walked to the side of the pool that was the most shallow. There was a long gently sloping bottom where the younger kids could play without fear of getting in too deep.

Sharon began to walk into the water with Molly Sue at

her side. The water was cool and felt good. When they were in deep enough that Molly could feel the water's force move her, she reached out and grabbed for Sharon.

Soon, she was laughing and splashing Sharon. Leslie and Sherry joined them. When the young girls moved away from the adults, Leslie said, "Molly Sue has never been to a pool before, has she?"

Sharon shook her head. "Doesn't appear so. Every day I learn a little more about what her life was like before. Today I found out she and her mommy had a garden and grew vegie-tables." Sharon smiled. "And, she doesn't like onions unless they are in the middle of something."

"You've been good for her, Sharon."

As she watched the two girls play, Sharon grew serious. "I think so. I think under the circumstances she has done well. But I don't know if that will be enough to convince them to let me keep her until we find her mother."

"Has there been any progress on that front?"

"None that I know of. It just seems like we have exhausted all resources. You would think that when Molly Sue didn't return, someone would have missed her and reported it."

"If they could have reported it, couldn't they have asked for help rather than send Molly Sue?" Leslie slathered her mixture of baby oil and iodine on her legs. "I suspect they must have lived so primitively that there was no way to contact anyone and Molly Sue's mommy was too ill to go."

"I agree. I often wonder just how ill her mommy was and if she is even still alive."

"Do you think we will ever know?" Leslie looked at Sharon with her hand held shading her eyes from the sun. What she saw was deep-lined concern crossing Sharon's face.

"I don't know Leslie. I just don't know."

Sharon - December 1971

The ridiculous party dress Sharon had bought to wear to the New Year's Eve party was a poor choice. The black backless halter dress was beautiful and looked amazing on, but it was December and cold. Patty had assured her that everyone would dress up for the party and it was her first date with Will so she had splurged on the dress.

The borrowed black shawl did little to keep her warm, but it provided some cover for her bare skin. She paced a worn strip in the carpet in front of the picture window in her living room. Upon the sound of a motor shutting down and a door shut, she froze. *He's here*, she thought.

Her entire body began to tremble slightly. Against her better judgement, she had agreed to a date with Will. She had not actually met him yet, only speaking on a brief phone call when he invited her to the party. Sharon felt The New Year's party was a good choice since there would be an evening filled with people, booze, and music. She could avoid herself and the tormenting thoughts of her past all evening long.

The knock on her front door sprang her from her

frozen state and she quickly opened the door before she had time to back out.

Will Yates stood there before her dressed in a tuxedo. His sandy blond hair was slightly tussled as if he had walked straight from the beach, even though there was no beach within a hundred-mile radius. When he smiled, rows of perfect white teeth lit the darkness of the night. He was so handsome, that it caught Sharon's breath.

"Hi, I'm Will."

Sharon nodded.

Will grinned. "Are you ready or shall I come in?"

Sharon nodded.

Will laughed and it broke Sharon from her reverie.

"Yes, I'm ready." Heat from embarrassment rose up her neck as she grabbed her fussy little party purse off of the end table and walked out onto her door stoop.

Will reached for her hand to help guide her down the steps. The chariot that awaited them was a sleek black BMW. It was brand new. Anxiety flooded Sharon's senses. *Is this his car? Is he rich? I don't know how to act.*

"You look lovely," said Will.

Lovely. I've never known a guy to use the word lovely. Am I dreaming? Is this a fairy-tale?

"The car should warm back up quickly." Will smiled over at Sharon as he brought the motor to life. The leather seats held Sharon firmly and smelled so new, she felt like she was royalty.

The New Year's Eve party was being held at Lenny's boss' house. It was a large sprawling estate that overlooked

Lake Pinnacle. They held the yearly event for as many people as they could invite. It was as much a show of ostentatiousness as anything. The evening wear was an understood necessity should you be privileged enough to be invited. Sharon knew they had only invited her because she was Will's date.

Footmen waited to valet park the car, their red jackets punctuating the night. Will opened the door for Sharon and led her up a curved stone path to the grand entrance. Lights bathed the majestic home and the walkway with halos of warm light.

At the door, Will slid his arm across Sharon's lower back and guided her into the entryway. The room was brightly lit with candles and grand chandeliers. The marble tile underneath her feet gleamed. Sensing her hesitation, Will gently guided her forward into the main room.

Activity bustled in every corner. Groups of three and four laughed, sipping glistening liquid from crystal goblets. Sharon's concerns about the sparse covering of her dress quickly faded. The room was bathed in warmth from the crackling fireplace that was as large as Sharon's entire living room.

When Will moved forward, eyes spun around and instant smiles greeted him. It appeared the entire room knew and loved him. Sharon tried to not feel insignificant and out of place. Beautiful women draped their hands on his shoulders as they greeted him. It was clear that he was a very desirable catch. *Why on earth did he ask me out on a date? Was it some kind of bet or dare?*

They each accepted a flute of champagne as the waiter slipped past. It gave Sharon something to do with her hands, something to busy herself with. Across the room, a large grand piano softened the staccatos of laughter with Christmas music.

Will turned to Sharon and smiled. His gaze lingered on her face and she could feel him taking her in. "You look absolutely stunning tonight."

Sharon smiled. "Thank you."

"I saw you with Patty the other day and thought you were beautiful, but now I realize just how beautiful you really are."

Sharon fidgeted. She had never thought of herself as pretty, much less stunning. If he was sincere, he was warming her heart. He didn't seem to have eyes that were scanning the room at the treasure trove of other beauties though. His eyes were focused on her.

"Thank you," she blushed and looked down at her drink.

"Lenny can't say enough wonderful things about you. So, you are in business school correct?"

"Yes. But I just graduated. Patty and I both took the accelerated track where we went during the summer and instead of graduating in May, we graduated this December."

Will was nodding as he listened intently. "What are your plans now?"

Sharon looked out into the room nervously. "Well, I need to get a full-time job. I just don't know where. It seems I've put in a ton of applications, but I've only had a couple of interviews. I'm working part-time still at the drugstore, but they can't even give me a full-time position."

It was clear to Sharon that Will came from money and to admit her financial shortfalls was quite embarrassing.

"Sharon, it seems to me that you are an intelligent and dedicated young woman. The right position will come along and the person who hires you will know they got someone special."

Sharon looked up into Will's eyes. They were intense. She felt feelings she had packed away long ago begin to beg for revival, but she wasn't sure she wanted to let go and indulge them. Will wasn't like the silly high school boys she had known and he was not even like the guys she had met since. Will was a gentleman and being with him made her feel like a woman.

"Thank you Will," Sharon said smiling broadly. "I appreciate the vote of confidence."

"Will you dance with me?"

Before she could answer, he took the empty flute from her hand and sat it to the side. He took her hand and led her with grace to the dance floor.

The pianist was playing Have Yourself a Merry Little Christmas, and she thought he was leaning to a much slower and moodier rendition of the song. Or maybe it was just that time had stood still as Will pulled her close to himself. His arm was strong across the small of her back, but he still held her with gentleness. He was about six inches taller than she and her cheek would rest just under his chin, should she choose to do so.

He held her much closer than necessary for a Christmas tune, even a slow one. She could feel the stiffness of his wool tuxedo and smell the scent of his aftershave. Her body began to feel weak as their bodies swayed close together, and she could feel desire beg to rise up inside.

At that first tingle of once lost desire, her mind began to challenge her. *Stop! What are you doing?* But the feelings didn't stop and truthfully she didn't want them to stop. And then way too soon, the song stopped and Jingle Bell Rock filled the room with joy.

Will led her once again to the side of the room. "They have a buffet set up. I'm pretty hungry, how about you?"

Sharon nodded. The buffet was an extravagant display of all types of food. You could fill your plate with a five-course meal or simply choose from dozens of hors d'oeuvres. They filled their plates and Sharon followed Will to a quieter room in the house, pondering how well he seemed to know the house.

Down the hallway towards the back sat a nice cozy study. The fireplace was lit there as well. The dark leather furniture and elegant wood-paneled walls were inviting. It had been designed for comfort and Sharon welcomed it.

They sat at a small game table to the side of the fireplace. "I hate trying to stand in a crowd of people and eat while holding my plate," Will said.

Sharon smiled. "Yes. You have that trade off at parties. You get a ton of great food, but then you usually have to stand to eat it. I'm thankful you found this little nook. Are you sure that it's okay that we are back here?"

Will smiled. "Yes. See, they lit the fire and turned on the lamps so that guests would feel comfortable here."

"You seem to know your way around here quite well? How is that?"

Will's smile dropped, and he hesitated before answering. "I live here."

SHARON - AUGUST 1978

Sharon stood looking at the guest room that Molly Sue had never slept in. Molly Sue walked in with Fuzzy and looked at Sharon.

"I think it's time that we turn this room into your room." She looked at Molly Sue when there was no response. "We need to get you your own room. Wouldn't you like that?"

Molly Sue continued to look at Sharon. Finally, Sharon got down on Molly Sue's level and looked at her. "What was your bedroom like at your home with your mommy?" No response. "You did have a room of your own, didn't you?" No response.

"Tell me about your house."

"I slept with mommy."

"In her bedroom?"

"We only had one room."

Sharon frowned. "Only one room?"

Molly Sue nodded.

"What was in that one room?"

Molly Sue shrugged. "A bed, a table, a stove. A cupboard."

"What about a bathroom?"

"We went outside for that." Molly Sue was losing interest and began fiddling with Fuzzy's neck bow.

"Well, we're going to paint and fix this room up. You'll be starting school soon and you will need your own room, bed and things."

The bed would do. It was a full size bed. It would need a new bedspread and of course they needed new curtains.

"Let's go shopping."

Sharon drove to the city to go to one of those new large chain stores where they sold a little of everything. Hopefully, she could get almost everything they needed in one place.

"What is your favorite color?"

"Pink."

"I like pink too."

"No, maybe blue," Molly Sue replied.

Molly Sue was brushing Fuzzy's fur with her hand.

"I like blue too."

"I like yellow too," said Molly Sue.

"Well, maybe we can find a bedspread with lots of colors."

It was a Saturday afternoon and the parking lot was full. It seemed everyone wanted to try out the new store.

When they walked through the swishing glass doors,

Molly Sue jumped and clung to Sharon. Looking into the vast store was overwhelming. She held on to Sharon and tucked her head into Sharon's leg.

Sharon picked her up and slid her into the seating area of a shopping cart. Molly Sue was on the small side of five and still fit well. "Here you can ride in here." Molly Sue nodded as she hugged Fuzzy.

They walked up and down the aisles. There were so many things to look at and soon Molly Sue grew comfortable with their environment. On the aisle where the bedroom sets were displayed in clear bags, it was a sea of color.

Sharon took Molly Sue from the cart and let her walk down the aisle looking at each one. Finally, she stopped in front of a pink floral spread and looked up at Sharon and smiled. "So, I guess pink really is your favorite color." Sharon laughed and Molly Sue nodded.

They bought sheets, curtains, curtain rods, a little bookshelf that had to be put together, a desk lamp with a pink frilly lampshade, and a few other knick-knacks.

With the few other items Sharon had thrown in the basket she shouldn't have been surprised with the cashier said, "That will be $124.58." She nodded and wrote out the check. The monetary cost of raising children had never occurred to her. She was glad she had been putting a good sum of money away into her savings account for several years.

"Now we need paint." She said to Molly Sue as she rolled the full cart out to her car. Getting everything into the Mustang was tricky, but with a little creative arranging, she managed.

At the hardware store, she held a pillow case up to several colors of pink to see which one worked best. "You know, it may just be too much pink. What if we paint the walls a fresh coat of white paint?"

Molly Sue just nodded. *She does not understand what we are doing*, thought Sharon.

It was three in the afternoon by the time they arrived back home. "I'm almost too tired to do anything else today. What if we paint tomorrow?" Of course, Molly Sue nodded in agreement.

They took all the pieces out of the packaging and spread them all out. Sharon laid the spread on the bed and put a pillow in the case. "What do you think?"

Molly Sue smiled and ran her hand along the pink flowers. "I like it."

"Will you sleep in here with me?"

Sharon looked at Molly Sue and thought before answering. "Well, no. This is your room. I'll sleep in my room and you will sleep in here in this room." Molly Sue looked frightened.

"I'll be all alone? I don't want to sleep all alone. I want to sleep with you Miss Sharon." Tears threatened to burst from their holding.

"Well, Fuzzy will be here sleeping with you. You won't be alone." Molly Sue nodded, but didn't look convinced.

"We will take it slow. You won't be alone. I don't want you to be afraid." Molly Sue walked over to Sharon and hugged her legs. "I love you Miss Sharon. I love you so much."

Sharon knelt down and hugged Molly Sue back. "I love you too, sweet girl. So very much."

The sofa felt very comfortable when Sharon and Molly Sue finally relaxed there. They had bought a new book at the store and Molly Sue was eager for Sharon to read it. Half way through, the phone rang.

"Hey girl, can you watch Sherry and Brandon this evening?"

"Of course. What's up?"

"Mike got a promotion at work and he decided at the last minute that he wanted to take me out on a date. You know, a grown up date." Leslie laughed. "I don't think we have been out just the two of us in ages."

"Of course. My goodness you keep Molly Sue for me every day. Will they be spending the night? It is fine if you want an all night date..." Sharon teased.

"Ooooh I hadn't thought of that. Would you mind?"

"Of course not!"

At six that evening, Leslie came in Sharon's front door dressed to the nine's carrying two small overnight bags. "You look gorgeous, but I think you need to reconsider your accessories."

Leslie rolled her eyes. "Thank you, but I thought I wasn't going to fit into this dress. It's a pre-childbirth beauty."

"You look lovely. Really." Just then Mike honked the horn.

"Well, I guess I'd better go. Here is some money for pizza." Sharon waved her off.

"I've got this. Now go."

Leslie hurried out the door and Sharon stood watching them drive off. Her heart longed for love, but fear was a careful guardian of her heart, and it dutifully drew her back in.

They ate pizza and played board games that Leslie had brought. By nine o'clock, Molly Sue and Sherry were yawning. *This might be a good time to try Molly Sue sleeping in her own room. She and Sherry could sleep in there together.*

Brandon, I'm going to let you sleep on the sofa or on the floor if you prefer, and the girls will sleep in the bed in Molly Sue's room.

"Can I watch television?"

"I'll have to think about that. Maybe."

Once everyone had their teeth brushed and their jammies on, Sharon took the girls into the spare room. "You two ladies are going to sleep in here together. Won't that be fun?"

Sherry jumped up and down clapping and squealing. "Yes. Yes."

Molly Sue stood clutching Fuzzy closely, saying nothing.

Sharon pulled the new bedspread off that they had laid on there and turned back the current covers. She got them both tucked in and lit a small night light near the bed. Molly Sue had still not said a word.

Sharon got Brandon situated and said he could watch

television if he kept it low so it didn't bother the girls. He complied.

As soon as Sharon had had her nightly two glasses of cabernet, she peeked in on the girls. Sherry was sound asleep, but Molly Sue lay rigid on her back holding Fuzzy. She looked straight up at the ceiling. *She'll go to sleep if I don't bother her*, thought Sharon.

The bed felt good to Sharon, and she fell asleep soon after sliding under the covers. Soon though, movement woke her. From the opposite side of the bed, in slid Molly Sue very quietly.

"Molly Sue, are you okay?"

"Yes. Me sleep with you Miss Sharon. I keep you from being lonely."

"Okay sweet girl. Okay."

Sharon reached for the small girl and pulled her into her arms, secretly glad Molly Sue had chosen to come sleep with her. She had grown used to her small body lying in the bed next to her. Until then, she had never realized just how lonely her life was.

CHAPTER 6

*S*haron - January 1972

The shock of realizing Will lived in the great mansion on the lake soon passed as he explained that Lenny's boss was his uncle and while he was getting his master's degree, he was living with them. Yes, his mother's family came from money and yes, he had grown up in a wealthy and generous home, but; they had raised him with strict discipline.

He had chores even though most could have been done by a cleaning lady or cook. It had been important to his parents to teach him to work for a living and to take care of himself. He actually had very little money at his disposal, on purpose.

January had brought a bought of bitter cold and then the sun would break free and force warmth into the frozen land. It was on one such beautiful day that Will had come to Sharon's apartment and swept her away, not taking no for an answer to head out on a weekend road trip.

"You will love this little B&B. It's cozy and the drive will be great." Will was dancing her around the tiny living room.

"Okay. Okay. Let me throw a few things in a bag."

With minimal thought, she threw a few things in a bag and they hurried out the door.

"So, how far away is this place?"

"About two hours. But the drive is beautiful." Will smiled at her and Sharon felt her heart melt.

"It's the dead of winter. Unless we are in Hawaii, there is no beautiful drive." Sharon snorted a laugh.

Will reached a hand over and pulled up her chin and turned it to look his way. "You make any drive beautiful."

Sharon swiped at him. "Stop it! You're too charming. I just don't buy it."

Will laughed. "Am I laying it on too thick? Isn't that what the ladies like?"

"Not if it isn't sincere."

"How do you know it isn't?"

"Well, only time will tell if you are sincere or not."

"Okay, Sharon Paulson. I'll just have to show you that my talk isn't cheap." He winked at her and turned up the radio. Soon they were singing to Maggie May, Don't Pull Your Love, and I Feel The Earth Move.

Sharon took a deep breath. It was easy to be with Will. She liked it and hated it. Would he break her heart? Was she willing to be vulnerable enough for him to do that? Was it too late?

"I'm hungry."

"Hmmm," Sharon replied.

"What?"

"Well, look around. Where on earth are we going to eat way out here?"

"There's a place a bit up the road."

Sharon watched, and for the next several miles she saw no sign of a city or town coming up ahead. Then Will began to pull off the road up to a small old building that looked like it had been a gas station years ago. Like fifty years ago. One car sat off to the side.

"What on earth is this place?"

"You'll see."

They walked to the door and Sharon wondered if the slat board porch would fall through. The old screen door rebelled with a screech when Will pulled to open it.

A blast of warmth, almost too much warmth, blasted her as it hurried to escape the tiny establishment.

"Lawdy mercy, boy. Where you been too? Ain't seen you in ages." A large man lumbered from around an old counter and pulled Will into a huge hug. His dark skin glistened with the dew of sweat. "And who this beautiful lady be? Mm mm."

"This is Sharon. Sharon this is Earl. He makes the best BBQ in the entire state. Hell, in the entire country."

Earl turned and swiped the air as if brushing off Will's

comment and walked back to the stool he had vacated when they had walked in.

"Two specials, Earl. And two beers," Will said as he unwound his scarf from around his neck. Sharon had already peeled her layers off.

Will walked toward one of three small tables in the room. Sharon wanted to laugh at the typical decor of red-checked vinyl on the tables and the stacked bottles of various hot sauces next to the salt and pepper shakers.

The walls were adorned with... well, junk. But very interesting junk and old metal signs. Behind the bar were neon beer signs.

"Well, what do you think?" Will asked. His eyes sparkled as if he had presented the Hope Diamond to Sharon.

Seeing the look on Will's face, Sharon laughed. "You crack me up."

"What?" He feigned incredulity.

"Let me just say that the food better be good."

Then as if on cue, two large plastic baskets lined with red-checked paper appeared before them. A mixture of pulled pork, ribs, and a chicken breast filled the baskets to overflowing. Sides were set on the table in individual brown bowls. There was red beans, coleslaw, and fried okra.

"I'll never eat all of this." Sharon looked at the enormous amount of food that sat before her, not knowing where to start.

Will was already halfway through his first rib. Sauce rimmed his mouth, and he didn't care. Sharon reached for the pulled pork and piled it on the butter toasted Texas toast. "Here." Injected Will. "You have to have some of this." He grabbed a dark red plastic bottle and squeezed a generous portion of fragrant and spicy sauce on the pork. "There you go."

Sharon tentatively took a bite, unsure of what she would experience. Flavor exploded in her mouth and her eyes went round. Will nodded without missing a beat gnawing on a bone.

So they ate, and they ate. When Sharon thought she would die from overeating, Earl slapped down two large servings of peach cobbler swimming in heavy cream.

"No. No. No. I can't. I will explode."

"Taste it."

"Will, I can't. I'm serious. I'm - going - to - bust - wide - open."

"Taste it. One bite."

So she did, and one bite led to the next. She made it four bites before she dropped the spoon into the plate. She was shaking her head. "You were right. It is amazing, but I'm going to have to lay myself out on a slab to let this food digest."

Earl slid the ticket on the table. Sharon glanced, and it read, $5.50. "Are you kidding? That's all he charges for all this?" Sharon was stunned.

Will got up and tossed a twenty on the table. "Low overhead."

The ride the rest of the afternoon was a struggle. Being full to the brim with amazing food, and the warmth of the sun coming through the windshield, had created a comfort coma. She kept repositioning herself each time her eyelids grew heavy.

"It's okay if you nap." Will said.

"No. I'm fine." But soon her eyes were closed and her head was leaning on the doorframe of the car.

When Sharon woke, gravel was popping underneath the tires. She looked up as the sun was dipping behind the trees bathing the ground in long exaggerated shadows. The long driveway that Will had slowed down to navigate led to a large Victorian house. It was massive and elegant. Intricate details were each one painted, and Sharon thought she could count at least four, no five different colors.

The front door opened at the sound of their car coming up the drive and a man and woman in their fifties stood with smiles to greet them.

"Welcome," the woman said immediately as Sharon opened her door. "You are just in time for dinner."

"Oh, I'm sure it is wonderful, but I ate such a big lunch." Sharon caught Will's face and the slight shake of his head.

"We would love to join you for dinner," Will said.

As soon as they stepped inside, Sharon's body betrayed her. The scents of a home-cooked meal drew her further into the house. The dining room held a display of large soft hot rolls, fried chicken, mashed potatoes, and gravy. There were green beans, and a host of other sides.

She looked woefully at Will, and he smiled with a wink.

It surprised Sharon that she could entertain the idea of

eating again. It had only been five hours since she had eaten the huge BBQ feast, but the fresh home cooked food was irresistible.

After dinner, a large rich chocolate cake was set on the table and they cut huge slabs from it against Sharon's protests. The rich butter frosting, thick with cocoa and sugar, made Sharon close her eyes in divine ecstasy.

The couple had been very pleasant during dinner. They were obviously versed at small talk that was not overtly probing or intrusive. They allowed their guests to determine the depths of personal details that were discussed.

After dinner, Will and Sharon spent the evening bundled on the front porch swing snuggled next to each other.

"Do not. I repeat. Do not feed me one single meal tomorrow." Sharon tried to feign a scolding.

Will leaned his head back and roared with laughter.

"You laugh. I had to unbutton my pants after the second bite tonight."

Will's eyebrows dipped up and down. "Oooh, so your pants are unbuttoned?" He reached a hand down to where her zipper lay. Sharon pushed his hand away.

"Oh, no you don't. I'm not in the mood for anything but a stomach pumping in the emergency room."

Will smiled and pulled her close. For the next hour they didn't say a word, only gently relaxed to the swaying of the swing. When Will felt a shiver run through Sharon's body, he rose and pulled her up.

"I hope you've recovered. It's time for bed." He pulled

her close, wrapped the old quilt around her and kissed her long and deep.

SHARON - SEPTEMBER 1978

Labor Day weekend had been nearly as hot as Memorial Day weekend. Two hot sweltering weekends that sat as bookends encompassing summer like sentinels guarding the passage of time.

Bill had laid out his case for Sharon being designated as Molly Sue's temporary guardian to Judge Abernathy over eighteen holes on lush green grass. A decision was rendered over two tall glasses of sweet tea on the veranda of the country club.

Judge Abernathy looked at Bill through slits. "I don't like it Bill. What will the town think? A child needs two parents. If we let a single lady keep her, it just won't look right." He turned to look out on the course they had just conquered and took a lengthy swig of his tea.

Bill didn't want to push his long-time friend, so he let him have his say. Bill only nodded.

"Oh hell, if you say it's best for the girl, then I'll sign off on it. Get the paperwork over to me in the morning and I'll sign it." No more was said about Molly Sue, and the conversation turned to predictions of local high school sports for the fall season as the two men sat wiping sweat from their brows and the child already forgotten.

The next morning, the Tuesday after Labor Day, Sharon

took Molly Sue to kindergarten. She had not yet been officially designated as her guardian, but the school had allowed her to attend until they could complete the final paperwork.

Sharon had spent the entire weekend taking Molly Sue into the city and shopping for school clothes. They had eaten out and Sharon had spent almost an entire week's wages on her sweet charge. Molly was wide eyed through it all.

The discussion of school was foremost on Sharon's lips. She hoped that the more she talked about it the less anxious Molly Sue would be, but somehow she didn't think she was achieving her goal.

"Molly Sue, you do know what school is, right?" They were sitting in a booth at Woolworth's deli sipping on large milkshakes in tall clear glasses.

Molly's big blue eyes just looked at Sharon. Finally, Molly's head shook back and forth slightly, her blonde curls bobbing.

"So I have been talking to you for days about school and getting ready for school and you've had no idea what I've been talking about?" Sharon was so exasperated at herself for taking something as important as this for granted.

"No, Miss Sharon," Molly's eyes watered. "I'm sorry."

"Oh Molly, it's okay. I should have asked if you knew. Don't cry. It isn't your fault." Sharon reached into her bag and pulled out a white handkerchief from her purse. It was one from a stash her mother had given her. But when she saw it, she paused. There was something about it that triggered pain deep inside her. But, she couldn't remember what.

She handed the handkerchief to Molly Sue and helped her dab her eyes. "Pretty," said Molly Sue as her little finger followed along the purple scallops and violets along the edge. "I like it."

Sharon watched Molly Sue with the handkerchief feeling a deep sadness inside that she couldn't quite understand. She smiled a forced smile at Molly Sue, and nodded.

"You like that color?"

Molly looked up and nodded. "I like the flowers too."

"That color is purple and those flowers are called violets."

"Pretty."

They sat drinking their milkshakes and Molly played with the handkerchief. "Would you like to have that for your very own?"

Molly eagerly bobbed her head and smiled.

"It's yours. Keep it in your pocket for now, okay?"

Upon leaving Woolworth's, Sharon drove over to the grade school. The kindergarten room was on the opposite side of the school building from their police station. Molly would still be close if she needed Sharon.

They got out of the car and Sharon led Molly to a bench where they sat down looking at the school. "Molly this is the school building. Right now it looks just like any old big building, but in two days, there will be lots and lots of kids just like you running in the playground and sitting in classrooms learning things.

"You will learn how to read books just like I do. You will make new friends…"

"Like Buddy?"

Sharon frowned, then nodded. "Tell me more about Buddy."

It was Molly's turn to frown. "He took care of momma. He brought her things." Molly turned to look back out at the playground.

"What kinds of things?"

Molly shrugged her shoulders without hardly thinking as she continued to look around the vacant school yard.

"Did you like Buddy? Was he good to you and your momma?"

Molly looked up at Sharon and nodded.

"Did he live with you?"

Molly Sue thought for a moment then shook her head no. It was like this each time she tried to get more information from her about her momma and Buddy and their life as it had been.

"So, in a couple of days, I'll bring you here and you will stay until noon, or lunchtime. Then I'll pick you up and take you to Miss Leslie's for the afternoon. I promise you will like it. School is great fun. And if you need me, I'll be right over there on the other side."

"Miss Sharon, are you my momma now?" Molly's eyes searched deep into Sharon's soul.

"No Molly. You still have a momma, we just can't find her. We're still looking though. Have you thought of anything that might help us find her?"

Molly shook her head. Her expression was very sad, but she was long past the point of her big blue eyes spilling over with tears at the mention of her momma.

"Can Fuzzy go to school with me?"

"I think Fuzzy should stay with me or Miss Leslie. He is too young for school. But he might visit from time to time."

Molly Sue's brow furrowed.

"You can't go to school until you are five years old. Fuzzy is less than one-year-old. He's still a baby and needs taken care of."

The gaze that met Sharon was one of skepticism, but Molly didn't mention it further.

"So, I am five?"

They had no formal birth certificate, but the doctor had done tests that determined her age to be from the five to six-year range. "Yes, you are. Such a big girl."

Molly sat up a little straighter and looked out at the schoolyard again. Sharon thought her heart would burst. She hated the thoughts that came hoping they would never find her mother. The guilt was heavy and convicting. Bill was right. It would tear her apart if they found her, but she couldn't help it now.

What do you say we go home and then tomorrow we will go to the swimming pool? I have the day off and we can make it a holiday?

Sharon smiled and hugged Molly close. "Oh, my sweet girl. You have so much to learn. But you need to tell me every time I say something and you don't know what it is.

Promise?" She held Molly Sue at arm's length to see her response.

A huge smile preceded a vigorous nod of her head. "I will Miss Sharon. I will."

∽

SHARON - MAY 1972

The months between January and May seemed to blur past as though Sharon were on a carnival ride rushing fast and laughing heartily with every shifting bump and turn.

Will had not disappointed. He was every bit of what he appeared to be and his devotion to Sharon was genuine.

Sharon often felt as though she were living someone else's life. She felt as if she were waiting for the other shoe to drop and her fantasy to disappear as if it were fog hit by the heat of the sun.

But, as each day came and went, Sharon could see a life with Will. Each day he kept coming back and showering her with love. His calm and easygoing demeanor was comforting to her.

Thoughts of her past abortion still haunted her. She had not told Will yet and battled in her mind when and if she should. She felt deceptive, but then she would question if it really mattered. What would he really think of her?

She was still working at the drugstore. Even though she was getting more hours than before, she was still not working full time. Her applications for employment were in every file cabinet in every office within a twenty-mile radius. So, she settled in and worked hard where she was, but never neglecting the want ads. Each morning before the ink was even dry, Sharon was scanning for new job postings.

Will didn't seem to mind that she worked at the drugstore. It didn't seem to matter to him at all. *What would he expect from her if they got married,* she often wondered? *Would he want me to stay home and not work? What would he want?*

Patty had not worked since graduating business school. Evan was now running and into everything. He was her full-time job. Lenny's salary had increased and their family seemed to have found its groove.

The four of them, Lenny, Patty, Will, and Sharon often went to dinner or the movies together. They were an easy group to be friends with.

"Have you told him yet," asked Patty as Sharon reapplied her lipstick in the restroom mirror.

Sharon looked at her friend in the mirror. Instead of answering she looked down, recapped her lipstick and dropped it into her purse.

"Sharon, he loves you. He may ask you to marry him. He should know." Patty had turned to face her friend who continued to avoid her gaze. The outside door swung open and the noise of the restaurant ushered in two women laughing at a private joke. It broke the moment of tension and Sharon turned to go.

Patty reached out and stopped her friend. "Sharon, what are you afraid of?"

Sharon turned to face her friend. In a harsh hushed whisper, Sharon said, "I hate myself for having an abortion. I allowed them to kill my baby." Her face was wracked with pain and anger at herself. "How can Will see me as anything other than a baby killer when he finds out?"

"Sharon, you have to forgive. This anger and bitterness is eating you up. You know you had no choice. Forgive your father. Forgive yourself."

Sharon looked away. She thought about forgiveness. It eluded her and she had no desire to search for it. Gently shaking her head, looking back at her friend, "No. I can't. I won't." Then she turned to re-enter the restaurant.

As she walked back toward their table, she drew up the happy persona from deep inside that she kept for just such occasions. She had spent countless moments practicing the fine art of emotion suppressing. Sometimes she did it so well that she even fooled herself.

The remainder of dinner was enjoyed, but then with dessert, Lenny ordered champagne. Sharon felt the room shift as if a typhoon were coming. She could sense it long before the words were said.

With four glasses poured, Lenny lifted his, glanced at Patty and announced, "We have an announcement. They have selected me to head up our new division in Portland. It is a huge promotion and we are so excited."

Lenny's words swirled in Sharon's mind. Did she hear what she thought he said? Portland is thousands of miles from here. Patty smiled lovingly at her husband and avoided eye contact with Sharon. *She knew and didn't tell me.*

They would not only be taking their friendship away but also baby Evan. It seemed like he was as much hers as he was theirs. How could they take him away?

The room began to swim and Sharon sat her glass down without taking a drink. She trained her eyes on the candle in the center of the table and stared at it in an attempt to stabilize herself. Hardness as familiar as her own name began to creep back up from its lost place deep inside her. Once, it was firmly re-established inside of her; she looked up at Patty and attempted a smile.

Words of congratulations were uttered, or at least she thought she had uttered them. She had meant to. The explanation of plans to pack and move seemed to float through without attaching themselves to Sharon's mind.

The two couples said their good-bye's for the evening on the sidewalk. The night was still light out with the beautiful glow of dusk.

Will could sense Sharon's distress. "Let's walk." He guided Sharon down the sidewalk and around the corner to the park. The bench he chose faced the west, so the sunset was in full view. Sharon had no energy or desire to do anything but comply.

"I can't imagine how hard this news must be for you." Will's voice held sympathy, and he simply sat and waited for Sharon to respond. He reached out and took her limp hand.

As Sharon sat, words didn't come, couldn't come.

Would Will leave her too? Would everyone she ever loved leave her?

"I... I... I can't really talk about it right now." The lump in Sharon's throat made forming words nearly impossible. The beauty of the sunset seemed only to remind her of all the beauty that kept fading from her life, just as the sun faded into the horizon.

Silent tears fell then, and she did nothing to stop them or to explain them. Then she knew, just knew that it was time to rip the bandaid off and just get it over with. Why delay the pain? She couldn't hurt any more than she was right at that moment, so if Will were to leave her, there was no better time.

"I had an abortion."

Confusion muddled Will's thought. *Did she say abortion? When?* He pulled his hand away and Sharon closed her eyes. *Here it comes*, she thought.

"When?" Will's words no longer held compassion, but shock.

"Two years ago."

Relief edged out shock from Will's mind.

"My father made me. I wanted to keep the baby, but I was just graduating high school and... he made me." The tears were no longer silent. Sharon wrapped her arms around herself and her body shook.

Will wrapped his arms around her and pulled her close, but she was stiff and non-compliant. He did his best to hold her, but could feel the cavern between them.

Through her sobs she wailed, "I don't know if I can

even have another baby. Evan was my baby too. I love him and they are taking him away."

Will searched for something, anything to say. This was out of his personal realm of encouragement and he feared he would only make matters worse, so he just sat trying to hold her tightly.

Finally, she resisted no longer and allowed herself to relax into Will's arms. He wrapped her with both his arms and pulled her close, resting his chin on her head. As he gazed past the bench into the park, sadness welled up. This could change everything.

CHAPTER 7

Sharon - December 1978

Sharon couldn't remember a Christmas she had been more excited about. As she pulled out her meager supply of Christmas decorations, she saw the tiny stocking she had so lovingly made for baby Evan. She stood up slowly and ran her finger across the needle-pointed name.

Overwhelmed with memories, she walked to the sofa and sat down as if her body had suddenly become robotic. Tears escaped, and she brushed them aside. Memories of little Evan were bittersweet.

With a deep breath and resolve to forget the past, Sharon stood and continued emptying the few small boxes of ornaments and decor. Molly Sue would be up from her nap soon and she was eager to decorate with the precious girl.

Once all the items were out and ready to go, Sharon searched through her records for an old Christmas album she remembered having. Now, she only bought eight-track tapes, but the Christmas one was an LP. As she flipped through her collection, she hummed the melody of White Christmas.

Soon she found the album she was searching for near the back. Pleased at her find, she pulled out the album and turned to place it on the stereo. Molly Sue stood in the door to the hallway with tousled hair and her Fuzzy in tow.

Sharon set the needle on the vinyl and turned to smile at Molly Sue. She swept the girl up into her arms and said, "Let's sing Christmas songs." As usual Molly Sue just looked at Sharon.

"Do you know what Christmas is, Molly?"

"Yes," she said.

"Do you know any Christmas songs?"

"Yes."

"Do you know the one playing?"

Molly Sue tilted her head slightly to listen. Sharon nearly laughed and the intense look on her face as she put serious effort into remembering the song.

She sat Molly Sue back down on the floor and moved the needle on the album over two songs. The intro to Jingle Bells came happily through the speakers and Molly Sue's face lit up and her head bobbed eagerly.

Soon, both were laughing and singing Jingle Bells. By the end of the album it seemed that Molly Sue knew about three of the songs. When the stereo pulled up its arm and rested, Molly Sue was still singing to Fuzzy.

"We have to go buy a Christmas tree! Let's get our shoes and coats on and go see what we can find."

In the car, Sharon turned the heater on high, hoping that it would warm up quickly. Molly sat in the passenger seat with her red wool coat and white stocking cap which Sharon had bought only the previous week.

"Tell me about the Christmas trees you had." Sharon had had many such conversations over the past months hoping to learn more about the little girl's past. At this point she had lost most of her apprehension of losing Molly Sue. With each passing day which revealed no sign of her mother, Sharon felt increasing comfort. Even though she would often chide herself for such selfish thoughts, it was true none the less.

Molly didn't answer Sharon's question about a tree. She was too busy peering out the passenger window at the stores clad in Christmas decor. Multi-colored lights were strung everywhere and evergreen garlands and wreaths abounded.

"Ho Ho Ho," said the side-walk Santa as they drove past, and Molly Sue craned her neck to keep him in sight as they passed.

Once she could no longer see him, she turned and looked at Sharon quizzically. "That was Santa." Molly Sue's eyes got round.

"What's a Santa??"

Sharon parked the car and turned to look at Molly Sue.

She told her all about Santa and the stories about how he would bring good little boys and girls presents Christmas Eve while they slept. Molly Sue asked several questions and Sharon attempted to answer them all.

Molly Sue climbed out of her door. As soon as Sharon rounded the end of the car, Molly Sue grabbed her hand and began to run, pulling Sharon along.

The little plaza where Santa was taking requests had a line of about ten children of all ages. They took their place in line and Sharon watched as Molly Sue kept peering around the other kids to see Santa. She would dance from one foot to the other and then shuffle to look from another vantage point.

Finally, they were up to Santa and Molly Sue climbed up on his lap.

"What is your name little girl?"

"Molly Sue."

"What do you want for Christmas?"

"My mommy."

The look on Santa's face grew confused and Sharon felt like someone had punched her in the gut. Heat flushed up her neck as she stumbled to explain that she was Molly Sue's guardian, not her mother. But the reality left her feeling cold and hopeless. Molly Sue was not her child, and she still loved and wanted her own mother.

Once done, Molly Sue hopped down quite content and grabbed Sharon's hand. She looked up at Sharon and smiled. "Santa will bring me my mommy for Christmas."

With all the courage she could muster, Sharon smiled at

Molly Sue. "I'm sure he will do his best." Sharon squatted down to Molly's level. "But Molly, we've been looking and looking. Lot's of people have. Santa may not be able to find her either."

Molly didn't cry, she just looked at Sharon. Almost intuitively Molly Sue said, "I love you, too Miss Sharon." Then she plopped a kiss on Sharon's cheek, and started down the sidewalk once more.

A huge sob stuck in Sharon's throat, and her hand flew to her mouth. "I love you, too. Now let's go get that tree."

The tree lot was just around the corner, so they walked hand in hand. Ahead of them was a lot of all types of evergreen trees both short and tall, thin and full. Since it was the Saturday after Thanksgiving, the lot was full of customers searching for the perfect tree.

Suddenly Molly Sue's hand pulled from Sharon's as the little girl took off running towards the smallest most scraggly tree. They had pushed it aside at the very back of the lot. As Sharon walked up, the salesman was telling Molly that that tree was to be put in the wood chipper for mulch and was not for sale.

Molly turned to look at Sharon and then back at the man. "But we want this tree for our Christmas tree." She looked back at Sharon.

"Molly there are lots of trees out there. Why do you want this one?"

Molly turned to look at it and patted it. "Buddy gave us Christmas trees just like this one."

Sharon stood and looked at the man. "How much?"

He laughed, snorted and waved his hand as he turned to leave. "Lady you can have that one for free."

Sharon looked down at Molly Sue. *She has led such a curious life that I know nothing about.* "Okay Molly, this one will be easy to take home." Sharon picked up the sparse little tree, and they walked back to her car.

She had brought an old quilt and some ropes to tie a tree to the top, but thought maybe she could just get this one in the backseat even though in her Mustang there was little room. But sure enough, it fit.

They filled the ride home with squeals of delight as they drove past more decorated stores and houses. Sharon took the long way home so they could drive past more businesses decorated for the season and the churches with nativity scenes.

At the sight of the very first one, Molly Sue shouted, "Baby Jesus. Baby Jesus. Baby Jesus." She pounded the window and looked back at Sharon so she pulled into the parking lot.

When they walked up to the life size nativity scene, Molly Sue's mouth was a round 'O'. She crept up to the manger and knelt down looking at the baby doll someone had swaddled in an old sheet.

"Hello baby Jesus. My name is Molly Sue. My mommy told me about you." She paused and gently patted the baby. "Mommy told me to come here, and I did, but I can't find my mommy now. Will you take care of her for me? And Buddy too?" Molly Sue bent down and kissed the baby on the cheek. "I love you baby Jesus."

Sharon stood watching the scene. If she thought what she had witnessed with Molly Sue on Santa's lap had affected her, this brought her near devastation. She stood with a trembling hand to her mouth as tears ran down her cheeks. Emotional conflict tormented her as she battled with her own desires, hoping, and wishing for the best outcome for Molly Sue. Yet still hoping that outcome would be with her.

Before she knew it, Molly Sue was standing at her side, smiling up. "Baby Jesus loves us Miss Sharon. He will watch over mommy, and Buddy, too."

All Sharon could do was nod her head. Faith of any sort, her faith in God had died years ago along with the baby inside of her. She had lost all hope in God and humanity, but watching Molly Sue's genuine and pure faith in this moment brought Sharon up short. Would the girl's faith bring her mommy home, or would it destroy her when her prayer was not answered the way Sharon's had not been?

Molly confidently took Sharon's hand and led her back to the car. Once inside, Molly Sue turned to look at Sharon and beamed. Sharon smiled at the little angel. Maybe she was a gift from God to her. But if Molly Sue was a gift to her, then it would come at the expense of Molly's prayer. If Sharon really loved Molly Sue, wouldn't she want, hope, that her prayer would be answered over her own selfish desire?

Back at the house, the tree was easily erected. It took less than half the Christmas lights Sharon had and only one strand of the garland. Molly Sue marveled over every ornament that she picked up before placing it on the tree. Each one seemed to be a new and unique treasure that she had never experienced before.

When the tree was finally decorated, Sharon pulled out the box with the star. It looked too big and weighty for the small tree. "I think our star is too big for this little tree."

"I can make an angel."

"Okay."

Sharon got out the art supplies and sat with Molly Sue as she labored over each detail. To Sharon's surprise a beautiful angel soon took shape on the paper. As soon as she finished, Molly Sue picked up the paper and began carefully tearing the angel out of the page. Sharon sat holding a pair of scissors but halted her offering of them to Molly. The girl was painstakingly tearing the angel away almost perfectly.

Her little tongue stuck out the side of her mouth and her brows furrowed in concentration. Sharon sat awestruck. Finally, when the angel was free, Molly Sue said, "There." She looked over at Sharon and smiled.

The angel held a striking resemblance to the picture Molly Sue had originally drawn of her mommy when first arriving, however this time she had lovely angel wings.

With some thin Christmas ribbon, and tape, they were able to attach the angel to the top. Molly squealed with glee and hopped up and down clapping her hands.

Sharon turned from the girl and the tree and walked to her liquor cabinet. She pulled out a thick crystal glass and poured it half full. This was once the only thing that had helped her get through the pain. Her need for it once more was stronger than ever.

Her thoughts of Molly Sue at the nativity scene talking to the baby Jesus resurfaced as the amber liquid settled into the glass. As she swirled the liquid in the glass, she secretly hoped that Molly Sue's hope would not be crushed the way hers had been so many years ago.

She had prayed, begged God to help her against the cruelty of her father, and in the wake of hollowness afterward. *Where was God for me? What prayer did he answer for me? I stopped praying then. It just hurts too much to hope.*

Molly Sue hopes her mommy will be found. Will her hopes be crushed too? Will God let her down too?

SHARON - JUNE 1972

The day that Sharon had been dreading for an entire month had finally arrived. The moving truck was loaded and pulling away from the curb. Lenny had given her a hug and walked to the car. He knew this last few moments should be private between Sharon and Patty.

Evan twisted in his mother's arms and reached for Sharon. Her heart lurched, and she took him. Her arms wrapped tightly around his small familiar body and she memorized the feel. Her head rested on his and she closed her eyes. She soaked in his smell and movements, subtle as he too rested against Sharon.

"Sharon," Patty began, "our family is all here. You know we will be back. And you can come to Portland and stay with us and visit. I'm so sorry. I will miss you so much." Her words were heartfelt and meant to be true, but they both knew that distance changes things.

Lenny hated to, but he honked the horn. They had a long way to go, and they were already behind. Sharon opened her eyes and looked at her friend. "Patty you are my dearest friend. I've never had a friend like you. I don't know what I'll do without you."

Patty smiled and reached for Evan. Sharon reluctantly unwound her arms and released her hold. As Patty took him, Evan began to fuss and reach again for Sharon. She leaned to him and kissed his cheek. "Be good for mommy. Auntie Sharon will see you again." Evan only fussed louder and struggled against Patty's arms.

Sharon reached and quickly hugged Patty and turned to walk away. She did not look back until she was seated in her car. By then Lenny and Patty's car was a block away and Sharon watched as it turned the corner.

It was hot in the car, but that was more desirable than using strength she didn't have to turn the car on. This feeling of complete emptiness was almost exactly the same as after the abortion. Evan had been aborted, in a sense, away from her.

Finally, she turned the key and hot air blasted out over her face. Still, she sat unwilling to move from in front of the SOLD sign in the yard of Patty and Lenny's house.

She breathed deep, knowing she couldn't sit there

forever and put the car in gear. At least she had her date with Will to look forward to that evening.

Consciously she shifted her thoughts to Will. Things were going very well, and she had high hopes that this might be the one bright spot in her life; the one thing that could make all the other pain and suffering worth it.

Law school was going well for Will. *I could be an attorney's wife someday*, thought Sharon, and she smiled. She was slowly getting used to being in the mansion at the lake, but Will seemed to prefer to spend time other places. He said the overdone extravagance of it all didn't set well with him.

She had been to his parents' home and even though they had as much money, if not more than his uncle, they lived far more modestly. They lived over three hundred miles away, but Will had taken Sharon there twice in the past six months. *That's a good sign*, she mused.

That night they were going to the country club for dinner. Potential law firms were beginning their courting dance and tonight was one such affair. A law firm from the city was sending two of its partners to treat them both to dinner. Will called it an informal interview of sorts.

By evening, the joy of life with Will had dampened the sorrow of losing Evan, Patty, and Lenny. Sharon turned back and forth in front of the full-length mirror. The simple form fitting black dress did exactly what she had hoped it would do, show off her curves.

As she stood looking in the mirror, she placed her hands over her flat abdomen and thought of all the times

Patty had complained that her pregnancy with Evan had ruined that part of her forever.

There was a knock on the door and broke Sharon away from her thoughts. With one last look to confirm she had pulled herself together well, she turned to let Will in.

"Wow. My how beautiful you look." Will's eyes were lit with adoration and he took her hand and twirled her for a three hundred sixty degree look. He whistled sharply and pulled her in tight. "You are gorgeous."

"Thank you." Sharon smiled.

Will gazed into her eyes. She was beautiful, and he knew he was in love with her. But was that enough? He'd had his future planned for years. He knew just what he wanted and had worked hard to achieve it. Even though he loved Sharon, was she the best fit for a wife, his wife?

The country club was beautifully lit in the dusk evening. As they exited the car, and the valet drove away, Sharon felt like she was in a fairytale. When she was with Will, everyone treated her with the utmost respect and deference. It caused her to rise in response and behave as a person of status.

The large round table seated six comfortably and two couples were already seated. The men rose to great them and Sharon nodded cordially to all. Will pulled out her chair and then sat as well.

The other two women were at least twenty years Sharon's senior. They seemed nice enough on the surface, but Sharon couldn't help wondering if they were judging her. Yes, she looked good, but sometimes that was not well received by the wives. Then came the inquiries of her employment and family.

Admitting that she still worked at the local drugstore usually caught in her throat. Having severed ties with her parents over a year ago was also something she had learned to skirt around. None of it ever seemed to phase Will, though. He subtly defended her and sang her praises to whoever might be in earshot. It was the way Will treated her that gave her the courage to attend one informal interview after another at the country club.

After the first time, when she had poured out her woes regarding the searing looks of the wives and their sometimes snide remarks, Will had laughed. "You know they are just jealous? Right?" He had listened, understood, and encouraged her that she had absolutely nothing to be ashamed about.

With each dinner, her confidence grew. The glances and remarks were taken in stride. She liked who she was becoming. She was a strong and independent woman. And she was dating a man who was not threatened in the least by her strength or her growth, on the contrary, he encouraged and nurtured it.

Just before dessert, Sharon excused herself to the ladies' room. Soon, the other wives did as well. Sharon stood looking in the mirror, tucking in a loose end in her upturned hair. She patted it and turned to make sure all was well and once again in place. At the end of the vanity, the other two wives stood.

"You know Sharon, Will is being groomed for a political

future?" It was more of a statement than a question, or was it?

Sharon didn't respond immediately, but then turned and with cool eyes trained on the wives she smiled and acted as though she had known all along. "I am supportive of whatever Will chooses to do."

A slightly knowing look was shared between the two and then a condescending giggle, "Well, yes, but do you really think you are material for the wife of a congressman or senator?" At that remark they huddled together and left the room.

All the confidence she had felt growing inside her the past several weeks seemed to have disappeared in a snap. All it took to bring her down was one well placed snide comment. She hadn't known of Will's plans for a political career. Was he hiding that from her? She felt sick in the pit of her stomach.

She gripped the edge of the counter and shut her eyes, willing herself to be strong and not let those hussies get to her. Finally, she felt her courage rise and a breath of confidence return.

When she walked out of the ladies' room, she held her head high and smiled at others as though she was the queen, all while her stomach churned and threatened to take her down with nausea.

At the table, she motioned for the waiter to fill her flute. As the men sat and talked, she lost track of just how many flutes came and went. She did not engage in conversation so it was easy to hide inebriation.

Finally, Will turned to look at her with concern. He had noticed that she was suddenly thirsty and had almost consumed the equivalent of an entire bottle of wine. He ordered two coffees, one for him and one for her.

As the other two couples began to grow restless and ready to end the evening, Will continued to sit causally as the second cup of coffee came for both him and Sharon.

At the end of the second cup, Will stood and thanked everyone for the wonderful evening and dinner. Sharon stood as well. The coffee had taken the edge off of the fog of the wine and she could stand firm and shake each hand.

Once out in the night Sharon relished the feel of the air on her bare skin. She had grown hot from the alcohol and it felt refreshing to be out in the cool evening air. As they stood waiting for the valet to bring Will's car, he stood looking ahead. Sharon noticed a slight twitching of his jaw and he said nothing.

The car came and once inside, Will began, "Sharon, what happened in there?"

She turned to him and wondered what he was referring to. She had not said a word and had played the part well, or so she thought. "What do you mean?"

"I mean, why all of a sudden did you feel the need to drink an entire bottle of wine?"

She had never seen Will angry like that before. Their lives had been simple, but now he was not happy and more specifically, he was not happy with her. She looked at his face, now rigid and exercising control.

"I... I... Well..." Then anger shot through her as she

remembered feeling betrayed that he hadn't told her of his political aspirations. "Why didn't you tell me about going into politics? I would think that I would be the first you would tell. I had to find it out from the two snarky bitches in the ladies' room who think that I'm not fit to be a congressman's wife." There, she had said it.

His face softened, and he looked away. "That is their story, not mine. I want to practice law."

They rode in silence back to Sharon's small garage apartment. Will parked and turned off the key but both sat unmoving. Questions filled the void, but neither one brought them into the open.

Finally, Will took the lead. "All I've ever wanted to do was practice law. Yes, others have mentioned that I would make a good congressman, but I think it is only because they think I can be a pawn for them. I won't be a pawn for anyone."

Sharon sat quietly, feelings of regret for misjudging Will loomed large. "I'm sorry. I hope I didn't embarrass you. I just kept wondering why you hadn't told me and then wondered if it was because I am not what you need." Her voice trailed off and Will reached for her hand.

"Sharon, I love you. Right now, all I know is that you are what I need." He raised her fingers to his lips and kissed them.

"Will I always be?" Her eyes questioned him but the only response was when he leaned in and kissed her with hunger and desire. All questions were forgotten and passion carried the night.

Sharon - December 1978

Molly Sue had been a snowflake in the school Christmas program along with several other kindergarteners. She had danced around on the stage with the others mimicking a snow flurry as the choir sang, I'm Dreaming Of A White Christmas.

Sharon sat with pride in the audience. It was moments like that when she forgot Molly Sue was not her child. Leslie and her husband sat to Sharon's left and Bill had sat to Sharon's right. He asked if he could come see Molly Sue's program and Sharon had welcomed it. She was a special child and the entire police department loved her dearly.

"Have you gotten all your Christmas shopping done?" Leslie asked Sharon.

"I keep wanting to buy more and more. I've never had a child to buy Christmas presents for before. But I don't want to be ridiculous about it." Sharon blushed when she thought of her extravagance.

Leslie smiled. She understood and was thankful that her friend had finally found the joy a child could bring. But secretly she was concerned that Sharon would once again be devastated in the end. The entire town constantly gossiped about Molly Sue and Sharon, wondering where this child could have come from.

At twenty-six, Sharon seemed like an old maid to the town. They all wondered why, and questioned whether she would ever get married and have children. This always led them to question Sharon's suitability in raising Molly Sue. Leslie often wondered if this constant gossip would someday escalate and cause Sharon to lose Molly Sue altogether.

They served refreshments in the gymnasium and Sharon stood holding a glass of hot chocolate watching as Molly Sue sat with Leslie's daughter eating Christmas cookies. The two had been friends from the day they had met. Sharon often wondered if Molly Sue talked of her past life to little Sherry.

"Leslie, does Sherry ever mention Molly Sue talking about her life before here? I just wondered if she shares things with Sherry that she doesn't share with us."

Leslie stood and watched the girls a moment, thinking. "I can't really recall anything Sherry has mentioned. It wouldn't surprise me. I'll ask one of these days when it seems appropriate. Does she still cry for her mommy?"

"Sometimes. She sometimes wakes up in the night and cries out for her. It breaks my heart."

"The whole thing is just odd. What mother wouldn't be searching for her child? Even if the mother sent her here, when she didn't come back that should be a concern."

"Except that she may have sent Molly Sue for help because she was too sick or injured to come look for her. For all we know her mommy may be dead."

"How awful. I can't even imagine. Does she still believe Santa is bringing her mommy for Christmas?"

Sharon nodded. "And that baby Jesus is going to watch

over her mommy and the mysterious Buddy, in the meantime."

"You should have seen her Leslie, when we drove up to the nativity scene. She was far more excited than when we saw Santa. She walked up so slowly and in such awe. Once she was up to the little manger, she knelt down and just sat silently looking at the doll who was supposed to be baby Jesus. It was as if it didn't matter to her that it was only a doll.

"Then when she talked to it, she was so reverent. Can a five or six-year-old be reverent? Whoever her mother is must have taught her about Jesus. I only hope that it doesn't come back to hurt her. Believing in something that will only disappoint you is harsh."

Leslie listened to her friend. Sharon often talked this way and Leslie felt challenged to find words to say. She knew Sharon had suffered one huge disappointment after another and had reached the point of near hopelessness.

"We should never stop hoping Sharon."

Sharon only shrugged her shoulders and tipped her cup to drink the rest of its contents. "It's easier to not hope." She crumpled the cup and tossed it into the trash as she walked away.

On the drive home Sharon asked Molly Sue what she talked to Sherry about. "Do you ever tell Sherry about your mommy?"

Molly Sue nodded. "So what do you tell her?"

The little girl looked over at Sharon and studied her profile in the light of the passing streetlamps. "I tell her my mommy is nice and plays with me and reads to me. She tells me stories and draws pictures with me."

"What about your home, where your mommy is?"

Molly Sue studied Sharon's face before answering. "Hmmm?" A frown of confusion clouded her face.

"You know, do you talk about your toys, or your house? What was your house like?"

"Little. Mommy and I slept together. I have a dolly I play with and I draw a lot."

"What is your dollie's name?"

"Bonnie."

Sharon slowed the car and pulled into the driveway.

"Miss Sharon can we go to the baby Jesus program with Sherry?"

Sharon looked at Molly Sue. She knew she meant the Christmas pageant at Leslie's church. She hadn't stepped foot in a church in years and just wasn't sure she wanted to foster Molly Sue's hope in baby Jesus. But then, she hated to disappoint the child.

"Yes, we'll go." Sharon smiled. She would see that this little angel got whatever she wanted.

CHAPTER 8

*S*haron - June 1972

The week of Will's law school graduation was filled with one party after another. The bar exam was still ahead, but a week off to celebrate was called for. He had narrowed his offers down to two prospective law firms.

"Have you made a decision yet?" Sharon asked.

"I'm still trying to figure out what will be best in the long run. If I just had a crystal ball so I could see the future." Will laughed and kissed the end of Sharon's nose. They were nearly inseparable now and Sharon had finally begun to relax and just enjoy being with him. She had grown confident in many ways, one of which was in his love for her.

"Okay, so let's talk about it. Give me the pros and cons." Sharon sat cross-legged on the back patio of the mansion at the lake. It was a beautiful day, and they had thrown together lunch and brought it out to enjoy.

"Well, one is more money and maybe more prestige, while the other may get me to full partner quicker."

"Which will mean more money and prestige," said Sharon laughing at the irony.

"Yes. So you see my dilemma."

"Why don't you just start your own law firm? You know, work for yourself."

"Not yet. I need the experience of working in a solid firm. I need to build my reputation and client base. Maybe someday I will. I would really like that, but I have to pass the bar exam and get a lot of experience and clients first."

Sharon leaned back on her elbows and stretched her long tan legs out in front of her. "Well, which law firm will give you the tools you need to get out on your own quicker?"

Will sat looking at her. He hadn't quite thought of his choice in that light before. "You're right. If my end game is really to have my own law firm, I want to choose one now that will prepare me for that regardless of whether or not I become a partner." He sat looking at her bare legs and reached out, running his hand from her knee to the bottom of her shorts. They were short and tight and he wiggled his fingers to slide them underneath, but Sharon stopped him.

"Not here. You know that people are in and out of here like Grand Central Station." She smiled coyly at Will.

He pulled his hand away and slid it around her waist, then leaned in to kiss her. Sharon loved the way he looked at her. His eyes spoke volumes of love and respect like she had never known from anyone before.

"Will." His uncle's voice came bellowing through the open doors.

"Yeah?" Will answered as he reluctantly pulled away from Sharon.

"Come into my study. We need to talk about your plans."

"My plans?" He looked through to doors to see his uncle's frowning face.

"It is time to make some life decisions." On that comment he turned and walked away.

Sharon's stomach did a flip, but she told herself it meant nothing. However, the smile on Will's face had faded, and he rose to follow his uncle. Before stepping through the doors he turned to Sharon, "Maybe you should go on home and I'll call you later."

Sharon nodded and smiled at the back of Will's head as it disappeared through the doorway.

Her thoughts on the ride home were consumed with worry. When she was with Will, she had no doubts about how he felt about her. So, why was there this lingering feeling of dread? It was because for all of Will's good intentions; he was still a puppet on a string that his powerful uncle pulled. His uncle had been tolerant of Sharon and her low social status, but now that Will would enter the real world, it was time to get serious and that meant get serious about choosing an equitable mate.

Will had issued reassurance after reassurance that he

was his own man and knew what he wanted for his own life and was determined not to let anyone stop him. But he hadn't asked Sharon to marry him yet, and really there had been no talk in that regard. Maybe that was why there was such uncertainty circling Sharon's heart.

Sharon's phone didn't ring until much later in the day. Just when she thought she couldn't take it anymore, her phone rang at five-thirty. "Sorry I didn't call sooner."

"It's okay, but I was a little worried. It's been five hours." Sharon tried not to sound needy, but it was difficult. She stood twirling the phone cord around her finger and then off again.

"I know. I know. Sorry."

There was a strained silence over the phone that Sharon didn't know how to approach. "So… what did your uncle want to talk to you about?"

"He's still pushing me towards politics. He has my life all mapped out. He made it clear which law firm he wants me to join and then how long I will practice a specific type of law, then at what point I will begin my campaign for state representative, then a national senator for the state, then on and on and on." Will's voice was tense and frustrated.

"What makes him think he can rule your life like that? It's your life. You have the right to live it the way you want to." Sharon was angry and afraid that his uncle would convince Will to bow to his desires.

"Sharon, you don't understand. He has a lot of money, money that has helped me in a lot of ways. I know my father paid for my college, but my uncle had a lot of influence getting me into the schools I wanted to go to. My grades were good, but not that good."

"You don't owe him Will."

"Yes, Sharon. I do." Sharon felt punched in the gut. If Will bowed to his uncle on his career path that would leave Sharon out in the cold. She was not part of his uncle's plan.

"Will, I love you and I want you to have the life you want. Everyone should live the life they really want." She had lowered her tone and softened her voice to diffuse the tension.

"I know," he replied.

She had hoped for more. She had hoped to hear that he loved her too. "Hey, I need a night off with the guys. Do you mind if we don't go out tonight?" What could she say?

"Yes, that's fine."

"Okay, I'll call you tomorrow. We have that graduation party at the lake in the afternoon. I'll call before then."

"Okay."

"And Sharon, I do love you, too."

SHARON - DECEMBER 1978

Sharon had dreaded the Christmas pageant all day long. So much so, that she had mixed up a large batch of eggnog and had been sipping on it the entire day.

It was the last Saturday before Christmas which was Christmas Eve. She had already wrapped all the presents she had bought for Molly Sue and had them tucked neatly under their little tree. She had withheld a brand new bicycle for Santa to give her.

A knot that could not be dislodged from Sharon's stomach told her that Molly Sue would not prefer a shiny new red bicycle over her mother, but Sharon had no power over that.

It was the third Saturday in a row that Sharon and Molly Sue had baked cookies. They had made several large batches the week before and boxed them into colorful Christmas tins and delivered them to various friends and a few older people who she knew would appreciate them.

Molly Sue loved delivering the cookies. She enjoyed everyone, but the little lonely old ones she seemed to adore. She would get close and pat their frail hands as they talked. She would tell them about baby Jesus and how it was his birthday coming up. Then, she would ask them if they knew about baby Jesus and they all nodded that they did, often with tears in their eyes.

Today, they were making a small batch of gingerbread cookies for themselves and to leave for Santa.

Molly Sue listened intently with large round blue eyes as Sharon discussed with her that it was customary to leave cookies and a glass of milk for Santa on Christmas Eve. Sharon wanted to ask how she had spent Christmas in previous years, but always feared opening a wound in the young girl's heart, wondering if discussing her life with her mother brought pain.

"How will Santa get into our house?" Molly Sue asked quite matter-of-fact.

"Well, no one really knows how Santa gets in. Some say that if you have a fireplace, he comes down the chimney, but he comes to all houses even if they don't have a chimney."

"He didn't come to our house."

Sharon looked at Molly Sue. Her heart skipped a beat, and she struggled to find the perfect response.

"Tell me about Christmas with your mommy."

"And Buddy."

"Yes, and Buddy."

Molly Sue went back to picking up tiny round sprinkles they were using for buttons and placing them on the icing outlining the gingerbreads jacket. "Buddy would get us a little tree. Mommy and I would color ornaments and put them on the tree. Buddy would get us a cake with fruit in it and we would all eat it before bedtime. Then before bed, Mommy would read from the big book that tells about baby Jesus."

She looked up at Sharon and with the sincerity of an adult said, "He is our greatest gift, you know."

Sharon smiled and nodded.

"He was our greatest gift every time," said Molly Sue as she went back to work.

"Did your mommy give you presents?"

"Mommy gave me a dolly. She made her"

"A dolly. That's nice." Mollie Sue's head was bobbing up and down in agreement.

"I loved her."

"What else did you do for Christmas?"

"Buddy would get us a turkey and we would eat turkey and the cake."

"I see."

Once the cookies were decorated, and they had cleaned the kitchen, Sharon sat with another large glass of eggnog in the living room. Molly Sue crawled up on Sharon's lap.

"Today is Christmas Eve. Are you excited?" Sharon asked.

Molly Sue just looked at Sharon and then shrugged one shoulder.

"What's the matter sweet girl?"

"You don't have the big book about baby Jesus. How can you read the story?"

The big book. Molly Sue was referring to a bible. No, Sharon didn't have a bible.

"I can get one. Will that make you happy?"

Molly Sue smiled and hugged Sharon. As she slid down from her lap, Sharon downed the remainder of her glass.

They had filled the church sanctuary to the brim with people and there were very few remaining seats. Leslie had hoped however, that Molly Sue could persuade Sharon into coming and had saved them two seats near the front.

The play was sweet and endearing. Sharon wasn't sure at what time during the play she had relaxed, but she eventually found herself laughing at the little actors on the stage. Near the end, they shifted from the gaiety of the folklore of Christmas into a more serious mode. Elaborate riggings had been made to lift little angels slightly into the sky and they even used a few real animals.

Molly Sue stood when they lifted the huge curtain revealing the scene with baby Jesus in the manger. They had a newborn baby, well a nearly two-month-old baby, for baby Jesus. Her eyes were focused with intensity and her mouth hung open as she gripped the backs of the pew in front of her.

Sharon watched Molly Sue watch the show, more than she watched the actual show. When the children's choir began to sing, Molly Sue's face was soon damp from tears and she sang quietly with the choir. Her reaction amazed Sharon, when she herself felt nothing. Even when the pastor stood at the end to invite others to know baby Jesus and a few went to the front, Sharon just sat numb.

"Sharon, why don't you guys come to our house for hot chocolate and cookies?" Leslie invited.

Sharon smiled and Molly Sue jumped up and down with joy.

Leslie's and her husband Mike's home was cozy and filled with signs of love everywhere. They had two children, a girl that was Molly Sue's friend and a boy two years older. Handmade garlands roped the tree and plaster of Paris ornaments hand-painted by the little ones hung haphazardly.

The floor had random bits of scattered tinsel that had escaped the branches, but no one cared. Mike lit the fireplace and threw an extra log on, and the flames shot upward.

"The hot chocolate is wonderful, but I can't even think about eating another cookie. Molly Sue and I have made and eaten so many cookies the past few weeks that I'm not sure I will want another one until next Christmas."

Mike turned the television on and Rudolf the Red-Nosed Reindeer stopped the children in their tracks. Alone with only Leslie in the kitchen, Sharon asked her friend, "Molly Sue wants me to read to her tonight about the baby Jesus. I don't have a bible. Could I borrow one?" Sharon felt embarrassed that she had to ask. Everyone was supposed to have a bible, right?

"Of course." Leslie didn't miss a beat or act as though the request was anything out of the norm.

She wiped her hands on the hand towel and left the kitchen. In just a minute, she returned with a leather-bound bible and handed it to Sharon.

"I'm embarrassed to say, but I have no idea where to find that story in this big book." Sharon thumbed through the thin pages with thousands up on thousands of words.

Leslie pulled a slip of notepaper from a drawer and jotted down where to look and then tucked the note near the front.

The weightiness of the bible resembled the weightiness of Sharon's heart. Leslie could see it reflected on her friend's face.

"Sit down. We can have our hot chocolate in here." They both sat and Sharon carefully laid the bible on the table, not taking her eyes from it.

"Okay, what's wrong?" Leslie asked.

Sharon focused on the cup in her hands before looking up at Leslie. "I should be happy. I have so much. I have Molly Sue in my life and she fills it more than I ever thought possible. I have a great job, and great friends. But I feel so empty inside.

"Tomorrow Molly Sue is expecting baby Jesus to answer her prayer and have Santa bring her mommy to her. What am I going to do when that doesn't happen?"

Leslie knew the young girl would be heartbroken. "Have you tried to talk to her about the situation? You know, about the probability of her mommy not being there on Christmas morning?"

"Of course I have, well tried to anyway. She won't have it. She's so optimistic that it will happen, after all, she prayed to baby Jesus." Sharon dipped her head and focused again on her cup, her sarcasm tainting each word.

Leslie didn't know what to say and had no words of wisdom. "Well, after you guys get up on Christmas morning, come over here for breakfast and then Christmas dinner. Spend the day with us. The children will love it and hopefully it will distract Molly Sue."

"I hate to impose on your family," said Sharon. Leslie slid her hand across the table and placed it on Sharon's. You and Molly Sue are our family. Please come." Sharon nodded.

Molly Sue and Sharon pulled into their driveway about nine-thirty and hurried inside from the cold. Molly plugged in the tree lights and pulled off her coat and stocking cap. As she stood in the living room waiting for Sharon, she yawned and rubbed her eyes.

"Let's get our jammies on before we read, okay?"

Once they were both snug in their jammies, they prepared Santa's plate of cookies and a glass of milk, and placed them by the tree.

Molly Sue climbed up in Sharon's lap. "Can you read me the baby Jesus' story now?"

Sharon smiled and nodded. She picked up the bible from the end table where she had laid it. As she did, Molly Sue took it from her and began flipping the pages until she found the right spot and held it there where Sharon could read.

Stunned, Sharon looked down and sure enough they were right where they were supposed to be. "How did you know what page to turn to? You can't read yet."

Molly Sue took her finger and ran it under the name at the top of the page and carefully said the word, Luke. Then she turned and smiled at Sharon. When Sharon smiled in return, Molly Sue turned back to the page where the big number two was next to the number one.

"Luke two verse one. My mommy told me. We read this story a lot."

Sharon settled back and began to read the story, when she struggled with some of the King James vernacular, Molly Sue was prompt to correct her. She knew the story by heart. When she had finished, Molly Sue begged her to read it again, which she did.

"Okay, that is twice. It's time for bed now. But first,

Molly Sue, I need to talk to you again about hoping that Santa will bring your mommy in the morning. Santa doesn't bring those types of things, only toys.

"I know you prayed to baby Jesus, but sometimes our prayers don't get answered. I don't want you to wake up tomorrow morning and be disappointed if your mommy isn't here." Sharon watched Molly Sue's face as she explained. There was no disappointment that registered on the little face.

"Do you understand?"

"I understand. But baby Jesus will bring my mommy to me. I know he will." Then she jumped down off of Sharon's lap and hurried toward her bedroom with Sharon close behind. Once she was firmly tucked in, Sharon went back to the living room. She sat in the room's dark lit only by the Christmas tree lights and thought about her life, and the Christmases she had experienced through the years. The highs and disappointing lows.

"I have no idea what I'll do in the morning when her mommy isn't here. God, she prayed to you. You have to help me deal with this. I don't know what to do." The prayer was spontaneous and surprised even herself as she uttered it.

The next morning, Molly Sue quietly slid from her bed and tiptoed to the living room. There in front of the little tree was a shiny red bike with a big bow. She walked further into the room, with Fuzzy gripped to her chest. She stood in the middle of the room and turned slowly looking all around.

"Where's my mommy?" Molly Sue's quiet voice asked with tears rising and sobs breaking free. Then she turned and looked and saw Sharon coming down the hall. At that moment, baby Jesus placed a promise in her little heart, and it filled her with hope. But she would tell no one, not yet anyway.

Sharon - July 1972

Will popped the cork on the champagne and laughed as froth spewed up and out. Sharon stood by glowing with pride. He had defied his uncle's wishes and had taken the job he had wanted to take. The next day, Will had moved into his own garage apartment, just like Sharon.

"So, you have the job you wanted. It feels good to celebrate, Will." Sharon was thankful for more than one reason that Will had the courage to stand up to his uncle.

His father had helped. A down-to-earth man who loved his son deeply. When Will had poured his heart out to his father, he received the confirmation he needed to tell his uncle a firm no. When his uncle persisted, Will's father made a call, and it was all over. Will moved out the next day.

They were sitting at a small table they had scoured from Will's parent's old cast-off's in their storage shed. They had cleaned it, sanded it, and had attempted to stain it again. It was not a great job, but they had enjoyed doing it together.

They would move it from her deck where they had worked on it, to his apartment tomorrow. But, they decided to enjoy the summer night on the deck before they did. It barely fit on the tiny deck outside Sharon's garage apartment, but it was nice to be dining alfresco for a change.

"Tell me about the job." Sharon bit into a cracker laden with cheese.

"Well, I will be the lowest man on the totem pole. Actually, I think that phrase is a misnomer. I think in truth the lowest man on the totem pole is the most important, but anyway." He was babbling from excitement and Sharon laughed.

He looked at her and his face softened. "You know for the first year I will be working long hours, right?"

Sharon nodded and smiled. She knew. They had talked about it. She was willing to be patient and had expressed that to him multiple times.

"I don't want you to think that I am avoiding you. I just have to concentrate on work. But, please know that I'll be missing you and thinking about you." He reached across the table and picked up her hand. He held eye contact with her as he kissed each knuckle, then gently laid her hand back down.

He picked up a cracker of his own and popped the whole thing in his mouth. As he chewed he talked around it. "And, I'll be broke. They don't pay first-year attorney's much more than the janitors."

Sharon laughed. "Will, you will never be broke. Your family is loaded."

Will's smile faded slightly and his tone became serious. "Yes, my family is loaded, but I want to do this on my own. And my father wants that too. He has tightened his purse strings."

"So, is he taking back the BMW?" Sharon toyed with him.

"No, he isn't taking away my car. That was a gift."

"Thank heaven." They both laughed. "I guess if it gets really bad you can always sleep in it."

Will leaned over the table and whispered. "Or, I could always move in here with you." The words hung in the air with unspoken connotations. Did Sharon dare assume? No, she wouldn't let herself.

Instead of commenting, Sharon sipped her champagne. She had grown to love the bubbly liquid over the past few months of living the high life with Will. But, this would be the last for a while. A budding lawyer can't afford champagne.

"I got a job interview scheduled." Sharon didn't want her almost news to overshadow his. Well, if it was even possible for an interview at the police department to overshadow his news.

Will looked up at her and grinned. "That's awesome. Where?"

Sharon looked down and fiddled with placing cheese on another cracker. "It isn't a big deal. It's at the police department. They have an opening for a file clerk."

"Sharon, that's wonderful. Are you excited about it? Is it something you think you will enjoy?" Will was genuinely interested, and that warmed Sharon's heart.

She bit the corner off of the cracker as she thought. "It will get me out of the drugstore. It will give me some experience in business. That has been my biggest problem. I had the schooling, but no experience. I've been passed over so many times by people who actually had experience. I don't know if I will like it, but I am excited that it might lead to something that I will like."

Will nodded. "You'll get it and you'll do great!" He popped another whole cracker topped with cheese into his mouth.

They spent the evening eating crackers and cheese and a bottle of wine when the champagne ran out. Sharon finally felt she could let her guard down with Will. He had battled and won his voice to follow his career his way. It filled Sharon with enormous confidence that he would fight for her.

Between the giddiness of new opportunities and the intoxication of the alcohol, passions flared and soon they were in a passionate embrace and well on the way to satiating their hunger for each other.

An hour later in the dark of night, Sharon rested in Will's arms as he slept. It was in that moment that she thought life was turning a corner. All the loss, all the pain, could now be forgotten and packed away in the past where it belonged.

She pondered how the physical touch of his arms

around her could cause such a tangible emotional high. She rolled towards him and snuggled deeper into him. The movement aroused Will and another round of lovemaking began.

Sometime around five in the morning, Will rose. He needed to get home and get ready for his first day on the job. He watched Sharon sleeping and his heart was full. He would ask her to marry him one day, but first he had to get through this first year and get a place of his own, a real place.

He bent down and brushed a soft kiss on her brow. She barely stirred, no doubt exhausted from their near sleepless night of reoccurring passion.

Sharon woke two hours later. She did not need to be at the drugstore until nine, so she still had two hours. The bed felt empty with Will gone. It was rare that he stayed the night, but it was hard to imagine being in bed alone after last night. It had been perfect.

She stretched and then rolled over, gazing to where the sun emphasized the dip in the bed where Will had laid. The sheets were cool as she slid her hand over the area, his heat long gone. She pulled his pillow near and breathed deep. The smell of his cologne mingled with the scent of their lovemaking filled her and she hugged his pillow tight as if it were him.

Her morning routine beckoned, and she finally rolled out of bed, padding to the bathroom. She reached for her pill box and flipped open the top. Initially confused, then stunned, she kept looking at what she saw before her.

Threads of her memory fought to fix what she saw, but all they could do was confirm, not deny. She had missed a pill.

She shook it off, popped out a pill from its foil confinement, and downed it with a glass of water. It was just one pill. What could be the problem? And soon, all was forgotten.

CHAPTER 9

Sharon - February 1979

Winter had been cold, and they had had record snow falls. Molly Sue loved playing in the snow and Sharon showed her how to build a snowman.

Their days were filled with work and school, and then warm dinners at home in front of the television. In kindergarten there was no homework, but Sharon loved to read to Molly Sue each evening. Now that they had a bible, Molly Sue urged Sharon to read more and more stories from there.

Sharon pondered some of the parables and stories, but felt they had to be just fairytales. The book of John seemed to draw her as it talked about the love of Jesus, yet the stories felt foreign to her. She could not feel his love for her.

"Here is another big heart," said Sharon as she and

Molly Sue sat at the kitchen table decorating her Valentine's Day box for school.

"Who is your valentine Miss Sharon?"

Sharon didn't respond right away. "I guess you are, sweet girl."

Molly Sue smiled as she glued crepe paper swaths of pink and white to the cigar box. Her little tongue hung out to one side as it always did when she was concentrating. A dab of glue was stuck to one cheek and a bit of pink glitter to her nose.

"My valentine is baby Jesus."

Sharon sighed and resisted the urge to roll her eyes. How could this child still talk about loving Jesus when her prayer to have her mother back on Christmas had not materialized? She never understood why she had been so calm that morning. Sharon hadn't brought it up for fear of pointing out the obvious, and Molly Sue never spoke of it.

The sweet girl never stopped talking about Jesus. She loved it when Sharon read stories from the bible above all other books. Even Sharon herself had grown to enjoy reading some of them, even while guarding herself from believing them.

Valentine's Day morning was a challenge. Sharon was trying to juggle the cigar box, the cards Molly Sue had done for her classmates, and a large Tupperware container of cupcakes for the party.

She delivered Molly Sue and took everything in. "I'll be back at ten for the party," Sharon told Mrs. Patterson.

Then ten minutes later, Sharon walked into the station

relieved to be at work. That place had been her home and these officers her family for several years now. When she needed someone, there were usually several available to help her.

She shrugged her coat and scarf off and hung them on the hook by her door and shivered as the colder office embraced her. When she turned, she noticed a large vase of pink roses on her desk. A large card sat beside it. She turned and looked for the culprit. *Who would possibly be giving me a bouquet of roses on Valentine's Day?*

Her fingers trembled as she pulled the card from the envelope. It was a lovely Hallmark card and spoke of being someone's dear valentine. The word love was not used, but a poem of how much she meant to the sender was beautifully written. It was only signed, an admirer.

She studied the writing. She knew every officers handwriting at a glance. She had read countless case files and reports each one had written over and over again. This writing was not one she recognized.

She laid the card down and touched the soft blooms. They felt comforting to her fingers as she glided them over softness as smooth as silk. As she bent to smell them, her nose was filled with the scent of airborne joy. She couldn't help smiling. It had been a long time since she had felt loved, admired, or appreciated. If she just knew who had sent them.

She stepped out into the empty hallway. When she approached the front desk, Anthony was on the phone, taking notes. She waited patiently until he hung up the phone.

"Anthony, do you know who sent the roses that are on my desk?" Sharon asked as she watched his face closely for signs of deception.

He looked straight back at her, and holding her gaze he said, "No. I didn't know there were roses on your desk."

Sharon tilted her head and looked at him skeptically. "Hmmm. Not much gets past you. Are you sure you don't know who sent them?"

He simply shook his head and reached to answer the now ringing phone.

Bill wasn't in yet and there were only a couple of new officers back in the bullpen. She barely knew them and didn't feel either would send her flowers, much less roses.

At a loss, she went back to her office and got right to work. She sat the roses to the side of her desk where she could see them as she worked and continue to smell their intoxicating scent.

Bill, tapped on her door at nine a.m. When she looked up he smiled and nodded toward the roses. "I see you have a valentine."

Sharon's eyebrows rose. "Well, I guess. I just wish I knew who they were from. It would be nice to thank them."

He chuckled and headed towards his office. As an afterthought, Sharon called after him. "Hey Bill, you didn't send them did you?" Before he could answer she heard him pick up and answer his phone. How silly of me. Bill didn't

CHAPTER 9 | 143

send them. He wasn't even here when I arrived this morning.

She had to admit; it was hard concentrating on work with the mystery of who sent the flowers, lingering in the back of her mind. Then she had the thought to call the florist.

"Hello. Yes, this is Sharon Paulson at the police station. I received a lovely bouquet of pink roses this morning. The card was only signed, an admirer. I was wondering if you could tell me who sent them."

"Just a minute." Papers shuffled then muffled shouting in the background regarding her question took up about a minute or two.

"Ma'am we didn't make a delivery to the police station this morning. We sold several bouquets of pink roses yesterday, but most were cash and I have no way of knowing who bought that specific one. Are you sure they came from us?"

"Yes, the vase has a little gold sticker with your logo on it. Well, thank you for your time. They are wonderful."

Sharon sat staring ahead racking her head trying to remember anything that indicated that she had a secret admirer. Of course if she knew who it was, then they wouldn't be secret, right?

When she suddenly realized what time it was, she jumped up and grabbed her coat. It was ten minutes until ten and she didn't want to be late for the kindergarten party.

She quickly stuck her head in Bill's office and

announced where she was going. "I'll be back this afternoon." Bill smiled and nodded. "Take the day if you want."

Sharon smiled in return. "I have way too much work to do. I sat daydreaming about my secret admirer this morning and didn't get nearly finished."

Bill laughed and waved her out the door.

Sharon - August 1972

Sharon hung onto the side of the toilet as she wretched. It was the third day in a row this had happened, and she knew what it was. She flipped the handle and sat on the cold tile floor. Foreboding thoughts fought to ravage her mind, but she pushed them aside.

It was different this time. Will loved her and he would be overjoyed with the news. Yet, if she really believed it, she would have told him days ago.

They had seen very little of each other the past few weeks. As predicted, Will arrived at work pre-dawn and crashed in bed past midnight. They allowed him to go home early on Saturdays and he didn't have to work on Sunday's, unless he didn't want to get behind. So, he always treated Sharon to a Saturday evening date and only worked on Sunday afternoons.

He had become consumed with work. Maybe not so much with the work itself, but with achieving the best possible outcome in each case. He wanted recognition. He wanted to be known for his excellence and his strong work ethic, so he pushed himself. When he was with Sharon, he fought to keep distractions at a minimum.

Each case, each client's needs presented complex situations that needed creative solutions. Will's mind worked overtime on them even when he was away from work.

But at least there was one thing that eased Sharon's mind, she knew that she could get pregnant again. After the abortion, there were concerns that might not be the case. She had heard so many horror stories about women not being able to have children after having their abortions, and she carried the fear that those stories would be hers.

She pulled herself up and turned on the shower to heat. Telling Will was not something that she looked forward to. He had so much pressure as it was, this would only add more.

Her hand slid across the mirror as she wiped the condensation away, revealing dark circles under her eyes. She hadn't been sleeping. Worried thoughts of how Will would respond tormented her. She had to take care of herself though or she would lose this baby. From the moment she knew she was pregnant, she resolved to do whatever she had to do to take care of herself and it.

Today was her first day on her new job. She had been second in line when they selected a new file clerk over a month ago, but for whatever reason, whether it be the environment or the job itself, the one they had hired had quit. They had called Sharon two days ago and offered her the job if she still wanted it, and she did.

Her closet proposed another quandary. She would be the only woman in their small town station. She did not want to appear enticing to the men, but not stern and stuffy like an old matron either. Professional. That is what she wanted, to appear professional.

As she moved first one hanger to the side and then another, her mind went to what to wear as her pregnancy increased, and then to thoughts of what people would say. Pregnancy in and unwed state happened in this day and age, as it always had, but was still frowned upon. How would her new employer feel about it?

Pulling out a navy skirt and white blouse she turned to lay them on her bed. She told herself it didn't matter anyway because as soon as Will found out, they would get married and move in together. She was only about six weeks along and wouldn't show for awhile; she hoped.

She arrived at the station thirty minutes early. As she pulled into the parking lot she stopped, unsure of where she should park. Were there assigned parking spaces? What if she parked in someone's place?

As a horn blared behind her, she jumped and pulled her car forward. The Ford Galaxy 500 pulled in and stopped abruptly in a spot by the front door. Sharon pulled in the spot farthest from the door on the far side of the lot. Surely no one would have this as their personal spot.

Standing on the pavement outside her car door, she surveyed her surroundings. The day was crisp and clear and the trees were changing. The maple trees across the street at the brand new elementary school were bright red.

Sharon smoothed her skirt down and slid her purse strap upon her shoulder. The black pumps she had chosen were the most sensible shoes she owned, but at the drugstore she had worn tennis shoes and her feet were already starting to hurt. If she had to stand a lot in this job, her feet would be killing her by the end of the day.

The glass and aluminum door swung open to Sharon's push. She stood just inside the door unsure of where to go. It was still early, and the station was quiet. A man walked up to the front counter and asked if he could help her. The nametag on his uniform said Lt. Anthony Sproul.

"Yes, my name is Sharon Paulson. They hired me to be the new file clerk." She rubbed her hands together and felt the sweat between them.

"Oh yeah! Nice to meet you." A broad smile greeted her, and she relaxed, just a bit.

The lieutenant picked up the receiver of the big black phone and punched one of the buttons. "Chief we have a lady up here name Sharon Paulson. She said she is the new file clerk."

Resting the receiver back on its cradle, he nodded down the hall. "He said come on back. His name is on his door. Chief Bill Jacobs. It is actually William, but he doesn't like to be called William. We all just call him chief."

"What are you prattling on about Anthony?" The chief had walked down the hall to meet Sharon rather than wait for her to come to him.

He was a large man, not fat, but tall and stout. Sharon had to look up to look him in the eye, and she had always considered herself to be tall at five feet eight. He had a kind face and Sharon's shoulders released their tension just another small notch.

He gripped her offered hand and shook it with purpose. "Well, let's get started, shall we?" He led her back towards his office and motioned for her to take a seat in the chair in front of his large oak desk. It was full. There were files and papers, a photograph or two, pencils, and pens, and little tchotchkes all over it.

The wall behind him held wall to wall built-in custom cabinets in the same oak finish. They too were filled haphazardly with no rhyme or reason to them.

When Sharon heard him say, "I know it's a mess. I'm not real good at that sort of thing." Sharon realized her mouth was hanging open. "I don't have a file clerk and my secretary left too. I'm in a mess."

"I'll do it," Sharon blurted out without thinking.

"You'll do what?"

"I can do both. I can be your secretary and the file clerk." As she heard her own words come tumbling eagerly out of her own mouth she thought she might be sick again.

"Well, I don't know. It's a lot of work." The chief looked her over as if sizing her up.

"How about I give you one week of doing both? If you can't hack it, I'll have to hire an additional person." Sharon was nodding as if she understood, but was also wondering if he would hire a file clerk or a secretary. She wanted the secretary position even though they had hired her for the file clerk position. She had to prove to him she could do it.

By noon, Sharon's feet were hurting as if daggers lined the insides of her shoes. She looked down to see the tops of her feet pillowing out like rising dough. She moaned and sat down in her chair. The priority had been to get the filing caught up before she could learn the daily routine. She had been standing for three solid hours digging through file cabinets searching for correct file placement.

Her cuticles were bleeding from being caught on the tops of file folders as she dug to separate the folders. No wonder the other file clerk had quit, and now she had volunteered to take on two jobs on her first day. What a fool.

The chief popped his head in the door. Lunchtime. I'm heading out. You have an hour for lunch. You can take it here or out. It doesn't matter. And then he was gone.

Home. I'm going home. *I have to change into other shoes,* she thought as she pulled her purse from the hook on the wall and headed out the front door.

At home she fell into her only comfortable chair and sighed with relief. As she pulled off her first shoe, she knew she would never get it back on. With both shoes off and her feet propped up, she thought about what shoes she could wear that would not hurt her feet. Then she thought about food. She was starving.

The first peanut butter and grape jelly sandwich didn't satisfy, so before she had stuffed the last bite in, she had made two more. *I can't keep doing that,* she thought.

A quick glance at her watch let her know she had a mere fifteen minutes to get back to work. She padded in stocking feet to her bedroom and began digging through her shoes for something, anything to wear. A pair of black flats, ballet flats, they were called, was the only choice.

By the end of the day, Sharon had shoved the last file into place and closed the drawer.

"Wow!"

She spun around to see the chief standing in the door. "You're done?"

Sharon was exhausted, but she was done and proud of it. "Yes, sir."

He walked in with a stunned look on his face and shook Sharon's hand. You're hired.

"For what?" Sharon asked.

"For whatever you want." And with a wink, he left the room.

SHARON - APRIL 1979

Bill stood in Sharon's doorway a moment watching her work, before tapping lightly on the doorframe. The small office was filled with Molly Sue's drawings, impromptu photographs of Sharon and the girl, and simple craft items Molly had made. Sharon immediately looked up and smiled, but as soon as the look on Bill's face registered, her smile faded.

She laid down her pen and shifted in her chair. She knew bad news was coming. Bad news always came to her and she should be used to it by now. But, it seemed as with each passing year it hadn't become easier to take. On the contrary, she often wondered just how much more she could take.

Sharon remained silent as Bill pulled out the chair in front of her desk and sat down. "We still have no sign of Molly Sue's mother. The FBI has searched for leads as well, and there is nothing. It's time that a long-term solution to Molly Sue's guardianship be established."

Bill let the first blow sink in before continuing. When Sharon sat silent, he continued. "The Judge feels that Molly Sue would be best served in a two parent home. He has asked a case-worker to evaluate her current home situation and to begin formal long-term guardianship proceedings."

Sharon had dreaded finding Molly Sue's real mom, but this was just as bad. She was going to lose her just like she had lost everyone else in her life she had ever loved. Her head merely nodded, and she picked up her pen again. Her body was operating on its own apart from her conscientious. She didn't even remember Bill standing and walking from her office or turning to ask if she were okay.

Her work spun before her. Concentration was impossible. Dark thoughts rose to prominence, and she didn't attempt to push them away. *Let them come. Let the darkness come. What does it matter anyway?*

By ten-thirty Sharon could take no more and left her office telling no one. It was still an hour before she had to pick up Molly Sue from kindergarten and take her to Leslie's, but she wanted, well needed to talk to Leslie in private.

Surprise crossed Leslie's face when she saw Sharon so early at her door. She opened the door wide welcoming her friend inside.

"Can I get you a cup of coffee? The kids are all quiet. We can talk in the kitchen." Leslie led the way and Sharon followed along without a word. In fact, she hadn't said a word to anyone since Bill's announcement earlier this morning.

Leslie began the routine of making coffee, occasionally looking back over her shoulder to Sharon. Should she ask or wait for her to say what is on her mind?

As the water heated to a boil in the coffeemaker, Leslie sat at the table across from Sharon who still sat quietly. She sat rigid in the chair with her purse planted firmly in her lap. Her knuckles were white from the tight grip which held it.

Sharon focused on the old Formica-topped table and mentally traced the little boomerang shapes in her mind. The numbness was debilitating, and she didn't know if she had the ability to form words.

Leslie slid her hand across the table and touched Sharon's arm. "Tell me. Tell me what happened."

As Sharon breathed in to begin, her breaths were jagged and fierce as they fought back emotional pain. Sharon looked at Leslie and all she could do was cry.

Leslie rose and went to her friend. "Oh sweetie, did they find her mother?"

Wrapped in her friend's arms, all she could do was shake her head. At the unexpected response, Leslie pulled back from Sharon and looked at her questioningly. "Then what's wrong?"

"The judge has determined it is time for a social worker to get involved and start formal guardianship proceedings for Molly Sue."

Leslie sat back in her chair. Her mind was rapidly working to solve the problem or at least find a silver lining in all of this for Sharon. "But can't you just adopt Molly Sue?"

Sharon took a deep cleansing breath. "The judge believes that it is best for all children to have a two parent home. One with both a mother and a father. I can't say I disagree completely, but Molly Sue and I have created a little family with just us two and I can't believe that she would be more loved and cared for somewhere else." As she spoke, courage rose and with each breath Sharon felt stronger.

"Sharon you have to fight this. It's 1979 after all. Things aren't done the way they always have been. I'll stand up and testify for you. I mean, just look at how Molly Sue has flourished. She had come from... who knows what, and she's going to school and doing so well. She plays well with the other children. I think if they take her from you now it could do real damage."

The coffee maker beeped and Leslie rose to get their coffee. She sat two steaming cups on the table. "I have a friend, you know, Mike Yates?" At the name Yates, Sharon's head popped up from blowing on her coffee to look at

Leslie. Then in a quick attempt at recovery, she again busied herself with it.

Leslie hadn't noticed. "Mike does family law. He can help you get custody of Molly Sue."

Sharon thought, then reconsidered. "No. I don't have the money for an attorney."

As Leslie continued to encourage her to call Mike, Sharon's mind drifted back in time to another Yates, Will Yates the love of her life. They may not be related. It had to be just a coincidence, a cousin maybe.

"Sharon. Sharon, are you listening to me?"

"I'm sorry, Leslie. My mind was wandering."

"I insist that you talk to Mike. He can let you pay it out." Leslie stopped and sipped her coffee while watching Sharon closely.

Sharon was overwhelmed. What defense did she have against the system? What did she have that could prove she would be a good parent to Molly Sue? Nothing had ever gone her way, why should she even entertain the thought that it would for her now?

Silence filled the room for several minutes. Both Sharon and Leslie were lost in their own thoughts. Then Sharon sat her coffee down on the table and looked at Leslie.

"I need to fight this. I will never forgive myself if I don't fight it. I can be... I am... a good mother to Molly Sue. You are right. She has flourished with me."

A broad smile bloomed across Leslie's face. She jumped up and retrieved a business card from the kitchen drawer.

Handing it to Sharon, she said, "He's in the city; part of a large law firm. He has resources and handles primarily family law. I know he can help you."

Just them four bright eyes peered around the corner and Leslie motioned for the two toddlers to come to her. "We're hungry Miss Leslie."

"Okay. I'll get lunch started. Molly Sue and Sherry will be here soon." She looked at Sharon and winked.

Sharon took a deep breath and rose to leave. She felt stronger. A little scared still, but stronger. *I can do this. I can,* she told herself as she left to go get Molly Sue.

CHAPTER 10

Sharon - September 1972

It had been an entire month since Sharon had impressed her new boss with her skills. The thought of having to go back to life at the drug store terrified her and fueled her to do more than she thought was required of her.

She still had not told Will that she was pregnant. His work schedule was grueling and every time that she would be on the verge of telling him, fear shouted out in her mind that it was not the time. But, then she would question that he would be angry for not telling him sooner. The turmoil was constant.

"I'm really impressed with the job you are doing." Bill stood in the door.

Sharon looked up from her desk and beamed at him. "Thank you."

He walked further in and looked around before sitting down. "I'll be honest. When you said you wanted to take on both jobs, I was skeptical. Oh, let's face it, I knew you wouldn't be able to do it. I knew you would try your best, but I didn't think anyone could do both jobs. You've surprised me."

"Honestly, there were times that I didn't think I could get this place under control," Sharon replied.

"So, now let's talk. It's still a lot of work. I've seen you come in early and leave late. I want to offer you the administrative job which will be my personal secretary primarily, but also overseeing the file process."

Sharon's heart sank. He was taking duties away from her already. Her disappointment must have resonated on her face.

"What's wrong?" Bill asked.

"What do you mean?"

"You look devastated." Bill's face was creased in a scowl.

"I thought I was doing a good job."

"You are. Let me finish." Bill smiled. "You will oversee someone in a supervisory role to handle the files. You will train them and supervise them. You've earned the right to delegate the grunt work to someone else." Bill winked.

Elation replaced disappointment. Then her mind shifted to the pregnancy. What was the point of succeeding when she would soon be let go? Telling her boss before telling Will wasn't right, but then she needed to tell Bill before they made more changes.

"Okay, you still don't look excited. What's wrong?"

Sharon got up and shut her door. Her mind was racing, searching for the right way to say what was so horribly wrong. She sat down like a stiff log in her chair, unable to look at Bill. Nervous energy caused her to reach for a pencil laying on her desk. Suddenly she looked up at Bill. Her stomach knotted up, and she blurted out what she didn't want to say.

"Bill, I have to tell you something. I think before we go any further, you have a right to know. I'm pregnant. I've put off telling you because I haven't even told Will yet. I'm so sorry. I'll help you train my replacement." Sharon ducked her head and a large tear plopped on her desk blotter. She angrily swiped it away. She wanted a baby, but the timing sucked.

"Why would I need to hire a replacement?" Bill looked confused.

"I'm not married and I'm pregnant. The morals clause..."

"Humph. Don't worry about that. I'm not going to fire you over that. Unless you have decided you want to stay home and take care of the baby. I would understand that."

"I need the job. I love the job." Sharon laughed. She would love nothing more than to stay home with the baby she had so longed for, but she would have to support that baby until she and Will could afford a different arrangement.

"Then it's settled. As of today, you'll have a twenty percent raise on your next paycheck and I want you to think about a file clerk. Now, there is a possibility that you could delegate those duties to the officer at the front desk, but then when things get busy, he would probably neglect those duties. Anyway, put your thoughts together, and let me know."

Bill rose to leave and with his hand on the doorknob, he turned and smiled at Sharon. "We will get through this. No one has to know right now. I understand the confidence you've placed on me. I won't say a word." He nodded a quick nod and turned to leave.

As he closed the door behind him, Sharon exhaled the breath she had been holding. Had she really heard what she thought she had heard? Had he really said he wanted her to stay? Not only that, but he had promoted her and given her a raise. Had she earned it? She knew she had. The long days and diligence to get things in order had paid off.

Now she had to tell Will. Maybe it would take some pressure off of him knowing that Sharon could keep her job. Yet, she couldn't escape the fear that knotted in her stomach.

She pushed thoughts of telling Will out of her mind and grabbed the legal pad that sat to the side of her desk. At the top of the page she wrote, 'Filing Strategies'.

For the next hour and a half she poured out one idea after another. Some were absurd, but they had fueled other thoughts that seemed very doable.

One of her greatest challenges had been the lack of diligence on the officers part. They put little effort into their file reporting and organization. But Bill hadn't put her in charge of the officers and she knew they wouldn't listen to a secretary.

During lunch at her desk, she began to cross through the ideas she knew would not work. Then, she numbered the most favorable ones in order of how she would prefer they be done. Some ideas could be combined, making things very efficient.

Finally confident in her plan, she tapped on Bill's door.

"Yep?"

Sharon sucked in a deep breath of courage and opened Bill's door. His welcoming expression eased her nerves somewhat. He really was a kind man. Most men who had achieved as much as he had at his young age would be arrogant and proud, but Bill was humble. Maybe that is why he had made chief so young.

He motioned for her to sit. "Got some ideas already?" One side of his mouth lifted in a grin.

"Yes, but I want you to hear me out all the way before you decide."

He nodded and leaned back in his chair.

She lifted the legal pad and tried to control her trembling hand. She sat it on the front edge of his desk to anchor it. For the next thirty minutes she laid out her plan.

"The files are so incomplete when they come to me. I've seen that they have even gotten worse since my arrival. I think the officers feel that they don't need to fill in all the reports since I am here now. If they will be more diligent about the paperwork on their end, then it will make a file clerk's job so much easier.

"And the officers really are the ones who need to fill in their own paperwork. They are the eyes and ears of the cases and for me it's time consuming to research what they could easily put in while working the case." She paused momentarily to gauge Bill's response.

"Then if they will complete the files, we can have baskets on top of each file cabinet for that specific file cabinet, broken up in alphabetical groups. So if they have a file on someone named Smith, they would drop the file in the basket for the 'S's'. It would be easy for them to do rather than just dump them on a desk in a huge pile.

"Then each day, I, or when we get a file clerk, she, can quickly scan through the file making sure it was complete and then filing it away."

"I like the idea, but you know the officers will complain."

Sharon wilted. "I know. But, they'll do it if you tell them to." Her eyes were pleading with him.

Bill just sat and looked at her for a while. "I agree that it will help everyone if they can be more diligent about filling out their own case files. I've needed information out of some of them months later only to find missing information. Let's start there. I can leave you completely out of it and tell them that is a new mandate."

Hope rose in Sharon's chest. "Thank you. Then, afterwards we can look at hiring a file clerk. I'm thinking that with so much work being done by the officers, and then the new sorting system, a part-time entry level person is all that we will need. It will save the department money and make things far more efficient."

Bill smiled and nodded. "Great job Sharon. I fully agree. You know, you are so smart. I hope the world doesn't find that out and some large corporation comes by to steal you away from me."

"Thank you, sir." Sharon rose to go, her hand now holding the legal pad steady.

"Write me a memo regarding exactly what the officers need to do to complete their files and then get the baskets purchased and in place. I'll hold a meeting on Monday morning and break the news to them."

"Sir, I really want you to know how much I appreciate my job. Thank you for taking a chance on me."

Bill looked at Sharon standing before him. She was a beautiful and highly competent young woman. But, there was a shadow that lingered somewhere behind her eyes. Something that seemed to keep her from being completely happy. Maybe that would change. Maybe he could help make that change.

"Sharon, thank you for taking a chance on us. Men can be stubborn, but down deep inside we know we need you."

Sharon - May 1979

The initial meeting with the caseworker in Sharon's home had gone well, or so Sharon thought. She had kept her home tidy for years and Molly Sue was not a difficult child to clean up after.

"So Miss Paulson, Molly Sue has been with you for how many months now?" She shuffled through her notes as if she didn't know the facts by heart. She was a small woman with slightly unruly long dark hair that hung loose.

"Ten months give or take a few days." Sharon tried not to fidget.

"Ten months. I see." Marcia Wallace looked up and smiled at Sharon. "Can you tell me how it has been with Molly Sue here?"

"Wonderful. She's a joy to have around. She is very well behaved." Marcia did not come across as aggressive, in fact she was pleasant in tone, but there was an unsettling edge to her that was hard to relax around.

"Yes, but haven't there been some… issues about her lack of… understanding?"

"Well, I'm not sure what you mean." Sharon thought she knew exactly what Marcia meant, but didn't want to make it easy for the caseworker.

She looked back down at her notes and read. "Child appears to have been raised in an uncivilized environment with limited mechanical and physical comforts." Marcia looked up and waited for Sharon to respond.

"She is a very content child. Yes, I guess that statement could be true, but I've just learned to patiently explain things to Molly Sue. She's very smart and learns easily. The car was the first thing I taught her about. As soon as I realized it was new to her, an unknown experience for her, I explained it to her. Then, she was fine.

"Now each time I suspect that something is new to her, I take the time to teach her about it." Sharon thought her response sounded good and intelligent. She hoped Marcia would feel the same.

"Hmm… I see." Marcia looked back to her notes, then up again. "You have never been married, is that correct?"

Resisting the urge to fidget again, Sharon responded, "No, I haven't been."

"Why is that?"

Sharon looked at Marcia's dark brown eyes which were enlarged by the prescription lenses that they sat behind. They sat looking unblinking, waiting for Sharon to answer. All Sharon wanted to do was run screaming from the room.

"Well, I guess I just haven't found the right person… to marry."

"I see." Marcia continued to look at Sharon as if she expected her to continue.

"I'm not against marriage or anything, but I guess I just feel it is too important to just marry for the sake of marrying."

"I see."

This woman was getting on Sharon's every nerve. Sharon knew this interview would get under her skin and that she would have to keenly guard her answers, but this staring thing that she had going on was more than Sharon thought she could endure.

She had felt she could play her game and so she just sat calmly and held Marcia's gaze, smiling.

"Could I see Molly Sue's room?"

Sharon welcomed the change and stood motioning for Marcia to follow her. Molly Sue was at Leslie's. Marcie thought it best to visit the first time alone with Sharon. She would have plenty of time with Molly Sue on upcoming visits.

The guest room that Sharon had turned into any girl's dream had white walls, pink ruffled curtains and a pink floral bedspread. The room was orderly. A doll bed sat in one corner with a baby resting quietly there. On the bed with the pillow sat three stuffed animals with Fuzzy front and center. A small bookcase next to the bed held dozens of books.

Marcie opened the closet to find it full of dresses, pants, tops, and shoes. After a cursory look through, she shut the closet door, made a few notes and turned towards the door. Sharon wanted to ask what she kept writing down, but knew it would make her look weak and nervous, which she was. Not weak, just nervous.

Sharon followed Marcia back to the living room, where she returned to her place on the sofa.

"Sharon, why do you think you are the best choice for Molly Sue, not being married and all?"

"I love her. I've cared for her since she came. I've helped her transition from… somewhere, to here. She is happy and healthy.

"She came from a home without a daddy, so I believe

that made the transition easier. There is also no competition here with other siblings. She can learn and grow in an emotionally safe place."

The words she had practiced with Leslie came out with confidence, not because she had rehearsed them, but because she felt them to be true.

Marcia sat once again looking at Sharon, then finally nodded, made more notes and rose to leave.

"I'll be in touch." And just like that, she was gone.

Sharon closed the door behind Marcia and leaned on it. She felt weak in the knees. She should go to Leslie's and get Molly Sue, but she needed to gather her strength first. Last night's bottle of wine was nearly empty, so she opened another as she downed the old.

A glass or two would calm her nerves. She honestly didn't know how she would make it through this. Her life had been filled with one catastrophic disappointment after another so she had no idea how to hope, knowing that hope would not be satisfied.

She carried her glass and the open bottle to her favorite chair and quickly downed one glass to take the edge off, then poured another which she intended to sip. After three glasses of wine, Sharon's phone rang.

"Hello," answered Sharon.

"It's Leslie. Did the case worker leave yet?"

"Yes. I'm a wreck. I don't know how to endure this." Her words were slightly slurred. She had fallen asleep from the wine and the phone had startled her.

"The other kids are gone now. I'll bring Molly Sue home."

"Thanks." Sharon hung up the phone and went to sit back in her chair. She leaned her head back and cried. How on earth she had any tears left to cry, she did not know! If she lost Molly Sue, she was done. She knew she would not have the will to go on. It was all just too much.

In a half hour, Leslie opened the front door and Molly Sue came bounding in. She stopped long enough to give Sharon a hug, then ran to her room.

"That bad huh?" Leslie said nodding towards the empty wine bottle.

"I don't know. She was so calculating and quiet. I felt like I answered all the questions correctly, but it just seemed like she kept waiting for more. I didn't want to ramble. You kept telling me not to do that. But I don't know that she is convinced."

"Sharon, while this is unresolved you need to stay away from the wine. I'm not saying you have a problem, but it might be construed that you do. You don't want to give them anything that they could use against you." Leslie was concerned. She didn't really think Sharon drank too much, a couple of glasses of wine a night before bed, but the stress of this situation had increased her drinking.

"I'm about to crumble under the pressure of all of this. Bill warned me not to get attached to her, but the moment I saw her, I was. My heart is breaking into a thousand pieces. And to make it worse, Molly Sue is still praying, still believing her mommy, her real mommy will be found."

Sharon leaned forward, wiped the tears from her eyes, and took a deep ragged breath. "It is what it is and I just have to prepare myself for the worst."

"I don't believe that. You have to hope for the best. God brought Molly Sue into your life for a reason. Be thankful for that."

Sharon huffed. "Brought her into my life just to rip her away again. I've spent a lifetime of punishment from God. I get my hopes up and then they are just as quickly dashed. I think God takes great pleasure in seeing me tormented by one painful situation after another."

Leslie sat speechless, not knowing what to say. She had heard most of her life that the things that happened to us must be ordained by God. But, it was hard to see the purpose in all that Sharon had suffered through.

"It isn't over yet, Sharon. Have you talked to the attorney yet?"

Sharon shook her head. She had thought about it, but fear kept her from actually doing it. "I will."

"You have to do it soon. The quicker you call, the quicker they can start working this out. Don't wait until they…" Leslie caught herself.

"…until they decide against me? Until they decide to take her away from me?" Sharon's hopeless eyes pierced Leslie's heart.

"Call now. Right now while I'm here."

Sharon closed her eyes, blew her nose on the tissue she held, and drew up strength from somewhere inside like she had done so many times before. "Okay."

She didn't want to do this. She didn't want to face this. It was all too hard.

The little white card shook as Sharon held it in her trembling hand. The only sound on the line was one shrill ring after another. "No one is answering. It's too late. They've left for the day." Then suddenly someone answered, out of breath as if they had hurried to catch the phone.

"Yates and Crawford Attorney's at Law. Matt Yates speaking." Sharon slammed down the receiver and dropped to the floor.

"I can't. I can't do this."

Molly Sue had heard the commotion and came running into the room. When she saw Sharon on the floor, she walked over and placed her small hands, one on each side of Sharon's face. "It be okay Miss Sharon. It be okay."

SHARON - OCTOBER 1972

Sharon loved her new job. She excelled at every task the chief handed her. He had told her she was the best secretary he had ever had, even though he had only been chief for less than a year. He had allowed her to hire a part-time file clerk and supervise her.

Will seemed to love his new job as well. He didn't have an office like Sharon. Being a lowly first-year attorney he had a cubicle in the basement. Sharon had given him a desk photo of the two of them, but it was still packed away. He barely had room for the stacks of files he had to go through each day, much less trivial personal items.

Now so far along, Sharon knew that it was critical to tell Will about the pregnancy. She had wanted to before now, but each time she had planned to, something came up. He had a meeting here and there, and he had even cancelled a date or two. But it was Saturday night, and he had promised her a nice evening for just the two of them.

It was customary that they spent more time at Sharon's small garage apartment but tonight she was driving to Will's. Inside it was a mess. Clothing was strewn everywhere and a week's worth of newspapers were scattered about as well.

The smell of garlic wafted through the mess to Sharon's nose. Spaghetti. She loved Will's spaghetti. He turned to greet her with a loving smile. Setting the sauce covered wooden spoon down, he scooped her up into his arms and held her tight.

"I've missed you so much." He kissed her hungrily and she let him. She had missed him too.

Sizzles from the stove tore them away as the spaghetti sauce bubbled over and onto the stove. Sharon cleared the tiny table they had restored and set it with two plates and a small candle she found in the cabinet.

"It's just spaghetti and garlic bread."

"Sounds wonderful." Sharon was just excited to be with Will. She had brought a small overnight bag planning to spend the night with him.

He presented the wooden spoon to her to taste and

when her eyes lit up he smiled. "Yum. Wonderful as always," she praised his handiwork.

Once settled at the table and the first bites consumed, Will asked, "So, tell me all about your new job."

He hung on every word as she told him about volunteering to take on two jobs, but that her risk had paid off. Sharon glowed as Will rested his full attention on her the way he always had when they were together.

When she asked about his job, his face clouded over, and he looked down at his plate stabbing and twirling another bite. He didn't speak for a moment, clearly gathering his thoughts. When he had, he laid his fork down on his plate and looked at Sharon.

"I wish I could say it is wonderful and that I love it. I guess someday I will. I guess someday it will be what I thought it was going to be when I was in law school." Then at a sudden thought he jumped up and said, "Hey, I have something to show you." He took off into the other room and came back with a large framed document. "I'm legal now."

Sharon ran her hands over the law license he had framed. He had passed the bar with flying colors and now here was his license to prove it. Only two months earlier he had done the same with his diploma. "Wow. I'm impressed." She looked at him with such pride, so thankful that he was hers and that he loved her so very much.

He replaced the frame back in the other room and as he sat back down Sharon said, "I have a surprise for you too."

Her face beamed with happiness, but it belied the fear that hovered inside.

"Really? What?" Will's eyes searched her face for telltale signs that would give her secret away.

"I… I'm… Well, we are going to have a baby."

Will's face looked like he had been hit with a bucket of ice water. His mouth fell open and his eyes kept blinking slowly as if on some kind of mechanical loop. "A… baby?"

Sharon waited for him to recover and become overjoyed, but he simply sat in shock. The longer he sat, the more somber she grew.

He finally looked down at his plate and tried to say something, but he only stuttered nonsense. Then, when he realized how his reaction was affecting Sharon, he got up and came to her. He wrapped his arms around her, but he felt her stiff defensiveness. "I love you," was all he could say.

She laid her head on his shoulder telling herself that it was just a huge shock and that everything would be okay, but deep inside she knew she was lying to herself.

He finally released her and sat back in his chair. He once again began to eat, and then rethinking his hunger after only one more bite, he pushed the plate away and looked at Sharon.

"How far along are you?" She was watching him and her face was neutral, unsmiling.

"Two months."

"Okay, Okay. Well…" The wheels in his mind were

churning and the longer they churned the angrier Sharon got.

"Well, there is still time for you to have an abortion, right?"

"Abortion?" Sharon screamed at Will. "I... will... not... have... an... abortion..." she said through gritted teeth.

Fantasies of him being overjoyed, getting down on one knee and proposing dissolved. She stood up and threw her napkin in her plate splattering spaghetti on the candle. She watched it smolder and die. When it did, she huffed an acknowledgement of the sign that it gave.

Will stood and reached for her. "Sharon, wait. Let's talk about this."

"Will, just exactly what is there to talk about? I thought you loved me?"

"I do love you. I do."

"Then I don't understand." She was crying now and couldn't stop.

"Look, the firm has a strict morals policy. Even if we got married right now, they would know that you were pregnant when we got married. Just have an abortion this time and then we can get married and have more kids." He was pleading with her now, realizing that he was stuck between the woman he loved and a job he had waited his entire life for.

"No, Will. I won't have an abortion. I don't know how you could ask that of me. You know my greatest tragedy was my father forcing that on me. I won't let you force that on me now." She turned to leave, and he followed her raking his hand through his hair.

"Please, sit down. Let's talk about this. There has to be a solution." He reached for her again and she pulled away.

"I will not have an abortion." She stood rigid in the middle of the room. "I don't see a solution."

Will paced a circle in the room. He solved problems all day long, he could solve this one. Sharon was hurt that she and the baby had suddenly become another problem to be solved.

He turned to her. "We could elope tonight and get married. Then when the baby comes, we can just say it came early. That might work, right?"

"No, Will. It won't work. You know it won't work. I'm more like two-and-a-half months along and you can't pass off a full-term baby as a premie. They will all wonder why we eloped. The wonderful up-and-coming attorney eloped instead of having the wedding of the year. They will know Will. They will all know.

"Now you just have to decide if your baby and I are more important to you than your career." She stood waiting for the answer she knew was coming, while hoping she was wrong.

When nothing at all came, not a word either way, she quietly turned and left.

CHAPTER 11

*D*onna - June 1973

Donna swatted at the mosquitos as she walked down the slight path that wound through the tall grass. The grasshoppers and katydids rivaling choruses worked to drown out the rumble of the nearby stream. It was a beautiful day, but the heat of the sun was working to dominate the day.

She had been drawn to the woods spontaneously, just grabbing her bag and hurrying out the door, barely taking the time to throw in a couple of apples. The large bag now rested slung across her body from shoulder to hip. Its long fringe was swinging back and forth, and brushed her leg as she walked.

Slap! Her hand left a large red handprint where she slapped at a black fly. Noticing that her skin was growing red under the light of the sun, she thought, *Good. I'll get a tan while I'm out. I just wish I had my bikini top on instead of this halter. I'll have hideous tan lines.*

The denim halter she wore was homemade. It covered her ample bosom, but just barely. It tied around her neck and also in back. It stopped about six inches above the low top of her hip hugger cutoffs.

"Ouch! Dang it!" A goat-head shot through her rubber flip-flop and punctured the bottom of her foot. She wobbled to maintain balance as she pulled her foot up to remove the small intruder. A tiny trickle of blood spilled out and pain shot through her foot as it came loose.

She stood looking around and rethinking the hike. *This might not have been the best idea.* But then the sound of the stream as it rushed over the rocks encouraged her, so she continued.

Her mind was no longer on the beauty and wonder of the woods and stream, as she hobbled down the overgrown path attempting to guard her foot. She was bug bitten, sunburned, and now her foot throbbed. But, in only a few more steps, she entered the shade of the huge tree next to the stream's bank. The temperature immediately dropped, what felt like to Donna, five or more degrees.

The coolness of the shade immediately drew her mind from the minor irritations which had plagued her just seconds before. She sat next to the stream and pulled off her flip-flops, sticking her feet in the cold water. The stream was noisy here as it encountered the large boulders protruding in random clumps. The rush of the rapids tried to suffocate out all other sounds, but to Donna it was soothing.

She stretched her arms out behind her and locking her elbows, rested on her arms as supports. The grass was short in the shade of the tree and she laid further back onto the ground and rested as the water continued to wash over her feet.

It really is a beautiful day, thought Donna. She was happy, joyful even. The small growing mound beneath her hands raised prominently as she laid on her back. The low-slung jean shorts rested easily under her abdomen when she stood and her short halter allowed it room as well. Laying down, it was easy to see that Donna was six, maybe seven months pregnant. She wasn't quite sure which.

Jared knew about the baby and he was cool with it. They had no plans to marry and neither of their parents were pushing them to either. The freedom her own laid back parents felt, allowed her the same freedom. She would have the baby, take care of it, and if Jared wanted to be involved he could, or not.

Donna had graduated high school the year before and instead of going to college, her parents let her continue to live at home on their small acreage outside of town. They grew their own food; chickens, vegetables, and eggs. Her dad worked in construction so they also had plenty of meat and other essentials.

Her mom stayed home and tended to the property, gardens, and the home. When she was done with her chores, she spent her time painting. The far corner of their living room had large windows which let in ample light and her mother had spent countless hours there painting one beautiful scene after another..

Donna had attempted to learn to paint from her mom, but hadn't quite seemed to develop a talent or skill for the art. When she had spare time, she wrote. She loved to wind and weave stories and could get lost for hours in her character's lives.

As she gently rubbed where the growing baby sat, she wondered if it were a boy or a girl. She would have to name it and considered names, both new and old that she knew. *Would I rather it be a little boy, or a little girl*, she asked herself? *A little girl. I want it to be a little girl.* Donna closed her eyes and as she drifted off to sleep, she smiled at the thought of holding her tiny newborn.

Long before she opened her eyes, she felt the presence of another person near to her. Her skin prickled, and she purposely kept her eyes closed hoping they would just go away.

The sound of feet scraping against the ground and a slight grunt as a body plopped to the ground, caused Donna to open her eyes just slightly. Could she see through the slits without turning her head? No, her head was turned the wrong way.

She tried to wait it out, but her feet were now freezing from being in the cold water for so long and she was growing stiff and needed to pee.

Slowly, she rolled her head to the other side and there a mere three feet away, sat a large man clad in overalls, old work-boots, and a t-shirt. He sat cross-legged with his forearms resting on his knees.

As Donna turned her head to look at the man, he sat quietly watching her. He didn't feel threatening to Donna, and he made no move to approach her.

She struggled against her growing midsection to sit back up, pulling her feet from the stream. As she herself sat cross-legged, her belly spilled over the top of her shorts and she reached down placing her hands underneath for support.

All the while, the man only sat and watched, never speaking. Donna sat watching him in return. He was a man, but he was younger than she had first thought, having an almost boyish quality about him.

His hair was tousled and curly, dark brown. He was large, but not really fat, just large. His face was round and fleshy, but not unattractive.

"My name is Donna. What's yours?" Donna finally asked.

His eyes blinked suddenly in surprise as if he was not expecting her to talk to him.

"I'm Buddy."

"Hi Buddy. Do you live around here?"

Buddy nodded.

Donna looked around for her bag and pulled it to her. She reached inside and pulled out the two apples, handing one to Buddy. "Here, you like apples?"

She bit down with a loud crunch on her apple as she held the other towards Buddy. He looked at the offered apple and then at Donna. He seemed unsure whether or not to take it.

She wobbled it and said, "Here. You can have it."

Buddy reached out and took the apple from her hand. It was then that she realized with their hands in such close proximity, just how large his hand was in comparison to hers.

They sat quietly while they finished the apples. Once done, Donna threw her apple core into the stream and watched it bobble off over the rocks.

Her back was aching. She had been sitting on the hard ground far too long. Rolling to the side in an ungraceful attempt to stand, she nearly fell. Buddy jumped to his feet with the speed of a gazelle and steadied her.

"Thank you Buddy." Donna smiled and Buddy smiled.

"I have to go home now, but it was nice to meet you."

Buddy's forehead wrinkled and his mouth turned down. Then he slowly began to shake his head. "No. You can't go."

A rush of adrenaline flooded Donna's nervous system and she tensed. "What do you mean I can't go?" She tried to keep her voice steady and calm, but there was still a slight tremble to her words.

Buddy pointed to her blossoming belly and said, "You can't go. Buddy will protect you."

Donna's mind raced to reconcile Buddy's words with his actions. Why did he think she needed protecting just because she was pregnant?

She smiled once more attempting to appease Buddy and hopefully help him to understand that she was fine.

"Really, Buddy, I'm fine." She slung the long strap of her bag over her head and adjusted it to drape just right on her side. With one foot, she flipped her flip-flop right side up and slid her foot in. With both feet now shod, she looked back at Buddy who still stood frowning.

"Well, good-bye." And as she took a step towards the overgrown path, Buddy reached out and gently grabbed her shoulder. His hand was so large that he held her entire shoulder joint in the palm of his hand.

Fear rocked through Donna's body. She turned her head to look at Buddy. She didn't want to anger this huge man-child.

"I need to go Buddy." Donna's eyes pleaded with him.

Once again, Buddy pointed with his free hand towards her belly. "Buddy has to take care of you. No one will hurt the little baby. I will take care of you."

Donna's mind raced to make sense of what Buddy was saying. He was obviously mentally challenged, but there would be no way that she could escape his might if he was determined to hold her.

She thought for the time being it would just be best to go along with his plan. Once he fell asleep, she would go.

However, before she knew it, she was swooped up into the air and cradled in Buddy's arms. She watched as he walked, noting every tree and landmark that she could see. It was only by a sheer force of her own will that she could override the fear and think rationally.

"I take care of you. I take care of the baby." Buddy repeated this as his heavy footfalls trampled down the overgrown path.

After what had felt like over an hour of walking, a weathered white farmhouse loomed before them. The siding was coming loose and there were signs of neglect everywhere.

Once upon the front porch, Buddy gently sat Donna down on her feet. He looked at her and with what Donna could feel was deep sincerity said, "I love the little baby. I not hurt it like my daddy hurt me."

Gears began to turn and click into place in Donna's mind. "Your daddy hurt your momma when she was pregnant?"

Buddy nodded and a tear rolled down his weathered cheek. "He hit my momma there, and it hurt me. I take care of the little baby so no one can hurt it."

Her heart wrenched from her chest as she saw the deep pain in Buddy's eyes. He had had an abusive father who had beat his momma. Those beatings had caused him mental damage. But he was intelligent enough to know, or maybe he had been told, what had caused him to be how he was.

"I love the little baby. I take care of the little baby."

Donna stood on the porch stunned with no idea of what to do.

∼

Sharon - May 1979

It had been four weeks since Marcia Wallace had visited Sharon's home. The lack of word from her was unnerving, to say the least. Sharon filled her mind with the joy of taking care of Molly Sue. Her entire world now rotated around this young girl.

She had attended the second parent conference of the year the previous night. She loved walking the hallways filled with other parents and all the excited children. Molly Sue had stayed with Leslie for the evening, however. Sharon wanted to ask her teacher about her visit with Marcia Wallace.

"Molly Sue is a joy to have in class," her teacher Mrs. Patterson said. "Her grades are slightly above average. She was quite behind when she started, as you know, but she is bright and has caught up quickly. She loves to learn. I think she will be very good at reading."

Sharon was relieved to hear those words. "That is wonderful. We read every night." Sharon hesitated, squirming in her seat, then said, "I don't know if Marcia Wallace has come to speak with you yet or not…"

Mrs. Patterson was nodding at the mention of Marcia's name. "She has. We spent about thirty minutes discussing Molly Sue."

"Did you discuss any concerns with her you might have?" The teacher's demeanor appeared that all had gone well, but Sharon lacked confidence that she would be so glowing to the caseworker.

"I told her that I thought Molly Sue was doing very well

with you." Sharon breathed a sigh of relief and closed her eyes.

"I do have one concern." Mrs. Patterson's eyes darted about the room looking at the other parents admiring their students art work.

In a lowered and hushed tone, she continued. "I have seen Molly Sue standing at the back fence of the playground a few times. You know, it's that tall chain-link fence that looks back into the woods? Well, she just stands there looking. She holds the fence and just stands there." Mrs. Patterson's face was pinched in concern.

"What does she say when you ask her about it?"

"Nothing. I didn't ask anything at first, then when it happened again, I did. But she just looked at me and smiled."

"How many times have you seen her do this?"

"I think two, no, three times that I've seen. I don't know how many more times though, that I have not seen."

"Okay. I'll talk to her about it." Distracted, Sharon gathered Molly Sue's artwork and other papers and left the school.

What is going on, she wondered. She pulled into Leslie's driveway and walked to her door. It was still early, and the kids were circled in front of the television.

"Can we have a cup of tea in the kitchen?" Sharon asked Leslie as she entered.

Leslie nodded and led the way. Once in the kitchen, Sharon told Leslie about the conversation with Mrs. Patterson.

"What do you think she is looking at," Leslie asked.

"I don't know. I wonder if she is thinking about where she came from. If she maybe came through the woods back there to here." Sharon took a sip of the hot tea. "Maybe she's remembering things."

Leslie sat down across from Sharon. "But that could be good right? You've been trying to get her to remember where her mother is. She said her mother was sick, and that's why she came here."

"Yes, but that was months ago. Her mother would be better by now, right?"

"Or dead."

Leslie's words struck Sharon, and she instantly felt horrible. Had they tried hard enough to find Molly Sue's mother? What if they hadn't and now she was dead? She had depended on the girl bringing help and now it could be too late.

"I'll have to talk to her about it. If she is remembering, then I have to help her."

"Have you heard from Marcia Wallace?"

"No." Sharon picked at her sleeve.

"Have you called the attorney back?"

"No."

Leslie was exasperated. "Sharon, I know you don't want to lose Molly Sue and Matt is the best attorney around for this type of thing. You have to call him. I'm serious."

Sharon only nodded and looked away. The thought of seeing an attorney made this situation real. It would mean that Sharon would have to face the story of her life and bare it to another individual. They would want to know why she hadn't married. They would want to know if she had any skeletons in her closet that Marcia Wallace could drag out and use against her.

She rose to leave and gathered Molly Sue's things. "Thank you so much for all the help you give keeping her for me. I couldn't do it without you."

"I know."

Almost as an afterthought, Sharon turned. "You never mentioned if Marcia came to visit you."

"She did. I thought I mentioned it." Leslie stood nervously shifting from one foot to the other.

Suddenly suspicious, Sharon said, "No, you didn't."

"It went well." Leslie smiled but her eyes betrayed her.

"What?" Sharon couldn't imagine what Leslie would have to say that would be negative. They had been friends for a long time and had always gotten along well. Leslie had never criticized Sharon's treatment of Molly Sue.

"Well, I kept feeling like she knew something I didn't know and was trying to pry it out of me."

"Like what?"

Leslie shrugged her shoulders and shook her head. She wrapped her arms around her waist. "I have no idea. That's probably why I never mentioned it."

As Sharon turned back around to go, Leslie blurted out, "She asked me about your drinking."

Sharon whirled around. "My drinking? Why would she ask about a thing like that?"

"Did you take your trash out before she came?"

Sharon thought back to the day of the visit. Her kitchen trash sat just inside the door from the living room to the kitchen between the refrigerator and the wall. It would have been easy for anyone to peer into it as they passed the doorway. Then she tried to remember if she had taken it out and what if anything incriminating had been in there.

But that was ridiculous. She didn't drink too much. If there had been a wine bottle in there, that was no big deal.

"I don't know. I don't know what was in there."

Leslie looked at Sharon apologetically. "I only said that you sometimes have a glass of wine at night after you put Molly Sue to bed. There's nothing wrong with that." Sharon nodded woodenly as she gathered Molly Sue and helped her with her jacket.

"Can you call the attorney and make an appointment for me? And can you come with me?" Sharon's eyes pleaded with Leslie. It was time to do whatever she could to keep Molly Sue, no matter how hard it might be.

"I will, I promise." Leslie smiled reassuringly at her friend. But they both knew that this was far from over.

On the drive home, Sharon tried to shake the conversation with Leslie from her mind so she could focus on Molly Sue. "Molly, Mrs. Patterson said that she has seen you standing at the fence a few times on the playground. Why is that?"

"To see Buddy." Molly Sue was matter-of-fact in her response as if it were no big deal and there was nothing to hide.

Sharon frowned. "To see Buddy. You've seen Buddy?"

"I think so." She looked over at Sharon and nodded.
"I don't understand. Why do you just think so?"
"He hides in the trees."
"What makes you think you saw him?"
"I heard him call my name."

Donna - June 1973

It had been three days since Buddy had *rescued* Donna from the stream. Her plan to escape once he fell asleep hadn't worked. The tiny old farmhouse was creaky and at each slight sound he became alert and immediately attentive at her side.

Lengthy discussions of why Donna was safe and how there were others waiting to protect her, others that would be worried when she didn't come back home, were fruitless.

The cabin resonated with emptiness. Not from inanimate objects like chairs, tables, plates, and such, but with the absence of a family that once was.

Buddy filled his days working to take care of Donna. He did his best to cook simple meals and fussed over her when she ambled from one place to another.

"We go get more meat." Buddy stood before Donna as she sat on the worn sofa.

"Okay. Can I stay here while you go?"

"No. You go with me. I keep you safe."

They trudged through the dense forest, Donna still in

her flip-flops and Buddy in his heavy boots. As they walked, Donna was searching her mind for a plan to get away. The truth was, they had walked so far and in such an erratic path that she had no idea where they were. But if she could just get away, she was confident she could find her way back to town.

Deep in the shadows of the trees, Buddy motioned for Donna to squat down as he was doing. His beefy finger rested on his lips and his eyes were round. Ahead of them, Donna saw a rabbit. She did her best to squat, but toppled over in the process and the rabbit scurried away.

"I'm sorry Buddy. I can't squat down anymore."

His sympathetic eyes looked at her and the pat he gave her shoulder shook her. "It's okay Donna. You just stand still next time."

They continued quietly through the light mottled woods, stopping when a shadow was thought to be a morsel, then moving on when it wasn't. Finally, they came upon another rabbit and as Donna stood still, Buddy squatted and pulled the trigger.

The rabbit received the impact and shuddered as its nerves felt the last thing it would ever feel. Black eyes lay still as Buddy reached out and scooped up his kill.

"We eat rabbit tonight."

Donna's father often hunted for their meals and so eating rabbit was nothing new to Donna. As they walked back, Donna stopped and said, "I have to pee."

Buddy nodded his head, but as Donna started to walk off, he reached out and stopped her. "Right there."

Using the restroom as a way of escape had been Donna's first thought after Buddy had taken her. She had tried and failed. Now he stood watch right by her each time.

As they stepped out into a meadow that Donna had not seen before, the thought came to her that she could run and escape. The open expanse would not hinder her as the woods did. She had run track in high school and was an excellent runner. However, she had never run while seven months pregnant.

The flip-flops would have to go, but if she could slide them off in one swift movement, then scoop them up as she took off, it might work.

Buddy shifted his gun from one arm to the other and repositioned his hunting bag which held the rabbit. Donna knew that it had to be now or never.

She had already worked her feet as far out of the flip-flips as she could and yet still walk, so now she slipped them the rest of the way out, grabbed them up quickly and took off running as hard as she could.

Buddy was startled and stood for a moment as she ran. Then, he dropped his gear and ran too. Donna was much faster, even pregnant. She willed herself to ignore the sharp sticks and goat heads that punctured her feet.

One hand rested underneath her large abdomen to support it as she ran. Her legs were long, and she was fast, however Buddy's size helped him to cover ground quickly.

The air in Donna's lungs rebelled and the stitch in her side became almost overwhelming. Then suddenly the ground assaulted her as her running came to a halt and she slammed downward.

Pain shot through her ankle and up her leg. She had stepped in a hole and twisted her ankle. The pain was so intense that she could do nothing but writhe on the ground. She clutched her knee up to her as far as she could.

Buddy did not scold her as he knelt beside her, only gently scooped her up and held her close as you would comfort a baby. "It be okay Donna. I take care of you."

Wracking sobs wrenched from Donna. The damaged ankle had been the catalyst, but the true depths of her pain was from the entrapment this poor addled soul had created for her.

With one hand, Buddy grabbed the abandoned gear and as he continued to hold Donna tightly. Despair threatened to overtake Donna for the first time as they journeyed back to the house. In Buddy's effort to protect her, to help her, he had no idea just how much he was really hurting her.

As Donna laid on the old daybed in the open living and kitchen area, and watched Buddy clean the rabbit, she began what she hoped was a convincing argument for him to let her go. "Buddy, did your momma love you?"

His back was to her and his movements, and at the mention of momma, there was only a slight hitch as he worked. "Momma loved me."

"Where is your momma now, Buddy?"

A loud sniff could be heard, and a hand raised to his face. He was crying. "Momma went to the angels."

"Where's your daddy?"

"He died a long time ago."

Donna pondered the different descriptions he used in describing two deaths. His choice of words communicated the depth of his love for his momma, or maybe the depth of her love for him. On the other hand, the cold word died, was the only descriptor for the man who had hurt the one Buddy had loved.

"If you were lost and didn't come back home, your momma would have been sad, right Buddy?"

He only nodded.

"Buddy, I have a momma who will be terribly sad when I don't come home."

His movements stilled for a moment. Then, they resumed without comment.

"Buddy my momma and daddy love me and take care of me. No one hits me at my home. They will cry and be so sad if I don't come home."

Still no word from Buddy as he continued to work on the rabbit.

"What if you go with me to my home? They would love to meet you and know how you took care of me. They would be so thankful to you Buddy."

When still no words came, Donna began to once again sob. "Please Buddy, take me home."

Buddy laid down the now skinned and bare rabbit and turned to look at her. "Buddy keep you safe here. Buddy keep baby safe too."

Donna's mind raced as she worked to determine if he understood what she had said or if he was just defying her wishes. Whatever the case was, he was determined to keep her.

As he stood watching her, she felt the atmosphere in the room change. Something in his eyes, something in his demeanor shifted subtly. Donna had never once felt threatened by Buddy. His simplistic speech and calm actions had comforted her. But now something was different and her body tensed.

She gripped the covers and braced herself as Buddy wiped his hands on the rag he held. His smile was gone and she could tell his thoughts were internally focused. He dropped the rag onto the table and walked heavily towards her.

Donna winced and braced herself, but he only knelt in front of the daybed and looked her in the face. "You will not leave. Momma left Buddy to go to the angels. You will not leave Buddy too."

As his words began to sink in, Donna saw the pain leach from his broken and lonely heart to his face. She knew in that moment, there was nothing she could say to convince him to either let her go or to come with her. Buddy would keep her here, no matter what it took.

CHAPTER 12

Sharon - May 1979

Leslie had called and made the appointment for the attorney's visit and then had rescheduled twice at Sharon's insistence.

As they neared the door to the attorney's office a deep unexpected calm settled on Sharon. She knew it was resignation from somewhere deep inside her soul. She paused at the door to the attorney's office and ran her fingers along the black and gold lettering embossed on the frosted glass. W. Matthew Yates, Esq. A memory flashed through her mind of a framed document she had once admired. She smiled slightly with a sad and yet knowing smile and nodded for Leslie to open the door.

As the door swung open, Will stood behind a massive walnut desk. His hair was shorter and the thin, lean body of his youth was now one of a solid and sturdy man.

He had begun his practiced and professional greeting as the door began to swing open, but he stopped mid-sentence upon seeing Sharon. Leslie had made the appointment with his secretary and he had no idea who would be coming for the meeting.

They stood, just taking each other in. Leslie felt the atmosphere in the room shift, but didn't know why. Sharon had never told Leslie about Will, just that she had once nearly gotten married, and no more.

Leslie, suddenly very uncomfortable said, "Sharon, this is Matt Yates."

"Matt," said Sharon in a near whisper, a slight smile on her face.

Will suddenly very uncomfortable looked down at his desk and straightened the desk blotter, and then back up. "Yes, my wife preferred it to Will. I've gone by it ever since."

As Will spoke, the glint from the gold on his finger caught her eye, as did the photograph of a happy couple on the credenza behind him. Then, her eyes darted about searching for other pictures, pictures that were glaringly absent. There were no pictures of children. She looked back at Will and without speaking a word, Will responded.

"We never had children." He coughed and Sharon gave a light nod.

He motioned for them to sit in the two leather chairs before him. As Sharon slid into the soft but firm leather, she looked back up at Will.

"We were only married for two years. She became ill

with cancer and passed away a year ago. I've just never taken my ring off." He turned the gold band absentmindedly as he spoke. He then glanced at Sharon's bare fingers resting in her lap. Feeling his gaze shift, she folded her hands into each other.

Leslie watched as the silent unspoken conversation unfolded beyond the cordial one she could hear. She felt as though she were intruding in a very intimate and private moment, but had no idea why.

"How may I help you?" Will began.

Sharon took a deep breath and began. She told the entire story of how Molly Sue had come to them and how she had cared for her from the beginning. She explained the situation with the judge requesting a formal guardianship hearing and the visit from Marcia Wallace. Will dutifully took notes.

"Why do you feel concern about not being approved for final guardianship?"

"I never married. They seem to feel that only married couples are suited to give guardianship to."

Will nodded. He wanted to ask about other children, his child, but held back. "It's true that in general the court favors two-parent homes, but it sounds as though you have given Molly Sue good care. She is flourishing in school and is happy. That will go a long way towards proving you are the best fit for her guardian."

"I don't know how much this is going to cost, but whatever it is, I will have to work out a payment plan." Sharon said with shame filling her words, while looking at the edge of Will's desk. It was difficult enough asking him to serve as her attorney, but completely demoralizing to have to ask for charity too.

"That won't be a problem."

Sharon looked up and with hard eyes looked at Will. "I'm not saying I won't pay, or can't pay. I'm saying that I will just need a payment plan in order to do so."

Will's face saddened, and he nodded. For the remainder of the hour he asked questions about their daily routine, any problems that might surface in the hearing, and who they might call for character witnesses. After the initial difficulty and awkwardness, they settled into a flow and were able to cover ground.

At the end of their appointed hour, Will's desk phone buzzed and his secretary reminded him his next appointment was waiting.

Sharon and Leslie rose as Will reiterated the next steps he would take and confirmed he had Sharon's contact information correct so that if he needed anything he could contact her.

In the hallway, Leslie shut the door behind her as Sharon leaned against the wall for strength. She placed her arm around her friend and led her out to the car.

"I don't know what that was all about, but you must tell me everything." Leslie's face was lined with deep concern for her friend.

Sharon rested with her head back and her eyes closed. As Leslie waited, a single tear slid from the corner of her eye.

After a few quiet moments, Sharon began. "He was the love of my life."

"Oh no." Leslie felt sick inside. "The name on the card? You didn't know?"

"I tried to tell myself it wasn't him, but I had seen his law license when he had framed it. It said William Matthew Yates, Esq. When I saw the door with the W before Matthew, I knew."

"The voice on the phone?"

"He had run to the phone and was out of breath. It was hard to tell, but it was so close. Mostly though, it was becoming real that I was having to take legal steps to keep my sweet girl."

Leslie reached over and took her friend's hand as they both sat in silence.

"I suppose he will call once he had worked through the file and needs something else." Sharon wasn't sure she wanted to talk with him in private. A phone call seemed too intimate.

"Yes, I'm sure he will. I suppose he will file with the court to gain formal guardianship for you before the social worker can file her motion. I only wish the temporary guardianship you have was done permanently from the beginning."

Sharon nodded. She barely heard Leslie. Her thoughts were lost in a time gone by. They were snagged on memories of laughter and love. They were replaying a time when Sharon felt her life had turned a corner and that life before her was going to be her dream come true. A time when she thought everything would be okay.

"I sometimes wish Molly Sue had never come here. I honestly have no hope that the court will give her to me and the pain will be unbearable. I don't know how I'm going to endure losing her."

"Sharon, you have to have hope. You have to. If you don't, you are right, you may lose her forever. You can't fight this and you can't take care of Molly Sue the way she needs you if you don't snap out of this. If you can't do it for yourself, do it for Molly Sue."

"Maybe she would be better off with someone else. Maybe they are right, maybe she would be better in a home with a mother and father. Maybe I'm not the right choice."

"You don't believe that."

"I want her so badly I can't see the truth. I want her so bad I almost don't care what is right or wrong."

Leslie turned the key and when the car came to life, she began backing from the parking spot. "Yes, Sharon you do. It's just too painful to think about right now. You love her and love always wants the best for a person. If you love her and it is best to let her go, you will."

Sharon glanced out her window as they drove past the imposing stone building where her past had just come crashing into her present. As she did, the placard on the side of the wall confirmed it had not just been a nightmare. Yates and Crawford Attorney's at Law glinted in the sunlight and she closed her eyes from the piercing ray.

Donna - July 1973

The last four weeks had resulted in multiple escape attempts as Donna continued to grow in size. Buddy's patience seemed to be growing thin. After each failed attempt, she expected wrath to greet her, but he would just gently retrieve her and took her back to the old farmhouse.

He insisted that she accompany him for everything, even when his need to use the restroom came. He would tie a thin rope around her wrist and hold it as he relieved himself. He would let her stand just outside the door and then shut the door holding the rope tightly.

Several times she had reached up with her other hand in an effort to hurriedly untie the knot. But Buddy's strength always pulled the knots so tight that her small fingers couldn't separate the loops before he would once again emerge.

When she needed to go to the bathroom, he stood in the doorway. There never seemed to be any sign of sexual tension coming from Buddy. He seemed to have no interest in her in that way. One day her need to bathe became so overwhelming, that she found herself just stripping and bathing with him standing there. Not once did he seem to react to her nakedness. He would stand there and look away giving her a small bit of privacy, if only visually.

There was no electricity in the old house. It had been built for electricity, but she assumed that when his parents had died, lack of payment had caused them to shut it off.

There was an old well pump outside they hauled water from. She bathed in the tub, putting a stopper in the drain and dumping water in that they had hauled in.

Donna did her best to fall into a routine. She had been born with a naturally positive attitude and throughout her childhood she felt happy, hopeful, and optimistic. Even when she had learned she was pregnant, it hadn't diminished her sunny disposition. She immediately turned her thoughts to all the pleasure the baby would bring to her life.

The month in the old farmhouse had worked hard to diminish her core optimism. The hope she had felt so keenly in the beginning now came and went just as the night faded to light each day and then back. *What would I do if I lost hope all together*, she thought? So, she worked hard to make the best of her days.

Then suddenly one day Buddy announced, "I take you to your home."

Donna's skin prickled with anticipation. "Home?" Her eyes searched his for more. *Dare I hope he means what I think he means?*

"You and baby need a home. I take you to your home."

Donna frowned. "What home?"

"Buddy has you a home. It real close." Donna's heart sank. She wasn't going home, yet. She knew that her parents and Jared would be looking for her. But where were they and where would they look? She knew, hoped really, that they wouldn't give up looking.

Buddy took Donna by the upper arm and marched her

out the back door. A small path curved through the woods to the right. Then suddenly as if appearing by magic, a small cabin, less than half the size of the old farmhouse, stood before them.

"Daddy and Momma lived here first," he said as the door hinge creaked.

The room was darker than the farmhouse, but it did have a few small windows. It was one room and had very few furnishings, primarily a small bed and table. The metal frame of the bed had peeling paint, but looked otherwise clean. In fact, the entire room looked clean.

A vase of wildflowers sat on the table. "When did you do this Buddy?" Donna looked at him stunned.

"When you was asleep." Buddy ducked his head almost as if he were feeling bashful.

"It looks very nice Buddy. Thank you." Donna was ecstatic. Now she could escape.

"Here. You put this on." Buddy held up an old, but clean house dress. It must have been his mother's. The tiny flowers that had once graced the thin cotton fabric were nearly gone now from countless washings. The front buttoned from collar to hem.

"I'm not sure I can right now Buddy. It may not fit." Donna patted her now huge middle.

Buddy looked caught off guard, then nodded as he carefully folded the dress back up. She could tell he was trying hard to think of what to do. Then suddenly he grabbed her wrist and back to the old farmhouse they went.

He hurriedly walked to an old chest and threw it open.

Pleased, he stood holding clean, but old men's shirts and overalls. Donna couldn't help but smile at his childlike enthusiasm. They were much smaller than Buddy. *They must have been his father's*, thought Donna.

Buddy scooped up a stack of old shirts and overalls, grabbed Donna's wrist once again and back to the cabin they went.

In the cabin, Donna looked around. Out the back window she could see a stream. Was that the stream she had first met Buddy at? If so, all she needed to do was follow it to civilization.

Even though the cabin was tiny, it had both a back and front door. Buddy instructed her that the back door led to the outhouse and the creek.

After a few elementary instructions from Buddy he motioned for her to sit on the bed. She now wore an old thin cotton shirt with the sleeves rolled up. It was long on her and came nearly to her knees. She would wear it as a dress for now, saving the overalls for colder weather. *Hopefully, I'll be home by then.*

While she sat on the bed, Buddy got down and reached way back underneath it. A strange clattering sound resulted in the appearance of a chain with an ankle shackle. Before Donna knew what was happening, he had clamped it around her ankle and locked it.

Horror ripped through her body as realization set in. Jumping to her feet, she tried to run, but Buddy's large arm scooped around her waist holding her firm.

"Buddy, no. Don't lock me in here." Time tilted and

Donna collapsed into a heap on the floor. As she wailed, the last wisps of hope drifted away.

Sharon - June 1979

A voice on the line cleared its throat. "Sharon." It was Will.

Sharon's body prickled with anxiety. "Yes."

"Do you have a minute to talk about the case?"

"I do."

A slight pause of silence broke the flow of conversation. "It was good to see you the other day," said Will.

His voice still felt as smooth as fine whiskey to her. It still cradled her in comfort, but she couldn't let it subdue her and entice her like it once had. She shook her mind free and responded. "Yes Will, but I need to focus on the case."

"Yes, sure. I have depositions set for several of the people you listed on your character witness list. They will be short, but we don't need any surprises, so I have chosen to depose them ahead of time."

"What do you mean surprises?" Sharon immediately became concerned.

"Just that I want to know for a fact what they will say in court. We can let some random, inconsequential bit of information be a fly in the ointment."

"I see." She sounded like Marcia Wallace. She leaned

forward in her chair and placed her free hand over her eyes.

"I would like to meet with you, not to depose you, just to talk about the case and what you should expect."

"Can't we just do it here over the phone?" Sharon didn't trust herself to be alone with Will. The flame wasn't dead. She could feel the faint embers glowing deep in her soul. She wanted nothing to do with anything that would fan the flame to reemerge.

"I think it would be best to do it in person."

Sharon took a deep breath. "Okay. Okay. When and where do you want me?"

"Could I take you to din…"

"No." Sharon blurted out before he had finished his sentence.

"Okay. Well then, let's meet at my office. Or I could come to your home."

She didn't want him there in her home. It was safer at his office. "I'll come to your office. When should I come?"

"I can meet you today after my last appointment. Would five thirty work for you?"

"Let me call Leslie and see if she can keep Molly Sue for a while longer today."

"Okay. I want to meet her. I mean, I should meet her."

"Not today."

"Yes. Sure."

When the call ended, Sharon tried to muster the strength for the hundredth time to get through this. She took a deep breath and dialed Leslie's phone. After a brief explanation, Leslie readily agreed to keep Molly Sue.

As Sharon drove to the city, she could feel her hands slippery wet on the steering wheel. She didn't like this. This meeting alone with Will. Yet she had to admit there was something deep inside that was drawing her in direct conflict to her good sense.

Her jaw clenched as her mind shifted to memories that made her hate him. Made her want to hate him. Had that really been seven years ago? It still felt like yesterday.

The reception area was quiet when she entered and the receptionist was gathering her purse in order to leave.

"Mr. Yates is in his office waiting for you," she said as she walked out the door.

Pausing at his door, Sharon pulled strength from somewhere and turned the knob. Will was looking out the window with his back to her, and the sunlight glinted off of a few random blond strands of hair. A flash of memory of her running her hands through his hair, came and went.

She cleared her throat, and he turned and smiled. "I saw you pull up. What a sweet car. It fits you."

"Thanks." *How could he know what fits me? He doesn't even know me and the person I've become.*

She sat in the same chair she had in the previous visit and he sat in his chair. He sat looking at her face taking her in. She sat quietly and let him. "You look good Sharon."

"Thank you, but I don't. I'm tired and this is beating me down. But, thank you for saying it."

He looked closer, but all he could see was the woman he

had fallen in love with so many years earlier. She had been his first true love. And even though he did love his wife, thoughts of Sharon often came to him. He had loved her, truly loved her and he had missed her.

"Well, okay, let's get started." He looked down and opened a file that laid on his desk.

He read off the list of people he had been able to schedule for depositions. There was Bill and three other officers from the police station that had been there for a few years. Leslie and her husband Mike. Mrs. Patterson, Molly Sue's kindergarten teacher.

"Is there anyone else that you can think of that we should call? Do you go to church, or are you part of any community groups?"

Sharon only shook her head.

"Do you have any reason to think that any of these people will say anything unexpected?"

"Like what? Just come out and ask me what you want to ask me."

Will sighed and laid his pen down. "Sharon, tell me about your life. What your routine is and what you do."

"I go to work, and I go home. I really don't do much."

"Tell me about your life since Molly Sue."

Sharon's face slowly came to life, and she leaned forward placing her elbows on her thighs. "Will, she is the most wonderful child. Her constant optimism is staggering. She is just happy, all the time. She is loving and kind and considerate. She puts me to complete shame, and yet, she loves me.

"When she first came we didn't know what to do. She said her mommy had sent her, but we couldn't find her anywhere. Molly Sue couldn't retrace her steps and tell us where she had come from. When talking with her, she said her mommy had sent her because she was sick. I assume she sent her to get help."

Will was caught up in the joy with which Sharon talked about Molly Sue. It drew him in and he wanted to meet the small child.

"When she arrived, she had only an old pillowcase for a makeshift dress with a thin rope tied around the middle. Her only shoes were rags tied around her feet. I took her and bought her clothes and shoes and took her home with me. My boss, the chief of police didn't want me to, but when I insisted, he allowed it.

"Then when her mommy didn't return, the judge gave me temporary guardianship at Bill's urging. But I guess my time has run out." She looked down having uttered that realization.

"Not if I can help it. It's true that in this state the tides have not yet changed and the courts look far more favorably on a two parent home, but you have taken good care of her and we will argue that to remove her now, would be detrimental.

"This is for guardianship only. They will not be able to satisfy the courts standard that willful abandonment has occurred. Molly Sue has shown no signs of abuse or neglect and it is believed that her mother sent her here for help. Now the matter of her clothing may be an issue, but extenuating circumstances will have to be considered."

"If I lose guardianship, what then?"

"We will fight this all the way Sharon. I promise. I will do everything I can to help you."

Sharon shut her eyes. She believed him. She believed he would do all that he could do to help her.

He let her sit for a moment to soak it all in. He had a burning question that had tormented him for years. Was this the time to approach it, or should he wait?

"Sharon," he began, and she opened her eyes. His demeanor was different. The professional cloak of an attorney was shed, and he sat with a painful expression on his face. She knew what was coming.

"Yes?"

"What happened after you left that day? You know, to the baby."

Sharon sat quiet and looked down at the floor. Swirls of paisley tapestry in reds and creams swirled beneath her. Could she just simply tell him in a brief answer? No. She would need to venture there another day.

Divots where her elbows had been, remained in her legs as she sat back in her chair. She crossed her legs and looked at Will.

"I want to tell you about my life after you left, but not today. I want to yell and scream at you for even asking when you didn't back then. But we are both older and I know we all have things we would do differently if we could go back.

"If you are still willing to take me to dinner, I'm willing to tell you."

He nodded, rose from his chair, and reached out for her hand. She hesitated for only a brief moment before taking it. It felt familiar. It felt like it had so long ago, as though it belonged.

CHAPTER 13

*D*onna - September 1973

The chain reached from its anchor on the wall beside the bed to the outhouse, the stream, and a small garden area. With both a front and a back door in the small cabin, she had more mobility, but no freedom.

The chain allowed her some privacy, though. Buddy didn't hover over her every second of every day this way. He was free to hunt and do whatever he did before he had found her.

She had tried everything conceivable to free herself from the chain and the chain from the wall anchor. Whoever had devised and built it had been equipped with more tools and had been much smarter than she. From the few conversations she had had with Buddy, she guessed this had been his home and his father had once tethered him with that chain.

The cabin was so sparsely furnished that she couldn't seem to fashion a tool from anything to free herself from the chain. A man had built it for a man. It had been built to withstand Buddy, and his strength.

Boredom was the worst. She paced back and forth until she couldn't stand the rattling of the chain any longer. With her fingernail she had scratched little hash tags on the timber walls beside the bed. She included all the days since her captivity.

The baby would come soon. She knew nothing about giving birth. Of course, at home she had seen their livestock give birth, but not a human. She was thankful for at least that now. It gave her a little knowledge of what to do. She knew there would be an afterbirth and that she would have to tie and cut it loose from the baby. That part differed from the animals, but her mother had explained that to her while they watched the mothers attend their young.

At the thought of the baby, she smiled. She could almost feel the weight of it in her arms and feel its slight squirms. But this was no place to raise a child. It would be in captivity with her. And once again her thoughts drew her to planning an escape.

The sound of heavy footfalls on the path drew her gaze up. The day was already hot, and the insects buzzed about noisily. Through the slightly waving tree limbs she could see first the boots, then the blue of his overalls as he drew through the trees and closer to the cabin.

He found her sitting on the threshold of the front door. She wished for a covered porch to sit on, but the threshold was the best she could do. He reached out to take her hand and help her up.

"Hi, Donna."

"Hi, Buddy." Half-way up a pain shot through her back and she doubled over.

As always at any sign of distress, Buddy scooped her up into his arms. Once in the house he gently laid her on the bed. His eyes were large and round. "You okay?"

Donna smiled. "Yes Buddy, I'm okay."

"The baby?" He asked through the groaning of the bedsprings as he sat on the edge.

She knew he feared the baby coming. She wasn't exactly sure why. "Buddy why are you afraid?"

He looked down and then around nervously. Light reflected off of the large pools of water that had collected in his eyes. His large fingers fiddled as they sat in his lap. His body was tense as his mouth opened and shut searching for words that didn't come.

She reached out and rested her hand on his arm. "It's okay Buddy. You have done a good job taking care of us. The baby will be okay." She hoped her words were true. She hoped the baby would be okay.

Her countless words attempting to convince Buddy to take her home so a doctor could check her and the baby to make sure it was okay, had fallen on deaf ears. She had even told him that afterwards they could come back to the cabin, knowing it was a lie. He seemed to know nothing of doctors or what they were for, so he did not trust her words.

Just then another pain shot through Donna's back and abdomen, an unfamiliar pain. "Oh, no! It's too early," she screamed out.

Buddy jumped up and turned first one way and then the other unsure of what to do. He began to moan and rock. "Buddy sorry. I don't how to help baby now." Between Buddy's agitated spell and the pain, Donna was about to reach the end of her rope. But something maternal she had never known surfaced.

She made it through the pain and then said, "Buddy, I can tell you what to do. I need rags, and more bed clothes. There will be blood, lots of blood. You will need a big pot of boiling water. Can you get those things?" Buddy's head began to bob rapidly up and down and he rushed out the door.

Between pains, Donna looked over at the marks on her wall recounting them again. By her best guess, she was close to nine months, but still two or three weeks away. *Close enough*, she thought.

As Buddy hurried back down the path towards the cabin, he could hear Donna's screams. His challenged mind surged with fear. He wanted to help the baby, but didn't know how to now.

Once back in the cabin, Donna quickly instructed him on what to do. She stripped off the sheets in case they were all they had. She covered the bed in two layers of quilts and then folded one in half that could catch the baby and the afterbirth.

Once the bed was fixed, she gave Buddy additional instruction about getting lots of water and boiling it so it would be clean. She explained that they would need something small to wrap the baby in. He nodded focused but quiet.

He hurried back out the door and she grabbed the back of a kitchen chair and gripped it until her knuckles turned white. She breathed and panted then as the pain came, a gush of water ran down her legs and onto the floor. "Momma, oh momma," she sobbed. She didn't want to do this alone.

Buddy didn't return for sometime. The water must be taking time to boil. While waiting, she had laid back on the bed and there had been several pains by the time he rushed back through the door. He carried a large pot of steaming water. As he stood in the middle of the floor looking at her, the boiling water sloshed on his hands without notice.

"Set it on the stove. We won't need it for a bit."

Just as the pot was firmly set down on the cold stove, another pain hit hard. She could feel the tiny life pressing through her loins. It felt as though she had no control over her own body or the pain. It would push the tiny life out with or without her help.

Her sharp piercing shrill filled the cabin and Buddy became nearly frantic. He paced in a circle and pulled at a strand of hair over his left ear. He glanced over at the bed now red with blood. He moaned and rocked as she wailed and then there was silence.

Before him on the bed lay a tiny baby girl. His eyes grew round and his mouth shaped a small oval. Donna was spent and knew the baby lay on the soft quilt between her legs, but she had to catch her breath before she could respond.

Then as Buddy timidly reached out for the quiet baby and picked it up, it squinted its eyes tight and bellowed out its first cry. He looked at Donna and laid the baby on her.

With a good cursory glance Donna realized she was healthy and whole. "She's okay Buddy. She's okay. I need a string and some scissors or a knife. I have to cut this cord from her."

He had retrieved them earlier as she had instructed. She tied the cord and cut it just as the afterbirth passed. Dutifully, Buddy folded up the soiled folded quilt and took it out of the cabin.

Big blue eyes looked up at Donna and her heart was complete. A pink fist worked to find its mark in the little mouth, but not providing satisfaction it was quickly rejected only for a retry.

Donna pushed herself into a sitting position against the headboard and unbuttoned her shirt. The first tug of her breast hurt, but it was the best hurt she had ever felt. The tiny life pulled and pulled and finally rested.

Buddy walked in and saw Donna there holding the sleeping baby. He didn't know what else to do.

"We will need to bathe her in a moment when she wakes again. You did good Buddy. You did good." Donna smiled up at the large man-child and tears rolled down his large cheeks.

"Buddy did good. Buddy did good," he said.

Sharon - June 1979

They took Will's car, a new and larger BMW, still black. They remained quiet as he drove her to a local restaurant where they could share some quiet privacy and eat a nice meal.

When the hostess led them to their table, Will's hand touched the small of her back the way it had countless times and emotion fluttered through her. She gripped the top of her purse with both hands until her fingers rebelled.

He pulled out her seat and like the gentleman he was, and had always been, he waited until she was seated before he himself sat.

The waiter came and introduced himself and offered the daily specials. They were long flowery names for above average dishes. A bottle of nice wine was ordered, and Sharon sat void of hunger.

With the mechanics of meal ordering out of the way, they were left alone to continue the conversation which had begun in Will's office.

"I was determined to have the baby. You know that. My greatest tragedy in life was the abortion my father forced me to have. I was not going to let anyone get in the way of having that child, our child." She looked down and fiddled with the napkin that she had laid in her lap.

"As you know, I got the job at the police station. The police department has a morals policy just as the law firm you worked at did. I had secretly begun looking for other jobs in acticipation of that.

"When Bill offered me the promotion, I told him about the pregnancy even though I hadn't yet told you. I didn't feel it was right to take it without him knowing. I was sure that he would want to hire someone else.

"Bill was kind. He came into my office, shut the door and sat quietly. He had such a compassionate face. I still remember it." Sharon smiled at the memory of how Bill had been there for her. She hadn't expected it, but she had desperately needed it.

"I told him what had happened. I also told him I was prepared to leave as soon as I could find another position. He reminded me that he was the chief of police and that if he didn't make it an issue, then there would be no issue.

"After that night, I told Bill. He knew something was wrong. I confided in him. He helped me get everything I needed and even put together a baby bed. A lady he knew that kept babies in the neighborhood agreed to keep the baby while I worked. I was all set.

"Then one day, out of the blue, I was standing on a ladder reaching up to place a box on a tall shelf and I began to cramp and bleed. It came on so suddenly that I dropped the box when I grabbed at my abdomen. It set me off kilter and I fell from the ladder. Even though I was only a few rungs up, it was enough to be critical.

"Bill heard the noise and found me. I was losing the baby. I was bleeding, but it wasn't until I fell that my uterus began to rupture. The baby might have been saved had I not fallen. It was a little girl. I was eight months along." Sharon reached up and wiped tears from her cheek.

"She had wisps of blond hair. I named her Carley Ann." Sharon suddenly pushed back her chair and walked to the bathroom.

Will sat stunned. The windfall of grief that came, came without warning. His child. Carley Ann had been his child and Sharon had had to bury her alone. She had done it while he had been in some corporate meeting somewhere fighting over legal nonsense.

The waiter came and sat a basket of beautifully baked hot rolls on the table and asked if there was anything they needed. Will was barely aware of his presence. He shook his head woodenly and breathed, "Thanks."

Will's mind raced from regret to excuses and back again. He was numb from head to toe. The numbness was debilitating and radiated from somewhere deep in his soul. He couldn't fix it. He simply could not fix this.

Finally, Sharon emerged from the ladies' room. She had dried her tears and had garnered some internal strength from an unknown source. Will assumed she was practiced at it. He on the other hand had no idea how to overcome and regroup.

She sat back down on her own and replaced her napkin in

her lap. When she finally looked up and made eye contact with Will, he was nearly catatonic. Had he suffered from military combat he might have been considered, shell-shocked.

"Will, I lost Carly six years ago. I understand this news is new to you, but I've had a long time to attempt to recover. I can't say that I have fully, or that I ever will, but I've learned to move forward. I will not be able to get pregnant and have children of my own now.

"I think this is why the issue with Molly Sue is so critical to me. I couldn't help fall in love with her from the second I saw her. I know, have known from the beginning, that she is not mine. My mind keeps telling my heart that very thing. But, it does no good.

"The possibility that her real mother is out there somewhere is a very real possibility. I understand that. But I have taken good care of Molly Sue and I believe that she should stay with me until they find her mother." By the time that Sharon had stopped, her face had gone from one of controlled neutrality to contorted anxiety. Realizing it, she forced herself to relax and lean back in her chair.

The waiter brought their meals. Will responded to his requests regarding their culinary needs, without thinking or engaging. Reading the mood at the table, the waiter simply left them alone.

Sharon's body gnawed with hunger at the scintillating food which lay before her. She hadn't eaten all day and her body insisted that she feed it. But her heart and soul couldn't be bothered.

Will too, had lost interest in eating. He was working to push through the mental fog which had buried him. "Sharon, I am so sorry."

She could tell he was sincere. Their time together had joined them, connected them, and she could feel his sincerity. It seeped into her soul and gave a tiny measure of comfort. All she could do was nod.

"Will, we need to move forward and focus on Molly Sue. We can discuss Carly another time if you feel the need to, but we have to do all we can to keep her."

It was not lost on Will that Sharon had said; *we need to keep her.* Had it been a slip of the tongue as if they were a couple, or as in attorney client? What did he want? He had always loved Sharon, even when married to his wife, who he had also loved.

He looked down at his perfectly done ribeye and realized he too was hungry. "Yes. Yes, well… let's eat and talk about it." He did his best to shift back into warrior mode in order to create the perfect strategy to win this battle, but his heart kept him drifting back.

"She looks like what I think Carly Ann would have looked like. It struck me hard that first day she walked into the station. She is close to the same age Carly would have been, and she has curly blond hair and big blue eyes. And…" Sharon sat for a moment trying to find the right words, "she is so happy and optimistic. You would think that the apparently simple life she had led would have affected her negatively, but apparently she flourished."

"I think maybe our complex lives often keep us from being happy," said Will.

"She has been good for me, but I'd like to think I have been good for her too."

"Why do you think that you might be in danger of losing guardianship of her?"

"Small town, old-fashioned stereotypes. They believe that she should be in a two parent home. I can't say that wouldn't be ideal for a child, but she came from a single parent home. She has transitioned easily, or I think she has."

A mental cloud drifted over Sharon's face. "What?" Will asked.

"Well, there is Buddy. He isn't her father, brother, or… But, he provides a male figure for her."

"Tell me about this Buddy."

Sharon sat thinking, replaying all that Molly Sue had said about him. "Well, she loves Buddy, that is clear. She has never said anything negative about him at all. I think maybe he looks after them and helps them. Maybe since it is a single parent home, Buddy is a neighbor or someone who helps them out."

Will was listening and nodding. "That still isn't a father. Has her teacher or anyone else mentioned that Molly Sue has shown any deficit from being in a single parent home?"

"Not that they have said to me. But that Marcia Wallace. She just irks me. She looked at me and my nerves come undone. I feel like she is looking at me with disapproval and I want to defend myself to her."

"They are all like that. They are trained to present a calm and detached front. I'll interview her and see if I can get a read on where she is leaning. It seems to me that there is nothing she could present other than you are a single parent guardian."

Will slid his hand across the table and rested it on Sharon's. She started to slide it away, but the familiar memory of his touch held her. She had missed that touch, but it had not been there when she needed it the most.

Finally, she closed her eyes from the pain of his absence and slid her hand away. But, those few seconds had warmed Will's heart. Maybe she was healing and forgiving him.

Once back at the office, they sat in Will's car next to Sharon's. She hadn't made any move to get out and so Will just sat still.

For Sharon, leaving his car would be akin to when she had walked away from his life that day so many years ago. She knew in her mind it wasn't. She knew she would see him many more times over the course of the next few weeks and months. But the intimacy that they had regained over the last couple of hours, held her captive.

As if Will felt the words only her own heart could say, he reached out and took her hand, pulled it to him, and he kissed it. "I've missed you. I truly have."

Sharon could only nod.

"I want to kiss you. I want to hold you, but, while I am acting as your attorney I can't. I want you to know though, how I feel."

Sharon pulled her hand away and looked forward. "I don't know how I feel Will. You must understand that this, all of this, is bittersweet. There has been so much of me that wanted this moment, but then the anger and pain of loss and rejection hasn't completely gone away."

"Sharon, I never rejected you."

She looked over at him, angry all over again. "You chose your job over me and your baby. You - rejected - us."

His face folded in on itself and he nodded. "I am so sorry. You're right. I would give anything to go back and make another choice, the right choice."

Sharon reached for the door handle and as she pulled it, she said. "I know, but choices are like rivers that once fallen into, take us so rapidly downstream that we suddenly arrive at places we never knew existed or where we never desired to go, and there is no way back upriver."

DONNA - DECEMBER 1973

The joy of her new baby was the most genuine, and currently the only light in her life. Donna sat on the threshold of the back door in awe of the sweet baby girl resting in her arms. She had named her Molly Sue.

Life in the tiny cabin, in captivity could have been much harder than it was, but Molly Sue was a good baby. She ate from her mother's breast well and slept contentedly afterwards. The time she was awake was spent with Donna's full attention talking and singing to her.

As Donna sat in the open doorway of the cabin facing out back towards the stream, Molly Sue rested on her lap with Donna's forearms providing a snug fortress on each side of the tiny swaddled body. Light danced in the big blue eyes that looked up at Donna, so full of trust and love.

Sorrow like a lightening bolt shot through her heart. *I have to get out of here. I owe it to Molly Sue. Oh God, please help us.*

Donna's mind had worked overtime to devise a plan of escape, but none presented itself to her. The chain was steel and heavy. She could walk to the stream and bathe and get water and walk to the outhouse. The contents of the cabin were simple: an old twin size iron bed, a potbellied wood stove, a small table and two chairs, a small cupboard in the corner, a bucket for washing and drinking water.

There was a pillow, a couple of sheets, and a few old quilts stored in a trunk that Buddy had brought in. He would bring food on plates and then take them back when he left. She had asked for a pair of scissors to cut down some quilts making them more manageable to swaddle Molly Sue in. He sat and watched as she cut a quilt down then stitched the edges to keep the batting tucked inside.

He sat right next to her and never took his eyes off of her the entire time. She knew there was little she could have done with a mere pair of scissors, anyway. They would be fruitless against the heavy chain and the bolts that anchored it to the wall.

Finally, the blue eyes grew heavy and Molly Sue drifted

off to sleep. Donna looked up and out at the landscape before her. It had been a secluded paradise that did its best to comfort her when she had first arrived. Sun dappled the sparse grass underneath the barren elm trees as the wind toyed with them, causing them to sway back and forth.

The leaves had been turning when Molly Sue was born. They were now scattered about brown and dry and the trees stood empty and lifeless. The cooler weather of December had Donna now wearing the overalls and heavy socks which Buddy had brought to her.

Today the sun was working hard to heat the day and seemed to be winning. It was warm for December and Donna sat in the open door soaking as much of it in as she could. Molly Sue had turned two months old the day before and Christmas would soon arrive.

The creek of the front door behind her revealed the presence of Buddy. Donna looked back and placed a finger over her lips to indicate silence. Buddy stopped just inside the door and nodded.

Donna gently scooped the tiny bundle up in her arms and rose to enter the cabin. "Hi Buddy."

"Hi Donna." Buddy continued to stand. It wasn't mealtime, so she had no idea why Buddy had come.

"I take care of you."

"I know Buddy. You have done a good job, but it is time for me to go home now. The baby is safe. The baby is good. You did good."

Mid-way through her sentence Buddy's head began to

shake as it always did. Discussing her release was always meaningless. He wouldn't even listen to her.

Turning, Donna walked to the bed and laid the small baby down patting her gently on her back to smooth the transition from arms to bed. *I have to resign myself to making the best of my life here for now and wait for an opportunity that will someday come.*

Donna stood and turned to see Buddy's eyes that held a sort of love which radiated from them to her, but not the kind that Donna could easily define. It wasn't the love of a lover, or a parent, but there was something that Buddy felt deeply for Donna and the baby. She wanted to hate Buddy, but she couldn't. The best she could do was hate the situation she was in, and now she knew she had to make the best of it.

Donna pulled out a chair quietly from the kitchen table and sat down. Buddy did the same mimicking Donna's careful attempt at silence. As he sat, the chair groaned from the weight of his body.

"Buddy where do you get money from?" Donna asked.

His brows furrowed. "Money almost gone." He looked at his lap and Donna reached out touching his forearm.

"Where do you get the money from?

The face that rose to look back at her was worried. "There was money in Daddy's dresser. I don't use it much. I hunt and get eggs from the chickens." Then his eyes lit up. "I take eggs to the lady in town and they give me salt and sugar and flour."

"I see." *A barter system*, Donna thought.

"I chop wood too. I take it to Mr. Pike and he gives me things too, but no money."

"I see."

"Does Donna need something? Buddy can take eggs or chop more wood." The heartfelt eagerness on his face touched Donna, but left her feeling an even greater sadness.

"Not now…" she began then reconsidered. "Buddy, I would like a notebook to write in and a pencil. I get bored here with nothing to do. I used to write stories. Can you get me a notebook and some pencils?"

It had been rare to see Buddy smile the way he did now. Discolored teeth from too little care sat between his open lips. "Buddy get Donna a notebook and pencils. Momma had a notebook. Buddy get you Momma's notebook." Previously he had thought to bring his momma's hairbrush and a toothbrush. She never thought she would be thankful for a secondhand toothbrush, but she was and used it immediately after boiling it in water.

"Thank you Buddy. Someday the baby will need things too."

"Okay," said Buddy.

Buddy rose and left the cabin, soon returning with a slightly used notebook and a handful of pencils in various lengths and sharpnesses. He excitedly placed the items on the table in front of Donna. It was clear he hoped for praise.

Donna smiled. "Thank you Buddy," she said as she picked up the notebook and thumbed through. There were only a couple of pages with random notes.

Looking up into Buddy's eyes she once again confirmed, "Thank you Buddy".

CHAPTER 14

*S*haron - June 1979

Will kicked things in high gear and submitted multiple motions and briefs. He petitioned to cease the Department of Human Services intervention and one to issue guardianship to Sharon Paulson. He was also extremely busy doing depositions with character witnesses.

"Leslie, before we start the formal deposition, I wanted to speak with you alone." Will didn't want there to be any surprises, and even though Sharon may think she was telling him the truth, he knew each person's version of the truth is always distorted by their own emotional lenses. Usually, the more pain and suffering a person had experienced, the more refractive those lenses were.

"How long have you and Sharon been friends?"

"For about four years."

"How did you guys meet?"

"My brother is on the police force. My husband and I came to a summer picnic someone had for the department and they invited us. She had a wry and sarcastic sense of humor and we became fast friends."

"I only want the best for Sharon. I'm working hard on this, but I need to know details she may not even realize she needs to tell me. Can you think of anything that might blindside us down the road?"

Leslie repositioned herself in her chair. Could she talk to him openly? He was Sharon's attorney so hopefully it couldn't hurt. "Well, Sharon has been through a lot. I don't even think she has told me everything, but I'm concerned that the fear of losing Molly Sue haunts her constantly.

"She loves that little girl and enjoys spending time with her and doing all the mother daughter things there are to do, but it is all overshadowed by the fear of losing her. You can't really live life with that kind of fear hovering over you."

"And… It seems like there is more."

"Well, that fear has caused her to drink a little more than usual. It was common for her to have a couple of glasses of wine at bedtime, but I've noticed that she drinks more often now. I know it is to push away the fear and dread. Not that she ever seems drunk. I've not seen that, but she is drinking more."

Memories of Sharon's love for drinking came back. He also saw how she had used the potentially toxic liquid to medicate life's deepest wounds. "Do you think there is reason to be concerned that it will harm this proceeding? Would others have reason to bring this up or feel it is a concern?"

"I don't know. I do know that Marcia Wallace asked me about her drinking. I have no idea how she knew, unless she happened to see empty wine bottles at Sharon's house. I suspect there may have been a couple in her trashcan when Marcia came to visit."

Will's mental wheels were churning. "It isn't wrong to have a couple of glasses of wine at bedtime, but it could be a nugget that could easily be misconstrued into a negative trait. Have you talked to her about it?"

"I mentioned it. She just became more fearful. I feel really bad telling you this. I have never seen her drunk, well a little tipsy only a couple of times, but never ever drunk. I do not want you to get the impression that she drinks excessively."

"Don't worry. You have to remember that I know Sharon, or used to know her well. Medicating life's wounds and fears with alcohol is nothing new for Sharon. But like you, I rarely saw it out of control."

"Could she lose Molly Sue over this? Surely not."

"Honestly, it depends on how Marcia spins it and how conservative the judge is. His belief on drinking will color everything. Unfortunately, the public opinion of a woman who has a couple of glasses of wine before bed is far lower than a man who has a scotch or two after a hard day's work. Couple that with her being a single parent guardian and it could be all they need to take her away."

Leslie gasped. Will was right. "What can we do?"

"We will paint the best picture of Sharon and Molly Sue's life with Sharon that we possibly can. But if you can subtly redirect her from drinking as much, that may help too."

"I'll do everything I can."

Will began and finished Leslie's formal deposition and did another two by the end of the day. The sum total so far showed Sharon to be a responsible woman who took care of what she needed to take care of and was considerate to others. No one mentioned her drinking, or any other habits or behaviors that might shed a negative light on her.

One thing that did however, bother Will was that even though she was thought well of, the picture also painted one where she was not a particularly happy woman. Dutiful, responsible, trustworthy, but no one ever painted her as happy, fun loving, joyful, or peaceful. But then Will wondered how anyone could be those things after all that she had been through.

Guilt ripped at his insides again as he worked to push the pain away. *She will never forgive me, and I don't blame her.* His act of selfishness had deprived Sharon of not only that child, but from childbirth forever. He as well had been denied. His wife had never been able to bear children. Was it God's punishment for what he had done to Sharon? *Maybe so.*

Will looked at his clock and saw that it was five thirty. His secretary had beeped in a while back and had said she was going home. He tried to work, but his efforts were spent corralling his thoughts back to where they needed to be.

Finally, he gave in and sat mindlessly sitting for the next thirty minutes. Then in a spontaneous move, he jumped up and started towards the door. He had talked to Sharon briefly a couple of times since their dinner out, but he had not seen her in over two weeks. He needed to see her. He needed to see her at home with Molly Sue.

The drive to Sharon's home was spent mentally teeter-tottering back and forth regarding his spontaneous act. Several times, he nearly turned around and went home. But he felt he needed to surprise her. He needed to catch her off guard to see her as she really was.

Having grown up in the small town, Will knew where the street was that Sharon lived on and the approximate location of her house. Dusk was approaching and the sun hung like a large orange ball in a pink sky.

Will crept down the street towards Sharon's home. It was a good size bungalow. The yard was carefully cared for and flowerbeds bloomed profusely creating charm. The paint was new and clean and it had all the signs of a well loved and maintained home.

Sharon's car was in her driveway, and the glow of light from her home welcomed visitors through the windows. He pulled up in front of the house next to Sharon's near her driveway entrance and turned the key. He sat for a moment once again attempting to gain insight on what he was really doing there. He could not afford to be driven by personal feelings until this case was over.

He opened his car door and walked to her front porch. He knocked on the door, but heard laughter from the backyard. He knew she wouldn't hear him from there, so he walked around to the chain-link gate. With the sun still high enough in the sky, he could see Sharon sitting with Molly Sue at a table eating their dinner.

He stood quietly watching the two of them. Molly Sue had blond ringlets and big blue eyes. Sharon had told him that, but until he actually saw her, the resemblance to him, had not registered. Then Molly Sue saw him and pointed for Sharon to look towards the fence. She did not appear to be afraid of a strange man looking in their backyard, just wanted to let Sharon know.

Sharon quickly recovered a look of surprise on her face, then rose to greet him. "Hi Will. Come on back."

She was dressed in white shorts that showed her still shapely long legs, browned by the sun. He remembered how it had felt to run his hand along her thigh.

"Will, this is Molly Sue."

As he turned to look at the little girl, he was greeted with a large smile filled with joy. It was true what everyone had said, that she was the happiest child they had ever seen. But Will realized it was much more than that. She radiated pure joy.

"Hi. I'm Will. Nice to meet you." Will reached over the table to Molly Sue and offered his hand for her to shake. She merely sat and looked at it hovering there in front of her, unsure of what to do with it. Then, she rose up from the bench and took his hand to lead him away.

She stopped at a flowerbed at the back of the yard. "This is the flowers we planted. This is the bird house we painted. See?"

Will laughed. "Yes. They are wonderful."

Dusk had finally faded away, and the dark had announced its arrival with a bevy of fireflies. Molly Sue squealed with joy and ran to catch them.

Sharon walked up to stand by Will. She watched him watch her, and she knew that he too had just fallen in love with Molly Sue.

∼

Donna - December 1973

It was only three days until Christmas. Donna kept working to push the sadness away. Her baby's first Christmas was being spent in captivity, not surrounded by beautiful decorations and the warmth of family and friends.

"Buddy, can you bring me some books to read?"

He looked at her for a brief moment. "I will." He turned to go and was soon back with a large family bible. It was heavy and thick, leather bound. He laid it on the table and dust whooshed away from the impact.

Donna lifted the cover and read the list of family members in Buddy's family tree. Then she gently lifted each page and soon saw vivid illustrations of biblical paintings. She smiled and ran her hand over the smooth pages.

"Thank you Buddy, it's perfect." She hoped her sincerity

resonated with Buddy. Of all the books he could have brought her, this was the only one she really needed. It had been a long time since she had read its words or heard someone preach the stories from within.

"Can you read?"

Buddy frowned and ducked his head in shame. "It's okay, I can read. I can read to both you and Molly Sue." He lifted his head at her words and smiled, nodding his head.

"You know it's only three days until Christmas. We need to celebrate. What did your family do at Christmas? Did you have a tree and decorate it? Did you give gifts and have a big meal?"

The influx of questions seemed to overwhelm Buddy. It was clear his mind was racing. Donna reached across the table where they sat and touched his arm. "It's okay, Buddy. Just tell me about Christmas with your momma and daddy."

"Momma liked to cook. We would have a meal." A shadow of memory crossed his face.

"What is it Buddy?" Donna could see the pain on his face.

"Daddy didn't want momma to put up a tree. She did one time, but he got mad and tore it down."

"I'm so sorry Buddy."

He sat lost in thought. "You know Buddy, now that your daddy is gone, we can put up a tree and decorate it."

As if the sun had burst through the clouds, Buddy's face lit up. "We can?"

"Yes Buddy, we can." Donna went on to tell Buddy that

they just needed a little tree. She had tried to seize the opportunity to go back to the large house with the suggestion of a large tree, but he had declined.

Donna stood on the back doorway and directed Buddy to a small cedar sapling, he took his axe and chopped it down.

"We need a way to stand it up. A bucket of dirt or boards nailed to the bottom." Donna called to Buddy as he carried the tree to the cabin.

"Buddy can get a bucket."

"We'll need dirt in the bucket to make the tree stand up." Donna reached out and took the small tree from Buddy as he approached. "This will do nicely. Where can we put it?"

Donna looked around. The tree was indeed short and even though it was scraggly, its width consumed the small room. "Here Buddy, cut these bottom branches off." The removal of the lower branches removed width and gave a nice trunk to anchor into the dirt.

Buddy and Donna worked together to get the tree ready and soon in a vacant corner of the room, stood the little Christmas tree.

Donna stood with her hands on her hips. "We need to decorate it."

Buddy just stood with his arms down to his sides.

"Did your momma have Christmas decorations?"

"Daddy threw them all away."

Donna saw the sadness of that memory on Buddy's face. "That's okay Buddy, we can make some."

He looked at Donna with hope. "We can?"

"Yes. We just need paper, and crayons, and maybe colored pencils and glitter."

Molly Sue began to squirm in her wrap. It was time for her to be changed and fed. "Buddy go get paper and crayons."

Donna went to the bed where Molly Sue lay with her face scrunched in a pre-squal state. "Here. Here, sweet girl." The sound of Donna's voice soothed Molly Sue for a brief moment, and Donna felt the cut up quilt that she had fashioned into a thick diaper.

The sheets she had originally used were not thick enough, and since Buddy's mother had left him dozens of quilts, Buddy had allowed her to cut them in small diaper size shapes. She had only cut up one large quilt for now. With nothing else to do, she could easily wash and dry them each day.

Buddy didn't have safety pins, and he wouldn't have allowed her to have such a sharp object, anyway. After several inquisitions, Donna realized that she was being captive just as Buddy's father had eventually kept him. He had not been allowed sharp objects either.

Donna used long strips of torn sheets to tie around the quilted diapers. For now, it worked to hold them in place. She wasn't sure what she would do later. Hopefully, she would be long gone by then.

Buddy didn't return quickly. Had he gone to town to barter something for supplies? Once Molly Sue was napping again, Donna sat down and began to write in her notebook. She had intended to write stories, but found she used the notebooks for journaling, more that writing stories. She spent hours writing down descriptions of her days, Buddy, Molly Sue, and prayers.

Pausing, she pulled the large family bible over towards her and lovingly caressed it. Her mother and father had both taught Donna about the Lord and his loving kindness. They had taught Donna that we were to love as he loved and to lean on and trust in God with all our heart. Maybe instead of feeling rage at Buddy, that is why Donna was able to look at him with compassion. He was doing what he knew to be love.

Donna had been reading for over an hour when she heard the doorknob rattle. Molly Sue had been awake on the bed for sometime and was reaching for her feet, which seemed illusive to her.

"Buddy got glitter." He beamed with pride.

Donna moved the bible and her journal to the side as Buddy sat a plain brown paper bag on the table. Inside was paper, crayons, colored pencils, glitter, and glue. He had remembered every single thing that Donna had asked for.

"Buddy, that is amazing! Thank you so much. Where did you get all this stuff?"

"Took money from daddy's drawer and went to get it for Donna."

Donna was wrought with emotion. "Did you use all the money?" Donna asked, terrified of the answer.

Buddy reached into his pocket and pulled out a fist of loose bills and coins. "No. Buddy still has money."

Donna looked at the wadded pile before her and quickly counted. Several one-dollar bills and a five lay before her. He still had nine dollars and sixty-three cents. That was it. All the money that Buddy had to his name was in the palm of his hand and he had spent some of it for Donna and Molly Sue.

"Do you want to help me make decorations for the tree?"

Buddy's face beamed.

"We need scissors too." Buddy hurried out of the room and was soon back with the scissors.

She sat Buddy at the table and explained to him as one would do a small child what they were going to do. She helped him draw geometric shapes that they would color and cut out.

His large hands looked so strange when attempting to hold the small crayons. He looked at the one that Donna had drawn and worked hard to draw the same lines and designs that Donna had. While he worked in deep concentration, Donna noticed the tip of his tongue stuck out slightly from the side of his mouth.

Soon after starting, the crayon that Buddy was holding snapped in two from the pressure of his large hand. He sat looking at the broken crayon then looked at Donna with watery eyes. "Buddy broke it. Buddy so sorry." Terror crossed his face. He feared her reprimand.

Donna placed her hand on his arm. "It's okay, Buddy. They will still work. Now we have two blue crayons."

Buddy looked back at his hand where the two halves of the blue crayon rested. "Now we have two."

S̲ʜᴀʀᴏɴ - Jᴜʟʏ 1979

Will's visits had become more frequent to Sharon and Molly Sue's. He felt as though he had come home.

"Do all attorney's visit their client's home this many evenings a week?" Sharon tried to not smile.

Will looked sheepish and rightly called out. "I think you know the answer to that."

Suddenly turning serious, Sharon said, "It's okay, isn't it?"

Will looked at her face. Fear hovered in the background. It was always there, even when she laughed and played with Molly Sue. She was always waiting for the other shoe to drop.

"There isn't anything going on between us, except friendship. I don't think it will cause any problems." Will hoped that was true. He had often questioned if he was just lonely and coming to spend time with Sharon and Molly Sue because it was easy, or if he hoped that after this was over, they would reconnect romantically.

Sharon stuffed the fear back down and nodded her head. Molly Sue brought Will a paper with brightly colored images. He wondered just how many of the different colored crayons she had used to fill the page with.

"Molly Sue, this is beautiful!" He turned to Sharon. "She really is good."

"I think in her previous life with her mother, drawing and coloring was one of the few things she had to fill her time. I don't think she had a lot of toys, or games. I think art was what she did, and she became very good at it."

Will held the page in his hands. It was a picture of Sharon's white house and an abundance of colorful flowers everywhere. He had learned that even though Sharon liked to plant and tend the flowerbeds, after Molly Sue had come, it began to be a prominent pastime. Molly Sue loved gardening and growing the flowers.

She would frequently break off stems and bundle them into small bouquets and bring them to Sharon and they would put them in water. Sharon had become Molly Sue's mother. Everyone needed to see this girl and how she flourished in this home.

Will didn't want his visits to feel like he was here to probe Molly Sue, but he would often ask her questions in an effort to gain more understanding of her and her previous life.

"Molly Sue, tell me about Buddy." The three of them were at the park and Will and Molly Sue were filling small bowls and tins with sand to make cakes and pies.

The little face found his eyes, and she watched them. "He was big, very big." She looked down, busy once again working to press the sand deep into the little tin cake pan.

"Did he live with you?"

"No."

"Was he a neighbor?"

Molly Sue's head tilted a bit. "I guess so. He lived in the white house next to ours."

"Did he live alone?"

"Yes. His mommy and daddy died."

"So, he lived alone."

"Yes."

"How old was Buddy?"

Again a slight tilt of her head was evident as she worked away at the sand. "I don't know."

"Was he the same age as your mommy or older?"

She shrugged her shoulders still hard at work. When the tin was satisfactorily packed, she turned it over and hit the bottom turning the sand cake out on the ground.

"Good job!" Will said. "You got it packed so tight that it looks just like a cake.

Molly Sue beamed. She looked around and found bits of leaves and twigs to decorate her cake. Will worked on his own creation in silence. There didn't seem to be any trauma from her relationship with Buddy, which was very good.

"Molly Sue was Buddy good to you?"

Molly Sue looked up and smiled. "I like Buddy. He is sweet. He looked after mommy and me."

"How did he do that?"

Her little eyebrows dipped slightly. "He brought us food. He brought mommy paper and me crayons."

Sharon walked over and stood slightly off, watching the two of them play in the sand. She wondered if Will was getting too close to Molly Sue or if this was all just research for the case.

When Will saw her, he smiled and stood dusting his hands on his shorts. "We made dessert if you brought dinner?"

Sharon looked down at the sand creations and raised and eyebrow. "I brought both dinner and dessert. Good thing too, by the looks of your creation." Will looked down, his sand pie had already fallen apart. He laughed at the sight of it.

Sharon had left to go get burgers and fries. The weather had been beautiful, and it just felt right to eat at the park. Molly Sue seemed to prefer playing outside. Sharon had showered her with tons of toys she could play with inside, but her favorite things were the things she found to play with in nature.

Will helped Sharon pull out the contents of the fast food sacks while Molly Sue continued to make picture perfect sand cakes and pies. He laughed. "She's better at that than I am."

"Oh, no doubt. Me too. I suspect she's had a little practice."

"Okay sweet girl. It's time to eat. Are you hungry?" Sharon walked over to Molly Sue and gave her a hand up. "Here let me help you wipe off your hands." Will watched as Sharon used a damp cloth to wipe the sand from Molly Sue's little hands. She was so nurturing and patient with her, but then Molly Sue was an easy child.

While eating, Will placed a French fry on his nose and

balanced it, looking at it cross-eyed. Molly Sue laughed and tried the same thing. "I don't think you'll be able to balance anything on that tiny button nose of yours."

"The fourth of July is coming up in two days. Do you and Molly Sue have plans?" Will braced himself for her to confirm that they did, but she shook her head.

"No. Not really. There is always an open invitation from Leslie. We have spent a lot of time with her family the past year. They are having a cookout and extended the invitation to you if you would like to come."

"I would like that very much." They finished their burgers and fries and Sharon opened the boxes of fried apple pies and they consumed those too.

"Well, it's starting to get dark. I think we should get home," said Sharon. Molly Sue was yawning and her eyes were heavy. While Sharon and Will cleared the picnic table, Molly Sue laid her head down and fell asleep.

Will picked her up and carried her to his car. *So this is what it is like to have a family*, he thought as he gently laid the sleeping girl in the backseat.

Back at Sharon's, they brushed more of the sand off and tucked her in bed without fanfare. Sharon assured him that she would change her sheets and bathe her in the morning.

She flipped off the light and as she started down the hall, Will grabbed her waist and pulled her close. His mouth found hers and his body came alive. Then he realized that after her initial acceptance, she was now pulling away.

"What's wrong? I'm sorry." Will's pained expression worked to sooth any error he had made.

"I… I… I don't know that I can do this again Will. I'm sorry if I have been misleading you. My word it felt good to kiss you, to feel you holding me. But.. I…" She shook her head and walked into the kitchen.

She retrieved a bottle of wine and a glass. Will watched as she poured a liberal glass and then promptly downed it.

"How much do you drink Sharon?" It was an even toned question but Sharon received it with hostility.

"What does that mean? Have some of my well-meaning friends said something about my glass or two of wine I have at night?" She was pouring her second glass as she spoke.

Will walked over and placed his hands on her shoulders. "I'm sorry."

She shrugged him off and walked into the living room, curling up tightly on the end of the sofa. Her eyes were hard when Will looked at them. She had shut the door to her soul once again.

He walked over and sat at the opposite end. "I remember how when things got too painful for you, you would always have a drink to help you get through." His words were soft in the hope that the message would land gently.

She shut her eyes and uncoiled slightly. A slight nod could be detected and Will slid down to sit next to her. He draped his arm behind her on the back of the sofa.

He took the glass from her and sat it on the coffee table,

then took her hand in his. "Sharon, you were the love of my life, and still are."

She continued to look down at her lap where their hands lay intertwined. "Honestly, I don't see a problem with the court allowing you to keep Molly Sue. I haven't found anyone who has had anything negative to say about you. It's clear that she is flourishing with you. When she meets with the psychologist, they will see it too."

"Is that why you've been hanging around, to see how Molly Sue really is?"

"No. I've been here because of you."

"I don't know how to break through the thick barrier of unforgiveness that covers my heart. It's been there too long, and it runs too deep."

"Time, maybe? Will you give me time?"

The love she had always felt for him was begging to be free, but the dark bondage of unforgiveness held it firmly confined. "I don't know."

"Well, let's focus on Molly Sue and getting past this."

Sharon nodded while studying their hands. How many times had they sat like this with their hands so intricately intertwined as if they belonged that way?

She leaned over and laid her head on his shoulder and closed her eyes. "Yes, let's focus on Molly Sue. That would be best for now."

CHAPTER 15

*D*onna - January 1974

Christmas had come and gone. Buddy and Donna had made enough paper ornaments to cover the little tree. Once they had been colored and cut out, Buddy had gone and gotten a ball of twine and they had poked holes in the tops and created loops to hang them by.

Buddy had hunted and had gotten a deer, and dressed it the way his father had taught him. Donna watched from her front porch step towards Buddy's house. He had a large pulley system where he would hang the deer and skin it.

He worked away with efficient movement. He rolled the skin and wrapped it in a white cloth after rubbing some type of gritty solution on it.

"What will you do with the hide?" Donna asked.

"Buddy will take it to town. The guy at the shop will buy it."

"What shop is it?"

"The leather shop. He makes saddles, and wallets, and stuff"

"How much does he pay you?"

Buddy looked at Donna for a moment, then began shaking his head. "He don't pay me. He gives me stuff."

Donna frowned. "What kind of stuff?"

"He gives me new boots, and stuff."

"He should give you money. That hide is worth more than a new pair of boots." The truth was, it was probably a fair trade. Donna had no way of really knowing what a deer hide was worth.

"Take me with you when you take him the hide and I'll make sure you get the right amount." Donna held her breath waiting for Buddy's reply.

After what felt like an eternity, Buddy shook his head.

"Well, let me write a note for him. I'll write down how much he should give you."

"No. You tell me. I'll tell him."

Donna shut her eyes, exasperated. She began to grind her teeth and seethed with frustration. It did no good to get this way. She sat in the door and laid her forehead on her knees; she drew a deep breath and let it go. She had to stay positive.

On Christmas Eve. Donna found the story about baby Jesus and had read it to Buddy and Molly Sue even though she was still a little baby. Buddy's eyes were focused and round as Donna read. When she had finished the story,

Donna asked, "Buddy have you ever heard about Jesus before?"

"Momma told me about Jesus. She told me he loved me but not like daddy loved me, like momma loved me."

"I see." Donna's mind began to work.

"So, you love me and Molly Sue, right?"

Buddy eagerly nodded.

"Then why don't you love me like your momma, and Jesus, instead of like your daddy?"

Confusion coursed across Buddy's face. He stood up quickly, knocking the chair backwards. He began to pace the floor twirling a shock of hair. This time, Donna did not try to interrupt his thought process.

When he finally stopped and looked at Donna, he said, "Mommy loved me and let daddy protect me. That is what I do for you and Molly Sue."

Donna looked at Buddy's face. "Okay Buddy. Okay."

Early Christmas morning, Buddy had come to the cabin. He had cooked a large roast of deer and brought a homemade fruitcake.

"Wow. Buddy where did you get the cake?"

"Lady who gets my eggs always gives us a fruitcake at Christmas."

Donna had taken some paper the previous week and had drawn what resembled two placemats. They were red ovals with green holly leaves on them. She had been saving them, not knowing what Christmas Day would bring.

Now, she sat their two plates on them and made a great

show of setting the table with the roast and cake. She was trying her best to make what she could out of her situation, but the desperate longing for her family tugged at her constantly, threatening to sweep her away in a sea of despair.

Donna lit the little candle in the center of the table and she bowed her head to pray. Buddy did as well after he had plucked his cap off of his head, leaving his hair standing out in all directions. Donna resisted the urged to reach out and comb it back down with her hand.

Donna gave thanks, and the two of them ate the meal in silence. Donna lost in memories of Christmas' past and Buddy, just lost. When the meal was over and while Donna was clearing the table, Buddy rose and went to the door.

Donna couldn't tell what he was doing on the little porch, but soon he came in and had a crudely wrapped package which he handed to Donna. "Merry Christmas Donna."

She was dumbfounded. "I don't have a present for you, Buddy." She felt truly sorrowful that she didn't. How she would have prepared one, she didn't know, but it still felt wrong nonetheless.

"It's okay." He was nearly hopping from one foot to the other in excitement. "Open it."

Donna sat back down on the chair and began to unwrap the package. Inside was a box and when she lifted the lid, she saw a stack of brand new notebooks and pencils. There was also a pencil sharpener like she had used in school.

"Oh, Buddy. Thank you. Can you anchor the pencil sharpener to the wall?"

"Yes." Buddy hurried out of the room and was quickly back with four screws and a screwdriver. It took him only ten short minutes to anchor the sharpener to the end of the little cupboard in the corner.

When he was done they sat down and each had another large slice of fruitcake. As she ate, Donna's mind was working overtime to try to figure something out to give Buddy for Christmas. But, the truth was, she had nothing to give, or did she?

"Buddy, I actually do have a gift to give you for Christmas."

"You do?"

"Well, I didn't say anything earlier because I didn't know if you would like it."

"Buddy will like it."

"I want to teach you to read. Would you like to learn to read?"

Genuine joy burst forth on Buddy's face. "Yes. Buddy would like to read."

Donna removed the food from the table, sat it on the cupboard, and wiped the table. She got out the older notebook he had brought earlier and opened it to the first blank page.

"First, you have to learn the letters of the alphabet." She sat next to Buddy and began to write a large capital 'A'. Then, she gave Buddy the pencil and instructed him to write the letter below and as he wrote to say it out loud.

By the time the sun was setting, they had covered several of the letters and were ready for a rest. "Each day, I'll teach you a little more, okay?"

"Okay."

As Buddy stood to leave, Donna took the papers he had done and with a red crayon wrote a large 'A+' on each page. She handed them to Buddy and said, "The A+ means you did a very good job. You take these home and when you want to, say them out loud. That way you can practice and learn them quicker."

Delighted, Buddy said, "I will Donna. I will."

He turned to leave the cabin and right before leaving, turned to Donna. "I... I... I love you Miss Donna."

"I love you too Buddy. I love you too."

Sharon - August 1979

Sharon couldn't stop trembling inside. They sat in the courtroom with Will by her side at the table. Several witnesses had already been called and questioned by Will. So far, only glowing testimonials had been given.

Leslie was currently on the stand and Will had turned her over to the state attorney.

"Mrs. Cramer, thank you for being here today. You know the petitioner pretty well, isn't that correct?"

"Yes, I believe so."

"Then can you tell me about her drinking problem?"

"Objection." Will belted out.

The judge's gavel rammed down hard on the bench. "This is not a trial, so we will hear all testimony."

Leslie looked panic-stricken. Her eyes searched Will's face for relief. He could give none.

"Mrs. Cramer, please answer the question."

"I don't know what you're talking about."

"It has been brought to my attention that Ms. Paulson drinks quite a bit. Could you tell us about that?"

"She might have a glass or two of wine right before bedtime after she has put Molly Sue to bed. Other than that, there is nothing."

The attorney made a show of shuffling papers, finally pulling out one to read from.

"I have an affidavit here from John Blankenship who owns the local liquor store. When asked how much liquor Ms. Paulson buys, he said she buys several bottles a week." He looked up to gauge Leslie's reaction.

"I don't know anything about that, but I would guess that two glasses a night times, say four or so nights a week, would be about two or three bottles. And that is if she were the only one drinking from it."

"Hmmm." He turned and walked back to his table and reached for more documents.

"Thank you, Mrs. Cramer. You may step down."

"That was our last witness, your honor." Said Will.

"Does the state have any witnesses they would like to call?" The judge asked.

"Your honor, I would like to call Marcia Wallace to the stand."

As Leslie walked past the table heading back to the galley, she glanced at Sharon with apologetic eyes.

"Ms. Wallace, can you tell me your concerns about Ms. Paulson?"

"When I made my initial visit to the petitioners home, I noticed there were several empty wine bottles in her trash container."

Sharon watched Will make a note and a large question mark, on his legal pad.

"In your interviews, did you question anyone who had concerns about her drinking?"

"It seemed to be widely known that she would have a few beers or glasses of wine at various parties or events. Along with her drinking at home, it could be considered a considerable amount."

Sharon was growing sick inside. She was not a drunk. She never drank more than anyone else.

The state's attorney asked Marcia several more questions. Once done, it was clear that Marcia Wallace felt that Molly Sue would be best served in a two parent home where the parents didn't drink the way Sharon did.

Will stood to take his turn at Marcia.

"Did you actually count the empty bottles in Ms. Paulson's trash container?"

"No, but I saw a couple."

"Was there any indication of how long they had been there?"

"No, of course not."

"Then we could also assume that they may have been

there for a week and that she had dinner guests that had shared the wine. Couldn't we?"

Marcia gave a small huff of air then said, "I suppose we could, but it was a weekday."

"Do people not have guests during the week?"

"Yes, I suppose they could."

"Did you find Molly Sue to be a happy child?"

"She seemed on the surface to be."

"On the surface?"

"She appeared to be happy."

"Would you say for a child who was separated from her mother, she was well adjusted?"

"She seemed to be well taken care of."

"So why then would you assume that another transition would benefit her, when she is lovingly being cared for?"

"Studies have shown that children thrive in two-parent homes. Ms. Paulson works and has to farm out Molly Sue for someone else to care for while she does so."

"Even though Ms. Paulson's work environment is so flexible that she can take Molly Sue to school each day, pick her up from school when she gets out and takes her two blocks away to her longtime best friend who watches children for a living. That she is not spending enough time with her?"

"I don't feel that Ms. Paulson is being fair to Molly Sue, by depriving her of a male role model in the home."

"Molly Sue came from a single parent home with only a mother, correct?"

"As far as we can tell."

"Then why is it unhealthy for her to be in the exact same home that she was previously in?"

"I believe that environment was not a healthy environment either."

"Did you see signs of trauma in Molly Sue?"

Marcia sat quietly thinking.

"She still shows a limited knowledge of civilized life."

"Could you elaborate?"

"I went through a bank of pictures of common everyday things, several of which she did not recognize or understand."

Will laughed. "I bet if you showed me a bank of pictures there would be things in there that I don't understand."

"Move it along, Mr. Yates," said the judge.

"Did her teacher Mrs. Patterson express any concerns with you?"

"No."

"Did she do well in her studies?"

"She was behind for most of the year."

Will pulled out a document. I have a statement here from her teacher that states, "Molly Sue arrived initially behind the other classmates, but she is a bright and intelligent student and by the end of the school year she was above average in everything and excellent in some areas."

"I would say that for her to begin so far behind and then not only catch up, but excel, she was in a nurturing home, wouldn't you Ms. Wallace?"

Marcia just looked at Will.

"No more questions, your honor."

CHAPTER 15 | 259

When all witnesses had been called, the judge asked that Molly Sue be brought to his chambers alone with the two attorney's and court reporter. He wanted to talk to Molly Sue one on one in a less intimidating environment.

Will assured Sharon he would watch over her.

Molly Sue's eternally joyful personality was subdued. The large stone and marble building terrified her. She could sense the seriousness of the situation, but had no idea what was wrong.

Leslie brought Molly Sue to the judge's chambers then left to sit on a bench in the hallway.

Seeing Will in the room, she smiled up at him. The judge had everyone sit and made a place for Molly Sue to sit by his desk where she could see only him.

"Hi Molly Sue. My name is Judge Abernathy."

Molly Sue just looked at the judge.

"I just want to talk to you for a little bit and ask you a few questions. Is that okay?"

Molly Sue nodded her head.

"You've been staying with Ms. Paulson since you came here, right?"

Molly Sue frowned. She had not heard Sharon referred to as Ms. Paulson before.

Will, cleared his throat and offered, "Miss Sharon."

The judge nodded and Molly Sue said, "Yes."

"Do you like living with Miss Sharon?"

Molly Sue nodded. The big man behind the desk frightened her. "I want my mommy."

"Are you talking about Miss Sharon?"

"No. My real mommy." Molly Sue's eyes began to tear up and they rolled down her cheeks.

"Where is your real mommy?"

"I don't know." Molly Sue began to cry in earnest now.

"Okay, Okay. Don't cry."

"We are looking for your mommy. You know that, right?"

Molly Sue nodded.

"So while we are looking for her, we are trying to decide where the best place is for you to live."

Molly Sue had stopped crying, but her eyes were still full of tears.

"Do you like staying with Miss Sharon?"

Molly Sue nodded vigorously.

"Can you tell me about your daddy?"

Molly Sue frowned.

"Do you remember your daddy?"

Molly Sue shook her head.

"At school, most of your classmates live with both their mommy and daddy, right?"

"Yes."

"Do you ever feel bad that you do not live with your daddy?"

Molly Sue shook her head no.

"You don't ever feel different from the other kids?"

Molly Sue just looked at the judge.

"Do you think Miss Sharon takes good care of you?"

Molly Sue continued to simply frown at the judge. Then she turned to look at Will. "I want to go now."

The judge relented and said that was all. "I'll review everything and let you know my ruling soon."

Will took Molly Sue's hand, and they walked from the room.

"I don't like that man," said Molly Sue.

"Sometimes, Molly Sue, I don't either."

DONNA - FEBRUARY 1974

Donna's determination to stay positive in her dire situation was hard to sustain. Molly Sue was now five months old and getting more active as the days progressed. She wanted so much more for her baby girl and felt powerless to provide it.

The grey February sky was reflective of the sadness Donna felt. The weather was colder and she couldn't leave the doors open the way she had on prettier days. It had been cold and dreary since the end of December and cabin fever was raging inside Donna.

She could tell that her moods, no matter how hard she tried to disguise them, affected Molly Sue greatly. So many nights after Molly Sue was asleep beside her, she had cried silent tears. All her effort seemed to be directed at pushing away despondency.

Teaching Buddy how to read had given her something to do. She couldn't hate this man-child. He didn't have a vindictive bone in his body. The abuse he had suffered combined with his mental challenges, created a thought process that convinced him he was doing the right thing for Donna and Molly Sue.

If she were to feel anger at anyone, it was towards his parents. His hard and angry father who had beat his mother, which had damaged Buddy in the womb. He hadn't had a chance.

Then Donna's thoughts would drift toward his mother. She pictured a kow-toed woman who bent from the abuse of her husband. Why hadn't she risen up and stood up for herself and her child? There was much that Donna didn't understand, but she knew that unless she had walked in her shoes, she couldn't judge.

The cabin moaned and creaked as the hard February wind beat against it. As Donna looked around the cabin she realized in truth, she had everything she really needed. She was surviving, but she couldn't say she was flourishing.

Molly Sue sat on the bed chewing on a wooden ring that Buddy had carved out for her. She was teething and slobbered on everything.

Plunk. The wooden ring went flying across the cabin for the dozenth time. Her little arms would go flying and the ring would bounce across the room. Donna would retrieve it and Molly Sue would laugh.

Had it not been for Molly Sue, Donna would not have survived this ordeal. She was a true joy. "Thank you Lord that you have given me a good, sweet, and docile child. I don't know what I would have done if she had been one that was naturally discontent."

A rush of cold wind suddenly blew in rattling through

the cabin. It was Buddy bringing food and firewood for the little pot-bellied stove.

"Hi Donna."

"Hi Buddy."

Donna took Molly Sue and sat her in a chair and tied a wrap around her to hold her in the chair. She began to bounce making it difficult to tie her in. She knew it was time to eat. Even though she still nursed at Donna's breast, Donna knew that was not enough nourishment.

"What did you bring us today, Buddy?"

"Potatoes." Buddy presented a big fat potato to Donna as if it were gold bullion.

"Thank you, Buddy." She had been encouraging Buddy to expand their diet. They all needed more nutrition. In the spring she had plans to plant a garden for vegetables.

"I need a way to cut the potatoes. Did you bring a knife?"

Buddy looked at Donna. He seemed once again, uncertain about whether he should let her have a sharp instrument. Donna could see memories flash behind his eyes as he tried to make decisions like this. She knew his father had never allowed Buddy to have a knife while he was captive out here in the cabin.

"I need it to peel and cut up the potatoes. I'll be careful with it."

Buddy's eyes darted around and finally nodded in agreement. "But you have to be careful." Buddy emphasized. He seemed more concerned about Donna's safety than he did about his own. She would have to kill Buddy to get away, and she knew she couldn't do that. And even if she were free from Buddy, the chain was the real problem.

Donna had spent countless moments studying the chain and the anchor. Buddy's father had been smart and knew that to hold someone as strong as Buddy, it had to be solid and anchored to the cabin. The last link of the chain had been fed through a large u-bolt as thick as Donna's little finger. From there it went through the wall of the log cabin and the end bolts were tightened down with nuts, now rusted solidly to the bolt from years of rain.

Donna had walked around through each door of the cabin testing to see if she could reach the backside of the anchor. She could reach it if she went through the front door, but the nuts on the bolts were seized up and there was nothing she could think to do to release them. She had tried countless times in the beginning and had finally given up when there was never any sign of progress.

So, even if Buddy were incapacitated, she would still be stuck, unable to get free. No, she needed Buddy to provide for her and Molly Sue until she could see a way out.

Donna stood with a pan of water at the little cupboard. She had placed the potatoes in the water and began peeling. Buddy was working to place pieces of wood not much larger than kindling into the stove. It was small and couldn't hold large pieces of wood. But, for the small cabin, it worked fine.

Buddy sat down at the table and leaned toward Molly Sue. Donna glanced over and saw his face. It radiated when he looked at her. And in turn, Molly Sue would bounce with joy when she saw him. A sad smile crossed Donna's soul.

Soon the potatoes were peeled and cut in smaller sections to cook faster. Donna put them on the stove and went to the table. Molly Sue was straining and reaching for Buddy. Soon, Donna knew she would be clever enough to escape the confines of the chair.

Donna untied her and handed her to Buddy. Sitting at the table, she watched them. Every single time that Buddy took Molly Sue into his arms, an air of exaggerated care came over him. It was as if someone were holding a fragile heirloom that could break with the slightest breath.

His focus was solely on her now and how he was holding her. At five months he would sit her on his knee holding one arm across her back to steady her. The other hand was usually ready to catch her when she wobbled or tried to move too fast. Today that hand held the little wooden ring. Her hands slapped at it as he held it in front of her.

"Buddy, we have to think about things that Molly Sue is going to need as she grows."

He looked up at Donna with sudden concern. "What will she need? I'll get it."

"She will need clothes and shoes as she grows. She will need toys to play with. There will be things, but I can't think of them all right now."

Buddy looked back at the angel on his knee. "Buddy will get what you need."

"Thank you, Buddy." A sizzle from the stove showed the

potatoes to be boiling over. Donna jumped up and with a square of quilt, she carefully pushed the pot further back on the stove so it got less heat. It was amazing how she had learned to cook simply on the tiny stove.

Molly Sue was no longer content to sit still on Buddy's knee and was squirming to get down. Donna reached over and took her from her perch. "Hey little missy." Donna held her in the air and wobbled her back and forth. Molly Sue grinned and a string of drool drizzled on Donna's face.

"Buddy I think she has a new tooth coming through." Donna sat down and put Molly on her lap. She tried to force her finger into the slippery mouth, and when she had achieved her goal, Molly Sue bit down hard on Donna's finger.

"Ouch. Yep, I felt a bit of tooth coming through her gum." She looked at Buddy and smiled. His eyes were round in wonder.

"Soon she will be better able to eat food. It will still have to be small bites that are fairly soft, but she'll be there before we know it."

Donna thought of her mom and how she would love to be sharing these milestones with her. And there was Jared, Molly Sue's father. He should be sharing this with her. At those thoughts, she couldn't hold back the tears falling silently from her eyes.

"Donna. Donna. You okay?" Buddy asked concerned.

Donna looked up at Buddy, not trying to hide her tears. "I was thinking about my mom and Molly Sue's father. He is a good man, and he is missing seeing his daughter grow."

Donna sat and watched Buddy. All he ever knew about what a father was, was mean and harmful. He could not understand that there could be another kind.

Buddy looked sad, but didn't know how to fix what Donna was saying. He knew he couldn't let her go. He had to protect her. So, he sat quietly saying nothing.

The remainder of the day was filled with eating and then working on reading lessons. Buddy was getting better and better at writing his letters. Then, Donna would read the bible out loud and Buddy would sit next to her and watch as her finger slid underneath the lines.

At around three o'clock, Buddy stood up and announced that he had to go do chores. He gathered the plates, silverware and knife and left abruptly. He would always do that. Somehow an internal clock triggered him to change course and when it did, he just did it with no fanfare.

And so her days went. Cooking meager meals, eating, and teaching Buddy. Oh, and watching Molly Sue grow. She was beautiful.

Her hair which had only been white fuzz at her birth was now little longer wisps of white blonde hair. It was going to be curly, just like Jared's.

I have to change what I think about. The more I think about what I don't have, the sadder I'll get and that will not do me or Molly Sue any good. I have to look at what we do have, what I have, and be thankful for it. I have to make myself focus on the good.

Donna reached for her journal and began to write. At

the top of the page she wrote the title, 'What I Am Thankful For'. At first the list was short. She was thankful for Molly Sue first of all, then food, then shelter, then she began to see the little things that she had. Things that she overlooked so easily when she was focused on her captivity, on the things she didn't have.

Soon, she stopped writing and sat back in her chair. She had filled the page with things to be thankful for. She smiled as she tore out the page. She was going to put it on the wall so she could see it every day.

The rough wood logs could be splintered if she worked at it. So, she picked at a sliver and pulled it out and bent it at a right angle. Using the pencil, she poked a tiny hole in the top of the page and slid it on the splinter.

She stood looking at the list and began to read out loud. "Lord, today I am thankful for, Molly Sue, food, shelter..."

CHAPTER 16

Sharon - August 1979

"The judge has made a decision, Sharon." Will had called the station to notify Sharon that it was time to reconvene back at court. With all that had been going on lately, Sharon had been away from the office a considerable amount of time. She was almost too nervous to work, but knew she needed to do so, while Molly Sue was at school.

At Will's words, the air was sucked out of the room and vertigo set in. "Okay."

"I'll come pick you up."

"Okay."

Sharon was sick in the pit of her stomach. She might be on the very precipice of loosing Molly Sue forever. *Why wasn't I with her hugging her and loving on her instead of sitting here at my desk?*

Bill had heard the phone and stepped in to see Sharon with her head in her hands. "Bad news?"

"No, but it's time. Will just called and said the judge has made a decision." With a ragged exhale, Sharon stood on wobbly legs.

Bill looked at Sharon. He felt such compassion for this woman who had done so much for him, and who had been his friend for so long. Was it possible that the face that looked back at him now had aged so much in such a short period of time? The weight of losing Molly Sue had stolen everything from her. It had stolen her peace, her joy, and had kept her from truly being able to enjoy each moment with the child.

"Thank you, Bill for all that you do for me." She meant it, but had no words to convey the depth of her sincerity.

"I know. I'll be right behind you."

As Sharon approached where Bill stood by the door, he reached out and drew her to him. "You look like you could use a hug." She needed one in the worst possible way, and her friend's arms felt solid and secure around her. It felt good to be held, but the time had come and she couldn't put it off any longer.

The trip to the courthouse was a blur. Will had been talking, but Sharon couldn't remember what he had said. It seemed like reassuring legal gibberish. It seemed like he was already preparing her for the worst outcome.

Leslie was waiting with Molly Sue on a bench just outside the courtroom. Leslie had gotten Molly Sue from school so should things go wrong, she could see Sharon one last time.

The realization that this may be her last moment with Molly Sue landed hard, and Sharon nearly buckled under the weight of the realization. Will reached for her to hold her steady.

Molly Sue ran to Sharon. Down on her knees, Sharon wrapped her arms around Molly Sue and held on for dear life. Molly Sue held tight, sensing something bad was about to happen.

Someone tore Molly Sue from Sharon's arms and she walked robotically to the table where they had sat the previous day. Rising to stand before the judge seemed impossible, but Will was there to support her.

The judge's lengthy explanation was muffled in the roar in Sharon's ears, but she did distinctly hear one phrase, and it was the one stating that Molly Sue would be removed from Sharon's home immediately and be placed in foster care in a two parent home.

Lights flashed behind Sharon's eyes, and the room went dark. As she dropped to the floor, Will was quick to scoop her up and set her in the chair. She opened her eyes to see Will's pained face. "We'll keep fighting this Sharon…" His words trailed off as Sharon began to shake her head. She couldn't hang on any longer. It was too hard.

When Marcia Wallace left the courtroom to take Molly Sue from Leslie, they heard a loud wail. Sharon shut her eyes, knowing that neither she nor Molly Sue would be the same again. The thought of getting up and walking out of the room seemed impossible to Sharon. Her body was numb and so was her soul.

She had known this would happen. Why had she allowed herself to care so much about Molly Sue? How could she have not? It was all too much. She needed to go home.

She must have said as much to Will because he ushered her to his car and drove her there. He kept talking of appealing and other nonsense, but Sharon couldn't bear to listen. "Will, please stop. Please. It's over."

Will helped Sharon into her house and helped her to her bed. She kicked off her shoes and curled up fetal style. "Please leave me alone Will."

"I can't leave you like this." Will was nearly as shattered at Sharon. He had grown to love Molly Sue and in some way he saw them as a family. Maybe that was the answer. If he married Sharon, maybe Molly Sue would be returned to them. Why hadn't he thought of that sooner?

"Sharon. Look at me." Will sat on the side of the bed and wanted Sharon's full attention.

She barely opened her eyes and looked his way.

"What if we get married? If we get married, then it will be a two parent home and they will give us Molly Sue back."

Sharon shut her eyes without responding. "Please, just go away Will. I can't think about anything right now."

Will watched as silent tears fell from Sharon's eyes. "Okay. Rest and I'll be back."

When the only response was silence, Will rose to leave. "Sharon, I do love you."

As he walked to the car, he berated himself for not doing a better job. He racked his brain to try to determine where he had gone wrong. But the truth was, in this area in this era, single-parent homes were still frowned upon. And the truth was, every child really needs both a mommy and a daddy, and Sharon couldn't give Molly Sue that.

Sitting in his car outside Sharon's home, Will wondered if that secret belief had held him back from presenting his best case. Had he subconsciously sabotaged this case so Molly Sue could be in a two parent home?

He didn't think so. But how could he know if his own personal beliefs had guided him without his knowledge? He turned the key and put the car in gear as the engine roared to life. He hated leaving Sharon like this, but she had insisted. And anyway, he had work to do.

As Will's car pulled away from the curb, Leslie's pulled onto Sharon's street. She parked and went in the front door, gently tapping and calling out so it would not alarm her friend. She tiptoed to the bedroom where Sharon lay.

Leslie stood and watched the rhythmic rise and fall of Sharon's body and knew her friend was asleep. But, she did not want her to be alone, so she sat in the living room and waited, and prayed.

After an hour, Sharon rose and came in and sat down. She couldn't say anything. Her words had all been stolen and held hostage. Her heart had been laid siege to, and it had lost. It's broken remains now shattered and barely beating.

Leslie looked at her friend. She too, had no words to repair the damage that had been done today. But she was there and that would be something.

Sharon rested her head on the chair back and closed her eyes. They felt gritty and dry as if someone had poured a beach full of sand in them. She remembered this feeling. This weightiness of distress that teetered on the verge of total and complete despair.

The first time was when her father had forced her to have the abortion. The second time when Patty and Lenny had moved and taken baby Evan away. Then, when Will had suggested another abortion to put their life on hold to save his career, and of course losing Carley Ann. She would not overcome it this time. She did not have the will to do so.

Leslie feared for her friend. She knew some of her background. Sharon didn't like to talk about it, but had confided a few things from time to time. She knew she didn't really know the depths of her pain. She could sense though, that her friend was in a critically dangerous place.

"Sharon, I want to call the doctor. He can give you something to help you get through this." Leslie rose to go to the phone.

"No."

Leslie turned and saw Sharon just as she had been. Had she not heard the word, she would have not even known she had said it. "You need something. You have to have something."

Leslie proceeded to the phone and called the doctor. As she hung up the phone, there was a knock on the door and there stood Bill. "How is she?"

Leslie snorted. "How do you think she is, Bill?" It irritated her that she couldn't help more, so directed her angst at Bill's question.

"I know. Stupid question. I just don't know what to say."

Bill walked into the room and sat on the end of the sofa closest to Sharon's chair. He was there as she sat with her eyes closed. He reached out and rested his hand on hers and her eyes opened. She wished she had the ability to express gratitude through her open eyes, but she didn't, so she closed them once again.

"I've called the doctor. He will come over and give her something."

Bill only nodded quietly.

Leslie paced back and forth across the small living room, winding up in the kitchen where she fumbled with the coffeemaker. She wasn't sure why; she didn't even think she wanted coffee, but it was something to do. Then when the coffee grounds spilled, and the pot sloshed water out, she broke down.

Bill found her sobbing, holding the coffee scoop in one hand the pot of water in the other. He gently took each one out of her hands and set them down.

"We will help her get through this. I think you need to

rest too. You kept Molly Sue nearly every day. Your heart has to be breaking too."

Leslie nodded as she wiped her eyes. "Will you stay with her? I think I do need a break. I hate to leave her, but I do need to see my family and hug them all."

She walked over to Sharon and knelt down by her chair. "Sweetie, I'm going to go home for a bit. Bill is here, and the doctor is coming. You won't be alone. I'll be back later to check on you." Sharon didn't have the strength or desire to even open her eyes and acknowledge Leslie.

The doctor arrived as Leslie was leaving. He attempted to question Sharon a bit, but soon realized that it was a fruitless effort. "Miss Paulson, let's get you to bed." The doctor stood and tried to help Sharon to her feet. She did not resist or assist.

Bill moved over and scooped up Sharon and lifted her out of the chair. She opened her eyes and saw his compassionate face. Long delayed sobs came ripping through her body and she melted into his chest.

"There you go. Let it out. It's okay to cry." Bill crooned and soothed her the best he could. His heart was breaking for her as he carried her to her bed. The doctor turned back the covers and Bill placed her inside. He found a nightgown she had thrown over a chair and stood looking uncomfortable.

"I'll help her with that," said the doctor as he took the gown from Bill.

"Let me know when you have her tucked in and I'll come back in."

Bill finished preparing the unwanted pot of coffee. As he stood waiting for it to brew, he noticed the refrigerator door covered with endless drawings by Molly Sue. He walked over to them and began looking at each one.

Was there something they had missed? Had she given them a clue in her drawings they had not been able to decipher? He switched gears from a hurting friend to a cop. But soon, he realized that these drawings were of her current life here with Sharon. There was no clue of where she had come from.

"She's all tucked in and I gave her a mild sedative. Here is a prescription for a few more should she need them. I'll stop back by tomorrow after office hours to check on her." He turned to go, then paused. "I don't think we should leave her alone."

"Don't worry, doc. I won't leave her."

Donna - May 1974

Spring had arrived and Donna welcomed it with open arms. At eight months old, Molly Sue had begun walking while holding onto the bed. She would stand looking out into the room. Donna thought she was trying to decide if she could take a step away from the bed. It was fun to watch her decide. So far, when she wanted to venture out into the cabin, she would drop to her knees and crawl.

With Molly Sue more mobile, Donna had to teach her about the stove. One day when Donna wasn't looking she had nearly touched it, but Donna had been quick and grabbed her hand. Molly Sue had cried and once comforted, Donna began teaching her not to touch it. She knew though, that she would have to be more careful now.

Their lives had a rhythm to them. She had learned to wash their clothes in the creek. The worst was Molly Sue's quilt diapers, which Donna also used for her cycles. Folded into three sections, they were bulky, but they worked.

She had encouraged Buddy to bring more variety in food. He worked to gather more eggs and chop more wood now. It seemed with the purpose of providing for Donna and Molly Sue; he worked harder. The increase provided him a way to buy foodstuffs they hadn't had before.

The list on the wall had grown. Each day Donna said a prayer and then stood and read from the list what she was thankful for. Often something new was added. Today she had written, 'living in the south'. She knew that had they lived in the north they would have to suffer long hard winters.

She opened the back door and sat down. She held Molly Sue on her lap and they sat looking out. The trees were fully green now and the blossoms on some were falling to the ground. She hoped that they would be fruit-bearing trees.

As they sat and listened to the birds, Donna began to sing a little song that she had made up.

"Let's all sing like the birdies sing, chirp chirp. Chirp chirp. Chirp chirp."

Molly Sue would clap and try to repeat her words. Each

CHAPTER 16 | 279

day as they sat, Donna would talk to Molly Sue about life. She would tell her what things were, the table, the bed, the door. When she ventured out, she would stop and pick up leaves and stones and she would show Molly Sue the lines on the leaves and the colors of the stones.

Her goal was to teach Molly Sue the wonder of the world around them. She was determined to live life, their life as it was, to the full. Right now, she couldn't change it, so for her sake and particularly for Molly Sue's sake, she wanted her to have the best life she could have.

Buddy worked longer hours since it was spring. He worked chopping wood until there were huge piles stacked around. Donna had encouraged him that others would also buy his wood. It took some doing to encourage him to the point where he went to another man he knew and offered his wood. That customer had agreed.

There was still time though to continue with their reading lessons. Buddy could write all the letters well now. Donna would call out a letter and Buddy could quickly write it without thinking. She had been teaching him small words as well, and as they would read the bible, he would grow excited when they came to a word he recognized.

Donna had also convinced Buddy to trust her with a needle, and scissors as long as he was right there with her while she used the scissors. He would always take them back once she was done. Molly was growing and needed clothes.

Buddy had brought Donna all the clothes his mother had in her closet and Donna spent hours going through them and figuring out how to cut and sew clothes. She knew Molly Sue didn't need many, two or three little dresses, so she saved the rest for later.

She had even taken a pair of Buddy's father overalls and made a little pair of jeans so her knees wouldn't grow sore crawling on the floor. For herself, Donna knew she only needed functional clothing and preferred to just wear the overalls.

"Today we start a garden sweet girl." Buddy had brought Donna some seed packets the last time he came. He had used some money from cutting wood.

She had watched and decided that the sunny patch in the back, but to the left of the back door would be good. Buddy would be here soon to help her turn the earth. In the meantime, she had taken some small sharp fallen branches and worked them into the ground to designate the four corners.

Thankful that she had helped her mom grow a garden all her life, she sat and wrote down all she could remember. What plants needed the most sun, which plants needed mounded, and which plants needed staked like climbing green beans and tomatoes.

She drew a picture of how she wanted to lay out her garden. She hoped to show Buddy so he would fully understand what she needed.

"I got a shovel Miss Donna."

"Thank you Buddy. I put sticks in the ground where the corners of the garden will be." She walked to each stake and showed him.

"We need to dig up all this ground and then remove any rocks and weeds. If you will start going in a line, I will come behind you and do that part."

Buddy nodded and began to turn over shovels full of dirt. It was rich and dark. Donna got down on her knees and began to weed through the upturned soil. She had brought a chair outside and had bound Molly Sue in it to keep her secure. She couldn't prepare the garden if she was constantly getting up to run after her.

Molly Sue bellowed. She wanted down on the ground with her mother.

"Molly, momma has to do this and you can't help." Each time Donna would get up to console her daughter, and then she would bellow when Donna walked away.

"Okay. Okay." Donna untied Molly Sue and plopped her down beside her on the dirt. As Donna took her hands and broke up the upturned soil, and pulled out weeds, Molly Sue watched. Then she reached down and grabbed a clot of dirt and shoved it in her mouth.

"Oh, Molly Sue. No baby girl." Donna pried the remaining dirt from her clenched fist and tried to dislodge what she had in her mouth. Once done, Donna sat holding Molly Sue where she was.

"How on earth am I going to be able to do this garden and watch Molly Sue at the same time?"

Buddy continued to work hard turning the earth with the shovel. He did not respond to Donna's question. Maybe he subconsciously knew it was not directed at him specifically.

"I need a playpen for you." Donna looked up at Buddy. "Buddy, can you make a playpen for Molly Sue?"

Buddy stopped shoveling and turned to Donna. "What is a playpen?"

Donna took her finger and began to draw in the dirt, explaining as she went. "It will keep Molly Sue in one place so I can work. It will keep her safe." She used that trump card often when trying to convince Buddy to do something. Above all else, he genuinely wanted to keep them safe.

He studied the crude drawing in the dirt. Donna could tell he was thinking. "Buddy can do it." He got up, dropped the shovel, and walked away."

"Well, no time like the present." Donna laughed to herself.

She got up and took Molly Sue to the cabin to clean her up. "You need a nap, anyway." She still breastfed her, so she sat on the bed and leaned back against the headboard and fed her baby. Soon Molly Sue's eyes grew heavy, and she fell asleep.

Donna gently eased out and went back to work on the garden. By the time Molly Sue woke, Donna had made great strides in clearing the garden. She had done all that Buddy had overturned and had begun to shovel some on her own.

It was almost noon when she heard Molly Sue's feet hit the floor beside the bed and then her scurry across the floor. It was time for a break, anyway.

She met Molly Sue at the open door and sat down with

her. Caked mud was all over. Her hands were raw and blistered and caked with dirt. She would clean herself up, but she needed to sit for a minute.

As she sat, she looked at the bracket clamped around her ankle. Her ankle had grown calloused where it had rubbed. Her ankle was much smaller than the bracket, but even though she had tried multiple times to free her foot, she couldn't.

In the beginning she had even briefly considered just cutting her foot off, but she would grow nauseous at the thought. Of course there wasn't anything that would have done that, anyway. Had her situation been more dire, she might have revisited that thought. But, for now, she would rather make the best of her situation. She hoped that her family was still out there looking for her somewhere.

After catching her breath, Donna got up and walked to the edge of the stream. The chain was strategically long enough to be able for her to get in the water, but not out too deep. She could fill buckets with water for cleaning and cooking and she could even bathe in the shallows on warm days.

She sat down with Molly Sue and held her so that her little feet kicked the edge of the water. She waved her arms excitedly and kicked both feet. She pulled to break free from Donna's grasp, but Donna held her tight. She stood Molly Sue up and placed her feet down in the water as she held each hand above her head.

Molly Sue strained to walk deeper into the water, away from Donna. About that time, a large bug slapped the side of Donna's face and her wet hands allowed Molly Sue's to slip from her grasp. Donna quickly recovered, but not before she witnessed Molly Sue's first steps.

She took two full steps into the creek before falling with a smack into the water. Even though the water was only a couple of inches deep where they were, she knew to be cautious. Once she had plucked Molly Sue from the water, she laughed both from the joy of the steps and genuine relief of retrieving her daughter.

"You walked baby girl! You walked." Donna hurried further up on the bank to flat ground and let Molly Sue's feet touch the ground. Carefully holding her hands once again, she waited while she wobbled on her tiny feet.

Just then, Buddy came around the corner of the cabin and Molly Sue surged forward and took four complete steps before falling into her familiar crawl. As Buddy approached, she stopped and reached up for him.

"She started walking Buddy. Just a few steps. But, she took them all on her own."

Buddy picked her up and held her in his arms. He beamed and kissed her on the top of her head. He laid his beefy cheek on the spot he had kissed and closed his eyes.

Conflicting emotions raged through Donna. It should be her father holding her right now. It should be Jared that she reaches for. She couldn't suppress the anger that raged through her.

"Give her to me. Right now. Give her to me!" Donna wrenched Molly Sue from Buddy's arms. The look of hurt and confusion on his face didn't faze her.

"Buddy is sorry." He looked at Donna wounded.

Donna began to yell and scream at Buddy all the frustrations that she had worked so hard to suppress and overcome the past months. After she had poured out her rantings, she fell to the ground with Molly Sue and cried.

Molly Sue had grown terrified with Donna's tirade and was bawling. Buddy stood looking stricken at the two on the ground crying. He didn't know what to do.

Finally, exhausted and her anger spent, Donna looked up at Buddy. All she could feel then was pity. Pity for the man-child who stood before her. "Buddy, I'm sorry. I just miss my family. I miss Molly Sue's father. I know you love her, I do. I'm sorry."

Buddy just continued to stand still. Remorse surged through Donna and she stood with Molly Sue. She reached out and touched Buddy's cheek. "I'm sorry. I really am." It was then that she noticed a tear track that had been drawn down his cheek.

Donna handed the sobbing Molly Sue to Buddy. "Molly Sue loves you too, Buddy."

He was not sure whether he should take her. He was still unclear on what he had done wrong and was afraid of doing it again. "It's okay Buddy. You can take her." Just then, Molly Sue reached both her arms towards Buddy and lunged toward him. He caught her and held her as her sobs subsided.

I can't change this. I have to get better at accepting and enduring this; she thought to herself. *I have to get better at remembering all the things I have to be thankful for.* She then turned and walked back towards the house, and the list.

~

Sharon - September 1979

Sharon had no will to go on. What was the point? Each time tragedy would strike in her life, others would encourage her to keep going, things would get better, there was so much to live for, and to be thankful for. It was all lies and nonsense. She had nothing to be thankful for, nothing to go on for.

The week after they had taken Molly Sue, she refused to leave her bed. There had been a rotation of friends coming and going to watch over her. She knew the general consensus was that they should not leave her alone under any circumstance.

They would peek in and ask if she needed anything. If she could muster the strength to say no, then she did. If not, they would simply be ignored. They brought endless food trays to her beside and for three days, they sat untouched.

"Sharon, you have to get up." Leslie was perturbed. She understood Sharon's grief, but life had to go on.

Sharon shut her eyes tighter, ignoring her friend.

"I mean it." Leslie grabbed the covers and flung them back off of her friend. Sharon didn't even flinch.

Leslie sat on the edge of Sharon's bed. "Sharon, I'm so concerned about you. Please sit up and talk to me."

Sharon didn't move or respond.

"I'm calling the doctor. Do you want him to put you in the hospital? Worse yet, a mental hospital?"

The words mental hospital struck a nerve deep inside Sharon, but was it enough to force her forward? Leslie stood at the door waiting to see how her threats would be received. Finally, Sharon took a deep breath and rolled partially over to look at Leslie where she stood.

"I know you mean well. But I just can't function." Leslie walked back to the bed and once again sat on the edge.

"Sharon, that's why I'm here. Talk to me. I know you don't think it will help, but it will. I will listen as long as you talk." Leslie reached out and took her friend's hand. She hid her shock at how desperately thin it was.

Sharon's eyes drifted closed, but she opened her mouth as if to speak, then shut it again. Leslie just sat, giving her friend time. Soon tears began to drip out of the corner of Sharon's eye. Then torrents came. She had not cried like this since she had collapsed into Bill's arms the first day she had gotten home.

"I hurt so bad. I hurt so bad. It all just hurts so bad." She sobbed out the words over and over again. She had curled back up in a ball, and Leslie rubbed her back. She felt her ribs through her skin and became worried. She must have not been eating for weeks prior to the court date. The stress and fear of what had been ahead had stolen her appetite.

Soon, the words and the tears subsided. Leslie knew better than to tell Sharon how to feel. She had not been through all that Sharon had been through. She also knew that no matter how much Leslie could see that Sharon was blessed with, until she herself recognized it, it would do no good to point it out to her.

"Sharon, I believe that Will can petition the court to get you visiting rights. You only cared for and loved her. They know that seeing you from time to time will be best for her. You may not be in a mother daughter relationship, but you can still be there for her."

Sharon listened to Leslie's words. "No. It's just too hard."

"You're being selfish." Leslie was furious.

Sharon looked up at her friend. How could she call her selfish after all that she had done for Molly Sue? The confusion on her face prompted Leslie to continue.

"You are only thinking about you. Think what this is doing to Molly Sue. First, she is separated from a sick mother who she can't find her way back to, then you take her in and now she is separated from you, and all you can think about is your own pain. Molly Sue still needs you. Get up and wash your face."

Leslie felt uncertainty assault her as she heard the words she had just spoken. What had she done? Was it the right thing?

Sharon's face relaxed, and she rolled Leslie's words over in her mind. "They won't let me see her. They will think it's best for her to make a clean break. They will want her to get settled and leave the past behind."

"You don't know that. Come on. Get up. You need to

shower, get dressed and eat something." Leslie pulled on her friend's hand. To her surprise, Sharon didn't resist. She slowly rose to sit up.

"Get in the shower and I will call Will."

Sharon nodded a slight agreement and rose to walk to the shower. Leslie watched and knew her friend was low on strength. Lack of food, and no motivation of the soul, were slowing her steps. She looked like she had turned into an eighty-year-old woman overnight.

Leslie waited until Sharon was in the bathroom and had started the water. Then, she turned and walked to the kitchen. Picking up the phone, she glanced at the clock. It was almost noon. The phone rang, and a receptionist put her on hold.

Soon, Will answered. "Is everything okay?" He was immediately concerned for Sharon. He had tried to go by at least once a day, but it was a bit of a drive and he had too much work piled up that needed his attention. He hadn't made it as often as he had intended and seeing her like she was, caused him so much discomfort that he would only stay for a short while when he came by.

"No, it's not." Leslie was trying not to let her irritation with Will come through. She had been surprised at how little time he had seemed to spend with Sharon when she needed him the most.

"What's wrong?" He could feel the tension in each hair as it prickled across his scalp.

"She has not eaten since the courthouse. I finally just

now got her up to take a shower. She needs you Will. She really needs you."

"Okay." Will knew Leslie was right, but there was a fear of something he didn't even understand that was pushing him away. He needed to think about Sharon more than himself right now. He couldn't let her down like he had in the past.

"You're right. I'm sorry. I'll be right there." Will asked his secretary to reschedule all his afternoon appointments as he headed out the door. He waved off her requests regarding when he would return, as he headed out the door and down the hall.

As he drove to Sharon's house his mind would not rest. He had said he would marry her to get Molly Sue back. But had he meant it? Did he want to marry her? He loved her, and he knew she loved him. So why had it not occurred to him to marry her before the court case?

As he pulled up to the curb in front of Sharon's home, the thought occurred to him that maybe he had never really forgiven her for leaving him before. But with that thought came the shame that always came. The shame that he had asked her to abort their baby for his career. He felt it every time he looked at her.

He loved her now as much as then, but if he had loved her as he should have then, he would have sacrificed for her, for his family, not demanded that she be the one to sacrifice.

He sat for several minutes unable to move from the car. He knew he didn't have the answers, but for now, she needed him and he would do his best this time to help see her through.

The thud of the car door as it closed in the quiet neighborhood resonated on the same frequency as the thud in his heart.

CHAPTER 17

*D*onna - September 1974

Donna sat writing in her journal. Molly Sue would be one-year-old in a few days. She had mastered walking and was now running. Donna's greatest fear was that she would take off and run further than Donna's chain would allow her to go.

There was the creek that she could fall into and Donna could not rescue her. There were wild animals in the woods. If she got too far and Donna could not reach her, they could take her as prey. Moment by moment she prayed for her daughter's safety and knew that she had to trust God to watch over her. He had proven faithful.

She had taught Molly Sue that she could not go further than the chain would allow her mother to go. Instilling fear in her child was not an option. Fear was the opposite of faith and she did not want her daughter to fear the things in this life, only trust and believe.

The sun shone in the cabin's window and highlighted the words that Donna had written. She had paused considering what she could do that was special for Molly Sue for her birthday. This was a first and would set a standard for birthday's to come. The truth was, she didn't have to celebrate it all and Molly Sue would never know that birthdays should be celebrated.

No, she wanted to celebrate the milestone, but in a way that marked the date and made a note of it, but not in such a way that it was overly accentuated. That brought her back to a gift or act to denote the wonder of her first birthday.

Then Donna began to wonder, *is the celebration for me or for her? I think it must be as much for me as for her. At this age she does not understand the importance of anything until I tell her it is important.*

That train of thought brought Donna to thinking that this applied in all things. She suddenly realized the critical importance that she teach Molly Sue only the things that were truly important. She had choices to make each day. Those choices would shape her daughter, so how did she want her to be shaped?

She slid the bible towards her and opened it to the New Testament and the first book of Corinthians. When she found chapter thirteen she stopped. This is how she wanted Molly Sue to be.

In her journal she flipped to a new page and at the top she wrote: Molly Sue Is. Underneath she wrote a list. She began with charity, which she knew was love. Above all, she would teach Molly Sue to love. Then came long suffering, kind, not boastful, not proud, not rude, does not demand her own way, not easily provoked, thinks no evil, does not rejoice about injustice, rejoices in truth, never gives up, never loses faith, always hopeful, and endures all things.

As Donna looked at the list she had just made, she knew that in order to teach Molly Sue these things, she herself had to be that way as well. Molly Sue would not just hear her words, but watch her and imitate what she did.

Then she began to read the list out loud. Molly Sue and I are loving, long suffering, kind, not proud, not rude, not demanding our own way, not easily provoked, think no evil, rejoice only in the truth. We never give up, never lose faith, we always hope and we endure all things.

She rose from the table and pulled another sliver out to hang the paper on, right next to her always growing list of things to be thankful for. Having the first list had already changed her life. She read it first thing every morning and often retreated to it in the day when she would feel herself starting to slip to sad or dissatisfied thoughts.

Being diligent to keep what she had to be thankful for, before her had changed her. She knew it. She could feel it. The new list would do the same. With both lists always before her and Molly Sue, they would make the best of the life they had until they were free.

Molly Sue walked over to where Donna stood reading

the lists. "Momma." She patted Donna's leg and Donna reached down to pick her up. The wispy blonde hair had grown some in the past year but was still like goose down, but the curls were clearly evident now. Her eyes were still at big and blue as they had been on their first day.

"Shall we go check the garden?"

Molly Sue nodded and squirmed to get down and quickly took off in that direction. She reached the mature plot of growing vegetables a moment before Donna and headed straight towards the tomatoes.

Donna grabbed her little hand right as she was about to pull off a not-quite-ripe tomato from the vine. "Not yet, sweet girl. It has to get red. It isn't ready yet."

Molly Sue frowned. She loved tomatoes. Donna took her hand and said, "Let's see if we can find one that is red and ready to pick. They walked along the rows and carefully pulled back vines and leaves on a treasure hunt for red gold.

The burst of red came through finally and Molly Sue saw it first. "Mato. Mato."

Donna laughed and helped Molly Sue to pull it off herself. The garden had been a great idea. Donna had almost given up a few times when the bugs seemed to overtake the tender new plants. Then she remembered that chickens would eat the bugs.

Buddy had agreed to allow the chicken a run in the garden and soon the grasshoppers were gone. She had also encouraged Buddy to move the chicken coop closer to her so that she and Molly Sue could gather eggs each day. They would gather the eggs, cook a few and leave the rest for Buddy to take to town.

With Donna's encouragement, Buddy had begun to build things. The first was the small playpen for Molly Sue. It challenged him at first, but then with Donna's continued encouragement and instruction, he had finally produced a nice and sturdy playpen.

From there, Donna suggested other simple things for him to make and encouraged him to take them to the general store as well. He would sell them for money so they would have it when they needed things for Molly Sue or during the winter months.

"Look Molly Sue," Donna was on the row where they had planted watermelon's. They were growing, but not yet ready. Then, Donna knew that would be the surprise for Molly Sue. Instead of birthday cake they would celebrate with a ripe red watermelon.

The discovery fueled more creative thoughts about what she could do to celebrate. She still wanted to give her a gift. Maybe she could have Buddy make something.

She filled the basket that Buddy had given her to gather from the garden. It was full of end of summer vegetables. In order to cook them, she had had to convince Buddy to trust her with a knife. He didn't want to, but finally one day, he brought her a small paring knife.

He had also left a few cooking utensils for her, a pot or two, a turner to turn meat over, and a potato masher. The thing she missed the most was butter, fresh creamy butter.

They had milk which Buddy got from the lady who took his eggs.

At the beginning of summer Donna had said, "Buddy, we need butter. You can either buy it or trade for it, but we need butter."

Buddy looked at Donna with large round eyes. "Okay." It was all he said, and he turned to leave.

The next day he came back with a tub of butter. Donna squealed with delight. "Thank you Buddy. Thank you so much."

Donna realized that she could make a list of things she wanted, within reason, and Buddy could usually come up with them. He didn't like going to most stores. He was familiar with the few he knew and refused to go to others. He had been made fun of his whole life and being kept in isolation had not helped him learn how to deal with the outside world.

But food items, were usually pretty easy. The lady who took the eggs often traded food, and now Donna had butter, real butter.

The entire summer had been filled with various vegetables smothered in scrumptious butter. Excited, sometimes she and Molly Sue would just eat them raw in the garden. Tomatoes were a favorite, and they ate them as they would have an apple. When the juice would run down their chins and arms, they would laugh.

The trees that Donna had hoped in the spring would bear fruit, did not. But sometimes Buddy would bring back a few apples and pears. The lady didn't send much as she felt the amount of eggs he brought would only trade for so much.

"Buddy, Molly Sue will have her first birthday soon." Donna was in the yard between the cabin and Buddy's house. He was chopping wood, and Molly Sue was taking a nap. Donna's chain stopped about five feet shy of the stump and axe where Buddy worked.

He stopped working and looked at Donna, waiting for what she might ask of him. "I want to give her a present. I want us to make her something." She knew if she requested a store-bought gift that it would set a standard that she didn't know she could sustain. Also, she doubted that Buddy would venture out to a store where he could purchase such an item.

"What do we make her?" Buddy creased his face in thought.

"I'm not sure. I'm still thinking about it."

"Okay," was all Buddy said, and he went back to chopping wood. Donna sat on the ground and leaned up against the nearest tree. She watched as he worked diligently. She had often thought there might be more intelligence there than she had first assumed. With no one to ever teach him, how would it have ever surfaced?

She had continued to teach him to read and he could now work his way haltingly through bible passages. Often though, he would stop and ask Donna what the words meant. Sometimes, it was a challenge for Donna as well. The old Elizabethan English often made things sound foreign.

To Donna's surprise though, with an ear listening internally, she would usually receive understanding and then would in turn explain it to Buddy in a way she thought he could understand.

There were tons of beautiful illustrations in that particular bible and they spent time looking at those as well, while Donna would explain what was going on in the picture. He had shown an aptitude to learn more than his parents had ever given him credit for.

By Molly Sue's birthday, Donna had planned a small celebration with the three of them. She had found a large ripe watermelon and sliced it in large round slices. There were no candles, but that was okay.

The gift that she had thought to do was a paper doll. Donna had taken one of the large white sheets of paper that Buddy had brought and drawn a figure of a doll that looked like what she thought Molly Sue would one day look like. The little doll had blonde ringlets and big blue eyes.

She had taken one of the stiff cardboard covers from the back of a journal and glued them together, making the doll stiff. Buddy had brought a pair of scissors and waited while Donna cut the doll out.

For Buddy's part, she had asked him to make a little wooden stand for the doll to stand up in. Then Donna made a dress or two out of paper and colored them in various bright prints. Buddy once again sat while she cut them out with the scissors. That was an item he rarely allowed her to use and was always close by waiting to take them away once she had finished.

It was a good day. They ate watermelon in celebration and Donna showed Molly Sue how to dress her new little doll and change her dress. Still lacking in motor skills, the one-year-old tore one of the dresses when trying to put it on the doll. But, Donna didn't care. She had plenty of paper and they could make many more dresses. It brought her pleasure to see her daughter playing.

That night as she lay in bed, Donna looked out the window and gazed at the stars. "Thank you Lord, for a wonderful day. I see all the stars in the heavens that you made and I know that you see me, and Molly Sue. I know I have to trust that you have a plan for us, and I do."

When Donna closed her eyes that night she felt at peace. A deep abiding peace that she had never really known before captivity. *How could this be*, was her last thought as she drifted off to sleep?

SHARON - OCTOBER 1979

Will had worked to try to gain visiting rights for Sharon to see Molly Sue. But, Sharon had been right. They felt a clean break was best for Molly Sue.

Will had made inquiries and Molly Sue was having a hard time adjusting. The once happy and joyful child was now sullen and withdrawn. But rather than admit that they had made a mistake in removing her from Sharon's home, they attributed her behavior as a result from having lived with Sharon. Further reason to keep them apart.

Little by little, Sharon had re-entered the real world. She went to work and did what she needed. Then she went home, ate little and drank her customary couple of glasses of wine, and fell asleep in her chair.

She had shut the room she had set up for Molly Sue, unable to even look inside. She had only looked one time and felt such a resurgence of pain, that she knew she could never look in there again.

Will called some and came by less frequently. There was a clear and evident wall between them, and neither cared to question why it was there or where it had come from.

Sharon simply didn't care about anyone or anything anymore, Will concluded. She knew on some level she blamed him for not being able to help her keep Molly Sue.

The thought of suicide was a constant cold wind that rushed in and out of her mind. She honestly didn't feel she had anything to live for. She didn't even want to breathe, much less live.

Leslie had been a source of gentle force in her life. She refused to let Sharon just sit and wallow in her self-pity. Bill had been much gentler with her. He had a tender side toward Sharon and feared saying or doing the wrong thing. He knew she was fragile, and he didn't want to be the one to further shatter her.

He would often find her staring out any window that faced the grade school. He knew she was waiting to catch a glimpse of Molly Sue on the playground. Bill didn't think she would see Molly Sue though. Reports that had drifted back to him said that Molly Sue kept to herself and rarely engaged in games with the other children.

"If you see her, what will you do? How will you feel? Better, worse?" Bill had walked up behind Sharon.

Sharon dropped her crossed arms and motioned indecision with her shoulders. "I don't know Bill. I just can't seem to stop. I'm sorry. I know I have work to do."

"It's not about the work. You always get the work done and do an excellent job. I'm just concerned about you."

Sharon didn't know how to respond. She felt obsessed with watching the school. She had also driven up and down the streets of their small town hoping to catch a glimpse of where they had placed her. For obvious reasons they had not disclosed who her foster parents were.

The thought to grab her and run away with her had crossed her mind. She would daydream about it, but soon discard it in despair, knowing that she could never pull it off long-term.

It was fall now and she had spent a complete year and a half with Molly Sue. Each day brought with it a memory of what they had been doing on that day the previous year. Soon, Thanksgiving would arrive and she would dwell on the laughter they had had around Leslie's family table. Then there would be Christmas and the wonder she had experienced through Molly Sue's eyes. And then, on and on and on, in an endless loop for the rest of her life.

She closed her eyes and walked back to her desk. She read the case file three times before she realized she had not comprehended a single word. It was complete. She shut it and tossed it on the pile.

Bill had followed her back to her office and had watched her read the file repeatedly before slapping it shut and tossing it aside. He didn't want to talk about personal issues any longer. It made him uncomfortable and he knew he wasn't making things any better.

"You know there is a new computer system being used in law enforcement."

Sharon looked up at him and frowned. "What are you talking about?"

"Well, there is a new system called ARJIS. It stands for Automated Regional Justice Information System. It contains information on cases and someone in law enforcement can do a search and find similar cases."

Sharon looked at Bill, momentarily drawn away from her personal trauma. Her mind was trying to contemplate this computer thing and how it could help in law enforcement. "I'm not sure I understand how it will work or how it could help. It can't take the place of a good cop who is doing their job."

"No… But if all the data from all those files were in a computer and then all the police jurisdictions from around the state were also entered, we could call another station and ask them to look on their computer for, let's say, missing women age twenty years old. Then they could do a search rather than have to rely on memory or take the time to search all the files. They could pull up a list and then pull the files and share them with us."

"How would that help us?" Sharon was struggling to put it all together.

"Maybe they were kidnapped victims, and they had a suspect. And maybe that same person might have kidnapped someone in our jurisdiction. That would give us a name and our guys could go out and question him."

Sharon began to see and soon her mind was thinking of many ways it could help. "Will we get one of these computers? We're such a small station."

"I've put in for one. But the thing is, we need someone to use it. Someone will have to be trained." He stopped right there. She was the only obvious choice, but he didn't want to push her. They had gone through a series of part-time file clerks through the years. None stayed very long. They were gaining experience for a more permanent job where they could move up.

"Could I do that?" Sharon asked. Bill wanted to smile, but played along.

"Well, I think that you would be the best choice to do that. The obvious choice."

"Okay." Sharon felt a small, very tiny, thread of something to challenge her. Something to motivate her to stay alive for one more day.

"How do all the files get into the computer?"

"Someone would have to type it all in. It won't be an easy or quick job. I suspect that it will take a long time to get completely up and running."

Sharon's mind was churning. It had been a long time

since it had had a challenge and it welcomed the distraction now.

"When do we get the computer?"

"As soon as you get back from training. I have to wait for you to get back so we can have your full input." Bill was trying not to smile. He had been planning this for a while now. Their budget was slim, but he had petitioned the city for an earmarked grant. It had worked.

"When and where is training?"

"In two weeks, for one full week, in the city."

"I think we will have to work on making sure we put each new file in as it occurs while also working on older files. Can I hire temporary people?"

"Yes. Within reason."

"What if I were able to hire two people straight from the vocational school who were at the top of their data entry class? They could work on entering older files. Our file clerk could work to enter new files and double checking the data entry files when they go in. We have to make sure our work is accurate or the data will be useless."

"I think that is an excellent idea." Bill stood. "I'll go get the information on the class and you can make your arrangements. Also, if you want to let the file clerk know, maybe she can get ready for the install."

"I will." Then just before Bill disappeared around the corner, "Thanks Bill."

"You're welcome."

Donna - November 1974

The weather was growing colder. Usually they still had pretty nice weather up until the end of December or the beginning of January, but lately the wind had been gusting and growing colder, and that meant more time in the cabin.

Donna had been journaling since the beginning, but lately she had been doing it more often. She had encouraged Buddy to make more things in his father's wood shop. He was getting better, but still needed some practice. She had told him that since Christmas was coming, more people might want what he made. With that, he was spending more time away from her and Molly Sue.

As the wind beat hard against the cabin, Donna stood reading her 'thankful' list. It was hard on days like this. She wanted to be out enjoying the world, even just her little world. It was easy to grow morose when the weather was bad.

She shut her eyes, as she gave a final thanks and turned away. She had learned to make bread. Buddy had been able to get her the necessary items, and a couple of bread pans. Her first attempts were horrible. Then she had a thought and had asked Buddy if he would look for any of his mother's recipes that she had written down or a cookbook.

He had brought a cookbook, with his mother's personal notes, and recipe cards. Donna was thrilled. Once she had that, she was able to make bread for herself and Molly Sue as often as she wanted. Since she now had butter, she was in dietary heaven. If she could now just make jelly. But she knew that would take more ingredients than she currently had.

She threw flour on the clean table and plopped the mound of dough on it to knead. It felt good to push and turn the doughy mound. Ideas began to run through her head. She could add cinnamon and sugar and make sweet bread. She made a mental note to ask Buddy for cinnamon and sugar.

Molly Sue walked over and began climbing up the chair and then tried the table. Donna stuck out her elbow. "Oh, no you don't missy. Momma's kneading bread. You stay right there on the chair until I'm done." Donna continued to work in the awkward position with her elbow stuck out to one side.

"There. We'll have bread soon." She divided the dough and placed it in the two pans and covered them with dishtowels she had also had Buddy bring her. Once again, she had tried to get Buddy to let her stay in the house, making a case that it would be easier than hauling so much stuff out here. But he had not acquiesced.

Donna walked over to the cupboard to set the bread down. When she turned back around, Molly Sue sat in the middle of the table and remaining flour. She was using both hands to swish it all around and all over her. When she looked at Donna, she dipped her head back and broke out with giggles.

"You little stinker." Donna walked back to the table and leaned down, placing her elbows on it. She looked Molly Sue straight in the eye, winked, and then kissed her nose.

She loved this little angel more than she ever thought she could love anything.

The remainder of the day she had planned to work on another pair of pants and a top for Molly Sue. She was growing and needed some new warmer clothes. Honestly two outfits were enough. She could wear one and then she could wash the other.

"Molly Sue, your momma used to think she needed an entire closet full of clothes. I now know that just isn't true." She looked at her daughter and smiled.

Buddy had finally brought his mother's little sewing kit. It was a padded floral box with two handles. When you pulled them apart, it revealed a hinged compartment with all types of threads, needles, random buttons, a tape measure, and even some embroidery thread.

Donna had once again requested her own pair of scissors, but Buddy still wasn't ready for that. So, she would decide how large she needed to make the items and would use pins to outline where she wanted to cut. She would then re-measure Molly Sue and compare that to what she had laid out before she had Buddy bring the scissors.

She would cut everything out, and then he would once again take them away. Sewing by hand had taken practice to get the stitches even, but Donna had always been good with her hands so she enjoyed the challenge, and soon she was doing a skilled job.

"There. The pants are done." She held up a little pair of denim pants. "These would look cute with some embroidery on them. How about some flowers?"

Donna went to work stitching little lines of green across the pants. Before she could start on colorful flowers, she could smell the bread and knew it was time to take it out of the oven. She dropped her sewing onto the bed and jumped up to pull the bread out before it burned.

"Yes. It's perfect." She was pleased by the site of the golden mounds. Suddenly she heard Molly Sue scream from behind her.

Donna whirled around to see her with the needle poking out of her little hand. "How could I have been so careless?" She rushed to the girl and with one hand, grabbed her wrist and the other, she swiftly pulled out the needle. She was thankful it hadn't gotten too deep.

She put the needle back in the fabric and put it up on the table, then pulled Molly Sue tight. "I'm sorry sweet girl. I'm sorry. Momma will be more careful." It was times like this that Donna wanted to regurgitate all the reasons why she shouldn't have to be in this situation and all the reasons she had to be angry and mad. But she had learned that would only create a dark cloud over her and Molly Sue.

So each time she was tempted to throw a self-pity party, she would take a deep breath, and if for no other reason than for Molly Sue's sake, she would walk to the 'thankful' list and read it out loud. Sometimes she found she had to read it through two or three times, but as she read, she would feel the angst decrease.

She had also found that reading it out loud was better. Her mind couldn't become distracted and it seemed as she also heard the words she was saying it had a more profound effect. So she would always read her lists out loud. She also wanted Molly Sue to hear how thankful they should be.

At peace once again, Donna closed her eyes and hugged the adorable little girl she held. "Let's get some warm bread. What do you say?" And, she tickled Molly Sue who giggled and tucked her head in the crook of her mother's neck.

Donna sat Molly Sue in her chair and wrapped the surrounding cloth to hold her in. Then, she retrieved one loaf from the cupboard and used the small paring knife to carefully cut two large slabs of bread. The steam rose as she cut and it smelled like heaven. "The bread of life. Molly, Jesus is the true bread of life. We should remember that each time we eat bread. The bread will nourish us, but only Jesus can nourish us fully and completely."

As Donna talked, Molly Sue shoved a large chunk of buttered bread into her mouth. "Chew that well, missy." Donna watched, making sure she hadn't taken too large a bite and pinched the next ones down to smaller sizes.

As she sat enjoying the fresh bread, soft creamy butter, and the presence of her baby girl, the wind finally rested, and a beam of light broke through the clouds. Donna sat and looked out the window at the dark cloud with a strong and solid light beam forcing its way through.

"Well Molly Sue, we made it through another day."

CHAPTER 18

Sharon - November 1979

The week of training had been grueling. Men who lived and breathed computers had taught the class. They seemed to frequently grow irritated by the class of novices who asked so many questions.

But their zeal for the new system was contagious and Sharon welcomed something new and challenging to engage her mind.

They had given each one in the class a large textbook for the class and stated that they were only touching the surface and that each person should take an extended class in the future. Sharon had also taken copious notes.

The Monday after class, Sharon arrived at the station and went straight to Bill's office. "Well, how did it go?" Bill asked.

She dropped the heavy book stuffed with a plethora of

notes, on his desk . When he saw the book, his eyes grew large, and he looked at Sharon, concerned about what she would say. She wasn't smiling. This couldn't be good.

Then she smiled. "It was wonderful. I learned so much and there is so much more to learn."

It relieved Bill to see some life back in Sharon. "I've ordered the minimum computer setup and the technicians will be here tomorrow. Tell me what you need."

For the next hour Sharon took Bill through the basics of the system, how it worked, and her ideas for making the best use of it in their station.

Bill felt like a hurricane had hit him square on. The barrage of new information regarding something he clearly didn't fully understand was hard to take in. "Okay. I am confident that you know what we do and don't need. Here is a budget based on the grant they have given us. We have to use our money wisely. I'm going to put you in charge of this."

Sharon nodded. During her time there, Bill had delegated more and more of the budgetary items to her and she had kept meticulous records, even scolding him a time or two to keep him on track.

"Let's have a staff meeting to share with everyone else what's going on. I'll let you handle it."

Sharon's mouth twisted briefly as if she had just eaten something distasteful. "You know they won't listen to me Bill."

Bill's stern look was reassuring. "Oh, yes, they will. I won't put up with their nonsense. This is too important, and it is mandatory. Anyone who does not want to learn the new system and keep up with progressive policies will be reprimanded and eventually terminated if they continue to refuse to comply."

Sharon wasn't sure, even though she knew Bill was sincere. The men all loved Sharon, but to them she was the station's token female. She had grown to even join in with their catcalls and teasing, knowing that it was their way of bringing her into the fold. She knew there was nothing aggressive or distasteful about it. They were just overgrown boys who really didn't know how to work with a woman.

But would that behavior transfer to them doing as she required them to do? Would they take orders regarding this new system from her? Completing files and putting them in the right baskets was one thing, but this was huge.

"The meeting will be mandatory, and we'll have it first thing in the morning." Bill continued to tell Sharon what he had set up and his thoughts about where the terminals should be. For the remainder of the day he and Sharon, along with Anthony's help, rearranged furniture and set up workstations for the computers. By six o'clock that evening both were tired and sweaty.

They sat in Bill's office exhausted. "I know that was a lot to get done in one day, but since the men are coming tomorrow to set up the computers we needed to get it done." Bill was apologetic for having pushed to get so much done in one day.

Sharon smiled. "It felt good Bill. You know... to actually

physically work at something. I still hurt, I still miss Molly Sue like crazy, but having such an intense class last week and something to focus on has helped. But I suspect you planned all of this. We're such a small station that we could get by for a while longer without a computer."

"Maybe a little of both. I want to have the computer system. When I first heard about it and how other cities were using it, I knew it would change law enforcement for the better. I want our town to be right there with them. I believe having one central place that is easy to search, will be a lifesaver on many occasions."

"We just have to make sure that the data gets entered correctly."

Bill was nodding. "Yes, but I know you will be diligent to get that done." Bill stood up and casually slapped the desk. "Well, I'm headed home for a shower and a cold beer."

Sharon felt suddenly deflated. She did not look forward to going home. While she was at work or away from home, it was much easier to push thoughts of Molly Sue away. "Yes. Me too."

On her drive home, Sharon's mind couldn't stop thinking about the best way to get the computer endeavor started at the station. She quickly headed home, showered, and then drove to the library. It wasn't as big a library as the one in the city, but hopefully she could find what she needed.

For three hours she searched for current articles on the use of computers in law enforcement. By five minutes until nine, her eyes were tired, and she was having to blink several times to see clearly. The light of the microfiche machine was taking its toll.

"Sharon, we will close in five minutes. If you want to print anything out, now is the time to do it." She nodded and leaned back in her chair. The notes she had written along with the few articles she had printed would be enough for now. It would give her ample ammunition tomorrow in the meeting against the men who would fight this every step of the way. She knew they would see the computer as a threat to their job.

The hum of the kitchen light was the only sound in the small house, and that only when Sharon flipped the light switch on. She laid the stack of notes and articles on her kitchen table and brewed a pot of coffee. She had her research, now she had to compile it along with her own discoveries from last week. She wanted to appear knowledgeable and formidable in tomorrow's meeting.

It was harder to work at home. When the house would creak and moan from the wind or settling, she would halt and listen. Listen for Molly Sue. It was a natural response from having lived with the precious angel for so long.

By midnight, Sharon felt she had what she needed to present her case in the meeting. The truth was, Bill had decided this was going to happen, so the officers had to comply. But, things would roll out and run much smoother if she could win their support.

Sharon stood looking in her bedroom at her bed. She'd slept there very little since they had taken Molly Sue. The bed seemed so lonely, and it was as if memories sucked in around her as she lay down to rest. But she needed a good nights sleep and knew that she needed to sleep in her bed.

She drew up and inhaled a deep breath of resolve. Fortunately, she was so exhausted, that she was asleep nearly as soon as her head hit the pillow.

Donna - December 1976

This would be Molly Sue's third Christmas. The toddler was active and precocious, but she was genuinely the light of Donna's life. It was now a full-time job to keep her close. Donna had taught her over and over again that she could not go further than the chain would allow. She was careful to not instill fear in her, but wisdom. She didn't want Molly Sue to fear anything.

Buddy had begun working long and hard days. In his limited way, he had become a good provider for Donna and Molly Sue. Life was simple, but honestly, life was good. Donna still missed her family, and Jared, but the memories faded into the past and were no longer painful.

Sometimes she would forget about the chain still clamped around her ankle and then laugh out loud when she remembered. "God it is only you that has made my life so sweet amid this absurd situation."

Reading from the 'thankful' list and the 'love' list every day helped and Donna knew it. She had also written down other scriptures that had resonated with her and had put them at various places around the room.

When Buddy had worked such long days, their lessons had slowed down, but he could now read the bible well, and Donna would often sit in the early evening listening to him read. She felt a great accomplishment hearing him pronounce the words clearly and with understanding. He rarely asked what a passage meant any longer.

Of course in the previous years when he would ask, Donna didn't always know. Sometimes she would guess, and sometimes she would just tell Buddy that she didn't know, but that she would pray about it.

Molly Sue talked about baby Jesus often. Sometimes Donna would watch her playing and she would talk to someone unseen. Several times she would ask Molly Sue who she was talking to, and the response was always, baby Jesus.

She had now gone through four paper dolls. She played with them so often that the paper would wear and tear and new ones would have to be made. Molly Sue was now so skilled at drawing that she would draw clothes for the doll.

They were always just like the ones Donna made for her. She had no other point of reference. Donna helped her design different colors and patterns, but Molly Sue would always dress the doll the way she dressed.

Donna's stacks of journals had grown, but Buddy was quick to provide when she needed more. She no longer just journaled, but wrote stories. She also made plans that she and Molly Sue's story would make a great book someday, so she continued to write their story and others as well.

She had expanded her garden each year. Some things

worked and others did not, but she kept experimenting. Her cooking had become more creative. She had limited ingredients and utensils, but could make some interesting dishes.

Buddy was good to take a list of spices, and other things to the general store and trade or purchase them. Donna often wondered if the man at the store wondered about Buddy and all that he bought. Did they know his parents were dead and that he was alone? It was certain that he didn't know about her and Molly Sue.

The thought had crossed her mind to write a note to the man at the store, but Buddy could read now and she knew if he read a note requesting help, that it would not end well.

Suddenly, a loud scream pierced the air. Donna came to full alert and listened. It was Buddy, and he was moaning and crying.

She bolted up and ran out the front door. Buddy was on the ground next to the stump where he chopped wood. He was holding his blood soaked leg. His eyes pleaded with Donna for help, but the chain would not allow her to reach him.

"Buddy, I can't get to you!" Donna pulled and pulled against the chain. But no amount of effort broke or stretched the chain.

Molly Sue had followed Donna out the door and now stood horrified next to her. The young girl's cries were as panic-stricken as Buddy's.

"Buddy, can you get to me? You have to get to me."

The puddle of blood grew on the ground below the wound. "Buddy, now. Scoot or crawl to me." Donna was now screaming in fear at Buddy. If he didn't get to her, he would bleed out and die.

It seemed to move him and he began to work his way to Donna. As soon as he was in reach, Donna ripped the tear in his overalls larger so she could survey the wound. It could have been much worse, but it was still serious out here in the woods.

"Take your shirt off." She commanded Buddy. He looked confused, but complied.

Donna slid one arm of his shirt underneath his leg and then tied the sleeves together around his leg above the wound for a tourniquet.

"I have to get you to the cabin so I can sew the wound closed. I can't carry you Buddy, so you will have to get up and walk with me. You can lean on me."

Buddy whimpered like a small boy and shook his head. "You have to Buddy. Please." Donna pulled on his hand and finally he complied.

He leaned heavily on Donna as they made their way slowly to the cabin. It was the closest she had physically been to Buddy since the day he had scooped her up from the creek bank. His bare arm was draped over her shoulder and the proximity to his underarm was suffocating. The reek of his body odor from having worked so hard, nearly made Donna gag.

When they got to the cabin, she led him up the few steps and then instructed him to lie on her bed. Molly Sue hovered in the background crying softly and chewing on her fingers.

Donna ripped the pant leg further up and worked quickly to gather water to heat, and her sewing kit. She had nothing to help him with the pain.

Molly Sue stood by the bed and looked at Buddy while Donna worked. It was as if two small children were staring at each other for courage. Their crying continued, but quieted.

When the water had boiled, Donna took clean rags and the hot water to the bed. "Buddy I have to clean this with hot water. I have to do what I can to keep germs out. Do you understand?" Buddy just looked at her and cried. He was terrified, but finally nodded his head.

The rag was so hot that Donna could barely hold it and wringing the excess water out scorched her hands. When she pressed the rag to the wound Buddy cried out in pain. He jerked his leg away from her, but with no place to go, Donna was able to follow and hold the rag firm.

When the heat of the rag began to subside, she pulled it away and repeated the process. "I don't think you hit an artery, but I will have to sew this wound or it will never heal. Do you understand?" She looked at Buddy and his eyes flitted about. Fear was preventing him from clear thinking. "I have to take my needle and thread and sew your leg. I have to. Do you understand?"

Buddy's face crumpled, and he cried harder, but he nodded. "It's going to hurt. I can't help it, but it is necessary." Buddy once again nodded.

Donna returned to the stove and heated the needle hoping that would sanitize it. She knelt beside the bed and took a deep breath. She didn't know if she had it in her, but knew she had to. *God please help me!*

As the needle pierced the skin and Donna drew the thread through, Buddy screamed and Molly Sue reached out for his hand. He grabbed the tiny hand as if it were his only life support.

Donna did not have scissors and had no real idea how a doctor would stitch a wound, so she did a running embroidery stitch called a blanket stitch. It served to pull the skin together, so she was pleased. Her hands were slippery with blood and it was often hard to hold the needle tight. When she tied off the last stitch and slid the needle off the end of the thread, she slumped to the floor.

Tears still streamed down Molly Sue's face, but she was now quiet. Buddy's eyes were closed, and he lay whimpering. "I'm done now Buddy. But I have to clean off the remaining blood and bind the wound." He did not respond.

Looking at the stitching there was something that made her think she should not get the thread wet. So, she took a clean wet rag and carefully wiped around the wound being sure to not touch the stitches.

She found a clean old sheet and ripped it into large strips and wrapped them gently around Buddy's leg. When she had finished all she could do for Buddy, she cleaned herself up out back. She watched as the blood ran from her hands.

What if Molly Sue or I were to get hurt? What would I do?

She couldn't seem to stuff down the anxiety. Until that moment, they had not had an illness or injury, except for the day Molly Sue poked the needle into her hand.

Her stomach knotted, and she felt nauseous. *What if Buddy gets an infection? What if he dies and we are completely alone out here? What will I do then?* Her thoughts were running rampant and her cold wet hands began to tremble.

Then torrents of tears and sobs broke through as the adrenaline of the moment gave way to relief. A small hand touched her back, and she knew Molly Sue had moved from comforting Buddy to comforting her.

"It be okay momma. Baby Jesus is here. He will take care of us." Donna sucked in sobs and looked with wonder at her sweet girl. She was so grown up, yet so innocent.

"Yes, baby, he will." She reached out for Molly Sue and held her tight. She sat for a long time in the open back door rocking her girl on her lap.

In the calmness of the late afternoon, the familiar red cardinal came to the branch closest to the cabin that traversed the back yard. He always came front and center when they sat there in the afternoons, and he sang to them.

That day was no different. Donna knew it was irrational, but she felt strongly that God sent the cardinal as a sign of comfort and support. She knew he sent it just to her, to sing just to her and Molly Sue. The bird was faithful and reminded her of God's faithfulness.

"Yes, Molly Sue. God will take care of us."

∼

CHAPTER 18 | 323

SHARON - NOVEMBER 1979

The next morning Sharon woke early, even though she had not had enough sleep. The anxiety of the coming day taunted her.

Bill had insisted that every person in the department attend the meeting. He made a statement that he had ordered a new computer system that would be installed later that day. From there he explained that Sharon had been thoroughly trained on it and that she would be in charge of setting it up and training the rest of them. He also clarified that this was mandatory and there would be consequences if they didn't comply.

He quickly gave Sharon the floor. Her notes rattled as her trembling hands laid them on the wood podium in the conference room. She felt a slight vertigo as she looked up into the room of navy and grey uniforms. She tried to smile, but wasn't sure she quite made it.

For a brief moment, the words just wouldn't come out, then she glimpsed Bill's encouraging face and courage came.

As she began to talk, her words grew strength. The excitement she felt towards the new endeavor showed and many of the men nodded in agreement. But there were also a few who were shuffling and quietly stomping around like discontent bulls.

The interested men asked questions. Some, Sharon could answer and some, she could not. She made notes of those questions and promised that when the technicians arrived to do the install, she would ask them.

"How on earth is a machine going to help us?" Sharon looked at the scowl on the officer's face. His hands were planted firmly on his hips and his stance was combative.

"When we compile all the information in all of our files we can search through without having to remember every case and every name. We can do searches for similar clues and other data. It will also have license plates that were collected on cases. If we get a new suspicious one, we can enter it and see if it popped up in any other cases."

The officer didn't look convinced. "Sounds like a lot of work for very little reward."

"I think this is only the beginning. At class they talked about future plans. Hopefully, in the future there would be a way to share data between stations and precincts so if a perpetrator had gone to another area and was committing the same crimes there they would know."

The officer frowned. "How on earth would we ever link them all together? There would be tens of thousands of them, more even." He snorted a sarcastic laugh and waved her off.

"I don't know about any of that. I just know what it can do for us and I am responsible for how it is set up and operates here."

Bill stood and Sharon moved to the side. "The bottom line is, we are doing this. There is no wiggle room. There will be policies and procedures written on how we use the computers. You will all be trained and if you don't comply, I will issue you a formal warning that will be placed in your personnel file. Three warnings and you will be terminated."

The faces of the men grew apprehensive, and moans were heard throughout the room. "What if we were never good at typing or such things?"

"I think the hunt and peck method will work. For now Sharon is getting a couple of data entry women to get our back files entered. Our current file clerk will be double-checking their entries. Sharon will train each one of you to enter the new files as they happen. You will not dump this on Sharon or the file clerk."

Sharon could already see the men devising excuses on why they didn't have time to finish or do a file at all. She knew they would do all they could to resist this new venture.

Bill dismissed the meeting and he and Sharon walked back to his office. "They are just as resistant as I suspected they would be," said Sharon.

Bill looked down at her. "But there are some that I think will embrace it. I saw a few faces intrigued by the challenge." Sharon nodded, leaning on his doorframe.

"You look exhausted. Did you sleep at all last night?"

"I showered and went to the library to do research. I became more and more fascinated on the way computers were being used in other cities. There is concern though about the security of personal data. Some feel that having so much in one place makes it vulnerable to identity theft."

Bill's face grew thoughtful and he shifted his head and tilted to one side. "Is it any more vulnerable in a machine than it is in a paper file in a locked cabinet that can be jimmied or picked open?"

Sharon laughed. "No, I don't think so. But you know how there are always people out there trying to find reasons why doing something in a new way is bad."

The arrival of the computers and technicians interrupted their conversation. They rolled in huge boxes of equipment on dollies and Sharon quickly began directing traffic. The officers on call jumped in and helped unload and distribute the new machines to the designated work stations. There would not be a computer for each person, but there would be one terminal in the bull pen which the officers could share. Then there would be one in Sharon's office, and one in the file room.

Sharon had contacted the vocational school and asked for their two best data entry students. She planned to put them on the bull pen terminal and one on the file clerk's terminal. Sharon intended to begin training on her terminal. Three terminals for a department their size was extravagant, but Bill had convinced the city council that it was to their benefit.

The morning rushed by so quickly that Sharon was surprised when Bill came in carrying bags of burgers and fries for her, the file clerk and himself. The technicians took that as their cue to go get lunch themselves.

It was nearly one o'clock and as Sharon sat unwrapping her burger; she realized she hadn't looked out towards the school playground once the entire day. The thought made her sad. Molly Sue was slipping further and further away from her.

Bill saw the shadow cross over Sharon's face. "What's wrong?"

Sharon avoided Bill's gaze, but when he persisted, she replied. "I just realized that I haven't looked at the playground once today."

"I think that's a good thing. You have to move on."

Sharon thought about Bill's words and sat silent for a moment. "It feels as though she is slipping further and further away from me."

Bill was void of words. He understood that Sharon felt that way and for her it was a sorrowful thing, but Bill knew it was a necessary thing.

The technicians returned quickly, eager to get their job done. When they had filled the station with foreign looking tan boxes which hosted dark screens with eerie glowing green type, and cables that would rival NASA, they announced that their work there was done.

Sharon's energy and adrenaline over having a new project, was long gone. She crumpled into her chair and felt as if she had been beaten. Training would have to start tomorrow, but for now, she just wanted to go home. It was the first time in a long time that she truly wanted her home.

Bill stopped at her door on his way out. "Great job today, Sharon. Can I take you to dinner?"

She had never had dinner with Bill and the suggestion shocked her. "Thanks, but I just want to go home."

"I just wanted to reward you for a job well done." Bill was concerned she would think he was suggesting something else.

"Thank you." Sharon smiled at Bill. He was an amazing boss. She couldn't have designed a better one had she tried. "But, I really am beat."

"Okay then. I'll see you tomorrow."

Bill walked on down the hall and Sharon sat watching the green blinking light on the small screen on her desk. The screen was so small compared to the large tan box that encompassed it. She would have to get used to working around the large monstrosities. Had she indeed embraced change that would be good for the department?

As she continued to look at the blinking cursor on the screen, her mind floated away thinking about how life continues to move forward whether or not a person wanted it to. Her life was moving on without Molly Sue.

What would she have done different that day the little girl walked into the station? Would she have put her in foster care immediately? Would she have forced herself to put up a wall between her and the girl? Could she have?

Would any of us choose to love another knowing that pain would be a certainty at some point along the journey? Or did love just choose us, sucking us in and holding us captive tightly against our will until we no longer resisted its pull and relaxed into naïve comfort?

Sharon reached up and flipped the black toggle button on the tan box. She walked through the station doing the same on each one. The night shift had just arrived and the day shift had all gone. It was quiet in the bullpen as the men who were to be on patrol gathered their equipment and joked with each other.

The dusk greeted Sharon as she exited the building. The parking lot was sparse and she could clearly see the playground, vacant and empty at that time of day. As she walked to her car, she thought how she knew vacant and empty so well.

CHAPTER 19

*D*onna - November 1976

Donna continued to monitor Buddy. She insisted he lay in her bed for a day or so to heal. With no pain meds, she had easily persuaded him.

She had changed the bandages often to keep the wound clean and dry. But, on the third day when she pulled away the cloth, she thought the wound looked a little puffy and red. Warning signs flared, but she had no idea what to do about it.

She laid her hand on Buddy's forehead and felt. Was he warm or not? It was hard to tell. She washed the bandage and hung it to dry. "Buddy I'm going to leave the bandage off for a bit so the wound can get some air. Don't move around while it is open like that."

"Okay." Buddy's spirit was dampened. He was still afraid, and she knew the pain must still be bad.

Molly Sue would stand by the bed and rattle on endlessly in her three-year-old dialog. She would pat his hand and tell him he would be okay. She would tell him how baby Jesus would make him well. She remembered the stories in the bible about Jesus healing everyone he met.

But Donna knew in real life that wasn't always the case, and baby Jesus wasn't here to lay his hands on Buddy, or to speak healing to him. When Donna pulled Molly Sue aside one day and had her outside, she sat with her and explained that Buddy was very sick and that sometimes here in this life, people didn't get well.

"But baby Jesus is here. He will heal Buddy." Donna was exasperated at her daughter's confidence.

"Yes… Jesus is here in our hearts, but sometimes people still get hurt and die."

Molly Sue just looked at Donna. She didn't say a word for several moments, then she looked over Donna's shoulder, smiled, and nodded. "Okay. But baby Jesus *is* here." With that comment, she turned and ran back into the cabin and began playing with her doll.

Donna glanced back over her shoulder to see what Molly Sue had been looking at, and saw nothing but leafless trees swaying in the wind.

Two days later, five days after the accident, the wound was inflamed and Donna paced the floor. Buddy was running a slight fever. She had no antibiotics, no other meds. She didn't know herbal remedies regarding plants that she could gather, if her chain would even have allowed that.

"God, please heal Buddy. Please, please, please. What will become of Molly Sue and I if he dies?" Then the thought struck her how selfish she was. Did she only want Buddy to live because of how his death would affect her, or did she really care about her captor?

Shame shrouded her, and she knew that she was being selfish. "I'm sorry. I do care about Buddy. God, please show me how I can help him." She rambled the same prayers over and over throughout the day. They were prayers fueled by fear and panic, not faith. But Molly Sue on the other hand, never doubted that baby Jesus would heal Buddy, and she stood by his bed frequently reminding Buddy of that very fact.

Buddy's fever grew and Donna placed cold compresses on his forehead. Molly Sue continued to talk to him long after he stopped replying. The night of the fifth day, Donna stayed by Buddy's bedside all night constantly monitoring his fever and tending to him. She had changed the compress constantly in an effort to keep it cool.

She wasn't quite sure when she had fallen asleep on the floor by the bed, nearly dawn by her estimate, but it was clearly mid morning now. The bright sunlight came piercing through the windows and she shielded her sleep-filled eyes.

With her consciousness came the reminder of Buddy. She suddenly turned to the bed only to see him smile back at her. "Good morning miss Donna." He was weak, but talking.

"Oh Buddy. You look better."

"Don't cry miss Donna."

"Buddy these are happy tears. I was so worried about you."

Molly Sue had crawled up on the end of the bed near Buddy's feet. When she heard their voices she sat up and smiled. "I told you baby Jesus would help Buddy."

Donna laughed an exasperated laugh and sat down onto the floor. "You did my girl. You did."

Buddy was still weak for a few more days and Donna encouraged him to take it easy. She had been carrying a bed pan back and forth, but he had eaten and drank little. Now that his appetite had returned, she helped him to the table to eat and then walk the short walk to the outhouse.

She would let him wrap his arm around her shoulder for support and then she would wait outside for him. One week after the accident, Donna took the paring knife, sanitized by fire, and cut away the stitches. The wound was still a bright pink line, but there was no sign of infection or further damage.

"You still need to be careful, but I think you'll be fine now Buddy." Donna said after removing the stitches.

"Thank you, miss Donna."

"You know if I'd had a pair of scissors it would have helped me." Donna took every opportunity to press for a pair of scissors.

Buddy was standing and had started toward the door when he turned around with fierce anger on his face. "You can't have scissors."

Donna jumped back startled by the ferocity in his voice.

"But, why Buddy? I don't understand."

"You can't run with scissors. It will hurt you. It could kill you." Buddy was yelling at Donna who stood bewildered.

"Buddy, I won't run with the scissors."

"No!"

Donna just stood processing the dialog they had just exchanged. "Buddy did you ever run with scissors?" Her voice was quiet and tender.

Buddy nodded. "My momma told me not to run with scissors. But I did." He slid his shirt and overall bibs aside and there on his stomach was an old pink scar. Two actually, from the two blades of the scissors.

It had obviously not gone deep enough to cut something vital, but enough of an injury to make it a serious one and certainly a reason for his mother to be overly attentive and cautious from that moment on.

"I'm sorry, Buddy. I didn't know." She decided to drop the issue of scissors for now. It was another moment of trauma he had experienced and the fear of scissors had been drilled deeply into him. He did not want Donna or Molly Sue to suffer the same fate as he had.

"I will bring you the scissors when you need them. Do you need them now?"

"No Buddy. I don't need them now."

Buddy turned and Donna stood in the door watching him walk back to his home. It was the first time in seven days and the bloody axe still lay on the ground next to a reddish brown stain. Buddy didn't pause to pick up the axe or even look its way.

As he rounded the corner, Donna continued to look in his direction pondering the strange man. She felt such an uncommon compassion for him that she couldn't describe. He was her captor. Yet, she felt compassion for him.

If she and Molly Sue were not here, he would be completely alone. He would have no one. If she had not been here when he had been injured, he would have died. It flooded her with thankfulness that she had been right where she was.

Molly Sue had walked up to stand beside her. "I like Buddy. He helps Jesus take care of us." And with that profound statement, she turned and walked back into the cabin.

Sharon - December 1979

The data entry clerks were still inputting data. For such a small department there had been tons to enter. Sharon had decided to start with the most recent and work their way back.

Their file clerk had worked her way to full-time status at least for now. In the beginning, she found multiple errors in what the data entry clerk had entered. Their lack of understanding of police terminology and the layout of the files hindered them. Within a few days though, they were making fewer mistakes.

Sharon had worked with the file clerk first. She felt it was imperative that she be the first one to learn since this was now an integral part of her job.

"Will this computer eliminate my job?"

Sharon searched her face. There was worry there. She had been the very first file clerk they had that had expressed any interest in the job long term.

"No, I can't see that it would. The officers will need help for a long time. There will always be a person needed to enter the data as well as someone to double-check what we have entered. We will still need to keep the paper files. Those will never go away."

Relief washed over her face and she turned to the screen to once again receive instruction.

Sharon's days were filled with work. She had welcomed the overwhelming consumption of it. It did not relieve the pain that still held firm inside, but it would force her mind to ignore it.

But November had turned to December and with it signs of Christmas everywhere. No matter how hard she had tried, she couldn't push thoughts of her last Christmas with Molly Sue aside. Everywhere she looked there was another memory.

Without a family, there were few she bought presents for. She would buy for Leslie's family and she always bought a little present for Bill to thank him for being such a great boss. She would also buy something for whoever was the file clerk at the time.

What about Will? Should I buy him a gift this year? Sharon sat and thought about their relationship. The resurgence of passion when Molly Sue had been the glue between them was something that Sharon was deathly afraid of, but at the same time desperately wanted.

When she had lost Molly Sue, she felt as though she had also lost Will. She knew she had pushed him away. Had she blamed him or were the memories of the three of them just too much to endure?

Will hadn't persisted either. It was as if he carried some kind of guilt that he had failed. He had dove back into his work, which could consume him twenty-four hours a day if not kept in check. It was a convenient out for Will.

They had gone to dinner a couple of times in the previous weeks, but their communication had grown stilted and forced. Neither one knew what to say. So, the time between seeing or talking to each other had grown.

Where are we? Do we still have something? Can we overcome it, and do we even want to?

Sharon was brought back from her rambling thoughts to the question that the file clerk had just asked. She internally chided herself to pay more attention. She was supposed to be teaching and needed to know what her student was doing.

At lunch, Sharon needed to get out of the station. She had taken lunch at her desk every day since the arrival of the computers and needed a break. The technicians had had to come back several times. Sharon could not write code and the operating system had shown to have several glitches that hindered their progress. Fuel for those who were adamant that they didn't need the machines.

The past week had gone well though, and Sharon needed air. The wind assaulted her when she stepped outside and she quickly pulled her gloves on and her coat tight. There were no children on the playground today, it was too cold. They would be in the gym or in their classrooms warm and snug coloring or playing board games.

The seats in Sharon's car were cold and seemed rebellious in warming to her body's heat. She cranked the heater to high and waited for her windshield to thaw. The cold winter wind had brought moisture and frost covered all the windshields in its path.

Sitting in her car, Sharon pondered where she had intended to go when she left the building. She knew she could do a little shopping, or go eat lunch, but she felt so lost that nothing sounded appealing.

She decided she would go visit her friend Leslie and put the car in gear. The streets were clear, the windshields on the cars the only victim of the frozen air.

Leslie's face lit up when she saw Sharon come through her door. They had long since stopped knocking and waiting for entrance. Since no one ever locked their doors, it was a common thing for friends to just come on in.

She hurried over and hugged Sharon before she could even shed her coat. "I'm so glad to see you. Come, have a cup of coffee with me. Have you had lunch?"

"No. I didn't want to go eat alone, but I had to get out of the station for a bit."

"I'm making soup. It is almost done."

Sharon welcomed the friendly chatter of her friend. She had missed her. She had missed so much. The kitchen was warm and the smells of the soup awoke Sharon's nose and stomach. She really was hungry and glad her friend had lunch almost ready.

"How are you?" Leslie asked, concern on her face. It was a common question and one that Leslie asked sincerely each time they saw each other.

"I'm better, I think. The work has helped. I think the timing of this computer install was no accident. I think Bill knew I needed something, anything to occupy my mind." She lifted the hot cup of coffee to her lips and tested the degree of heat. The warmth of the cup penetrated and soothed her cold fingers.

Leslie sat a large bowl of soup in front of Leslie and did the same for herself. "I don't have any little ones today. It's just us."

Sharon held the spoon mid-air. Thoughts plucking emotions from the box she'd locked shut flew out and collided in her mind. She sat the spoon back in the bowl and closed her eyes.

"I keep trying to push it all down and brush it aside. I don't know what to do. I don't know how to forget and how to heal." She opened her eyes and looked at the soup. Suddenly realizing her stomach had knotted and unable to accept food, she pushed the bowl away. "I can't eat."

"You were fine when you got here. Was it something I

said?" Leslie was concerned that she had opened a wound that should have staying closed.

Sharon shook her head. "No. It just happens. It comes from out of nowhere."

"I think you should talk to someone." Leslie had tried this approach before, but Sharon had never even heard her out. This time her friend sat silent, offering no denials or rebuttals.

"I talk to you, isn't that good enough?"

"But, you don't talk to me. Not really. The wound is so tender that anytime a conversation gets close, you steer away. I don't think you will ever fully heal until you get it all out. Until you open up that wound and clean out what is festering there."

Leslie reached across the table and laid her hand on top of her friend's. "Sharon, you have to talk about it, about it all. Getting it out will remove the burden of it all."

Sharon looked from where Leslie's hand lay to her concerned, but gentle face. "I don't know what to say. I don't know where to begin." She had experienced so much trauma and she had never fully unburdened any of it. Yes, she had talked to Patty about her abortion, but had she fully unburdened herself? She didn't think so. "Okay. I'll try. But it will take longer than the rest of my short lunch hour."

"How much overtime have you worked lately?"

Sharon started shaking her head. I'm in the middle of training our file clerk. I can't stay and talk.

"Yes, you can. I know she has duties she can be doing.

I'm going to call Bill." Without waiting for a response, Leslie turned and walked to the phone. Sharon didn't stop her.

Bill was more than accommodating. He only wanted what Sharon needed. He would direct computer traffic while she was out.

Leslie grabbed a box of tissue and guided her friend to the living room sofa. "Now talk. You've told me a bit about the abortion. Start there. Tell me more and don't just regurgitate facts. Tell me how you felt. Let me have it all."

Sharon closed her eyes and went back to that horrible day in her life. The terror of what was about to happen to her felt as real in that moment as it did then. She slumped forward placing her face in her hands and bawled uncontrollably. Leslie sat and waited, knowing that this was a necessary part of cleansing.

When Sharon had gained enough composure to talk, she went over every moment and how that moment felt. The feelings of betrayal by her parents, the feelings of guilt for killing her baby, the feelings of abandonment by the father of the baby, and more. She didn't rush through it, but took her time. Leslie just listened.

"I've been told so many times that I need to forgive my parents. I guess I don't know how to do that. I think somehow by forgiving them, I am betraying the baby they made me kill. Can I forgive them while holding my stance on what they did?"

"I believe you can. You will never agree that what they did was right, but you can forgive their actions."

Sharon sat pondering Leslie's words. She had already gone through a handful of tissues and reached for more.

"Jesus forgives us for all the horrible things we have done, but that doesn't mean he agrees with them. Forgiving us, does not mean siding with what we did."

Sharon thought she understood. Honestly, she never really felt that God had forgiven her. "What if God hasn't forgiven me?"

"He has to forgive you. It's his character to forgive. But, we have to come to him and ask him. I believe his heart yearns for us to ask."

Sitting on the sofa listening to Leslie's words, Sharon had new conflicting thoughts and emotions, some refreshing and hopeful. "I don't pray. I stopped because I always felt that God is disappointed in me. I just couldn't face any more rejection."

A mischievous smile crossed Leslie's mouth. "I believe that Jesus is in heaven right now holding both your babies in his arms and he wants nothing more than to tell them you have spoken to him and that you are fine."

Sharon looked at Leslie like she had spoken in a foreign language. "What are you talking about? Have you lost your mind?"

"Think about it. I have no doubts that your two babies are in heaven, do you?"

"No."

"Okay then. Can we both agree that Jesus is in heaven with them?"

Sharon reluctantly nodded.

"So, they are there together."

A shadow fell over Sharon's eyes and she nodded.

"Do you think that they want you to be okay?"

Leslie's words tugged at Sharon's heart. The problem wasn't so much that she felt they would blame her, but that she blamed herself. "I don't think they feel that way. I just can't forgive myself."

"Does that fix anything?"

"What?" Leslie was taking Sharon mentally to places she had never been. She was contemplating things she had never thought of.

"Does beating yourself up and not forgiving yourself help you or them?"

"No." The word was uttered so soft that Leslie could barely hear it.

"If Jesus died so that he could quickly and easily offer you forgiveness, then what do you think you are accomplishing by refusing it? If he doesn't hold it against you, who are you to hold it against yourself?"

"I hate myself for what I did."

"Yes, but he doesn't hate you and neither do your babies. No one wants you to hate yourself. It won't fix anything."

Sharon's mind was racing attempting to make sense of it all.

"Sharon, Jesus loves you and forgives you. Embrace it."

A ragged breath sucked into Sharon's lungs, then more torrents of tears. These were different. They were cleansing tears. The rest of the afternoon, Sharon told

Leslie every detail of her life and how she had merely survived going from one trauma to the next. She delved deep to pull out long hidden emotions.

More tears came with each new offering and so did the cleansing. "I'm worn out." Sharon finally gave a half-laugh as she folded and refolded the last shred of wet tissue she held in her hands. She felt a new sense of comfort having let it all out. At each new revelation, Leslie had encouraged her to give it to God and let it go by forgiving herself.

As she sat, watching the tissue slowly disintegrate in her fingers, she felt as though her pain had also disintegrated. There was still the sweet longing she held for Molly Sue, and her other two babies, but something about it all was different. She felt she could remember them and hold their memories dear without regret.

"Thank you Leslie. I feel better. I still hurt, but not like I did. It is softer and gentler. But, I think it is healing. Maybe someday it will be completely healed."

Donna - January 1978

Donna had read the 'thanksgiving' and 'love' list five times already that day. She had also walked around the room and read every scripture that she had posted on the walls. She couldn't break free from the agitation that she felt.

Today was a difficult day. She was irritable with Molly Sue and hated herself for it, pushing herself deeper into despair. It was amazing that she had not had more days like this. Usually she could read the list, pray, watch her precious daughter playing, and her emotions would settle and re-center themselves. Not today.

She lay on the thin mattress and silently cried. Molly Sue was working hard at the table coloring yet another picture. The tiny artist produced artwork profusely, and she never seemed to tire of it. Donna was thankful for that too. At least Molly Sue knew nothing of the outside world and therefore couldn't long for it.

Molly Sue was now five years old and had never spent a day in school. True, Donna had taught her letters, and how to write her name. But, she knew Molly Sue was still young, and she didn't want to push her. There would be plenty of time.

Without realizing it, Donna had fallen back asleep. At midday, she woke to Molly Sue patting her arm asking her if she was okay. Pulling herself from her daze, she stared at her daughter. She didn't feel right. She felt dizzy and foggy. But it was time to feed Molly Sue, so she sat up and reached for her child, hugging her tight.

"Mommy loves you Molly Sue. You know that, right?"

Mollie Sue smiled big and plopped a big kiss on her mommy's cheek. "I love you too Mommy."

The rest of the day dragged on and Donna continued to wonder what was wrong. She had no energy, and all she wanted to do was lay on the bed and fall back to sleep.

After five days of the lethargic behavior, Donna began to grow very concerned. She knew something was not right. She spent most of her waking time reading in the bible and praying for God to help her.

In the dark of night she would lay and wonder what would Molly Sue do if something happened to her? Buddy could not take care of her.

The man-child had grown in intelligence and maturity considerably since Donna had been taken captive; however, he was still challenged by the abuse he had suffered. He was working more and more and didn't come as often to check on Donna and Molly Sue. But, he always came and they would feed him and read the bible.

Donna's energy finally picked up, and she began to feel better, still not understanding what had happened to her. The vegetable stash had run out, and she thought that might have been the reason. A lack of vitamins could do that. Maybe she needed more sunshine and exercise. *It was just the winter blues*, she decided.

When the weeks went by and she again fell into the slump of lethargy, she became concerned. She had never, even in the wintertime become this sleepy and weak. Her appetite had diminished and even though she would cook for Molly Sue, she herself would barely eat.

With what energy she had, she would often pace the small cabin. It worried her, she couldn't shake it, and didn't know what to do. When the panic would seize her to the point she couldn't function, she would find herself back at the lists, reading them aloud.

Molly Sue was more of a priority than ever before. She

had to spend every moment loving on her and teaching her things that would build her character.

A favorite pastime with her mother had been to make paper dolls. Donna had showed her how to bend and fold the paper and then tear, not cut, since they still had not convinced Buddy to trust them with scissors. Once they had torn a few out, Donna would sew their hands together and there would be long strings of paper dolls.

Molly Sue didn't rush through the coloring process. She made sure each little girl had a pretty dress and different hair. None of them had shoes though, since Molly Sue had never had any, and Donna had given up Buddy's mom's shoes a long time ago. They had never fit well and were considerably worn when he had given them to her.

One day, they had made a list of all the girl bible names they could find. Then, Molly Sue had named each one a different name. She would often talk to them and tell them stories. They had become her playmates when Donna's energy would wane.

Donna often caught Molly Sue with the bible open to the beautifully rendered picture of the nativity scene, and her talking to the baby Jesus. For some reason, maybe her young age, she connected to Jesus as a baby. She would sit and talk to baby Jesus and ask him to help her mommy feel better.

When she wasn't praying for Donna to get better, she would just talk to him as if he were her best friend. As Donna slept on the bed after lunch, she would be half awake listening to her daughter. She felt peace at Molly

Sue's words and her confidence in the relationship she had with Jesus.

Donna often prayed herself. She felt that there was something not right with her health, and it was not getting better, so she prayed for answers about what to do about Molly Sue. She had no knowledge of the outside world. Donna had never taught her anything about it. Why tell her stories of a place and time she might not see for a long time, if ever.

One night in the early hours, Donna woke suddenly. As she lay in the quiet, she heard in her spirit, "Prepare Molly Sue to leave."

CHAPTER 20

Sharon - December 1979

The day that Sharon had spent with Leslie had started her on a journey of healing. She knew though, that it was a process. She still battled with thoughts that would come and anger would rise up. But she had learned to stop and shift her thinking.

Sadness still blanketed her from time to time, too. At Leslie's suggestion, she had made a list of people who she felt she needed to forgive. The list was long. Once she had experienced the initial pain of her parents' betrayal, it had been easy for her to take offense at even the smallest things.

As she sat and looked at the list, she felt shame at some of the small things she had held against people. People who had meant her no harm. It just seemed that everything that caused the slightest discomfort in her life pricked at her old scabs. Instead of realizing what it was, she would receive it as if it were a brand new wound that had been inflicted on her.

She still couldn't pray. When Leslie was with her, she would pray. Having her friend near, brought courage that she didn't have when she was alone. When she was alone, she had no idea what words to say. She still felt guilt, but now she felt guilty for harboring so much unforgiveness. She wondered if she would ever be free from the guilt and shame.

"So, on Christmas Eve, we are going to go to the evening service and you are coming with us. Then, you will spend the night with us so you can be here when the kids wake up. You are part of our family and we want you here. No getting out of it." Leslie's voice came over the phone with exuberance.

Leslie was more excited about Sharon's recent outpouring than she was. She hoped that Leslie didn't think she could just suddenly be okay. She wanted to be, but wanting something and it being so were not the same.

Sharon chuckled. "Okay. Okay. I will." She realized she was smiling. She still felt sad, but the angst was gone and a peace that she didn't understand had taken its place.

As she hung up the phone, she stood and looked out the window. It was snowing large soft flakes. Snow this far south was not common, and she knew the snow wouldn't last. She walked to the window and looked out into the front yard where only a year earlier she and Molly Sue had built a snowman.

CHAPTER 20 | 351

She lingered on the memory rather than run from it, smiling softly as she remembered the snowflakes that had rested on the tips of Molly Sue's long eyelashes. She took a deep breath and moved away from the window.

"I'm going to go Christmas shopping." She slid on her galoshes and bundled up in her coat and gloves. It was the Saturday before Christmas and the stores would be busy. *It will feel more like Christmas that way*, Sharon thought.

The Woolworth store was packed. The entrance was slick with melting snow and Sharon could smell the scents of pine wafting throughout the store. A large Christmas tree towered over the counters where children stood in line to talk to Santa.

Without thinking, Sharon began to slowly walk towards them. She had been warned that if she were to see Molly Sue, not to approach her or she could be detained. Since she worked for the police department, she wasn't concerned, but she didn't want to cause Molly Sue any undue distress.

She stood casually next to a counter lifting one perfume after another, while secretly scanning the line of children.

"May I help you?" A voice jolted Sharon. "That scent is new. Here let me spray you." Before she knew it, a fine scented mist of some floral combination drifted over her. She put up her hand as if to ward it off.

"No, thank you. I don't think I like that one." She moved along the counter to where the hosiery aisle was. She could look over it and hopefully she would be able to look as though she knew what she was looking for while really searching for Molly Sue.

The line of children wound around in a serpentine shape ending behind the beginning of the line. It prevented Sharon from seeing everyone that was standing there. As the line moved, new children would become visible. *I need to walk around in order to see the back of the line.*

She left the hosiery aisle and circumvented the outside of the displays. She could finally see where the line ended, but still not see all the children. It ended in the toy department. *They planned that strategically;* she thought.

I need to get toys for Leslie's kids, she thought, but then realized if Molly Sue were in that line it would be way too close to avoid detection. As she continued to meander through the store without drawing too close to the line, she suddenly saw the blonde curly hair of Molly Sue.

Sharon's gloved hand flew to her mouth. *Oh, my. She's grown so much.*

As she stood and watched her from afar, she realized she saw the little girl in a new way. She no longer felt a compulsion to have her, but a fondness for the girl herself. She watched for a few more moments, then smiled and walked out of the store.

DONNA - FEBRUARY 1978

The words instructing Donna to prepare Molly Sue were received with sadness, but a peaceful knowing. Her prayers had become questioning. "Why won't you just heal me, Father?"

Even though she felt at peace, it was difficult to fully accept the challenge before her. She knew that whatever was going on, Molly Sue's best interest was paramount. So, she began to think about what would Molly Sue need to be able to leave?

She would need to find help. She would need direction. But Donna didn't even know herself where she really was, so how could she direct her small child? She prayed and thought, and finally realized that if she could just get Molly Sue to go in a straight line, eventually she would find help. The worst thing was if she was just wandering aimlessly in the woods.

The stream and the sun were two things that Donna knew could help her. But the stream can meander and change course. If she told her to follow the stream, it might take her deeper into the woods and further away from civilization.

Donna began to write down in earnest what she felt she needed to do. She wrote all her thoughts down as they occurred and then underlined with finality the ones she knew were the right course.

So, what about when she got to another person? Molly Sue had never known anyone but Donna and Buddy. She had to teach her not to be afraid, but what if she came across someone who she shouldn't trust? Her mind raged as she turned the scenarios over and over in her head.

Who could Molly Sue trust? She could trust a cop. But

what if she came to other people long before she came to a cop? She would have to start teaching Molly Sue about the outside world. Donna had protected her so that she would be sheltered in a loving, peaceful environment. There had been no need to present ideas into her world that would only draw questions and confusion. Molly Sue had not been taught to fear, she would trust everyone.

But now, she had to decide what things from the outside world would be the most beneficial for her to know. To bombard her with massive amounts of data, would not be a benefit to her.

Donna had good days and days where she could barely get out of bed. Buddy had come to visit on some days when she had no energy. He was greatly concerned, but did not understand what to do to help her.

"Buddy, please take me to the doctor." Donna had begged as Molly Sue stood by wide eyed. She had no idea what a doctor was.

Fear contorted Buddy's face. "No!" He began to rock and shake his head. Donna closed her eyes, unable to argue.

By the end of February she knew it was time to teach her.

"Molly Sue, have you ever wondered what is out beyond the trees?"

The girl searched her momma's face as thoughts flitted through her mind. She was smart, very smart, but without being exposed to specific information, she had no resource to draw knowledge from.

"The birdies?"

They had talked about where the birdies go. How they fly away to warmer places sometimes or build their nests in different trees to be safe.

Donna smiled. "Yes, there are more birdies out there. There are also the deer, and rabbits too." Donna paused. "And… there are more people."

Molly Sue watched her momma's face earnestly listening.

"There are a lot more people."

Donna began to tell her about different types people. She drew pictures of farmers, the most likely she would meet on her journey. She told them about how they plant crops like she and Molly Sue had in their garden. They drew men in overalls and she even drew a picture of a green John Deere tractor.

In a few days, she talked to Molly Sue about police officers and they drew men with uniforms and badges on. They had dark caps and shiny black shoes, and they drove black and white cars. It took a long time for Donna to educate Molly Sue on cars, tractors, etc. Molly Sue had no point of reference. The best Donna could do, was get her to understand it was like the wagon that Buddy hooked to his horse and then loaded the wood on to take and sell.

Donna resisted the urge to push more information on Molly Sue than she could handle. The last thing she wanted was to overwhelm her or cause her fear.

As the weeks went by, Donna taught Molly Sue more, and more. They would sit in the backdoor's doorway and watch the sun and the shadow that it made as it dropped into the sky. This was by far the most critical thing that she could teach her. She drew a picture of how the sun rose in one direction and set in the exact opposite.

She drew a straight line and told Molly Sue that to find other people, a person could walk with the sun towards their back. Then, the sun would be high in the sky and they could sit under a tree and rest because without it, they would not know how to stay in that straight line. Then when the sun began to go down, they could walk straight towards it. Donna hoped that would help her understand how to walk in as straight a line as possible.

Donna talked to her about the stream. "A person should stay where they can see the stream for as long as they could. If it bends away and they need to keep walking, they should follow the sun, never the stream. If they get thirsty, they should find a shallow place and take a drink, then move on. They should not go near the stream when it is loud and white. They should not fall in. Whatever anyone does, they should not fall in.

How long would Molly Sue have to walk before she found someone, Donna wondered? What if she had to spend the night in the woods? Donna resisted the urge to panic, but often she would pace the cabin with the little energy she had.

"God, you told me to prepare Molly Sue to leave, so I am. I trust you to take care of her on her journey and to take her where she needs to go."

The anticipation of losing a daughter she had not yet lost, caused Donna intense grief. To push past it, she read the lists and scriptures frequently. She tried to prevent Molly Sue from seeing her tears, but she sensed that Molly Sue knew something was wrong and that something was about to change.

As the days turned into weeks, Donna often wrestled with the task at hand. She kept making excuses to push off the day she would set Molly Sue on her journey. She just couldn't bear to actually do it.

Donna had never said a word to Molly Sue about why she was suddenly teaching her all the new information about the outside world. Maybe God would change his mind and she wouldn't have to send her away. In that case, it would be best that Molly Sue never know that Donna had planned to send her away.

"Mommy." Molly Sue's sweet voice broke through the mental haze as Donna lay taking yet another nap.

Without opening her eyes, Donna reached for Molly Sue and drew her close. She climbed up on the bed and lay close to her mommy.

"Mommy, baby Jesus said it was time for me to go."

SHARON - MARCH 1980

The computer system was up and running. The men still grumbled, but the data entry clerks were long gone, so now the men had to enter their own files. Their hunt and peck style with their clumsy fingers made Sharon want to laugh. They would often look at her with her hand over her mouth hiding a grin.

"What?" Anthony said.

All she could do was shake her head. If she moved her hand or spoke, she knew she would burst out in laughter.

When he turned back to entering the file, she finally said, "You're doing so much better."

"Humpf."

"I'm going to talk to Bill about getting you your own personal terminal for the front counter so you can help everyone enter data as they create the files."

Anthony's head jerked around and seeing the big smile on Sharon's face, he realized she was only teasing.

"I'll never get the hang of this."

"Yes, you will. You are doing so much better than when you started. Keep working on it and I'll be in my office if you need me."

Sharon walked back towards her office. It was her birthday, but she hadn't reminded anyone. She tried to keep it a secret and since it was rare for anyone to send her a gift, really only Leslie, there was no reason for anyone to think about it.

As she turned the corner to her office, a large bouquet of spring flowers sat in the middle of her desk. Once again, no tag or a card from a sender. Over the last few years, from time to time, a bouquet would mysteriously appear on her desk. No one ever fessed up to it or knew where they came from. She had interrogated with fervor until finally giving up.

Now, when they would appear she would simply smile and smell the wonderful fresh scent. They didn't come often, but they were enjoyed when they did.

When she stood back up, the playground across the street caught her eye. The children were out playing on their lunch hour. She didn't stand obsessively as she had in the beginning, searching desperately for any sign of Molly Sue, but when she noticed children playing, she would look.

Blond bouncy curls caught her eye, and she smiled. She moved closer to the window and noticed that Molly Sue was not playing with the other children, but standing at the fence looking into the woods. Soon, though the bell rang, and they all ran into the building.

Sharon's phone rang, and she turned to answer it. "Hello."

"Hi. It's Will."

Sharon's breath caught in her throat. Could it have been Will that sent the flowers? A cocktail of emotions surged through her heart. "Hi."

"Happy Birthday."

"Thank you."

She stood lacing her finger through the coiled cord. Their conversations were still stilted and forced.

"Sharon, can I take you out this Friday night? I feel like we need to talk. I mean really talk."

Warmth flooded her. "Yes, I would love that." She hoped he could hear the smile in her words.

They made plans for him to pick her up and for a

moment their conversation eased and they were able to converse freely.

When she hung up the phone, she wondered if this was the beginning of true healing between her and Will. She let her mind daydream to what she hoped life with Will would be. He had been near the top of her forgiveness list. Had she forgiven him completely? She would need to tell him.

In her heart, she felt that she had worked toward forgiving her parents, yet she still couldn't bring herself to call them. Each time she thought of it, the pain would shut her down. The hardness towards them hadn't remained, only sadness for all the time lost.

When Bill stopped at her door, he watched her as she gazed off into space. He often pondered the change he had seen her. She seemed lighter in spirit, and happier. Her daydreaming now didn't seem to be anchored in grief or pain, but of quiet contemplation.

Bill cleared his throat and Sharon suddenly became aware of him standing there. She smiled and blushed, embarrassed that he had caught her daydreaming.

"Wow. What beautiful flowers! What's the occasion?" He walked in and bent down to smell the bright blossoms.

"You know what the occasion is. It's my birthday. You also know I don't know where the flowers came from." She watched him and a part of her wondered if he was the one who had been sending them. But it just didn't seem quite right. He was her boss, and even though he was an excellent one, he had never alluded to the fact that he wanted anything more.

"Did you call the florist?" Bill sat in the chair in front of her desk and crossed his legs.

"No. You know I've done that time after time, and they never tell me anything, ever. So, I didn't even bother today."

Bill nodded without comment. "How's the computer business going?"

"The machines and men are starting to play a little nicer with each other. Slowly. Some still balk at it, but I think they realize that it isn't going away and that they have to get on board whether they want to or not."

"There will be a section on the evaluation forms regarding their computer use and proficiency. I've told them all this, but I'm not sure they will believe me until it is time for the actual evaluations. I'm going to need you to help me assess that since I'm not actively engaged with it."

"They won't like a woman contributing to their job performance and evaluation," Sharon replied.

"They don't have to know where it came from."

"Okay, well let me know what points you want me to evaluate on and I will pay more individual attention."

The two sat in silence for a moment. Sharon's mind was off and running on how to evaluate the men, but Bill was still wondering how Sharon really was.

"Are you okay?"

Sharon focused on Bill's face a little shocked at the question. "Yes. Why do you ask?"

"You seem better lately. I see that something has changed, something good."

Sharon smiled. "Well, Leslie finally cornered me and made me talk about it all. She held me captive until I unburdened it all. Honestly, it felt good to let go of years of hurt and anguish."

Suddenly embarrassed by her confession, Sharon ducked her head away from Bill's gaze.

"I think that's wonderful. We were never meant to hold things in. I'm glad Leslie made you talk and forgive?" It was a question, not a statement.

Sharon looked Bill in the eye and nodded. "Yes. That was the hardest part. I'm still working on that. I think I've done it, and then it comes washing back over me in fresh waves. But, the waves seem to be lighter and lighter each time.

"Bill, I have to say that I am so thankful for you putting up with me all these years. I know my moods have been morose at times with all the garbage in my life weighing me down. I let it. Truthfully, I've had a good life, but now I feel I've wasted most of it by holding on to old hurts and wounds.

"If I had just forgiven sooner, or laid it all down quicker, I could have enjoyed so much more of my life. I feel like I cheated my own self and those around me from living life. I'm sorry if you got caught up in the hurricane of it all."

Bill smiled. "Sharon, it may feel like you were imposing your pain on others, but from where I sit, you didn't. You stoically held it inside while being good to all of us. That had to be a most painful way to live, holding it all inside for so long."

Sharon nodded. "Yes. But I didn't know anything else. Thank you for being there. You've been an outstanding boss."

Bill smiled and rose to his feet. "Thank you. I'll get you what I need for the evaluations by the end of the day. Take it easy today. It is your birthday after all."

The rest of the day sped by fast. From time to time though, the thought of Molly Sue standing at the playground fence and looking back towards the woods came to mind. *What was she looking at? Is she remembering where she came from?*

With no answers and no way to know, she would quickly discard those thoughts and go back to work. At five o'clock Leslie called.

"It's five o'clock. Your work day is over. I've fixed you a birthday dinner, you have to come eat with us."

Sharon laughed. There was no slick invitation, just her friend issuing a demand. Had she really become so slippery about begging off engagements that it had come to this? "Okay. What time?"

"How about five thirty? That will give you enough time to leave right now and go home if you really have to and then get here. Or, if you insist on staying at work, you'll have to leave by five twenty-five. Whatever the case, you can't stay at work too long. It's your birthday. Time to celebrate."

"Okay. Okay. I'll be there." Sharon hung up the phone

and let the comfort of friendship blanket her. "Thank you Lord for Leslie, and Bill. They've stood by me even at my worst."

She stood and began the routine of shutting down her terminal. The file clerk was still working, and she asked her to walk through before she left to batten down the hatches. She readily agreed.

It felt very strange to be leaving work this close to five. It was still light out, and the dusky day felt good. The glow of the sun considered setting and shot the sky with a vibrant hue of colors. *How many sunsets have I missed shrouded in my misery and discontent?*

She pulled into her driveway and hurried in her front door. She changed from her work clothes to blue jeans and a casual top. She wanted to be as comfortable as possible to have dinner with Leslie and her family. By now, she was one of them; they were her family.

She walked into Leslie's front door at five twenty-five. Suddenly, people jumped out from every doorway and behind every piece of furniture. Sharon's hands flew to her mouth, and she stumbled backwards in genuine shock.

"It's a surprise party." Leslie exclaimed.

With round eyes, Sharon looked at her friend. "You don't say?"

They had brought small gifts that they piled on the coffee table and Leslie had prepared tons of dips and hors d'oeuvres. The casual party atmosphere was fun and everyone was able to chat and eat at their leisure.

Will even came. He wasn't there to jump out and yell

'surprise', but he arrived soon after. Bill was there, a few of the officers from the station, and the file clerk too. There were other casual friends of Sharon's from around the community. She was sincerely overwhelmed with their love and generosity.

At around eight o'clock, they began to encourage her to open her gifts. She sat on the sofa and others sat where they could while others stood.

She received candles, and some costume jewelry. She even received a couple of funny gifts that made everyone laugh. Then when she thought she had opened them all, Leslie slid one last gift in front of her.

The mood in the room shifted for some unspoken reason. Was it because Leslie's demeanor had changed? Whatever the cause might have been, Sharon felt it and lifted the gift with care. She ran her hands over the beautifully wrapped package, hesitant to disturb the excellent job someone had done.

To rip the paper, felt like a travesty. So, she savored the experience. The ends of the rectangle box were taped, but they didn't clutch the paper, popping away easily. As she slid the white box from the paper, all mouths were silent, and all eyes were on the box.

Sharon set the paper aside, still holding the rectangle form of the box. The white box almost felt foreboding as if opening the lid might change her entire world. Then, she lifted the lid and moved the white tissue paper aside.

There in a beautiful silver frame was a vivid photograph of her and Molly Sue. Leslie had taken it one day when they were admiring the beautiful flowers they had grown in Sharon's garden. The photograph was professional quality, but had been taken by Leslie.

Sharon sat quietly and admired each detail of the photograph. Molly Sue's blond curls were scattered in an array around her small head. Her blue eyes were vivid and alive with excitement. Sharon was looking at the flower the young girl was holding up to her and smiling with joy.

A tear fell and plopped on the glass thrusting Sharon from her trance. She looked up at Leslie, and with tears in her eyes, mouthed the words, "Thank you."

CHAPTER 21

*D*onna - June 1978

Molly Sue's words had stunned Donna. She had not said a word to her sweet girl about sending her away or about her leaving.

Yes, she had discussed the direction of the people, and if one were to find them, they would have to walk in that straight line. But, she had never said that she would send Molly Sue away. She had always talked in terms of 'if' someone were to go see more people.

She had hoped and prayed that a miracle would come and she would not have to send her. But, it was obvious now that Jesus himself was also preparing Molly Sue for her departure.

Donna held her tight as tears fell onto the blond curls. She couldn't speak, but nodded her head. If whatever illness she had didn't kill her, then Molly Sue's departure surely would.

But maybe this was a way for God to rescue them both. If Molly Sue could get to the outside world, then she could bring someone back and rescue them both. Hope suddenly surged within her as this thought took concrete form.

She had always thought of sending Molly Sue away so that she wouldn't be left alone after Donna's death. But, what if this was a way to get a doctor back to Donna? Renewed hope brought energy to Donna, as her mind began to pull the final plan into action.

Donna had not felt like sewing the last few months, even though Molly Sue was growing rapidly. She had taken an old pillow case one day and found that it was the exact size Molly Sue needed for a little dress. It wasn't pretty, but it would function well.

Neither Donna or Molly Sue wore underwear. When Molly Sue had outgrown diapers, she didn't see a need to use their sparse fabric supply to make undergarments when it was only she and Molly Sue. She made pants for Molly Sue and as far as Donna had been concerned, that was enough.

But with the pillowcase for a dress, that would leave Molly Sue without underwear. The pillowcase covered her well enough, so that would have to work.

Neither one had worn shoes, but for the long trip, Donna felt that she might need something on her feet for protection or warmth. The initial surge of strength was now waning and as Donna surveyed the room for something to cover Molly Sue's feet with, she pulled off one of her sheets and began ripping it in strips.

Donna made enough strips that she could wrap them several times around Molly Sue's feet. The last portion of the strip, she ripped down the center and wrapped each one around her ankle tying them together in the back.

She then took a length of rope and tied it around Molly Sue's waist so that the pillowcase would not blow up and expose her daughter.

Then, instead of skirting around the issue with drawings and such, Donna sat Molly Sue down at the table with her and got serious about what she should do.

"Make sure you walk in a straight line. Mommy doesn't know how far you will have to walk, but don't give up and don't come back until you find someone. Okay?"

Molly Sue nodded. Her big blue eyes were focused intently on every word.

"If it get's nighttime, just sit next to a tree and rest. Don't walk in the night time, okay?"

Again, Molly Sue only nodded.

Walk until you see a person. Then tell them that Mommy is sick. I will write a note for you to give them. But, you will have to show them how to get back here. You will have to walk towards the sun when it is coming up, and walk with it to your back when it is going down.

Donna searched Molly Sue's face for verification that she understood. "Do you understand?"

And for a third time Molly Sue nodded.

"Baby Jesus will be with you. Do not be afraid. Do you

hear me? There will be a lot of things that may tempt you to be afraid, but always remember that baby Jesus is right there with you."

A knot formed in Donna's throat. She didn't think she had the courage to send her baby girl out in the world. Then in her heart she heard, "It's time." The words were familiar, soft-spoken, and peaceful.

The plan was to rise early the next morning and send her off at the break of dawn in order to give her as much time as possible. That evening, Donna sat down and wrote out a one-page letter explaining everything to whoever found her little girl. She hoped they would understand and that it would help lead them back here to her.

Donna laid awake all night while Molly Sue slept wrapped in her arms. She vacillated from peace to panic throughout the night. She talked to God non stop as she looked out the window next to their bed. The clear night was filled with millions of stars. The same stars that she had looked at for years. The same stars that gave her an understanding of just how big God was, yet how close he always came to her.

When the first hint of light crept in the window, Donna took in a deep breath and rolled over towards her baby. She watched Molly Sue as she slept. She wanted to believe that this wasn't the last time she would experience this precious moment.

"God, please bring her back to me. But, if you have another plan, all I ask is that you send her to someone who will love her and take care of her just as I would. If my role as her mommy is over, then please God, please send her a good mommy."

Donna pulled her sleeping girl tightly into her embrace. She wanted more than anything to believe that God would bring Molly Sue back to her with help, but there was something deep inside her that knew that would not happen.

Molly Sue began to stir and then rubbed her fist into her sleepy eyes. "Mommy?"

"Yes, sweet girl?"

"Good morning." Molly Sue gently smiled at her mommy.

Then, her perfect always cheerful girl grew sad. She knew too, even without saying it that this was the day that everything would change.

"Let me fix you a big breakfast."

Donna pulled out all the remaining strength she had to make their last breakfast together a party. She wanted Molly Sue to leave on a full stomach. Hopefully, they were not that far from civilization and Molly would not have to walk until she had gotten very hungry.

Once they had eaten, and made silly faces laughing at each other, Molly Sue stood up and said, "Okay."

Donna nodded and stood. She took the letter she had written the night before, folded it into fourths and reminded Molly Sue once more that she should hold the letter and then give it to the first person who would talk to her.

Donna walked Molly Sue as far as the chain would allow her to go. When the chain grabbed her ankle preventing one more step, she stopped with a lurch, but her heart walked on.

Molly Sue - June 1978

Molly Sue wanted to stop when her mommy had stopped, but she knew she had to keep walking. Baby Jesus had told her not to look back.

She had never been further than her mommy's chain had reached. She had never been anywhere alone. The woods were growing brighter as the sun rose higher overhead, and the stream had continued to flow slowly beside her.

Mommy had fed her a big breakfast and after a while of walking, she was growing very sleepy. She looked up to see if the sunshine was up high in the sky so she could sit down and take a nap by a tree. It was still behind her, so she kept walking like Mommy had said.

The rags on her feet felt funny. She would often watch her feet as she walked. *Why did Mommy put these on my feet?*

Suddenly, movement out of the corner of her eye caught her attention, and she stopped walking. She stood very still, and the movement resumed. It was a bunny rabbit. The sight of it filled Molly Sue with joy and she started to run off and follow it. Just as she started to step in that direction, she heard baby Jesus say, "No, Molly Sue. Don't follow the rabbit. Follow where Mommy told you."

"Okay, baby Jesus."

When the sun was finally high in the sky, Molly Sue had grown tired of walking. It was hot under the canopy of the trees, and she wanted to stop. She had started out walking quickly, but soon her steps had become slow and tired.

She sat down under a large tree with a thick trunk. As soon as her head rested back against the tree, she fell asleep. Her eyelids closed, her breathing grew shallow, and her fingers relaxed. The note her mother had spent hours writing and re-writing was picked up by the breeze and flew away like the birds.

Molly Sue only slept about an hour. The sun was far enough overhead though, that she could tell which way to walk. To her surprise, in just a few minutes the woods stopped and before her was a wide clearing. There were a lot of buildings and other things foreign to her.

Ahead and to the left was a large reddish brown building with a big high fence around it. The fence looked a little like the one the chickens were in at home, but it was much taller.

Molly Sue stood looking at everything and all the activity. For a moment, she panicked trying to remember her mommy's instructions. Then past the tall fence, she saw a black and white car, and she remembered the drawing they had made.

With her focus on that car, she walked straight ahead. The car had stopped next to other cars in different colors, and there was a man with shiny black shoes. He had opened a door and gone into the building. Molly Sue stopped just outside the glass door and looked down at her hands. The note was gone.

"It's okay, Molly Sue. I am with you. Open the door and go in."

Molly Sue pushed open the glass door and stood in the entrance of the police station. Then the kind face of a beautiful woman was there asking her where her mommy was.

Sharon - April 1980

The date with Will had gone well, but during the discussion, they realized that they should remain dear friends only. Sharon was healing, so was Will. Her dreams of a life with Will and what it would be like to be his wife, faded once and for all that evening. The realization had come gradually as they dined. She just knew it was something that she no longer wanted.

It was now her lunchtime and Sharon knew that if she stood on the sidewalk at eleven thirty each day, she would see Molly Sue playing in the school playground. She made sure that she was there as often as she could. She no longer felt the pain of the separation, but she missed her still.

As she watched, it appeared to Sharon that Molly Sue didn't engage with the other children the way she had seen her do in the past. She would like to think it was because they had separated her from Sharon, and missed her, but she knew Molly Sue was a resilient child and seemed to take any change in stride.

Today, Molly Sue was standing at the far fence with her back to Sharon as she had seen her do a lot lately. She remembered the previous year, her kindergarten teacher Mrs. Patterson mentioned that she would do that from time to time and when Sharon asked about it, Molly Sue had said that Buddy was back there.

All of Sharon's senses suddenly became alert, and she gradually began walking towards the playground. As she walked from the police station parking lot waiting to cross the street, she saw that Molly Sue had left the schoolyard and was walking towards the woods.

In sheer panic, Sharon ran back to the station, taking only enough time to stick her head in the door and give Anthony instructions.

"Anthony, get Bill. Molly is heading towards the woods and I'm going after her. Have Bill follow me." Anthony quickly nodded in agreement and lifted the phone to call Bill.

Sharon turned around and ran as fast as she could. Long before she reached the playground, Molly Sue had disappeared before her into the woods. By the time Sharon reached the edge of the woods, she doubled over panting. She gasped for breath and she pushed a hand against the stitch in her side.

There was no sign of Molly Sue. She opened her mouth to call out, but something told her not to. She didn't want to alert anyone who might put her in danger. But she had seen no one else. Maybe Molly Sue had remembered where she had come from and was walking back in that direction.

Looking down, she noticed Fuzzy off to the side. Horror ravaged her body. Molly Sue would never abandon Fuzzy. She grabbed the bear, clutching it to her chest and searched for footprints or any sign that might indicate where she had gone.

Her heart pounded in her chest and resounded loudly in her ears. The quiet of the woods only stressed the pounding. Sharon swallowed as big tears threatened to take over.

Pushing them down in order to help Molly Sue, she began walking straight back into the woods. It seemed the only logical path, and with no other indicators, Sharon took it. She hurried as quickly and as quietly as she could. Soon, she heard voices up ahead.

Finally, in the distance she could see random glimpses of Molly Sue. First her tennis shoes, then her blond curls. It was just the tiniest snippets of her through the trees. Then, she saw that Molly Sue was holding hands with a very large man. She did not appear to be afraid, and it did not appear that she was in danger. *That must be Buddy*, Sharon thought.

Sharon resisted every urge to run to Molly Sue, grab her, and run away with her. She knew though, that she could not outrun the man even without carrying Molly Sue. There was no way she could run from him with her in her arms. Realizing she was not in danger, her curiosity about where they were going, intrigued Sharon. She knew it would have to be back to where her mommy was, but exactly where that was she didn't have a clue.

The day was hot, and it soon exhausted Sharon. She had been following them for nearly two hours by her watch. She was not dressed for hiking in the woods, and her feet hurt. She had snagged her pants more than once on limbs and brambles.

Then suddenly, a clearing appeared and Sharon hid watching Molly Sue and Buddy enter a small log cabin. A stream was off to the left and the flowing water drowned out some of the sound, making it difficult to hear.

Sharon snuck to the door by circumventing the clearing, avoiding being seen directly from the cabin. Once at the back door, she looked in. There was an old twin iron bed where a lady lay. Molly Sue was bending down hugging the lady. That must be her mommy, thought Sharon.

The man stood quietly back away from them in the room's corner. Sharon stepped up on the threshold and walked into the room. Molly Sue whirled around.

"Miss Sharon. Miss Sharon. Help my mommy. Help my mommy." Molly Sue was screaming for Sharon to help her.

Sharon hurried to the bed and sat on her knees up next to the bed and looked at the woman. What Sharon saw devastated her. The woman was rail thin and her pallor was almost gray. Her hair was thin and sparse.

"Mommy this is Miss Sharon. She took care of me until they took me away from her. She tried to find you mommy, she tried." Molly Sue was overcome with fear and her face was wet with tears. She too, was now on her knees and scooted in close to Sharon.

The woman in the bed lifted her frail arm and reached out for Sharon. "Please take care of my baby girl. Promise me you will take care of her." Sharon took her hand. It was cold to the touch and so thin that Sharon feared hurting it by holding it.

Then the lady looked at Molly Sue. "Molly, mommy is going to go see Jesus now. Miss Sharon is going to be your mommy now. You be a good girl for her, okay? Will you promise mommy?"

All Molly Sue could do was bob her head up and down. Her little face was blotched red from crying and covered in tears. "No, mommy, don't go see Jesus. Not now. Don't go."

Sharon felt pain like she had never felt before. It shot through her entire body as though she had been suddenly shocked by the highest voltage of pure grief. Through all she had endured, watching Molly Sue hurt in this way was by far the greatest pain she had ever experienced.

God, please, please don't let her mommy die. I'll gladly give Molly Sue up once and for all if you will just let her mommy live. Please God, please, please, Sharon begged.

Then in the depths of her soul Sharon heard, *"Now you are ready. Now you know what true love is. It is sacrificing your own selfish desires for another, no matter how painful that sacrifice may be."*

"It's okay Molly. It's okay," said Donna, and the woman closed her eyes and rested, a peaceful smile on her face.

Sharon could tell by the lifeless feel of the woman's hand in hers, that she was gone.

Sharon gently laid her hand on the bed and turned to Molly Sue. She wrapped both her arms around the young girl and drew her in close. "She's gone now, Molly. She's gone to Jesus."

From the back of the room a loud wailing noise arose. The large man had slumped to the floor and was rocking back and forth, wailing at the top of his lungs. It was then that Sharon noticed Bill had arrived and was standing to the back of the room. She had been so consumed with the moment that she hadn't heard him arrive.

Bill walked further into the room and squatted down by the wall anchor where the woman's chain was attached. Sharon glanced over and as they watched, the rusted chain dropped with a clatter to the floor. She was free.

SHARON - APRIL 1980

Bill had Anthony notify the paramedics to be on standby. He had brought his radio and had given them a generalization of the cabin's whereabouts, so they waited.

Sharon sat in a chair at the table rocking Molly Sue and holding her close the entire time. As she did, she noticed the sparsity of the small cabin. But the entire room was filled with drawings Molly Sue had done, dried flowers, and handwritten pages by Donna.

Predominantly throughout the room were long strings

of paper dolls. None were cut, but each one torn precisely outlining the shape of young girls holding hands. All were brightly adorned with vividly colored clothes and various hairstyles.

On the table were stacks and stacks of notebooks, next to a large leather bible. Next to the journals was a larger single paper doll with several dresses that could be laid on and folded over to dress her. The doll herself had been made from one of the stiff cardboard covers from a notebook, but stood in a little manmade wooden stand.

She was well worn from hours of playing. The paper doll looked just like Molly Sue with curls drawn in ringlets of yellow, and big blue eyes.

Sharon reached out and slid what appeared to be the newest journal over to her. She began to read as she sat holding Molly Sue and rocking her.

Buddy's wailing finally diminished to a low whine, but the rocking didn't stop. Bill stooped down in front of him and tried to talk with him, but the traumatized man-child did not appear capable of responding. It was clear to Bill that this man may be large, but he had the mind of a small child. So, Bill sat down by Buddy and patted his shoulder while he rocked, and they waited.

After an hour, the paramedics could finally find the cabin and two men entered the front door with a stretcher. Once inside, they realized that the emergency equipment they had brought would not be needed.

Molly Sue had cried herself asleep in Sharon's lap and Sharon didn't want her to wake up and see them carry her mommy away, so she gently rose and carried Molly Sue out the back door. Bill rose from a now nearly catatonic Buddy and went with Sharon.

"How much did you hear?" Sharon asked Bill.

"I think all of it. I arrived right after you did. I heard her clearly say that she wanted you to be Molly Sue's new mommy." Bill smiled and Sharon studied his face. It was a face that had been with her for a long time. He had been her boss, but so much more. She was just now at that very moment seeing him as he had truly been. Her heart seemed to blossom and feel lighter, healed.

Wrapped up in her bitter pain and spiraling further away with each passing year, she had not been capable of seeing this wonderful man that God, yes God, had placed in her life as a steady rudder to help her stay on course.

Bill reached down and scooped Molly Sue out of Sharon's arms, knowing that the weight of her small body would have grown difficult for Sharon to hold.

Sharon released Molly Sue to Bill and smiled. Something seemed to suddenly fall into place. It was as if a missing puzzle piece had suddenly been found, or as if a gear that had been off its track had miraculously found its groove.

Bill reached out for Sharon's hand, and she took it. "Let's go home."

EPILOG

In the weeks after they had found Donna, Sharon had read every notebook from cover to cover. She had been transfixed to every page. Instead of growing bitter and contemptuous in her captivity, Donna had chosen to flourish and lean on God. Through it all, she had looked for the good in each day and focused on making life for Molly Sue the best that she could.

Her compassion for the man-child Buddy was one to be admired. She had seen him for who he was from the very beginning. A simple, lost child.

It was easy to see why when Molly Sue had arrived that day in the police station, that she was so peaceful, calm, and loving. Her mother had taught her to be all those things.

"Bill, listen to this." Sharon held one of the earliest journals in her hand.

Each day that I wake up I stand before a fork in the road. I have a choice to make. I can go down one road that leads to dark thoughts, self-pity, and despair. Or, I can go down a path of thankfulness of what I do have and see the joy that each day holds. It is up to me each day, each moment, to decide which path I will take.

Sharon had marveled at how despite all the hardships Donna had suffered in her captivity, she had made the choice to be thankful, kind, and loving. Sharon on the other hand, with so much to be thankful for, had chosen to grow resentful and bitter when any hardship came her way.

"I want to be better Bill. I want to change. I want to live with the freedom that Donna lived with inside of her."

Bill wrapped his arms around Sharon. "You know the only way that can happen is if you tap into the true source of love the way Donna did. You have to forgive God and let him love you or you can never truly love others."

"I know."

Sharon continued to read and to learn from Donna. At some point, Donna began to realize that she was critically ill. Her attempts to get Buddy to take her to a doctor were fruitless, and she began to worry about Molly Sue. Her notebook was filled with writings of different ideas to help Molly Sue get free, but then she would quickly see how they would fail. She didn't really know where she was in relation to civilization or exactly which way to send her.

Finally, out of desperation one day, when Buddy had mentioned taking a load of chopped wood to sell, she wrote a note and sent Molly Sue away. She had coached her for days on end about what she was supposed to do. She told her to follow the sun when it was going down to the earth. Somewhere along the way, the note had been lost. So, when Molly Sue arrived, she did not understand how to tell them to get back to her mommy or why she had come.

First, the days turned into weeks and then weeks into months. With each increasing day gone by, Donna realized that Molly Sue would not be coming back. She had prayed that God had led her to safety, and she took comfort in knowing that her darling little girl was no longer in captivity. She had held on as long as she could, hoping each day that she would see her baby girl again.

When Buddy had returned, and it was obvious Molly Sue had gone, he began to look through the woods for her. Donna, of course, did not tell him she had sent the girl away. Buddy thought she had merely wandered off and had gotten lost. He looked for her almost every day.

When days turned into weeks, then months, he ventured close to the woods by the school. To his challenged mind, he thought the tall chain-link fence around the school playground was a cage that the children were being held in after capture.

He came often to see if he could see Molly Sue, and then one day he did. He was terrified of the large cage she was in and even more terrified of the vast clearing between the school and the woods. So, he would stand just inside the dense woods and watch her.

Then, one day when he went, there were no children in the cage. For weeks he would go back and still there were no children. He didn't realize what school was, or that they took a break during the summer.

He told Donna one day when school resumed that he had seen Molly Sue. He had called out to her previously, but was unsure if she had heard him. When he saw her again, he ventured out into the clearing just a bit, and finding a gate, Molly Sue ran to meet him.

Donna had grown much worse and Buddy had used all the courage he had to go get Molly Sue and bring her to her mother.

Sharon, Bill, and Will advocated for Buddy and they took him to a group home for mentally challenged adults. It was a home where he would feel nurtured in a safe home environment and Molly Sue could visit often. Buddy had not taken Donna from malice or ill will, so there was no criminal case. His childlike mind had told him he was keeping her safe. The abuse he had suffered as a child was the only pattern of love he had ever known until he met Donna.

They removed Molly Sue from the foster home and placed her with Sharon. Bill testified of her mother's dying declaration that Molly Sue should be with her. It had been clear that Molly Sue was not happy in the foster home, and it took very little coaxing to get the court to give full adoption to Sharon.

Life did not go back to normal for Sharon, though. Her life had been a bondage of her own making that she had endured every day. But in that cabin in the depths of the greatest pain she had ever known, she had found genuine love.

The final tethers of the bondages had broken from her and all the years of bitterness and rage finally faded away. All that mattered, really mattered at that moment had been Molly Sue, and she was fully willing to sacrifice anything she had for her. It was in that moment that God had healed her heart completely.

The freedom to love and entertain joy, was a new experience for Sharon. She looked at people differently. She saw them, really saw them, for the first time. And she saw Bill. Often her mind would drift back to little acts of kindness that he had shown her through the years, that she had callously disregarded or ignored. The flowers had always been from Bill, but Sharon had never really believed that they had come from him, even though she had always asked.

When she had taken the job working for him, he was only six years older than she, but in a small town, it had been easy for him to climb to the position of chief of police. In love with Will at the time she took the job, she had never considered Bill as anything other than her boss. But he had fallen in love with her the first time he'd seen her.

When Will and Sharon had broken up soon after she had taken the job at the station, she had hardened her heart to the point where everyone and everything she saw was filtered through her own pain. But, Bill had patiently stood in the background silently loving her all those years.

One month after Sharon had received full custody of Molly Sue, Bill asked Sharon to marry him, and she said yes. The ceremony was small and Molly Sue was the flower girl. Leslie stood with Sharon and Anthony stood with Bill.

As Sharon stood looking into Bill's eyes, she felt a bit of sadness that the captivity and death of a young woman had been the catalyst that had worked to set her free. But as Sharon said her I do's, she remembered the rusty chain falling to the floor and was reminded that Donna too, was now free.

AUTHOR'S NOTE

This novel was intentionally set in a nondescript town somewhere in the middle or southern part of the country. I didn't want to give it a name because it is any town, anywhere, during that time.

The characters in this book are all completely fictional. I have never heard of something like this event happening in real life and honestly the concept of the book changed drastically as I wrote.

I must say that writing this book, changed me as a person and as a child of God. I realized I needed to become so much more thankful and filled with gratitude. I've had many challenges in my life, but when faced with the reality of the characters in this book, I felt humbled.

As I wrote, God poured this book into me and so I experienced it much the same way that you did, a word at a time, a chapter at a time, and when the last word was written, I was crying. My heart was forever changed.

I experienced the same roller-coaster of emotions that I am sure each reader also experienced. As much as I love my previous series, The Redemption Series, this book stole my heart! I hope that you loved it just as much as I did.

If it moved you, please consider leaving a review.

ABOUT THE AUTHOR

Nancy Jackson is a true Renaissance woman. A prolific writer, she has written 4 novels in just over one year. She is also a successful Oklahoma Realtor, metalsmith and jewelry instructor, as well as a business coach.

Her novels are rich and full bodied. They take the gritty parts of life and roll them up into mystery, love, and all the emotions we each experience everyday. She considers her favorite complement to be when people say, "You're characters are so real. It felt as if I knew each one!"